Cut to the Chase

T0352180

ALSO BY ELLE KEATING

Thrill of the Chase

Cut to the Chase

ELLE KEATING

New York Boston

Copyright © 2016 by Elle Keating
Excerpt from *Thrill of the Chase* copyright © 2015 by Elle Keating
Cover design by Christine Foltzer
Cover copyright © 2016 by Hachette Book Group, Inc.

Forever Yours
Hachette Book Group
1290 Avenue of the Americas
New York, NY 10104
hachettebookgroup.com
twitter.com/foreverromance

First Edition: March 2016

Forever Yours is an imprint of Grand Central Publishing.
The Forever Yours name and logo are trademarks of Hachette Book Group, Inc.

The publisher is not responsible for websites (or their content) that are not owned by the publisher.

The Hachette Speakers Bureau provides a wide range of authors for speaking events. To find out more, go to www.hachettespeakersbureau.com or call (866) 376-6591.

ISBN 978-1-4555-3503-3 (print on demand edition)

E3

*For Mike—my brother and truly my best friend
in the world. I love ya.*

Cut to the Chase

Out to the Chase

Chapter One

Chase Montclair stared out the window at the world below and prayed that the evil that yearned to infiltrate their lives would just disappear. But it would take more than prayer to lure the sick son-of-a-bitch out of the hole he had successfully hidden in for the past year. Erin and her brother had been on the defensive too long. It was time they took action and put an end to the madness.

Chase walked over to the bed and looked down at the sleeping woman, the woman he was determined to make his in every sense of the word. He pulled back the covers and slipped in behind her. As if by instinct, she nestled in closer, pulling his arm around her, though she was still peacefully asleep. The valiant part of him told him to let her rest. But as he held her naked body close, breathing in the scent of her hair and feeling her soft curves shift beside him, all he could think about was having her all over again.

He rolled her onto her back and gazed at her perfect body against pure-white sheets. His breathing hitched as he envisioned her in white, walking toward him, smiling only at him and because of him. Soon, he thought. Erin Whitley would be his wife.

Chase pulled back the sheet, exposing her breasts, which seemed to heed his attention. She began to stir, which was a relief, since his cock throbbed and longed to be deep inside her heat. Not yet. He wanted to hear her. Nothing pleased him more than when she screamed with pleasure. He gently spread her legs and took in the glorious sight. She was beautiful…and wet. Even in her sleep, she was ready for him. He licked his lips and knelt down so his face was only millimeters from her tight, glistening nub. Chase inhaled her scent, which made him mad with desire. He suppressed a groan as he enjoyed the erotic silence, and licked at her clit. He felt her bottom buck into his hands and her fingers grabbed his hair in apparent need. With his tongue circling her clit, he looked up and she met his gaze. Though she had been asleep just moments ago, her eyes were crazed and it was clear that she was going to come very soon.

"Oh God!" she whimpered.

He wasn't going to last either. Her cries of ecstasy were enough to make him spill even before he had a chance of getting inside her. Chase lapped at her, tasting her once more before standing up and pulling her to the edge of the bed. He lifted both her legs onto his shoulders and entered her in one determined thrust of his hips. In this position, he was so deep he swore he felt the lip of her womb with the tip of his cock.

"Erin…baby!" He slid in and out of her, which prompted sounds from her that he had heard before, just not as loud, or as uninhibited. Her body thrashed against his as he pounded into her.

She reached around and cupped his balls as they slammed against her with each forceful stroke. "Never enough. I want it all," she panted.

The combination of her words and the jolting sensations that tingled through his sack from the touch of her hand sent him into a frenzy. He knew exactly how she felt. He could never get close enough, never burrow deep enough. He would never get enough of *her*.

"I love you," he groaned.

He felt her body quake and clench around him as she found her climax. With his name on her lips, he released his seed deep inside her, hoping one day very soon it would take root and grow into something, someone, he would cherish for the rest of his life.

Chapter Two

I could wake you up like that every morning. Just say the words."

Erin snuggled even closer, inhaling Chase's heady scent and basking in the afterglow of yet another round of lovemaking. A girl could definitely get used to Chase's version of a wake-up call.

"I mean it. Every morning could be just like this," Chase said, his tone serious.

Erin didn't realize that his initial statement warranted an answer. She thought he was just being playful before. Lying in his arms, she looked up at him and peered into eyes that matched his tone. She didn't know how to respond. Or if she was even reading him correctly. Was he asking her what she thought he was asking? If she was wrong, she would feel like a total idiot. But just lying there saying nothing wasn't productive either.

She bit her lower lip and then just went for it. "Are you saying…asking me if we…" Erin stared into his dark blue eyes and noticed that although the seriousness still remained, it was joined by deep warmth and a hint of laughter. She swallowed as she gathered the courage to complete her question.

"I'm asking you to move in with me. I want this every morning. Every moment of the day," he said, his lips curling into a small smile.

Erin exhaled as relief poured over her. She'd wanted so much not to be wrong. There was nothing she wanted more than to be with Chase morning, noon and night. She was just about to wrap her arms around his neck, smother him with kisses and exclaim, "Yes!" when reality set in. In her apartment, high up and secluded, it was easy to forget. There were things, ugly game-changing things, that needed to be discussed.

"There are things we need to talk about first," Erin said.

Chase started to say something when Erin cut him off by putting her finger over his lips. "If, after our conversation, you still want me to move in, well…"

"Okay, that's fair," he said, his voice muffled due to the finger that was still covering his lips.

Erin smiled. He could be so damn sexy and commanding one moment and irresistibly cute the next.

Focus. She had to focus. Lying in his arms was definitely not helping matters. She sat up and crisscrossed her legs. He too shifted in bed and replaced his smile with a look that told her that she had his full attention.

"That last day in your lab…when I told you good-bye…I received a text from *him*." Erin inhaled deeply. Chase's hand covered hers, as if for encouragement to continue. Treat it like a Band-Aid, she thought. Just get it over with. He already knew the bulk of it and he was still here. That had to mean something. Didn't it?

"He told me that if I don't stop seeing you, he will…" It's not like she couldn't find the words, she just didn't want to hear herself say them aloud. But again, she realized that it was best if she opted for full disclosure. "He would hurt you…kill you." Chase sat there, his expression revealing nothing. Erin cleared her voice as she prepared for the second part of the horrendous tale. "I believed him then and still do. He will follow through on his threat. He's not just a rapist, Chase. He may be a killer. We don't know for certain if Gabrielle committed suicide."

Chase's eyes narrowed. "I want to see the text. All of them," he said, his voice firm and businesslike.

Erin stood and retrieved her purse. She pulled out her phone and handed it to Chase. It took only a moment for Chase to find the string of texts between herself and her rapist. Erin watched his hand clench the phone as he scrolled through her messages. The stoic, unwavering expression he had been wearing morphed into one of fury.

"Paul told me that the police are no further along in catching this guy than they were last year, which is why, understandably, you are hesitant to continue to trust them with your life and sanity. But things have changed. This bastard has to be stopped." Chase stood and threw her phone onto the bed.

Erin nodded. She knew Chase was right. The situation had gotten out of control. It was too large for her to handle. She had been a fool to think she could have solved the problem on her own by buying a gun and luring him out of the city. She suddenly felt like that helpless woman in the cemetery again. Damn him!

Chase must have sensed she was silently beating herself up because he sat down next to her and took her in his arms. "We'll get through this. And when it's over, you'll never have to fear him again. I'll make certain of it." Erin didn't want to cry. She didn't want to shed another tear over what had happened to her. But she found herself sobbing as he embraced her.

"But…but he promises to kill you if we're together. I could… never live with myself if anything ever happened to…you," she said, between stuttered breaths.

"Nothing will happen to me." He reached up and tucked a stray lock of hair behind her ear. "And no one will keep us apart."

Erin nodded, though she kept her eyes closed in hopes of thwarting the tears from flowing.

She felt two fingers lift her chin as he said, "But we need help, Erin. Even I can admit that."

Erin finally looked into his loving blue eyes. "I'm scared, Chase. For you…for Paul…for me. He's a ghost, Chase. The police couldn't help me then and as recently as this month, they have prepared me for the possibility that this piece of shit may never be caught."

Chase released her gently and stood. He walked over to the French doors that overlooked the balcony. "Okay, no police. But would you be comfortable talking to Andrew? He is ex–secret service and most likely has contacts within who are still active. I think he could help us nail down what we are up against."

Erin had known about Andrew's previous position, but at the time she didn't think it was wise to bring him in on the current situation. Of course he knew that she had been raped and was currently being stalked, but that was the extent of it. Up until this point, his only job was to protect her with his life, not dig, not analyze or compose a profile. But like Chase had said, things had changed. Relieved that they were bypassing the police, Erin nodded, giving Chase the go-ahead to involve Andrew even more than he already had been. But before she would disclose a solitary detail surrounding her rapist, she needed to talk to Paul.

"I want to talk to Paul first. I want him to be on board with this," Erin said.

"I'll call him...while you start packing," Chase said with a smile. He walked toward the door, his cell phone in hand.

* * *

As Chase discussed the text that directed Erin to stay away from him and the possibility that Gabrielle's death may not have been a suicide, it was clear from Paul's expression that Erin had withheld some things from her brother. But Paul didn't seem angry; instead, he appeared relieved, as if he was able to finally put some of the pieces of the puzzle together. Chase looked back and forth between Erin and her brother. This was definitely a conversation that should have been conducted over something stronger than morning coffee. But time was of the essence and it was crucial that Andrew was brought into the fold as soon as possible.

"He will be discrete. I can promise you that," Chase said with confidence.

"I don't doubt his competence, Chase. But..." Paul stopped, reached over the kitchen island and held Erin's hand. "Is this what you want, Erin? Are you ready for this?"

Erin gave Paul's hand a squeeze. Chase marveled at just how close they were. He was thankful that she had had such a supportive and caring brother to lean on over the years.

"Yes. If sharing what happened to me with Andrew will help stop the bastard and keep the men I love safe, than I am definitely ready for this."

Chase couldn't hide the small grin that began to form at the mention of how she felt about him. He could never get tired of hearing Erin declare her love. And he would never tire of telling and showing her just how much he was in love with her.

Paul sighed and then smiled. "About time you finally fessed up, Erin. I was getting worried that I was going to have to be the one to tell Chase you loved him. And believe me, that would have been awkward."

The sudden lighthearted comment from Paul was a welcome distraction from the seriousness of the conversation and the three of them laughed. Chase placed his arm around Erin's waist and pulled her to his side. "As much as I appreciate your willingness to take one for the team, I must admit that I am thankful those words came from Erin and not you. No offense."

"None taken," Paul said, chuckling. Paul shook Chase's hand, as a symbol of final approval of the relationship.

Erin's smile seemed to brighten the entire room. Chase didn't want that moment to end, but it was time. Chase looked at Erin and said, "Are you ready to talk to Andrew?"

Erin took a deep breath. "With my two men at my side, how could I not be?"

Chapter Three

"Last night, my mommy told my daddy to not let the door hit him where the good Lord split him. What does that mean?"

Mia Ryan looked at her five-year-old student and searched her brain for the appropriate response. Mia had come to realize early on in her short career as a kindergarten teacher that nothing within the home was sacred. Embarrassing family secrets seemed to make their way into her classroom and were often shared at show and tell.

"I think your mommy wanted your daddy to be careful not to walk into the door as he left your house," Mia said, staring into Jessica's big, round eyes.

The little girl seemed to buy Mia's quick response and smiled. Jessica then turned and joined her friends at the Lego table. Mia took a mental note to keep an eye on the child. Just in case.

Mia shook her head, realizing that she would never shed her suspicious nature. Though she had left the police force over a year ago, she found herself always on alert and never accepting anything at face value. Ninety-nine percent of the time, comments and questions like Jessica's were harmless and never materialized into anything of concern. But she needed to be ready and vigilant if that one percent ever walked into her classroom.

Mia thought that her insatiable need to keep people safe would have been quelled when she left her position at the NYPD and started the career she had always dreamed of, even as a little girl, as a kindergarten teacher. But she had miscalculated the facts. Her unfinished business had followed her from one lifetime and into the next. She was on edge all the time, always looking over her shoulder for the one who got away. She had failed and those around her had paid dearly for her incompetence.

* * *

Andrew hadn't seen his niece in over a month and was definitely feeling the guilt mount as he ascended the steps of the bungalow she had acquired when his brother, Tim, had passed. Even now, Andrew still couldn't believe Tim was gone. He should have seen it coming.

Tim and his wife, Joyce, were that picture-perfect couple that others strived to be. It was difficult to determine by just looking at them if they had been married for three weeks or thirty years. They had always seemed like two lovesick teenagers, never able to keep their hands off each other.

When Joyce was killed, his brother withdrew from the world and as much as Andrew had tried to convince Tim that life was still worth living, the more Andrew pled life's case, the more Tim would retreat into his dark place.

The tragedy of it all was that Tim didn't live long enough to discover the identity of his wife's killer. Mia had worked day and night on her mother's case, rarely sleeping, barely eating. The day Mia had solved the case, she rushed home to tell her pop that the killer had been identified and was in custody. Mia had walked into his bedroom and found him slumped over in bed. At first she had thought that he was just sleeping. But she quickly discovered an empty and unmarked container of pills on the floor beside him and knew that she would never feel the warmth of his eyes upon her or hear him say, as he so often did, how proud he was that she, his only child, had followed in his footsteps as a police officer.

Andrew gave his typical rhythmic tap on the door and uttered his niece's name. He heard the sound of nails scratching wood and a deep, husky bark. The door swung open, revealing a woman who had seen too much in her young life, but who was still strong enough to stand there with her hands on her hips and display a smile he had adored since she was a little girl. The screen door kept the furry newcomer from leaping into Andrew's arms. The bark had deceived him. He had expected a German shepherd, a Rottie perhaps. But as he stared into the chocolate-brown eyes of a yellow Lab that was in that in-between stage of puppy and adult, Andrew concluded that Mia's new sidekick was just a big old baby.

"Uncle Drew, meet Henry," she said.

Andrew loved that Mia always picked up from where they left off. A week, a month, six months could go by and it was as if they had just seen each other. Mia had always been special to him. He remembered his weekly visits. Sunday-night dinner with his brother's family had been a ritual he never grew tired of. The night had been spent talking about their past week and the days ahead. Tim would discuss his latest case and Andrew would share as much about his own experiences as he could without breaking confidence and scaring his young niece.

But it had surprised and intrigued him to learn that Mia was not only fascinated with the stories her dad and uncle told, but she seemed to crave the details surrounding particular cases, especially the ones that appeared to have gone cold. She would ask question after question, all the while jotting the answers they gave into a black-marbled composition book. When she had finished with her interrogation, she would give her opinion, her take on the kind of criminal they were dealing with. As a youngster, she had been quick and insightful; as a teenager and young adult she had been alarmingly accurate, to the point Andrew knew she had a gift at profiling.

Although Andrew kept his observations and admiration of her skill to himself, Tim made it obvious how proud he was of his talented daughter. His constant comments and coaxing about joining the force had started to wear on her, forcing her to make a decision between a career she had always wanted and one she saw as a hobby, although she loved participating with her dad and uncle on the weekends. In the end, her aspirations to be a teacher had prevailed and she left New York to attend Lehigh University in Pennsylvania. Andrew had made certain that they stayed in contact during her four years at college, even visited her on occasion when he found a break in his unrelenting schedule. She had grown into a beautiful young woman, with every opportunity within her grasp.

And then the unthinkable occurred and every nightmare was realized. Her mother's body was discovered under a large oak tree in Central Park. Joyce had been raped and strangled, as the hand marks around her neck indicated.

Andrew had been the one to make the phone call. His brother

had been too distraught, blaming himself for what had happened to his wife, for not being there to protect her. The night of the murder had been uneventful. Tim had been at work, patrolling. Joyce had just finished her twelve-hour shift at Jefferson Hospital as a NICU nurse. The cameras had time-stamped her departure from the hospital at seven eighteen in the evening. She was discovered in the park around midnight by two teenagers. The young couple had literally stumbled over her body while trying to find a secluded spot to make out.

Despite his numerous pleas, Andrew could not convince Mia to stay put, at least for that night. She had made the ninety-minute drive in a little over an hour. The moment she had walked into her parents' home, he knew something inside of her had snapped. Mia's eyes had been bloodshot and crazed. He had tried to console her, but she wouldn't have it. She had rushed into her parents' bedroom, where she found her dad crying. She had knelt down, taking his head into her arms, and wept with him.

Andrew had expected Mia to spend some time at home after the funeral. But the weeks turned into months and it was apparent that Mia had no intention of returning to Pennsylvania, despite the fact she had been offered her first teaching position at some picturesque elementary school in the mountains. His suspicions were confirmed when she blurted out over dinner one Sunday night that she was joining the force. He remembered the look on Tim's face. He had actually smiled, though his joy could not completely extinguish the despair in his eyes.

Four months had passed and the police weren't any closer to finding out who had killed Joyce. The case was growing colder with each passing day. A month prior, the NYPD had forced Tim's hand and made him take early retirement. At the time, Andrew had thought it was best that his brother was no longer in the trenches and had been removed from such a morbid environment. But the moment Andrew had learned that his brother had killed himself, he questioned whether all that extra time on his hands only expedited his death, significantly reducing his reasons to wake up in the morning.

Andrew remembered paying Mia a visit the night before she had left for training. He had hugged her, whispering words of encouragement. Alone in her bedroom, her dad safely in the kitchen cooking meatballs—an activity he hadn't engaged in since Joyce's passing—Mia finally had let her guard down and sobbed into his chest. She didn't tell him why she was crying. She didn't have to.

"Don't tell him, Uncle Drew."

"You don't have to do this. This is not your dream, Mia."

"But I have to find the bastard. He's out there somewhere. Besides, look how happy, how proud my dad is. I haven't seen him look so alive since my mom…" she said, not allowing herself to finish.

"You would make him proud in whatever you do, whichever field you choose. Can't you see that?" Andrew asked, pleading with her to understand.

Mia shook her head. "I can do this for my dad. I'm going to find him; you'll see," she said, wiping her tears with the back of her hand. Attempting to compose herself, she cleared her throat and forced a smile.

Her decision had been made. There was no changing her mind. Andrew knew from the look in her eyes that there was no turning back. "I'm here for you, sweetheart. You know that, don't you?"

"Yeah, I do," she said, hugging him tightly.

He embraced her, allowing the chapters of her life to play in his mind at a speed he wanted so much to slow down and repeat over and over again. He remembered her first day of school and how she waved at him and her parents as she galloped onto the school bus with confidence. He recalled the night Mia had come home from school crying because Jason Wyatt had broken up with her through a note passed during gym class. His frown quickly turned into a smile at the memory of her scoring the game-winning basket in the girls' state championship. She couldn't wipe the smile off her face for an entire week after that.

With no children of his own, Andrew felt that Mia was more of a daughter to him than a niece. Although Andrew struggled to keep it together, he knew he had to stay strong, for both of them. "You are most definitely my favorite niece," he said, trying desperately to lighten the conversation.

"Not a difficult feat since I'm your only niece," she said, chuckling and sniffling at the same time.

"Quite a watchdog you got there. I should be careful that he doesn't lick me to death," Andrew mocked.

"Henry can be intimidating when he wants to be," Mia said, patting the big galumph on the head. With the dog's ears plastered back and his tail wagging incessantly, he couldn't look any more submissive.

"I'll take your word for it."

Mia opened the screen door, unleashing the gentle giant. He jumped up. Just as Andrew suspected, he was mauled and licked repeatedly. "Down, Henry!" Mia scolded. When she realized that Henry's excitement was nowhere close to dying down, she bribed him with a treat and put him in one of the bedrooms.

Andrew looked around the quaint home and realized that Mia hadn't changed anything in regards to the décor, with the exception of Henry. He didn't know if it was a good thing or a bad thing that the house appeared as if it was trapped in time. Andrew suspected it was the latter. He decided he would talk to his niece about her living situation, but not now. At the moment, there was something he needed to propose. It was a risk; he wasn't going to waste a moment denying it. The assignment he was asking her to take on would either unleash the demons she tried desperately to keep at bay and send her spiraling, or free her from the pain and guilt she harbored. Even as he uttered the words, he was still on the fence as to whether he was making the right decision.

"I have a favor to ask, sweetheart."

Chapter Four

Scott Morris's attention was divided. And he did not like it one bit.

The scene before him should have brought him satisfaction, as it had on so many occasions. He had just informed the young man in his office that his cancer was in remission. The man stood and, with tears in his eyes, thanked his doctor. Scott smiled in return and told his patient that he wished to see him every six months from here on out. He would always need to be monitored, but for now, he was in the clear. The man shook his hand and practically skipped out of his office.

Scott had cleansed his patient of the filth that had infested his body. Another creature made clean because of him. That was what was important. Not the patient's happiness or appreciation that he would live to see another day. It made no difference to him that the young man had a wife with a child on the way. Or that now, because of Scott's skills and attention to detail, the child would grow up with a father.

Scott was growing restless, a state that he was not at all comfortable with. Because it was during these times, when his typical patient and meticulous nature was compromised, that he could make a mistake.

Control, Focus, Control...Act.

He repeated the words over and over. Scott had made up his mind in those early hours when Chase Montclair had not reemerged from his Angel's apartment building. Erin had blatantly disobeyed him. She and her lover needed to be punished. There was no way to avoid that outcome. He knew from experience that he wouldn't be able to move on to the next one until the current situation was resolved.

There was a knock at the door.

"Come in," he said.

"Dr. Morris, I apologize for disturbing you. But would you be able to take a call from a Dr. Dennis Thompson?"

Scott looked at his secretary. He had gone through three in the past five months. A combination of job incompetence and an aura of filth had surrounded each woman who dared to assume the role as his secretary. So he was pleased when Ms. Beatrice Foley had taken the job. She was a widow, and from his very brief encounters with her, she appeared to lead a simple life. She also minded her own business. A definite plus, considering.

"Yes, I had reached out to him earlier to discuss a case. Please put Dr. Thompson through," Scott said, returning Beatrice's smile.

Beatrice nodded and left his office. Moments later his phone rang. "Dennis, thank you for getting back to me." Scott consulted with the world-renowned doctor, asking his opinion on a treatment schedule he wanted to implement for a patient of his. The type of cancer his patient had was fast moving and all encompassing. He needed to eradicate it quickly, but wanted the other doctor's take on this rare and deadly form of cancer. Scott was able to swallow his pride and accept guidance, if it resulted in a clean patient at the end of the day.

"Scott, I'm glad you called. I was meaning to reach out to you. I apologize that I was unable to attend your father's funeral. Mitchell was a wonderful man and will truly be missed."

Scott sat back in his leather swivel chair. "Thanks, Dennis. I still can't believe he's gone," he said, giving the man the socially appropriate and expected response.

"Listen, Scott, a few of my colleagues are going hunting for a few days. Not sure if you hunt, but I was wondering if you wanted to get away for a while, get your mind off of things? I have a cabin upstate, nothing glamorous, but it has the necessities."

Scott's immediate reaction was to say no thank you. But before he blurted out such a knee-jerk response, he thought about it for a split second.

When one door closes, another opens.

"You know, I think I'll take you up on that. A little time away would be good," he said, his voice fitted with a touch of contrived sadness.

"Excellent. I'll call you later with the details. Unfortunately, I have a patient waiting for me."

"Not a problem, Dennis. We'll talk soon."

Chapter Five

Having second thoughts?"

Erin realized she had been attempting to hang up the same frustrating silk blouse in her side of the closet for at least a minute. Although the fabric would not cooperate and kept slipping off the hanger and onto the floor, Erin knew she was distracted, making the menial task at hand that much more cumbersome.

Erin dropped the shirt, allowing it to pool into a delicate heap on the floor, and turned to face Chase. She took him in, devouring him from head to toe. Though he wore his favorite worn jeans and a simple t-shirt, he looked beautiful and ready to be kissed. As much as she wanted to tear out of his closet, their closet, and tackle him onto the bed, she needed to get that worried look off of his face...and fast.

"Second thoughts?" she asked.

"About us moving in together?" he asked, his expression growing more serious by the second.

Erin sighed. He actually thought that she was reconsidering moving in with him? Well, if that was the case, she needed to clear up his misperception real quick. She closed in on him and wrapped her arms around his neck. Erin breathed in his scent, a combination of soap and pure maleness, and moaned in appreciation. She gave his ear a gentle nip before caressing his neck with strategically placed kisses.

"Erin, they will be here any moment. You know we won't be able to finish what we…" Erin cut him off with a kiss to the mouth and he groaned. Those admirable seconds of restraint were forgotten as he thrust his hands into her hair and reciprocated with his own hot kiss. She was so hungry for him, so needy, that she couldn't wait to get to the bed. She wanted him right there in front of the French doors, where the moon could spill in and illuminate his perfect body. Erin yanked off her tank top and easy-access yoga pants and stared at him.

"God, you're beautiful…and mine," he said, taking off his shirt and pants.

He was ready for her. He was always ready for her. She sank to her knees and licked her lips. The head was glistening with glorious anticipation. She needed to taste him, feel his essence on her tongue. With her hands firmly cupping his ass, she lapped at the mounting beads of liquid. Erin could feel her own wetness give way, and it shamelessly spilled over onto the insides of her thighs. She was just about to take him deep when he lifted her to her feet, bent her over the love seat, and slid into her.

Erin gasped, not from pain or shock, but from pure pleasure. His fingers massaged her ass while his cock found her core with each expertly driven thrust. She cried out, feeling every sensation at once. She started to look over her shoulder, to catch a glimpse of him as he worked her body and took what she happily offered, but stopped short when she caught a glimpse of their reflection in the glass of the balcony door. Though the image lacked distinct definition or detail, their lovemaking was firmly captured and she marveled at the sight.

"Oh baby," he groaned, rocking into her.

The sound of his voice was the only thing that could steal her attention from the couple in the window. "Go ahead and watch, my love. I want you to see how your body welcomes me in…how your body aches to be claimed." Her embarrassment for being caught was instantly replaced with burning desire when she looked into his eyes.

She didn't need to be told twice. Erin was anxious to return her gaze to the erotic image in the windowpane. She felt and saw Chase's hand release her ass and navigate to her belly and then lower. His breathing became labored as he continued to pound into her from behind. Erin felt two fingers gently stroke the taut nub between her folds. Her body had been on the brink of climax, but the moment he started to caress her clit, she knew she had only moments. She threw her head back and pleaded for him to come with her.

"Chase, come with me…please!" she begged.

"I'm with you, baby. Now watch how you make me come," he said, his voice strained.

Erin looked back at the window. She saw his eyes close as his thrusts became more intense. The look on his face, the raw emotion he made no attempt to conceal, brought forth her own orgasm and she finally let go. As he pumped into her, his warmth flooding her body, she watched him mouth the words, "I love you."

Chapter Six

Mia's instincts told her to run. Sprint was more like it. But she didn't. And how could she? Her uncle had never asked her for a favor before. In all her years, he had never once asked her for a single thing. There was no way she could turn him down. He needed her. Uncle Drew, a man who never seemed to need or want anything, needed her help now. Mia wasn't about to disappoint him, the man who had been like a second father to her.

Uncle Drew greeted her as she entered Chase Montclair's penthouse. Although he gave her a kiss on the cheek, she knew he was all business. She felt his firearm beneath his perfectly pressed suit as she hugged him.

"Thanks for coming, sweetheart. If this becomes too difficult for you, just tell me." His eyes grew soft. "I'll find another way to find this son-of-a-bitch if this case…brings up too many memories." Uncle Drew touched her chin with his two fingers and held it steady. Mia got the feeling that he was looking for something, a sign, perhaps, that she was too fragile, too vulnerable to take on the responsibility.

Mia held his gaze and smiled. Her demons might stir in the wee hours of the morning, interrupting her sleep with nightmares, but while awake and lucid she was somehow able to carry on with life. "Let's get to work," she said. His hand fell away. He returned the smile and led her to what appeared to be an office. Although the room had the essential office décor, computer, phone, desk and the like, it was also a space that required those occupying its walls to be comfortable. Her eyes were drawn to the two plush couches and matching chair positioned in front of a set of French doors. The room was saturated in earth tones, from the color of paint on the walls to the thick Oriental rug at her feet. While the office definitely gave off a more masculine feel, her sense of smell detected a floral scent, which complimented the room perfectly.

Mia walked farther into the room. She withdrew her composition book and a pen from her canvas bag and placed the bag on the floor next to the chair. Mia remembered how she initially felt when she received that bag as a Christmas gift from one of her students. She thought that sporting a bag that said *#1 Teacher* would make her feel self-conscious, as if she had bought it for herself and was bragging. It had taken her less than a day to carry that bag with pride and to realize how silly she was being.

"I'll tell Ms. Whitley and Mr. Montclair that you have arrived."

But before Uncle Drew could turn around, Mia was hit with a wave of that floral scent. "Ms. Ryan, thank you for coming."

Mia stared at the couple in the doorway and smiled. The woman—Erin, she could only assume—wore gray yoga pants and a fitted t-shirt. With her feet bare, her hair in a ponytail and her face free of any obvious makeup, she looked young and fresh. Mia took notice that Mr. Montclair's hand never left the small of her back as they walked toward her.

"Not a problem," she said, smiling at the couple and then at her uncle. Mia couldn't help but think that Uncle Drew appeared worried. She gave him a look, one that was meant to relieve him, one that told him: *I'm fine, I can do this.*

He nodded, though she was unsure if he really believed her. "I'll be right outside…if you need me," Uncle Drew said. He looked at the couple, but Mia knew the message was for her and her alone.

"Thanks, Andrew," Erin said, smiling warmly. There was genuine respect and appreciation behind those two words. Mia liked Erin already.

"Please call me Mia." she said.

Erin chuckled. "I can't tell you how many times I've asked, no begged, your uncle to call me by my first name."

"Stop trying. He won't budge on that. One of his many self-made rules," Mia said. "I imagine the formality enables him to stay focused. Whatever the reason, he is great at what he does."

"Very well, I will stop harassing him," Erin said with a sigh. "That is, if you call us by our first names."

"Done," Mia said, smiling.

"I trust Andrew expressed not only our desire, but our absolute need, to keep this matter between us. It is of the utmost importance," Chase said firmly. He led Erin to the couch. She immediately sat down, tucking her feet behind her. He put his arm around her and drew her close. He was her protector. A presence not to be reckoned with. His devotion to her was obvious, as was her love for him.

Mia sat in the chair opposite them. "I know my uncle told you that I was a profiler for the NYPD, but have since left the force." Mia eyed them closely, contemplating how much she should tell them. She knew her uncle. He would never have disclosed much more than that. He respected her privacy.

Despite just meeting this man and woman, she couldn't help but trust them. Although it was out of character for her to establish trust with someone so quickly. The years on the force, her mother's murder, and her father's suicide had left her guarded. And that was putting it lightly. "But now…well, now I teach twenty-five kindergarten children how to read, write and color. I show them how to play nicely and take turns. I am also assisting a handful of children in mastering the art of going on the potty consistently. My life has changed and I'm grateful for that." She cleared her throat. The next admission was a bit more difficult. "But I still think like a profiler…despite my time away. My uncle asked me to help you. You can trust that I'll do everything I can." Mia opened her composition book and dated the page. "And as for discretion, let's just say that my uncle and I are cut from the same cloth in that regard."

Chase squeezed Erin's hand and leaned back a few inches. He appeared satisfied with that response.

"It's essential for me to interview everyone involved. And it's of even greater importance that I speak to each person separately."

"Well, that shouldn't take too long. The only people who know about…about the rape are Chase, Andrew and my brother, Paul." Erin shifted in her seat, which only made Chase pull her closer to him.

Mia quickly secured her mask, her impenetrable poker face. Her heart quickened at the mention of the heinous crime, a crime that was too close to home. Breathe, Mia. You can do this.

Chase suddenly appeared uncomfortable. "I thought that you would talk to us…you know…as a group?"

Mia shook her head and closed the book. "Look, it took me all of two seconds to conclude how much you two care for one another." Erin smiled and her cheeks took on a rosy glow. "And it is for that reason that I need to talk to you separately."

Chase's eyes narrowed. He was not pleased. "I think I should stay…for support."

He was not going to win this. Mia had a feeling that it was a rare occurrence for Chase Montclair to be told no. "Your presence may force Erin to censor her recollection of the crime. Details may be omitted to spare your feelings. Chase, you need to have faith that I know what I'm doing." His jaw clenched as she stared at him. "In my experience, it's those details, those seemingly unimportant and many-times disturbing clues, which enable me to zero in on the suspect."

"Chase, I'll be just fine." Erin gave him a quick kiss on the cheek and a pat on the thigh.

With his jaw slackened only slightly, he didn't appear convinced. "Okay. I'll be in the kitchen if you need me. Can I get you ladies anything to drink? Water? Coffee?"

"I'm good. Thank you, anyway," Mia said.

"Me too," Erin said.

Chase sighed. His excuse to return to the office and be present for Erin's interview was squashed on the spot. Chase stood and walked toward the door. But before he made his exit, he turned and said, "Take care of my girl, Mia."

Erin blushed.

Mia couldn't help but feel envious of their relationship. She wondered if she would ever find something even remotely resembling the love and devotion she had just witnessed between Chase and

Erin. The chances were slim considering her tendency to shut out the world. The truth was that she was a functional hermit. She may go to a job she loved during the day, shop for food, and run errands like a normal person, but that was all a façade, an illusion that she was living a fulfilling life.

The sound of the door closing signified that the session had begun. Exhilaration and trepidation were competing for dominance. Mia had always enjoyed the challenge, the moment when all the pieces of the puzzle were laid out haphazardly, pleading with her to make them fit. But now the typical excitement she felt at the onset of a case was clouded by her own fear. It was impossible for her not to think about her mother. There would be similarities, details that would trigger painful memories she needed to keep tucked away.

Mia looked at the woman across from her. Though Erin's eyes radiated warmth, Mia couldn't mistake that familiar shadow, a shadow that threatened to snuff out the light. Erin needed her help. And that meant putting her own issues aside. Actually, it meant stuffing her demons further into that dark chasm, where they couldn't interfere and taint the present.

Chapter Seven

Erin watched Mia scribble furiously into her composition book and wondered what kind of person chose to profile. Mia's motivation and her skill to listen, analyze and identify intrigued Erin. She suspected that Mia had a story of her own, one that was rarely told.

They spent the first hour discussing the years leading up to the rape, which included her parents' passing. Erin told Mia about the night she learned they had drowned. She found herself going into vivid detail when she explained how her brother had looked as the police officer informed her that they were gone. With his eyes bloodshot, his body in shock, Paul Whitley had stood there as if the current reality was just a cruel delusion. Erin moved on and talked about how Professor Farrell, Josh Graham and a handful of other college friends had helped her through that dark period of her life.

"Talk to me about Josh," Mia said.

Erin instantly felt guilty. He had visited her a couple weeks ago and had helped her move into her apartment. They had spoken only once since then. Yes, she had a lot going on, between her relationship with Chase and the rapist at large, but still. Would it kill her to pick up the phone and say hi to an old friend? She needed to rectify that situation. Erin mentally put that on her to-do list.

"We met in Chemistry class during freshman year. We were both premed, so we shared a lot of the same classes throughout our years at Penn. He was, is, a good friend, though I have made little attempt to stay in touch."

"Were you always just friends?" Mia asked.

It was a fair question and she'd suspected that Mia was going there. "Yes, it was always platonic."

"Did he ever want your friendship to morph into something else?"

"No, I don't think so. If he did, he never let on." Erin laughed. "Let's just say that he never gave me reason to believe that he was secretly pining for me. He never hid his relationships, or encounters, with women from me."

"So, Josh was a player?"

Erin shook her head. The word "player" sounded so ugly. He may have dated many women, but he didn't dupe them or give them the impression that he was looking for anything long-term. "No, I wouldn't call him that. I mean, yes, his bed was rarely empty, but he never used manipulation to get them there. He didn't have to."

"Okay. Tell me about your other college friends."

It didn't take very long to discuss the friends she had acquired at Penn. It was a very short list, which was what Erin had preferred.

The conversation drifted to Erin's volunteer work at the Children's Hospital of Philadelphia. She spoke in greater detail about her original career aspirations and the wonderful opportunity she was given to work alongside Dr. Mitchell Morris.

"I attended his funeral this past week."

"Oh, I'm so sorry, Erin."

Erin smiled weakly. "Thanks. It was just so sudden. I saw him the night before he died at a benefit. Dr. Morris had looked pale and just…off. A few days later, his son came to my work and told me that his father had fallen down the steps in his home in Philly, where he succumbed to his injuries."

Mia's pencil stopped its mad scribbling and hovered over the lined paper. "Did you know Dr. Morris's son prior to this?"

"Dr. Morris's son, Scott, is also a doctor. We met at CHOP over a year ago in his father's office. I hadn't seen or spoken to him since. We were recently reintroduced at the Maya Montclair Foundation benefit last week."

Mia tapped the eraser end of her pencil against her book. "Describe him for me, Erin."

Erin hesitated.

"I estimate him to be over six foot, brown hair, brown eyes…clean-cut. He comes across as a little arrogant."

"Would you describe him as handsome?"

"Although he's not my type, I imagine he doesn't have difficulty finding women."

"So, he is attractive and a doctor. What makes him not your type?" Mia asked, her voice curious.

Erin shrugged her shoulders. She didn't know exactly, but something about Scott Morris turned her off.

"Is it because he's arrogant?"

"Possibly…not sure."

Mia turned a page in her book and sat up straight. Mia either sensed Erin's reluctance to talk about Scott Morris, or she found him not worthy to discuss further, because she switched gears and asked her about the night she was raped. Erin knew that this was coming, that everything they had discussed this past hour and a half was leading up to full and complete disclosure regarding the rape itself.

Erin must have appeared nervous, because Mia asked, "Erin, would you like to take a break?"

"No. I want to tell you what happened. It's just…"

Mia stared at her as if contemplating her next move, her next question to unload. Suddenly, Mia spoke. Erin's instincts had been correct. Mia most definitely had a story to tell.

Chapter Eight

Mia knew that disclosing a piece of her past would bring Erin comfort, putting her at ease and making her more willing to share critical information pertaining to the night in question. Mia rarely resorted to such a tactic. And it wasn't a tactic that was driving her now. Rather, it was the selfish need to share some horrible things with another breathing soul.

"Did my uncle tell you why I left the force?"

"No, he is rather tight-lipped," Erin said.

Mia nodded, knowing just how discreet he could be. "I joined the force shortly after my mother was raped and murdered. I worked on her case for two years before we found her attacker. But I was too late. My father, in his grief, took his own life. I resigned some time later and resumed my pursuit of landing a teaching position."

Mia expected to find Erin in a state of disbelief or a little shocked at what she had just admitted. Instead, Erin sat there, listening attentively, unfazed, as if she somehow expected that Mia's closet was riddled with skeletons.

"You see, it was in the details, those small, seemingly inconsequential details, that I discovered the identity of my mother's attacker. They often make all the difference, Erin."

Erin nodded. "I'm so sorry, Mia. I had no idea…I mean…I can't imagine that this is easy for you. Thank you for coming here to help me…to help us."

Mia smiled. She now understood why her uncle sought her out. Though the beautiful woman in front of her was intelligent and a fighter, she would never rest comfortably until the man who had raped her was captured, or better yet, silenced.

Erin exhaled and unleashed the events of that night in excruciating detail. Mia was thankful that Chase had kept his distance and had not insisted on staying. No boyfriend, fiancé, or husband should know the intricacies of how his woman had been violated. Erin described how he looked, smelled and tasted. She told Mia what he had whispered to her, that he knew her by name, that he had been waiting for her. Mia was impressed that she was able to recount so many details after a year's time. She jotted the details down in her composition book for future review. Right now, she just wanted Erin to talk, unload actually, everything she could remember.

But it wasn't without consequences. After two hours of interrogation and recall, Erin was spent. Mia didn't want to end the session, but she also knew that it wasn't wise to probe or question someone if her mind was tainted by exhaustion. It could skew Erin's recollection of events. It was best to come back when she was fresh.

"Erin, you did great tonight. I have enough to get started."

Erin stifled a yawn. "You're leaving already?"

Mia smiled. "We've been at this for over two hours."

Erin's eyes widened. "Two hours! Are you kidding me?"

"I'm not kidding you. We will need to put a little more time in, though. Can I come over tomorrow?" Mia put her book and pencil in her bag and stood.

"Of course." Erin rose from the couch and walked her to the door.

"I'll need to speak with your brother and Chase as well. Will they be available?"

"Don't worry, I'll make certain of it," Erin said. "But I must warn you, my brother isn't very forthcoming. He will give you the facts and answer your questions, but will not elaborate. And…well…he doesn't trust easily."

"Is he a lawyer by any chance?" Mia asked.

Erin laughed. "Andrew said you were competent at what you do."

Chapter Nine

Although Paul trusted Andrew's judgment, he wasn't completely comfortable allowing another person into the mix. But time was running out. His sister was in danger and threats were being made against the man she loved. Which made Paul feel helpless. Which made him feel like a failure.

It didn't matter that he had secured a great job at one of the top law firms in the city fresh out of college. He could not care less that he was apparently making a name for himself in a short time, as his salary and the bonuses he was earning proved. He had even fooled his sister into thinking he was pulling insane hours at the office because he was so in love with his career. The real reason he buried himself in his work was to avoid life.

Before his parents' death and his sister's rape, he had smiled more, laughed without considering the consequences and was optimistic about his future. He had always been a little on the "serious side" as his parents would say lovingly, but he could let loose from time to time, especially around his sister. Erin had the ability to make him feel at ease, which allowed him to just be himself. She loved him no matter what, even if he was in a mood.

But that night in the cemetery had changed him somehow. The reoccurring vision he had of that animal violating his sister left him in an eternal state of turmoil and unrest. There were other repercussions, like the fact he hadn't been with a woman since that horrific night or even attempted to date. It wasn't like he didn't have opportunities. There were plenty of women he had come in contact with over the course of the year, through work or in more casual settings, that in his other life he would have happily taken into his bed.

Despite those grueling days as a student in law school, he had found the time to pleasure women. Although his encounters had rarely progressed past a second date, he never disrespected the women he had taken into his bedroom by making hollow promises of forever. He had been honest with them, never allowing anyone to get too close.

He had always been a bit guarded, even as a boy. Unfortunately, his predisposition to distance himself from others served as the perfect foundation. Upon seeing his sister raped, he withdrew from the world completely and was content to stay away, refraining from intimacy or any situation that could invoke emotions. It was safer that way.

Andrew met Paul in Chase's foyer. Paul shook his hand firmly and then looked around for Mia Ryan. He couldn't help be a little skeptical and, to his embarrassment…sexist. In his experience, profilers were typically men. They also had more years under their belts. From Andrew's brief description, he estimated Ms. Ryan to be in her mid-twenties. He knew he shouldn't dwell on that too much. It infuriated him when people thought, and when the more brazen verbalized to his face, that he looked too young to have landed a position at Pierce and Stone. But still. How could he not be wary of Ms. Ryan's ability?

"Mia should be here any minute," Andrew said, as if reading his thoughts.

Paul nodded and then made his way into the kitchen. Chase was in the process of taking off a plastic lid to the most enormous sandwich tray that he had ever seen. Paul didn't need to see where the sandwiches had come from. He would know a Monty's sandwich anywhere. He and Erin were regulars at that deli. Erin was retrieving several bottles of water from the fridge. With her arms full, she shut the fridge door with a toss of her hip.

Paul had been worried that she and Chase might be taking things a little too fast, moving in together after only a few weeks. But Paul couldn't dismiss how happy Erin looked…and how at home she appeared in Chase's kitchen. He was thankful that he had kept his mouth shut. Who was he to give relationship advice anyway? He hadn't been on a date in over a year. The urge to be with someone and satisfy his most primal need was still there, that was for certain. He had no problem finding his own climax. He simply just couldn't take the risk of losing something or someone else in his life.

"Hey you! Perfect timing. Care for a sandwich?" Erin asked.

"There's enough food here to feed an army. How many people are you expecting? Or is Mia Ryan a sloppy-sandwich junkie like you?" Paul asked, eyeing the spread.

"I most certainly don't shy away from a messy sandwich."

Paul turned to face Mia Ryan. He hadn't known what to expect. Actually, he did have a picture in his mind of what she might look like, but this was not it. Holy hell, did he love being wrong! With her long brown hair cascading over her shoulders in thick, gentle waves against perfect skin, she was absolutely gorgeous.

Paul quickly summoned the gods to give him strength and composure. He could handle this. He was a lawyer. He concealed emotion and practiced neutrality for a living. Paul took a few short breaths and walked over to the young woman.

"Nice to meet you, Ms. Ryan. I'm Paul, Erin's brother." He reached out and shook her hand. Its warmth radiated throughout his body and for a second he couldn't breathe. With her deep blue eyes staring into his, she too looked to be at a loss for words. A glint of amusement had been replaced with another emotion, but what? It looked very much like desire. But he had been out of the game, out of touch with women for so long, he could be completely off and misjudging her response completely.

"Mia," she replied, her voice shaky. She had sounded so confident just a moment ago, when his back was turned, before their eyes had met.

He needed to pull himself together and quick. Mia appeared unsteady, giving him the encouragement to appear slightly more composed. "Thanks for coming last night and again tonight."

Mia withdrew her hand from his. He sorely detested the feeling it invoked. The sudden disconnect was unsettling.

"I'm happy to help," Mia said, looking from Paul to Erin and Chase. She smiled, but it did not bring him joy. Her attention had shifted from him to the happy couple in the kitchen.

What the hell was wrong with him? There was no rational explanation for why he was so captivated by her. He had been without a woman for too long. That had to be it.

Paul secured his mask, the one he wore in court, the only one he was comfortable wearing these days. "I don't have a lot of time and will need to get back to the office for a late meeting. Can we get started?" he asked, his voice firmer than he had intended.

Mia didn't get the opportunity to respond because Erin immediately jumped down his throat. "Paul, she just walked through the door." Erin glared at him. "Mia, are you hungry? We ordered from Monty's."

Paul felt the weight of Mia's gaze and looked over at her. That hint of desire he thought, hoped, he had detected just moments ago had morphed into something that resembled agitation. Actually, she looked pissed. With her brow raised, she responded, "No thank you, Erin. I had a bite to eat before I came."

With whom?

Paul had no idea where that thought came from or why he would remotely care who Mia Ryan, a woman he had just met, ate dinner with. He tried to fight back the urge to look down at her ring finger, but his curiosity won out. He masked his sigh of relief by clearing his throat. No wedding band, engagement ring, or any jewelry for that matter, adorned her perfect body. Worn jeans hugged glorious curves, while a fitted t-shirt emphasized breasts that were lush, but perky. God, she was stunning.

And still annoyed at him.

He realized that it was pointless to apologize for being rude. What could he possibly say, anyway? *Sorry for sounding so cold a moment ago, but it's the only way I know how to combat the fire that you seem to have ignited within me.* No, maintaining distance was a good thing. Mia Ryan would just have to deal with his clipped tone.

* * *

Erin gave Paul a dirty look and then glanced at Mia.

"Well, we will have plenty of leftovers. I'll make sure you take home a doggy bag," Erin said.

"That would be great. Should we use the office again, Chase?" Mia asked.

Chase held up a finger while he swallowed a bite of his sandwich. He wiped his mouth with a napkin and then answered, "Sorry about that, Mia. Yes, of course. The office is all yours." Mia watched Chase's arm disappear around Erin's waist and he gave her a squeeze. Erin gave him a gentle elbow to the side, but Mia could tell by the way she leaned in afterward and how she looked at him with affection, that she adored him.

The scene only brought Mia sadness. The stars would be aligned, hell would be firmly frozen over, and piglets would have sprouted wings to fly, before she found someone who looked at her like that. It wasn't self-pity that made her come to that conclusion. It was logic. In order to meet someone, you need to put yourself out there and trust that people won't disappoint you, that they won't leave you. And she wasn't ready or willing to take that risk.

"And don't worry, Paul. I can be thorough and conscious of the time. Are you ready?" Mia asked, grabbing her bag, not even giving Paul the courtesy of looking at him when she spoke.

"Please, by all means, lead the way," Paul said, his voice sounding smug and regrettably...sexy.

Mia gave Chase and Erin a wave and headed down the hallway to Chase's office with Paul at her heels. Mia got the sense that he was analyzing her, probably using his big boy lawyer skills to determine if she was worthy to complete the task at hand. Who the hell did he think he was to doubt her ability? Well, he had the right to question her credentials, but he didn't need to be an ass.

Mia walked into the room and took her seat from the night before. Paul removed his suit jacket and sat down on the couch directly across from her. He rolled up his sleeves and unraveled his tie a bit before folding his hands in his lap. Mia caught herself staring at him for a second before quickly looking down and fumbling for her composition book. She had noticed in the kitchen that he was handsome, but his rudeness had overshadowed his looks. But now, with him only a few feet from her, his tie not so severe, his body more relaxed, Mia couldn't dismiss the fact that he was the most tempting man she had ever seen.

She needed to get a grip. A big neon sign with arrows pointing to the words *CONFLICT OF INTEREST* may as well have been flashing over his head. Mia dated the page in her book. She had a job to do. She might not be getting paid for doing this, nor did she want to be, but it was important that Erin, Chase and Paul were considered clients, nothing more. And you didn't get involved, or openly gawk, at clients. Even gorgeous ones with haunting blue eyes and dirty blond hair that screamed to be mussed.

"Well, Erin and I got off to a good start last night, but we have some more ground to cover. Right now, though, I would like to ask you some questions. It will give me a more comprehensive look," Mia said, successfully shifting into the role of the professional she was. It wasn't too difficult to do when she thought about the woman in the other room.

"Of course. What would you like to know?" he asked, stiffly.

"The night Erin completed her last final exam, you texted her to stay put, not to walk home alone. Had you been concerned with her safety or felt that she was at risk for some reason?"

"Women are always at risk for the unthinkable." Paul shifted his legs. "To answer your question, no, there was no specific threat that I was aware of. Erin didn't have any enemies. She had a few friends in college she enjoyed hanging out with. But most of her college years were spent studying and preparing for medical school."

The frustration in his voice was evident and it was important that Mia help him simmer down, enough to get through the session. She feared that the next line of questioning was only going to anger him. But if she wanted answers, she had to plow forward. "Erin told me that you saved her."

"No, she was being kind. I was too late," Paul said.

"And that is as far as Erin and I got last night," Mia said.

Paul looked at her, a curious glimmer in his eyes. "Oh, you didn't get to the part where I interrupted the bastard from…" Paul stood and paced the room. He thrust his hands through his hair. "You didn't get to the part where I beat the fucker so severely…that I left him to bleed out in that cemetery."

Mia lifted her eyes from the page. There was no chance in hell she was going to be able to calm him down. He was like a caged tiger, aching to pace with no bars to keep him restrained. "No, but I hope you'll tell me," she said, trying desperately to keep her voice flat and unwavering.

He came to an abrupt halt and looked at her, his eyes boring into hers. "Mia Ryan, profiler turned kindergarten teacher. Amuse me. Tell me how one goes from studying horrific crimes and the perps that commit them to conducting story hour for five-year-olds."

Mia couldn't be certain if he was insulting her or if he was just trying to evade her questions and the retelling of his sister's rape. She wanted to tell him how she got to this point in her life. Maybe it would even make him feel like a real shit when she told him all the grisly details about how she was thrust into her profiling career as a result of her mother's rape. But she kept quiet, refusing to take the bait.

"I don't get to ask questions, Mia? How is that fair?" Paul said, his tone revealing that although he was annoyed, he was going to concede. He sat back down on the couch and continued where he had left off.

"After I beat him the first time, I checked on the woman. Until that point, I had no idea the cry for help had belonged to my sister. I looked at her. Her face registered, but the blood…it was all I could see."

Mia could tell by his softened tone that he was right back there, in that cemetery, like not a day had gone by. His emotions were in disarray and though he hid them well, she was able to get a glimpse of how vulnerable he could be when it came to someone he cared for. "As soon as the shock wore off, I went back to finish him off and unmask the piece of shit. But in addition to the blood that was coming from…well beneath her dress, she was bleeding from her side and it was then I learned that she had sustained another injury. She passed out in my arms as I carried her to the hospital around the corner."

Mia slowed her breathing, a method she employed to calm herself when she needed to appear in control. She was careful not to smile, frown or give off any emotion that would indicate that she was passing judgment.

"Are you profiling me now, Mia?" he asked with a smirk, though it was not at all playful.

"No, Paul. I'm afraid that I don't have time for that." She needed to keep the session moving along.

"Very well." He folded his hands again. "Once at the hospital, a rape kit was conducted and the police were called. We reported the crime and though the police immediately went to the cemetery to investigate, they only came back with blood samples, not a body, like I had hoped. Knowing that he was still out there, I packed up Erin's apartment and mine, and left for New York in the middle of the night. We stayed in a hotel for three weeks until the apartment we had planned to lease was ready. I started my job at Pierce and Stone, and Erin started hers at Montclair Pharmaceuticals a few months later." Mia didn't need to ask why Erin had changed her career plans. She knew personally that one's path could shift without notice.

"At what point did he make contact?" Mia asked. She continued to jot down notes, piecing together the thoughts in her head and memorializing them on paper.

"One year from the date of the rape. Erin went to a club with a few friends from work. Chase arrived at the club less than an hour after she arrived. He said she appeared wasted, which was not typical for my sister. Chase took her home, phoned a friend of his, who was fortunately a doctor and who took care of her. She had been drugged. A urine test showed that she had been exposed to HGB. The next morning a bouquet of flowers was sent by the bastard to Chase's penthouse."

"How did she know it was from him?" Mia asked.

"The asshole had the balls to wish her well…that he hoped she was feeling better."

"Anything else?" Mia asked. She had a feeling that he had omitted a critical piece.

Paul loosened his tie further. It was obvious she was making him uncomfortable. Mia felt guilty pressing him to remember, but it was of the utmost importance for him to continue.

"'Angel.'"

Mia's brow rose at the sound of a word that for many suggested wholesomeness, purity.

"It's what he calls her. It was printed on the card." A twinge of excitement surged through Mia. Killers and rapists often used nicknames when addressing their victims. More times than not, those pet names held a double meaning.

Angels represented innocence and virtue...cleanliness. Mia knew her next question would sting a bit, but she felt that she was honing in on a critical detail. "Paul, the night Erin was raped, you spoke of...of the blood beneath her dress."

Paul looked away, but responded, "I'm...I'm not certain she was a virgin. We didn't discuss our sex lives with each other, being brother and sister and all. But the blood...well I wouldn't have been surprised if she had never been with anyone until that night." Mia scribbled in her notebook, putting an asterisk next to the word "virgin."

Mia had been busy taking notes when she heard Paul shift on the couch. He rolled his sleeves down and buttoned them at his wrist. He readjusted his tie back into a perfect knot. Paul was transforming back into lawyer mode, which would most likely make him less forthcoming and even more abrupt than the "relaxed" version.

"This feels more like therapy than a question-and-answer session," he said curtly.

Yep, Paul the attorney was back. And it was obvious that he had had his fill for the night. He stood and reached for his suit jacket, not even waiting for a response.

"Oh, so you see a therapist?" Mia asked, unable to control herself. She didn't want to upset him further. It had taken a lot for him to dredge up such memories, but still. He didn't need to take it out on her.

Paul slipped on his jacket with two violent jerks of his arms. "We are finished here," he said, walking toward the door.

No. They weren't done. Not by a long shot. "For now," she said.

He didn't bother to look back at her. Paul Whitley stormed out of the office, slamming the door behind him.

Chapter Ten

I wouldn't take it personally," Chase said from the doorway.

Mia forced a smile. She had wondered if Paul had said something to Chase and Erin, maybe vented about the incompetent profiler who was handling their case before leaving for his meeting in a colossal huff.

"I understand why he is so…guarded. I'm a stranger…who is asking some very probing questions." She was sympathetic and recognized how difficult it was for someone to share something so personal. But she wasn't about to let him speak to her with disrespect, as if it took all that he had to just tolerate her.

Chase walked over and took a seat on the couch. "I guess it's my turn," he said, stretching his legs out in front of him.

Although Mia suspected Chase's session would be the shortest in duration, she had the feeling that she would have to do a lot of dancing, making sure that her questions didn't elicit the fury she knew she could unleash. His girlfriend had been raped and continued to be stalked. How could he not feel helpless, angry…grief-stricken over how she had suffered?

Chase had come into Erin's life just a few weeks before. That was where she would start. There was no need to discuss the details of that night with him. Not now anyway.

* * *

Chase told Mia everything he could remember about the last several weeks, from the morning after Erin had been drugged to the present. Which, of course, included Gabrielle and her involvement with the rapist. Chase showed Mia the text Gabrielle had sent him the night she supposedly had killed herself. He couldn't blame the police for coming to that conclusion. She had attempted before utilizing the same cocktail: alcohol and drugs. Chase was thankful that Gabrielle's family had kept their daughter's last arrangements private. A viewing or funeral would have been incredibly awkward for him to attend.

"Let's back up a little. Talk to me more about the benefit. Was there anyone in attendance that you found…out of place?" Mia asked.

Scott Morris's smug face flashed across his mind. Chase didn't like him. He couldn't pinpoint why. It was possible he loathed the man because he had history with Erin. Chase knew that it was incredibly selfish and immature to despise the fact that Erin had a life before he came along, but he didn't care. Chase just had to keep reminding himself that Erin's present and future belonged to him.

Mia must have sensed something, because she looked up from

her notebook and stared at him with a quizzical expression on her face. "Who was there, Chase?"

Chase didn't want to appear like a jealous boyfriend, making accusations with no evidence whatsoever. But he knew how important it was not to withhold information, even things that seemed far-fetched or based on gut feelings. "Erin's mentor from CHOP attended the benefit."

"And that seemed odd to you?" Mia asked.

Chase shook his head. "No, Dr. Mitchell Morris is…I mean, was a doctor. His work is well-known; his cancer research is groundbreaking. I was not surprised to see him there. But his son…"

Chase watched Mia flip back a few pages in her notebook. "Scott Morris?" she asked.

The sound of that name made him wince, just enough for Mia to notice. But what disturbed him the most was that Scott Morris had been brought up before, by either Erin or Paul.

"Yes. I had never met him before. But Erin knew him previously from her volunteer experience in Philly."

He didn't want to think about Erin discussing another man, but Chase couldn't resist. "Did Erin mention Scott Morris in her session with you?"

"Yes, briefly," Mia said.

Though Chase was grateful that Mia spoke the truth, it still infuriated him to hear that his girlfriend thought Scott Morris was important enough to discuss.

"Why does he bother you?" she asked, not pulling any punches. He was obviously not doing a great job of masking his disgust in regard to Scott Morris.

"Because the asshole vibe he gives off is overpowering," he said, his tone clipped and with more edge than he preferred when speaking to a woman.

Mia nodded and then looked at her notes. "Erin told me that Scott Morris's father died later that night. A few days later, Scott Morris came to her work, your building, and informed her personally that his father had passed. Does that sound accurate?"

"Yes. I watched him enter Erin's lab via camera. I couldn't hear their conversation, but I definitely didn't miss him hugging her."

Mia's eyes rose from the page. "Erin didn't tell me that."

"Well, she probably didn't think it was important. She told me that the gesture was a consolatory embrace, due to the fact he had just informed her that his father had died," he said, fighting desperately to suppress his mounting frustration and jealousy.

"But you didn't think it was so innocent?" she asked.

"In Erin's mind, she was being sympathetic, performing the ritual people do when they learn that a loved one has died. I trust Erin completely. But Scott Morris? Let's just say that I wouldn't be surprised in the least if he had seized that opportunity to move in on her."

"Has Scott Morris contacted her since that day?" Mia asked.

"No, I don't think so." Chase was going to assure himself that was the case the moment the session was over.

"Okay." Mia closed her notebook and set it on her lap. "I will need you to forward me the text from Gabrielle. I'm also going to ask Erin to send me all texts she has received from her attacker in the last several weeks."

Chase knew he was being dismissed. And he couldn't be more grateful. He was tired of talking about the horrors his girl had lived through and what she was currently battling. There was nothing he could do to erase what had happened to Erin. But he could be there for her now.

"Thanks, Chase. You've been helpful and…very gracious."

Chase knew that her previous session with Paul didn't go so well. Paul had hustled past him in the hallway, given his sister a quick kiss on the forehead and left the penthouse without saying a word. This situation was uncomfortable for everyone involved. But it was particularly painful for Paul. He had seen the monster, witnessed him violating his sister. How do you live with that memory?

"Like I said before, don't take Paul personally. Erin says he has always been more on the serious side. The death of their parents and Erin's incident only compounded his existing guarded demeanor."

Mia sighed. "Don't worry. I'll give him some latitude."

Chase was thankful that Mia had agreed to come and help. Before Andrew's suggestion to bring Mia on board, Chase had been tempted to take Erin far away from here, far away from the bastard. Mia was their last hope. But if they couldn't identify who was stalking Erin, Chase was going to follow through with his plans. They would disappear, forever fall off the radar, if that was what it would take to keep Erin safe.

Chapter Eleven

Paul could justify every lie he had ever told in his life. Some lies were uttered to protect people. Others were told to spare someone's feelings. But as he followed Mia Ryan home from Chase's penthouse more than three hours after his own session with her, Paul couldn't categorize the lie he had told Mia. There was no late-night meeting at his office, no pressing engagement that required his attendance. He had lied to escape *her*.

Sitting across from her on that couch in Chase's office, Paul had felt his defenses start to crumble. The way she had looked at him, as if searching for something, unnerved him. It was like she knew that it took everything he had to keep that mask he wore secure in her presence. He had hoped that once he left Chase's penthouse, his irrational thoughts and emotions would fall back in line. But that was not the case. In fact, it took only seconds after leaving Mia for him to realize that all he wanted was to see her again. Paul watched her pull into a small driveway. He parked two doors down and waited. For what exactly? He hadn't thought that far ahead. Mia exited the car and with keys in hand, ascended the steps to her porch. Moments later, each room was illuminated, as if she had the house wired to trigger the lights to turn on with one simple flip of the switch. The thought of her entering the house alone made him crazy. He should be searching her house, sweeping each room and giving the signal that all was well. It was a practice he had mastered over the course of the past year.

Why the hell did he feel so protective…possessive even, when he thought of Mia? Though she was beautiful, intelligent and so goddamned sexy, she was also the woman who had just learned his secrets and the violence he was capable of if given the opportunity. He had been able to set aside his lustful thoughts as he sat on that couch, discussing the events prior to and after his sister's rape. But the moment the session had ended, when Mia was no longer the interrogator, she once again became a woman, one whom he couldn't get out of his mind.

Paul wasn't proud of the way he had left Chase's penthouse, on the verge of a tantrum. At the time, he was unable to verbalize why he had to leave. He just needed to get far away from her. It was as if she possessed the ability to see right through him, and it was beyond uncomfortable.

Mia reemerged a minute later, but this time she had company. A high-strung, and from the looks of it, untrained, yellow Lab came barreling out the front door, dragging Mia along her front walkway with leash in one hand, and a plastic baggie in the other. She is not going to walk that animal through the streets at this time of night!

Paul couldn't believe what he was witnessing. She had been a police officer in one of the most dangerous cities in the world. She knew what lurked around its corners, saw it firsthand, and had even had the unfortunate privilege to speak with some of the sickest criminals about their crimes. And yet she continued with her stroll.

Paul had hoped that she would end her walk after the dog had relieved himself, but she had not turned around; instead she was picking up speed in the opposite direction from her house. She was halfway down the street when Paul decided that he had enough. He leapt out of his car and started walking briskly toward her.

He didn't want to frighten her, and just as he was about to call her name, Paul heard the chambering of a round and froze in his tracks. With pistol in hand, Mia turned and faced him.

"It's just me, Mia," he said, his hands outstretched, palms up.

"Goddamn it, Paul! What the hell are you doing here?" she said, tucking the gun away in some hidden pocket of her zip-up jacket.

He decided to lie for the second time in one night. It would be more believable and a lot less creepy. "I wanted to apologize for how I acted tonight at Chase's. You're trying to help us and I responded by being…well, a rude asshole."

"A phone call would have sufficed, Paul." She looked at him, her eyes boring into his. "Long meeting?" she asked.

Paul leafed through the scattered thoughts in his brain. Meeting? Oh yeah, that meeting, the one he had conjured up to avoid further exposure to Mia. "Yes, we wrapped up about an hour ago." He needed to regain control of the conversation. "Anyway, I pulled up just in time to see you walking…" He looked down at the Lab. The dog, which was still very much a puppy trapped in a grown dog's body, was wagging excessively, begging to be petted and paid attention to. "Is this why you carry a gun?" he asked, pointing to the dog.

"Henry. That's his name," she said, patting his broad head. "And I didn't adopt him for protection. He needed a home and I needed...well, he keeps me company." Paul didn't miss the inflection in her voice, the slight hesitation that spoke volumes. Mia must have detected her slipup because she stopped petting Henry and started in the direction of her house.

Good. At least she wasn't going to continue her midnight stroll through the neighborhood.

"Please tell me you don't make it a habit to walk Henry at this hour every night?" he said, trailing behind her.

Mia stopped abruptly and turned. Her about-face put him within inches of her. He stared at her, though she only kept his gaze for less than a second before looking away. But in that brief moment, when he could hear her sweet and quickened exhalations, he couldn't help but want to kiss those slightly parted lips. The floral scent of her perfume mixed with her shampoo was enticing him to make those inches between them vanish.

"He has yet to master using the men's room. So, yes. If nature calls, I walk him and let him take care of business," she said, taking two steps back, away from him.

Paul wanted to smile, maybe even let out a chuckle. She was witty and adorable when pissed off. But the thought of her walking around at night, gun or not, sobered him and all he could do was chastise her. "I don't think it's wise for you to be out here alone."

"I can take care of myself, Paul. I was a police officer, remember?"

"But you are also a woman and..." She shot him a look, cutting him off and making him want to recall his words. Where the hell did that sexist comment come from? The remark was out of character, even for him. He was just about to bite the bullet and apologize yet again, when he heard a screen door open and smack shut.

"Mia? Is that you, dear?"

Paul could hear Mia let out a barely audible groan.

"Oh, hi, Rose. Yes, it's just me…out walking Henry. He's a bit restless tonight."

Paul watched Rose rummage through the pocket of her pink ter-rycloth robe. She withdrew a pair of glasses and set them on her face. With her face now only slightly scrunched, she asked, "And who is your friend?"

"I don't believe this," Mia muttered, though not loud enough for the older woman to hear.

Paul decided to take advantage of the situation. He smiled at Mia and then walked the few short steps to Rose's stoop. "My name is Paul. Mia and I work together." He reached out his hand and shook her dainty one.

Rose blushed and then cleared her throat. "And I'm Rose, the nosy next-door neighbor." She released his hand and then looked over his shoulder at Mia. "He's quite handsome, Mia. Almost as handsome as my George…God rest his soul." There was just a touch of sadness in her hazel eyes when she mentioned George, a man he assumed was her late husband. The woman's ability to remain strong, even playful in a way, suggested that her George had been gone for some time.

Paul was dying to look behind him and catch a glimpse of the expression on Mia's face. But he resisted the temptation and decided to give the lovely woman before him his undivided attention. "George was a lucky man," he said. Rose's already-pink cheeks turned a violent crimson.

"Handsome and…charming," Rose said, chuckling.

"And leaving," Mia said from behind him.

Paul felt Mia's determined hand try to encase his. He adjusted and took her hand firmly in his and drew her close. "It was nice to meet you, Rose," he said, nodding. Rose gave him an abbreviated version of a curtsey.

"Good night, Rose," Mia said, practically dragging him down Rose's walkway. Mia didn't look at him, but she didn't let go of his hand either. Paul loved how her hand felt in his.

"Let me know if you ever need me to dog sit. You know, if you two need some alone time?" Rose called after them.

Paul couldn't stifle his laugher any longer. He chuckled, which only seemed to frustrate Mia even more. Mia gave her neighbor a wave, acknowledging the offer, and dragged him and poor Henry across Rose's yard and onto Mia's property. She wrestled with her keys, managing to open the door to her bungalow with one hand and entering the quaint foyer. Henry trotted off to the kitchen, probably in search of a drink. When they were securely in her house, with the door shut behind them, she attempted to let go of his hand. But his fingers only tightened around hers.

God, he wanted her.

He drew her close, knowing that she wouldn't be able to miss just how much. Paul noticed that her breathing matched his, quietly stimulated. Mia bit her lower lip, revealing that she may be nervous. But she didn't back away; instead, he felt her lean into him. He wanted to taste the lip that she desperately seemed to cling to. He lowered his head slowly, giving her every opportunity to turn him away. But she just stood there, her fingers still entwined with his when Paul heard neurotic barking coming from some room in the house. With the exception of Mia telling him to stop, he didn't think there was anything else that could make him switch gears so quickly. He instantly let go of her hand and ran in the direction of the barking.

Paul heard Mia cock her pistol as she followed close behind. Scratching accompanied barking and then...whimpering. Paul rounded the corner to Mia's kitchen to witness the world's worst watchdog in action. Henry had discovered a small colony of ants in his kitchen. But Henry didn't appear interested in the cluster of ants that were now making a meal out of a piece of fallen bread. No, what concerned him was the rogue ant that evaded every swat of his paw and then had the nerve to seek refuge beneath the fridge. Henry looked up at Paul as if seeking his assistance.

"I'm glad you have the gun," Paul said. He bent down and petted the dog between the ears.

Mia set the pistol on the island. "He has great intentions," she said, smiling at Henry.

He had to leave...now. He had been seconds away from kissing Mia, claiming her in her very own foyer. Henry's barking had been the wake-up call he needed. He couldn't get involved with someone while that madman was out there, terrorizing his sister. He was on an emotional roller coaster, on which his sexual desire for Mia would mount to an unhealthy extreme and then descend abruptly when reality set in.

Paul stood, leaving Henry wanting more. "I'm sorry for how I treated you at Chase's. I have no excuse other than it is difficult for me to discuss what happened to my sister. You asked me if I see a therapist. I haven't yet, but plan to with Erin. I agreed to go with her for a family session, just haven't gotten around to it."

Those deep blue eyes softened and her body seemed to relax as she leaned against the kitchen island. "I shouldn't have asked if you were seeing a therapist. It's really none of my business. You just have the uncanny ability to…frustrate me."

Her choice of words was interesting and making him…aroused. Time to leave before he showed her just how sexually frustrated *he* was. He could still feel her hand in his, her body pressed against him while they stood in her foyer. She hadn't said no, but she didn't say yes either. In hindsight, she had been like a deer in headlights. As if she had never found herself in a similar situation, one in which a man had made it crystal clear that he wanted her.

Impossible. Mia was beautiful, everything that a man craved. There was no way she could have made it to her mid-twenties without being…he didn't want to finish his own thought. Picturing Mia being intimate with another man infuriated him.

Paul didn't look at her for fear that he would be unable to control himself. He took the coward's way out and diverted his attention to Henry. He gave the dog a couple strokes and a good scratch on the belly. "Well, I hope we can start over. I promise to not be such an ass next time."

"And I will do my best not to take things personally and allow you to frustrate me. Clean slate?" she asked, bending down and giving Henry a couple scratches.

Now at eye level, hovering over Henry, Paul reached out his hand. "Clean slate," he said. She shook his hand, sealing the deal. Paul noticed that she didn't look at him. Interesting.

Time to get the hell out of Dodge. Before he ruined what he had just repaired. Paul rose to his feet and started for the front door. "So what is the next step in the investigation? You've talked to all of us. Now what?" he asked, purposefully steering the conversation in another direction.

"Well, I will review my notes from our sessions and analyze all correspondence to help develop a timeline, motive, and criminal profile. Speaking with the three of you this weekend was just the first step. There will be more conversations, more questions that need answers. I just don't know what those questions are yet. I will need to do my homework to see what information I may be missing. And that can take some time."

"Can I help you in some way?" he asked.

She shook her head. "Not at this stage. The next several days will consist of me up to my elbows in notes and evidence and comparing them with similar cases." He felt his face fall and he quickly tried to mask his disappointment.

"But I will need you. I mean…I know I will have questions and details that need to be provided," she said, blushing. "Also, I told Erin and Chase that I would like to meet with the three of you after I had some time to look at everything."

Flustered and embarrassed, she was absolutely stunning.

Leave…now. Just reach out, turn the doorknob to her front door and walk away.

"I look forward to hearing from you, then. Do you have my cell number, Mia?" he asked.

"Um…no. I don't think we exchanged numbers." Again, she appeared nervous, biting that pouty lip of hers.

He withdrew his phone from his pocket, careful not to brush by his cock. The slightest touch would awaken it and no doubt activate the launch sequence. After she gave him her digits, he called her phone so she would have his.

"Well, I'll leave you to your work. Good night, Mia." Henry came trotting up to him, wagging vigorously. "Good night to you too, boy." Paul gave Henry a pat on the head and then left Mia's home, a home he had not swept thoroughly. That thought left him unsettled. But what disturbed him more, what left him confused and wondering what the hell was wrong with him, was his unrelenting need to keep Mia safe.

Chapter Twelve

Erin couldn't imagine Heaven offering her anything better than this. She and Chase had spent over forty-eight hours in bed, leaving only to eat and shower. She nestled into him, wondering when the other shoe was going to drop. And it was most definitely going to fall; it always did.

"Tell me what you're thinking?" Chase asked from behind. He had been spooning her since their latest round of lovemaking.

"How did you know that I…that I was…"

"Your body went from relaxed to rigid in less than a second. What's on your mind, love?" he asked.

Erin loved how he could make her melt with just a single word. Who was she fooling? She loved everything about him, every side of him. He could be demanding and confident one moment and sweet and loving the next. And he was hers…despite everything. He still wanted her in his bed, in his life, even after learning her secrets.

"I'm scared for us," she said. She wasn't going to lie. He was learning to read her well.

He gathered her snugly into his arms. "I won't let him hurt you again, never again. This will all be over soon."

Erin had avoided asking the question that seemed to hover like some ominous cloud when she, Paul and Chase were together in the same room. It was time to dig her head out of the sand and just ask. "After Mia identifies the attacker, well, what then? Will we go to the police?"

Chase rolled her onto her back and she stared up at him... which was a mistake. With his mussed hair and sleepy, sexy blue eyes, Chase had the ability to distract her, even at a time like this. But she fought through her hormones and asked, "What's next?"

He brushed a golden lock of hair away from her face and then caressed her cheek with his fingers. "There will be no police. There's too much at stake. Paul, Andrew and I have decided to handle this in our own way."

"How, Chase? I would rather leave, hide away forever, than you three risk your freedom, your lives, trying to protect me."

His fingers stopped stroking her face. "I know you would. You were going to leave me that night if I hadn't come, weren't you?"

Erin nodded and looked away. "I wouldn't survive it... if anything happened to you. I thought if I left, well, he would come looking for me, leaving you here, safe in New York City. But I was foolish for thinking it could be that easy. You're already enmeshed in his plan. And I have no doubt that he'll follow through with his threat." She couldn't hold back the tears any longer. "Look what happened to Gabrielle," she whispered. "Maybe it was suicide, but what if it wasn't? What if he had gotten to her?"

"You need to trust me, trust that I will take care of you, Erin."

Erin thought about her life without Chase in it. How empty it would be. "It's not a matter of trust. It's a matter of keeping you safe and ensuring that you are not implicated if the bastard suddenly disappears or turns up dead." Erin wrapped her arms around his neck and drew him close. "Promise me that you won't put yourself in danger or do anything that would risk your freedom."

"You amaze me, Erin. At any time you could have asked me to take care of this situation, to put an end to it all. Instead, your concern is focused on my well-being and involvement. You are truly the most selfless person I have ever met."

Erin shook her head. Chase noticed the fresh tears that started to spill over and quickly wiped them away. "No, I'm not selfless. I need you to stay safe and out of jail so you can be with me...always. I can't think of a more selfish and more self-serving motive than that."

Chase smiled. "What you describe is love, not selfishness," he said.

"Love me, now, Chase," she said, brushing her lips against his.

He groaned against her mouth. Erin felt his shaft grow rock solid against the inside of her thigh. She responded swiftly, not giving him the chance to take control. Chase was a generous lover, always concerned that her needs were met well before his own. He needed to become accustomed to the fact that his pleasure was also hers.

Erin scurried out from beneath him and pushed him onto his back. She wrapped her fingers around the base of his cock, lowered her head, and sucked him in deep. Out of the corner of her eye she watched as Chase gripped the bed sheets. The thought that she could make him lose himself, that she could elicit such a carnal response, only made her want to pleasure him more. She quickened the pace, licking the velvet underside as she ascended and descended.

"Erin, just like that. God, you take it so good!" he moaned, placing his hand at the back of her head. Erin loved when his fingers twisted in her hair as he pounded into her mouth with his cock. In this position she could submit, without losing control. Though if she was really honest with herself, she loved being submissive with him. Considering her past, she never thought she would ever let or want to let a man to dominate her in bed. But Chase was different. He had the ability to take her any way he wanted without making her feel helpless.

"Come in my mouth, I want to taste you," she said, coming up for air.

"Ah...yes, baby," he yelled, releasing the sheets and grabbing her head with both hands. With three slow thrusts of his hips, he found his climax.

Erin looked up, expecting to see a heavy-lidded and very satisfied man staring back at her, but all she saw was pure lust. He scooped her up and carried her to the bathroom, where he drew a bubble bath.

Chase stepped into the steamy water and then lowered her into the tub, positioning her so her back was pressed against his chest. Erin leaned her head back and sighed, enjoying the relaxing lavender scent and the gentle rhythmic jets against her skin. She would have been content to remain as they were, her body encased by his, but then she felt his hands gravitate from her belly to the inside of her thighs. He kneaded her flesh, massaging the soft skin, until she felt like she was going to erupt. He hadn't even touched her clit, and she was on the verge of a powerful orgasm. She felt his lips trail softly from the nape of her neck to her left shoulder, which temporarily distracted her. The sudden brush of his thumb against her throbbing clit made her jolt with pleasure and she shamelessly let out a moan requesting more.

"I love how your body responds to me," he whispered, between kisses.

Erin lifted her body to increase the friction between his thumb and her taut nub. He chuckled mischievously. "Do you want more, Erin?"

"Y-yes," she stammered.

Erin felt his palm against her core and she shuddered. "I want you to come into my hand, to feel your release with just the touch of my fingers."

She didn't respond. She couldn't, actually. He was stroking her clit with one hand and cupping her breast with the other. He pinched her nipple at the same moment he entered her with two fingers. Erin gasped. She reached out and grasped the sides of the tub with both hands and watched as Chase ravaged her nipple. Erin wished she could see his fingers slide in and out of her, slick with her juices. Chase's fingers released her nipple and then dove beneath the suds. Seconds later, her back arched against him, as she took in the sensation of fingers sliding in and out of her in an intoxicating rhythm while his other hand circled her clit and caressed her folds.

"Are you going to come for me, baby? Like this?" he asked, his fingers grinding into her with expert precision.

"Oh…oh yes…Chase…yes!" she screamed, releasing into the palm of his hand.

Erin crashed back into him and it was then she discovered that he was ready for her…again. She slid to the other end of the tub and knelt. She looked over her shoulder and said, "I want you to fuck me right here, like this." She bent over, grabbed both sides of the tub and offered herself to him. Erin heard a splash from behind before she felt two hands grab her around the waist. He lunged into her with one smooth motion and she cried out. Erin knew he enjoyed taking her from behind. His cock burrowed deep into her core this way and he was never ashamed to let her know just how good it felt…and more importantly, how much he loved her.

* * *

Chase had intentionally toned down his language when he and Erin were making love. After learning about Erin's past, Chase thought it was wise to not appear so aggressive or demanding in the bedroom. But the moment that word slipped past Erin's luscious lips, he couldn't help but let the animal inside take over and claim her from behind.

Early on in their relationship she had showed him she could be gentle one minute and rough the next. And right now, she was giving him the green light to take her hard and fast. He entered her swiftly and felt her hot channel clamp down on his cock. He fought back the urge to spill in her right then and there and continued his quest to take her in the most primal way possible. Chase shifted his hands from her waist to her ass and squeezed her cheeks as he gained momentum. White-knuckled from holding on to the sides of the tub, Erin screamed his name and begged for him to come with her.

"You want it hard, baby?" he asked.

She was panting and gloriously flushed. But she still managed to answer him. "Yes…give it to me!" Erin could be demanding and straight-up ravenous when she was in the throes of ecstasy.

God, he loved her. The fact that Erin could submit to him, ask him to dominate her, told him that they had reached yet another level in their relationship. It was proof that she trusted him completely. She had gifted him with her heart, body and soul...and he would cherish them until the end of time.

Chapter Thirteen

Mia felt guilty calling out sick from work, but in her current condition, she decided she would be utterly useless in the classroom. The combination of hours studying the evidence and her vivid dreams of Paul had left her completely exhausted. The doorbell rang, jarring her from her thoughts.

Mia grabbed her pistol from the desk drawer and tucked it into her jeans. Henry trotted alongside her, wagging jovially. Mia peered out the front bay window and noticed that her visitor, who appeared barely out of his teens and was standing awkwardly on her stoop, was preparing himself to ring the bell for a second time. She quickly read the logo on his shirt and scanned the packages he was carrying. The logo on the grease-stained bag he was holding was familiar, as was the picture of the dog on the second bag. Though she relaxed somewhat, she kept her hand behind her back, firmly on her weapon.

Mia opened the screen door. "Miss Ryan?" he asked, his voice cracking. This kid was just a baby. She removed her hand from her gun and greeted the young man properly.

"I have a delivery for you, Miss Ryan," he said, nervously.

"Oh, who are they from?" Mia asked.

"I'm not sure. There's a card attached to this bag, here. The one with the dog on it. I didn't read the card; I would be fired," he said quickly. "And I don't want to be fired on my first day on the job."

That explained the jitters. Poor kid. Mia took the packages and set them on the moon table next to her purse. She withdrew a ten-dollar bill and handed it to the delivery boy. He blushed and thanked her several times, before running off and getting into a smart car. Mia couldn't believe he was old enough to drive.

Mia locked the door behind her and carried the packages into the kitchen. She set them on the counter and then removed the card, which was taped to the bag with the words *The Doggie Den*. She and Henry knew the place well. They were frequent flyers, stopping off at the chic little bakery for dogs just around the corner at least three times a week. Henry was addicted to the peanut butter truffles and gingersnap-shaped bones. She read the card and smiled:

> *I wasn't sure if you decided to forgo dinner the other night because you really weren't hungry or if you had lost your appetite due to my rudeness. You said you enjoyed messy sandwiches, so enjoy. The other bag is for Henry. Those dog treats looked so tasty that I almost tried one…almost. Again, sorry for being such an ass.*
>
> *See you soon.*
>
> *—Paul*

Mia peered into the doggie bag and was astonished over his choices. Henry's truffles and ginger bone cookies were mixed in with treats she was confident her puppy would not have a problem taste testing. She reached into the bag and pulled out a truffle and a treat that resembled a mini carrot cake. "Henry, look what Paul sent you." Henry sat at her feet and raised a paw before she even asked. "Take it nice," she said. Henry had a tendency to be over zealous and snatch food from her hand in a rather abrupt fashion. "Nice," she said, lowering the treat to his level. Whimpering with excitement, he controlled himself long enough to take the treat gently between his front teeth. "Good boy, Henry!" she exclaimed. He scurried into the kitchen to savor his snack in private. Mia took out a sandwich from the white Monty's bag and instantly felt her mouth water. She consumed the pulled-pork sandwich and the extra side of dipping sauce in less than ten minutes, not feeling even slightly guilty for ingesting so many calories in such a short period of time.

With her belly full and feeling rejuvenated to get back to work, Mia knew she first needed to tell Paul thank-you. Text or phone call? Mia weighed her options and decided that texting would be better. If she heard his voice, Mia feared she would never be able to give Erin's case the full attention it deserved.

She found Paul's number in her contacts and sent him a text: *"Henry and I are most grateful for our treats. It was very thoughtful and just what I needed. And…no need to apologize again. Clean slate, remember?"*

Paul's text came seconds later: *"Glad you two enjoyed them. And yes…I remembered. Just couldn't pass up the opportunity. Sleep well, Mia."*

Mia stared down at his text and was stunned by his choice of words. Paul had either found a way to invade her dreams at night or he was just incredibly lucky. She had hoped it was the latter. Because if he knew what her dreams consisted of the past two nights, she would be mortified beyond belief.

She had awakened from the most erotic dreams, ones which left her wet and wanting. In each dream, Paul started by holding her hand, like he had in her foyer. But in her dreams, no dogs barked, no ants interrupted or put a halt to what she wanted. In her dreams, he told her how beautiful she was, how he desired her, how he wanted to pleasure her until she begged. And then he would kiss her, slipping his tongue into her mouth and moaning with anticipation. In one heated dream sequence, he had taken her into her bedroom where he hastily removed her clothes, leaving her in just a bra and panties. He had commented on how much he loved her black lacy thong, though in reality she didn't even own a thong. She felt his fingers dip beneath her panties where he found the evidence of her desire.

The dreams were so real, she could feel her arousal in that unconscious state. On two occasions, she awoke to her own hand stroking her clit with untamed vigor. The need was so strong that she continued masturbating long after the dream was over, all the while picturing Paul's face, his hands touching her quivering body, his lips tasting her.

Thank God she didn't opt for the phone call. If a text could conjure up such naughty thoughts, making her replay those fantasies over and over as if on a loop, what state would she be in if he had actually spoken to her?

Time to get to work and be productive.

Mia worked well into the night, developing a timeline, formulating a list of questions to ask Erin when she saw her again, and establishing a preliminary profile of the rapist. She was thankful that her hormones could adjust so quickly. It was also helpful that Paul hadn't texted her again.

Chapter Fourteen

Scott was used to faking it. Mimicking human emotion and mannerisms that were deemed socially appropriate had become second nature to him. But maintaining the façade for several days, around the clock, was a bit of a challenge.

But as he envisioned the sniper rifle tucked securely away in the trunk of his vehicle, he knew the hunting trip had been worth the discomfort. In addition to securing a weapon that could never be traced back to him, he had been able to practice on a live target. He was quite pleased with himself by the end of the trip. Even Dennis, a diligent and seasoned hunter, was impressed with his skills behind the trigger. Too bad Dennis wasn't diligent enough to notice that one of his many rifles had gone missing.

Scott pulled into the parking garage and weaved his way through BMWs, a Mercedes and a few Rovers and then stopped abruptly. Erin's vehicle, a modest four-door sedan, stood next to Chase Montclair's Bentley. His blood boiled as he stared at his Angel's car, housed comfortably in Montclair's building. It was the final push he needed. Scott put his car in park, withdrew the GPS tracker from his glove compartment and exited his vehicle. Though he needed to do this swiftly and without drawing attention, he silently repeated his mantra: Control, Focus, Control...Act. He bent down on his hands and knees and tucked the magnetic box under the body of Montclair's vehicle. Confident that the device was secure and successfully hidden, Scott stood and reentered his own vehicle. His hands were shaking slightly, which irritated him. This had gone on for far too long. Now that he could track Montclair's whereabouts, it would make it that much easier to accomplish his task. Scott made his way out of the garage and drove a few blocks before pulling over.

Scott did not like to lose. But he also couldn't look past Erin's transgressions any longer. His Angel had completely disregarded his directions and, from the looks of it, was now sleeping with filth. He typed in his final text to the woman who had gone from pristine, the embodiment of purity, to an infested Whore.

* * *

Erin stared at her phone in horror. He had made the threat before, but now, as she stood in Chase's kitchen, about to prepare a home-cooked meal for the two men in her life, she heard that other shoe drop with distinct clarity.

Chase entered the kitchen just in time to see her lay the phone down on the counter, her hands shaking uncontrollably. His smile faded instantly as he looked from her to the phone. Chase walked over, grabbed the phone and went right to her messages: *"Good-bye, sweet Angel, for the Whore has taken residence. Those content to lie with filth, shall join it for all eternity."*

Hearing Chase say the words aloud was much worse than reading them. It was not a veiled threat. Her rapist couldn't have been clearer about his intentions. She and the man she loved would walk around, possibly forever, with targets on their backs if Mia couldn't help them narrow down what they were up against.

Chapter Fifteen

Mia arrived within an hour of Chase's call.

The rapist had sent Erin a message bidding her farewell, which meant that his days of taunting her via text were over. He wanted to move on. But in order to do just that, he would need closure, at least that is what Mia concluded based on her research.

"Okay, Mia, what kind of lunatic are we dealing with?" Chase asked, clenching Erin's hand. Erin was enveloped completely by his embrace, making her appear small and fragile. But Mia knew that looks could be deceiving. Over the last several days, Mia had learned just how strong Erin could be. She was a fighter, one who would rather carry the burden on her own than dump her problems on the two people on the couch to either side of her. Mia could definitely relate. She too felt the need to keep her feelings, her own demons, securely tucked away, where they couldn't be a nuisance to anyone.

Mia looked across the room at her uncle Drew. He nodded, as if he was giving her the green-light to speak freely. Mia shifted her gaze to Chase, Erin, and Paul. "We're not up against a madman. The man we're dealing with knows right from wrong. He knows exactly what he's doing…he just doesn't care. He doesn't feel remorse or show empathy, though most psychopaths can mimic both if the situation warrants it." Mia looked from Paul to Chase and Erin and saw their concern growing by the second. But time was clearly of the essence, as the rapist's latest text indicated, so she continued unloading the profile on them.

"Based on the information you were able to provide me in our sessions, we can conclude that our psychopath is of medium build and most likely Caucasian." Erin was able to rule out her attacker being of African American descent because she saw the color of his skin, unfortunately in the most private of places. Mia didn't want to dwell on that fact too much, as it would only make Chase and Paul uncomfortable.

"Although no two psychopaths are the same, there are a number of characteristics that most possess, such as the complete lack of remorse and emotion."

"How do they function, then, in society I mean?" Erin asked.

"They know what the social norms are, what is socially acceptable and appropriate. In other words, they fake it. They tend to have average to above-average intelligence and are master manipulators, working the system and the people around them to their advantage, and they can come across as…normal. That is what makes them so dangerous. Psychopaths aren't the individuals walking through the streets, unkempt, muttering to themselves, paranoid that the government is spying on them. No, they can hold normal jobs, be that next-door neighbor that gives you the creeps for reasons unbeknownst to you."

Mia watched Erin digest that information. Mia was thankful that the three of them remained silent. It was best she gave them the complete profile and then open up the floor to questions and discussion. "They can be calculating, patient even, if the end goal is that desirable. Our psychopath knew you, Erin, before that night, most likely for some time. He could have been waiting weeks or months for that perfect moment to strike."

"Do you think it was someone...like a classmate at my university?" Erin asked.

"I don't think so, though it's not impossible. I think this individual is a little older, more established." Mia got the impression Erin already knew that and was simply checking the possibility off her mental list. "Erin, his texts, the dialogue he had with you the night in the cemetery, indicate that he craves cleanliness, requires his women to be pure, unblemished. He seeks virgins or at the minimum, women who lead a lifestyle that strongly hints at the possibility that they haven't been exposed to 'filth,' as he calls it."

"How could he have known that...that I had never been with a man before? I find that information to be impossible to obtain," Erin said.

"He couldn't know that for sure, but he must have followed you closely, knew your habits, who you hung out with, where you slept at night, to feel confident that you had met his specific requirements," Mia said.

Mia knew that it was time to unveil and put a spotlight on the elephant in the room. "The text you received tonight refers to you no longer being his 'Angel,' but a whore in his eyes. You have been tainted, ruined because of your relationship with Chase. And it makes him grow increasingly uncomfortable that you may be infecting his world. You have fallen off the pedestal. And he will make it a priority to make sure you land with the rest of the women who have fallen from grace…women like Gabrielle."

Erin's eyes widened at the sound of Gabrielle's name. Chase also appeared shaken, as he gripped Erin's hand even tighter.

"Then you are convinced that our psychopath killed Gabrielle?" Chase asked.

"Could she have taken her own life? Of course. Her track record was not good. Her parents, the police…knew she was capable of committing suicide. But more importantly, he knew and could have used that to his advantage. The newspapers and the magazines reported that beautiful model Gabrielle Green had taken her own life after suffering from a mood disorder for over a year. There was no need for further investigation. No need to point the finger in any other direction. To the world, she was a depressed young woman who couldn't face what life had dished out. I'm not convinced that Gabrielle killed herself. She had seen his face, could have outed him at any time. I can only assume she had served her purpose in his eyes and then he discarded her."

Chase stood and paced the living room. "So, what now? We can't just wait and let him find us."

"No, we can't wait. It's obvious from his text that he wants closure, which can only be achieved if you and Erin are dead." Mia thought it was more productive to be blunt. "Erin, Chase, you both mentioned Scott Morris in your sessions. I was in the process of researching the young doctor when you called me tonight."

Erin grew pale. Mia thought she was going to be sick, maybe even faint. "Are you all right?" Mia asked.

Chase whipped around in response to Mia's question to Erin. He hustled over to the couch and sat next to her. "What is it, baby?"

"I…I don't know. I just…" she shook her head, cutting herself short.

"Say it, Erin. Remember what I said about the details?" Mia asked, referring to the conversation they had during their first session, when she allowed Erin in for a moment and told her about her mother's murder.

Erin nodded and it appeared that the blood was slowly returning to her cheeks. "I remember," Erin said, smiling gently. Erin closed her eyes, sat up straight and crisscrossed her legs. She exhaled and then said, "Scott Morris is the neighbor you described, the one that gives you the creeps for reasons unknown. I have no idea why he makes me feel that way. I only saw him once while I was in college, and that was when he introduced himself in his father's office over a year ago. The only other contact was at the benefit and in Chase's lab."

"Scott Morris left his position at Penn Medical Center along with two other oncologists and joined the Oncology Department at Overbrook Hospital here in New York. That much I know. But I need more information. If he is the one who committed the crime, his injuries would have prevented him from going to work for some time."

Uncle Drew had remained in the doorway, listening. He was probably two steps ahead of her, silently predicting what she was going to ask him next. "Uncle Drew, I think it's wise to put someone on Scott Morris. I want to know his schedule, who he associates with; frankly, I want to account for his whereabouts at all times. In the meantime, I'll go to Philly to learn more about Dr. Morris. I also want to analyze the scene of the crime while I'm there."

"You will do no such thing, at least not by yourself. I'm going with you," Paul said, his voice abrupt and demanding…possessive.

He had been quiet the entire time, his expression unwavering and very lawyer-like. His sudden declaration drew the attention of Erin, Chase, and Uncle Drew. They stared at him for a moment as if surprised over his commanding tone.

Erin broke the silence. "I'll go, too."

Mia knew how painful it could be for a victim to return to the scene. It would rip open the wounds that may have just started to scar over. "I don't think that's a good idea, Erin. It will evoke memories that I don't think you need to relive."

Erin didn't appear hurt, but frustrated…and remarkably strong willed. Erin was a fighter, a woman Mia admired more with each passing second. "I live with those memories every day, although they have lessened as of late." Erin smiled at Chase, as if silently telling him that he was the reason why her mind didn't go to that dark place more often. "Besides, you don't know where the cemetery is or the path I chose that night. It may be helpful if I come. You know, to provide the details?" Erin took her eyes off of Chase for a split second and stared at Mia, as if challenging her.

How the hell could Mia argue with that reasoning? Erin had used her own words against her. Smart girl.

"We will all go. I own a condo in Center City, though I haven't been there for a while. I stay there if and when I'm needed by my Philadelphia branch. Andrew, would you be able to come along with us? I'm reluctant to take Erin anywhere, especially into Philly, without proper security," Chase said.

Uncle Drew nodded, accepting the directive. "I think that's wise. If you don't mind, I would like to personally assign someone to Scott Morris while we're gone. He's in my line of work and will be discreet, if not invisible."

Mia knew how protective her uncle could be, but it was clear from their stunned but appreciative expressions that they were not used to Andrew taking control or uttering more than two words at a time.

"I would be willing to accept any support you could provide to ensure Erin's safety," Chase said, putting his arm around Erin's waist.

"Tomorrow, then?" Mia asked.

"Yes, the sooner the better," Erin answered.

Mia had already called out sick from work once this week. It would be easy to claim that she had come back too soon and her body had relapsed. She rarely got sick, so she was hopeful that her absences wouldn't raise any administrative eyebrows. "I'll be over in the morning, say around nine o'clock?"

"Sounds great," Erin said. Mia was surprised when Erin walked over to her and gave her a quick hug. "Thanks, Mia. I don't know if I could do this with anyone else. You make me feel…strong." Mia noticed that Erin was on the verge of tears and immediately empathized with what she was going through. The bond that was forming between them solidified with each shared secret and it felt eerily similar to real friendship. Mia had friends in college, but after her mother had died, those great, supportive friends seemed to drop off the face of the earth. Her mother's murder had attracted so much publicity that even her closest friends sought refuge, distancing themselves from Mia and the media circus.

Her friend Carina was the only one who remained in her life. However, even that relationship was starting to dwindle, which was solely Mia's fault. Carina had been the one to call, email, even drive into the city to see her on several occasions. The effort on Mia's end was embarrassingly less. It wasn't that she didn't want to see Carina or remain friends; she was just in a funk, one she didn't know if she would ever get out of. Carina must have gotten the hint that she needed space or something, because her friend's calls had ceased, making it a little over two weeks since her last valiant attempt.

"Good. You'll need that strength in the coming days. But if you feel that strength leaving you, we'll be there. We won't let you fall," Mia whispered, so only Erin could hear. Mia hugged her before heading to the elevator.

"I'll walk you to your car," Paul said from behind. His voice sounded strained, as if he was troubled.

"I parked in the building's parking garage, in the slot Chase assigned to me. I'll just take the elevator down. No need to walk me. Thanks, though," she said. She thought she had sounded appreciative of his gesture, but from the look in his eyes, he seemed, well, angry.

"Then, I'll ride with you on the elevator and see for myself that you have reached your car safely," he said, his tone dark. He entered the elevator and pushed the button for the appropriate level. The elevator door closed behind them.

"I need you to stop this, Mia," he said, his head bowed, those gorgeous blue eyes peering through long thick lashes.

Mia felt her face grow warm. Stop what? Thinking about him? Dreaming about him? Masturbating while envisioning him doing things to her, erotic things she had never in her innocent life experienced?

"What are you talking about? Stop what?"

"You need to stop putting yourself in danger. Taking Henry for a stroll at all hours, walking in a parking garage at night…alone. You're not being safe."

Oh…that.

"Paul, I know that you feel the need to protect me, well, women in general, considering everything, but I can take…"

Paul made the space between them disappear and he pressed her up against the elevator wall with his hard, and oh God, muscular body. "You can take what, Mia?" he asked, his thumb and forefinger lifting her chin, forcing her to look at him.

The sudden contact, her body perfectly molded against his, the scent of him, an intoxicating mixture of his soap of choice and cologne she was not familiar with made her legs weak. "I…I can take care of myself," Mia said, fumbling. She regretted her choice of words the moment they were uttered. She had been "taking care" of herself, in more ways than one, for years.

He smiled, as if enjoying how off-balance she was around him.

Shit.

"Why take care of yourself…when I'm right here?" he said, his smile fading. His eyes grew dark and heated, and Mia wondered how she was going to break free of him without incident. The elevator beeped and the doors opened, unveiling the parking garage. But he didn't move, or retract his fingers from her chin. Instead, he continued to stare at her, waiting for a response.

"Because it's…it's what I'm used to…what I'm comfortable with." Mia said, looking up at him with false bravado.

"But I'm not comfortable with that, Mia." Paul released her and stepped away, taking that heady scent and those gorgeous muscles with him.

Mia stepped out of the elevator, but Paul caught up with her and slid his hand to the small of her back to guide her through the garage. She loved the feeling of his hand, masculine and so blatantly possessive, on her, even if it was through two layers of clothing. She couldn't help but wonder how her body would respond if those hands she so admired touched her bare, heated flesh. She quivered at the thought.

"Are you cold, Mia?" he asked, mistaking her reaction to her naughty thoughts for a nonexistent chill in the air.

"Um...a little," she lied. Mia picked up the pace, fully aware that she was coming apart at the seams. This man was so beautiful, so tempting and so...off-limits. Paul was part of an ongoing investigation and as he demonstrated previously, was dealing with some dark and therapy-worthy issues. His concern, possible obsession, regarding her safety was a clear example that he continued to struggle with what had happened to his sister.

She withdrew her keys as her car came into view. Mia was careful not to look at him again, for it would definitely contribute to her undoing. But it was apparent that she didn't need to lay her eyes on him to become a neurotic mess because she dropped her keys. "Damn it!"

Mia bent over to pick up the keys, but Paul had already swiped them off the cement. He dangled the keys in front of her. "I make you nervous," he said with a delicious smile.

How could she respond to that? He was a lawyer. He would know she was lying. If she said yes, well, what then? Maybe she should find out.

"Sometimes," she said, barely able to look at him.

"And the other times?" he said, his gaze no longer heated, but scorching. "When you're not nervous, how do I make you feel?"

Wanton, anxious...hot. He had the ability to make her feel those emotions, sometimes all at once. She had been brave enough to tell him the truth, but Mia knew that the well was empty. She would never be able to elaborate further and tell him how he made her feel during those "other times." Times when she was all alone, when she felt her body grow needy and ready for his touch.

"I need to get home to Henry. I'll…I'll see you tomorrow morning." It was the cowardly way out, blaming one's rash departure on an innocent pet, but she didn't care. She needed to get away from him before she made herself look like an even greater ass, though she didn't know if that was possible.

Mia heard her car locks disengage behind her. Paul reached for her hand and placed the keys in her palm. "If you ever want to know how you make me feel…all you have to do is ask."

Paul released her hand and opened the driver's-side door. Mia got in and quickly shut the door with more force than necessary. She thought she witnessed a smug smile spanning his chiseled face. Mia couldn't take the risk to assure herself that was the case. She started the engine, kicked the car into drive and pulled out of the parking space. Against her better judgment, Mia peered into the rearview mirror, only to be met with, yes, a smug smile, one that was increasing by the moment.

Chapter Sixteen

Scott awoke to a subtle but easily distinguishable beeping sound coming from his tracker. According to his device, Montclair was on the move. Scott looked at his watch, which lay neatly on his night-stand, and was intrigued. Where was Montclair going at this early hour?

Scott quickly changed into his typical attire. His daily workout, shower and clean-cut shave would have to wait. The thought that Montclair was interrupting his schedule irritated him.

Scott secured the deadbolts, activated the alarm system to his apartment and retrieved his car from the parking garage. According to the tracker on his cell, the small dot representing Montclair's car was making its way toward the Lincoln Tunnel. Scott felt a sudden sense of panic. Was Montclair running...and taking his Whore with him? Scott slammed his fist into the steering wheel of his Audi and then pulled his vehicle over to the side of the road, just a few car lengths from Montclair's apartment building. What the hell was he doing?

Control…Focus…Control…Act.

Scott inhaled and exhaled slowly, coaxing his body to relax and his mind to clear. He was jumping to conclusions and losing control, the perfect combination to ensure his exposure. It was possible that Chase Montclair just had an early-morning meeting away from the office.

It took longer than usual for Scott to calm down and regroup, a sure sign that he had allowed the situation with Erin Whitley to get out of hand. He was already making mistakes and acting erratically. The fact that he had bypassed his exercise routine and shower this morning and flown over here because his tracker suddenly came to life told him that he had to end this and soon.

Scott felt his heart finally begin to stabilize. He shifted the gear into drive and was just about to pull out when he spotted Paul Whitley exiting a vehicle about twenty yards ahead of him, directly in front of Montclair's apartment building. Whitley greeted the doorman with a handshake but did not enter the building. He seemed to be waiting for someone. Scott slouched in his seat, taking cover but maintaining an unobstructed view of Whitley. Scott observed Whitley looking at his watch and then frowning at the street before him. Traffic was mounting by the second.

Whitley's scowl quickly diminished as he set his sights on a particular yellow cab that stopped abruptly, as a result of overshooting its destination.

"Mia," Whitley called, waving at the parked cab.

Scott sat up slightly, trying to get a better view of the woman exiting the vehicle. The rare beauty shut the cab door behind her and stepped onto the sidewalk. Scott sat motionless, in awe of what he was witnessing. Mia Moore had finally made her way back into his life.

Chapter Seventeen

Paul rushed over to pay her cab fare, but apparently she had beaten him to it. The cab sped off leaving Mia standing there looking as gorgeous as ever in a t-shirt and shorts. Paul couldn't help but stare at her shapely and well-defined legs. He hadn't the pleasure of seeing them bare before, since she'd always opted for jeans or yoga pants. But today was unbearably humid, a reminder that summer was upon them.

He felt his cock twitch as he reached for the bag she had slung over her shoulder. How the hell was he going to survive the two-and-a-half-hour drive to Philadelphia with her looking so...so fucking beautiful...so goddamned sexy? He needed to get ahold of himself.

"Oh thanks," she said, allowing him to take her backpack.

Paul loved how she could be strong willed and feisty with him one minute and shy and compliant the next. The sensual combination only heightened his arousal, confirming that the next few hours were going to be pure torture.

* * *

"Where are Erin and Chase?" Mia asked, adjusting her seatbelt.

"Chase called me late last night and asked me if I would mind driving separately. Your uncle wants to sweep the condo and Chase wanted to see if Erin was up to visiting her old advisor and professor, Dr. Farrell. Chase thought that tea with Dr. Farrell would be a good distraction, make the trip not so…overwhelming."

The realization that she would be travelling with Paul, alone, almost sent her into a panic attack. He would be within inches of her, his enticing smell surrounding her, making Paul's roomy SUV feel as cramped as that delivery boy's smart car. It also didn't help matters one bit that he looked like he had just stepped out of the pages of a J.Crew catalog. Wearing khaki shorts, a button-down cotton shirt with the sleeves rolled up and boat shoes, he appeared relaxed and painfully handsome. Mia couldn't afford to let her mind wander. It would just make the trip ahead that much more difficult.

"I think Chase is very thoughtful. He seems to really care for your sister," Mia said, praying that she wasn't blushing.

Paul pulled away from the curb and joined the mass of cars, which was moving steadily, not quite at a snail's pace, though rush hour was quickly approaching. "Chase makes her happy. But more importantly, he can be trusted."

Although Paul's tone sounded a bit clipped, Mia had learned, even in such a short time, that it was a result of him being overprotective, and rightfully so. Who in their right mind would blame him for wanting the best for his sister, considering everything that had happened and what he had witnessed?

Mia spotted a Dunkin' Donuts up ahead. She was craving some

caffeine along with a much-needed distraction. "Mind if we stop? They have a drive-through," she said, pointing to her home away from home.

"Don't mind at all. Could use a jolt of caffeine before braving I-95," he said, smiling. The tension her prior question invoked seemed to dissipate, leaving only the sexual tension between them to percolate.

With java in hand, they crossed over to the Jersey side of the river and headed south. Mia had just taken a gulp of liquid bliss when Paul asked, "So, Andrew must be your mom's brother? Since your last names are different."

Mia almost spat out her coffee. Instead, it went down the wrong pipe, causing her to cough and clear her throat.

"You all right?" he said. He reached over and rubbed her back. The heat of his hand penetrated the thin cotton of her shirt, causing her face to grow warm and her body to weaken with each stroke.

"Um…yeah. Just went down the wrong way is all." He gave her back a pat and then removed his hand. Her back stiffened, the sudden withdrawal of his hand leaving her body wanting more.

Mia could buy some time and evade his question, but it would be pointless. A simple internet search would answer any questions he may have. "My dad and Uncle Drew were brothers. I dropped the 'Moore' after my father died. Ryan was my middle name."

"I'm sorry, I didn't know that you lost your dad," he said, glancing at her for a moment and then back at the road.

"Erin didn't tell you about…about how or why I became a profiler?"

Paul shook his head. "Did you tell her it was okay to share that information with me?"

"No," she said.

"Then that is where it stayed. In the vault I lovingly refer to as Erin. She values her privacy and probably didn't think it was any of her business to discuss yours with anyone," Paul said. Mia already liked Erin; this new revelation only deepened Mia's respect and admiration for Paul's sister.

"It must be nice to have such a great sister," Mia said.

"After my parents died, well…she is all I have left," he said. Paul looked over at her, and though his eyes were sad, he forced a gentle smile.

Maybe it was because of the fact that his eyes appeared so haunted, so grief stricken that she felt compelled to tell him everything. Maybe it was because she knew what it was like to have both parents ripped away from you. Maybe it was simply that she trusted him. Regardless of the reason, she did just that and for the next hour she unleashed one demon after another. By the time they crossed the Ben Franklin Bridge into Philly, Paul had learned why she had switched careers, how her parents had died, and why she no longer went by the name of Mia Moore.

Chapter Eighteen

Think the owners will kick me out of this joint for bringing food in?" Erin said, tossing a box of Thin Mints onto the small table for two. Although Dr. Farrell didn't look up from his newspaper, she saw the hint of a smile beneath his bushy mustache.

"Then they will be tossing us both out on our keisters. Let them stand between a man and his Thin Mints and see what happens," he said, taking off his bifocals. Dr. Farrell looked up and smiled.

God, how she had missed him! How could she have waited so long to come see him? She covered her mouth and let out a half chuckle, half sob. Dr. Farrell gave her one of his fatherly hugs, firm and all encompassing.

"I was just thinking of you a moment ago and suddenly you appeared. You're a long way from New York. What brings you here?"

Erin thought it was best to keep things light. She and Chase had decided that if they ran into anyone they knew while in Philly, they would use the excuse that they had come to town to see the Phillies. It was an acceptable excuse since they were all Phillies fans. Well, she wasn't sure about Mia, but Erin was certain she could be swayed if she was, God strike her down for even saying the words, *a Yankees fan.*

"Two things actually. You and the Phillies. We are catching the afternoon game. But before we head over to the park, well, I was hoping that you still adhered to your daily ritual at Sawyer's Coffee House: midmorning tea, the funnies and a chocolate scone." Erin sat down and broke open the box of cookies she had brought. She eyed the chocolate scone in front of Dr. Farrell and frowned.

"I'll take the scone home for later. Now hand over the cookies," he said, his eyes twinkling. Erin handed him an entire sleeve of the chocolate mint cookies and smiled.

"And who is 'we'?" he asked, looking past her with a curious expression on his face.

"Paul took the day off too. He's visiting a few old friends before we meet up for the game," she lied. She had to keep reminding herself that keeping the conversation light was best for everyone. A little lie here and there wouldn't hurt anyone.

"And will Chase Montclair be accompanying you as well?" Dr. Farrell asked, nodding.

Erin looked over her shoulder and smiled at her beautiful man. Chase was standing just inside the doorway, speaking with Andrew. He discontinued his conversation when he noticed that she was staring at him. That irresistible smile appeared on his face and she felt herself melt. Erin waved her man over.

"Dr. Farrell, it's nice to see you again," Chase said, extending his hand. Dr. Farrell shook his hand and gestured for him to pull up a chair.

"Mr. Montclair, can I assume that Erin was awarded that promotion?" he asked with a mischievous grin.

Erin looked from Dr. Farrell to Chase, wondering who was going to let her in on the secret. What promotion? What were they talking about? She watched Chase's cheeks grow pink, as if he was embarrassed, and marveled at the sight. The transformation from confident businessman to a boy who had been caught with his hand in the cookie jar was both sexy and endearing.

"Unfortunately, we will never know. Erin resigned before I was given that opportunity," Chase said. A smile passed between the two men.

Chase had informed her that he had met with Dr. Farrell a few weeks back, and Erin couldn't help but wonder what that conversation had entailed. Best not to dwell on it. She decided to steer the conversation away from Chase and Dr. Farrell's initial meeting. "I did resign and it's because I'm planning to attend med school." Erin's resignation may have been expedited due to her breakup with Chase, but she had been planning, at least in her mind, to attempt to gain reentry into NYU.

"That is wonderful news, Erin." Dr. Farrell said as he sipped his tea.

Chase took her hand. "I agree, though I hate to lose such a hardworking employee." Erin felt herself blush at the compliment.

"It will be a loss to your company, but a definite gain in the world of medicine," Dr. Farrell said.

The sound of Chase's cell was a welcome distraction. Erin's face felt like it was on fire. She couldn't but help feel embarrassed over their abundant praise. But as she watched Chase look down at the display on his phone, Erin couldn't dismiss the feeling that he appeared concerned.

"I have to apologize. I need to take this call," Chase said. His smile had returned, but it failed to reach his eyes. Erin wanted to ask him who was responsible for making him go from playful to worried, but it was neither the time nor place. Chase excused himself and joined Andrew at another table. The sight of Chase and her bodyguard in the relaxed atmosphere of the coffee house left her unnerved. It was just a reminder of why they had come back to Philly.

Erin didn't want to spoil her time with Dr. Farrell. If her memory was correct, Dr. Farrell would need to leave soon in order to make his afternoon Ethics class. She decided to put that worrisome phone call on the back burner and give the professor her full attention and the apology he deserved, though she wouldn't be able to give him the details in regards to her sudden departure from Philly.

"I'm sorry I didn't say good-bye before I left," she said, fighting back the tears.

He reached over and gave her hand a pat. "No apology necessary. I'm certain you had your reasons." His selfless response only made the tears come to the forefront, and she reached for a napkin.

She should have known that he wouldn't pry and ask what those exact reasons were. It was what she loved most about him. He respected her privacy, but was more than happy to listen when she felt the need to unload. And she wanted to tell him why she had left, why she had put med school on hold, but she couldn't. It wouldn't be fair to burden yet another person with her baggage.

She had promised herself that she would keep the conversation light. It was clear that she was failing miserably. Erin dabbed at her eyes and forced herself to gain some control.

"So, I can't tell you how pleased I am to hear about your decision to return to school. It makes me feel like I did something right." Dr. Farrell popped a cookie into his mouth. "This year's graduating class was a bit of a disappointment… and so very dull."

It was like he knew when she was about to shut down. He had that uncanny ability to know when she needed a diversion, some levity to bring her back from the ledge. She smiled as he poked jabs at his mediocre students, comparing them to the ambitious super-stars in her graduating class. They spoke about the latest medical news and what treatments were gaining traction. It was refreshing to talk medicine again with someone in the field.

After a little while, Erin felt the conversation shift back to her, but this time it was natural and less anxiety provoking. She talked about her position at Montclair Pharmaceuticals and how she had met Chase, though she had to leave out and censor huge chunks of their unusual tale. Dr. Farrell sat and listened as she told him how relieved she was that Paul approved of her relationship with Chase. "Yeah, I had visions of Paul accompanying us on dates or giving Chase 'the talk.' But he actually has been very accepting, considering how overprotective he can be."

Dr. Farrell chuckled. "Paul has always been that way. He'll never change. Take it from someone who has lived it. I was quite certain that my three younger sisters were going to put me into an early grave. Between their boyfriends and the cruel fact that they were beautiful, I was constantly threatening scared teenaged boys with their lives." Erin laughed at the thought of Dr. Farrell, the reserved and easygoing college professor she loved, roughing up pimply-faced punks.

"But how could he not approve?" Dr. Farrell looked over at Chase. Erin followed his gaze and noticed that Chase was no longer on the phone. "He makes you happy…which, I must say, is so lovely to see."

Chapter Nineteen

Chase listened while his friend disclosed his findings. He was grateful that he had acted on his gut a few days ago and asked Sam to conduct a background check on Scott Morris. But the more Sam spoke, the more questions Chase had.

"Last April, Morris, along with two of his colleagues, was offered a position in New York City. Apparently, they were recruited to head the oncology department at one of the leading research hospitals in the country. Morris had accepted and was due to report to New York sometime last summer."

"Let me guess. Morris didn't start his new job on time," Chase said.

"No. It appears Morris didn't join the team in New York until December," Sam said.

The timeline seemed to make sense. Morris would have needed ample recovery time as a result of Paul's handiwork.

"Why the delay? What caused Morris to put his new job on hold?" Chase asked.

"Cancer."

That was the last thing Chase expected to hear. Chase looked over at Erin and was pleased to see the woman he loved catching up with an old friend of hers. He had caught her in mid-chuckle, which was always a beautiful sound.

"According to an article I found online, Morris was diagnosed with colon cancer last spring. He took time off from work to undergo treatment, which of course was a success. He returned to work months later in a new city, cancer-free."

"And the treating physician?" Chase asked, pulling his attention away from Erin.

"Well, that was the reason for the article. His father, Mitchell Morris, world-renowned oncologist, took on his case and nursed his boy back to health. The feel-good story was used to promote early screenings and the necessity of colonoscopies in both men and women. The heartwarming tale of a father saving his son was printed in several health magazines."

Chase felt his blood begin to boil. How convenient that the treating physician was now six feet under and not available to be questioned. Chase thought about the night of the benefit. Erin had said that Dr. Mitchell Morris looked off that night, as if he was anxious about something. A few theories were swimming around in his mind when he heard Sam continue.

"In regards to his phone records and banking statements, I found nothing of concern. Although Morris resides in a high-end apartment building and drives a luxury car, it doesn't appear that he lives a lavish lifestyle. He takes a vacation here and there, goes on weekly food-shopping trips to Whole Foods and other organic stores and belongs to some snooty gym around the corner from his apartment."

Chase scratched his head and allowed himself to digest everything that Sam had just told him. Morris was either really good at hiding his tracks or they were tailing the wrong man, plain and simple. And if it was the latter, well, that meant the son-of-a-bitch was out there, flying comfortably below the radar. Chase needed to consult with Paul, Mia and Erin and give them a recap of his conversation with Sam.

"Sam, I appreciate you looking into Morris. If you find anything else, please let me know."

"Absolutely. Is there anything else you need?" Sam asked.

Chase couldn't help but feel guilty. As of late, his friendship with Sam was very much one-sided. He didn't like that he was constantly asking Sam for favors, but he felt as if his hands were tied. There were few people Chase could trust, and even fewer who had the ability to make someone disappear.

"Sam, there is one more thing. There may come a time when Erin and I will need to live off the grid. If that happens, I'll need you, as my accountant, to transfer my funds to an account that can never be linked to me."

Chase was met with silence and for a moment. He thought his friend had disconnected the call. Sam sighed and then said, "Are you in trouble, Chase?"

Chase wanted to tell Sam what was going on, but he also didn't want to make his friend an accessory to whatever future crime might be committed. It was best to leave him in the dark. "I just need to figure a few things out. Sam, how long would it take to transfer the money, if it got to that point?"

"Not long…a day or two from the moment you give me the green light. But Chase, I don't think that…well, running…is such a good idea. You know you can tell me anything. You can trust me."

Sam sounded hurt, which only made Chase sick to his stomach. "I would trust you with my life and Erin's. For your sake, the less you know, the better. I need to leave it at that. I'm sorry."

"Okay. Just don't want to see you, or anyone for that matter, get hurt." There was a pause and then Sam said, "And no more apologies. The last time you felt sorry for something, I had to clear out my garage."

Chase couldn't help but let out a chuckle, despite the seriousness of their conversation. "I've been asking a lot of you lately, and taking you away from that pretty and very pregnant wife of yours. The 'I'm sorry' gift was more for Lucy, not you, jackass."

"A card, a pair of slippers would have made her happy, Chase."

"Are you telling me that she doesn't like her new minivan? With the baby coming, I wanted her to have the most up-to-date child safety features. If she doesn't like it, I can…"

"Chase," Sam said, cutting him off.

Chase laughed. "All I was going to say is that next time, I will send her to the spa, not send her a car."

"As long as the spa is in driving distance from our house and not on some luxurious island in the south pacific," Sam said.

"I appreciate you giving me the parameters." Chase wanted to end the conversation on a light note, but he also needed his friend to know where they stood. "Sam, thanks…and tell Lucy thanks for putting up with me."

"I will." And after a second, Chase heard his friend say, "And be careful."

Chapter Twenty

Scott had found himself in a conundrum of sorts. He had never deviated from the course or thought about redefining his rules before this morning. Mia Moore was no longer just an angelic face on television. She was real and more beautiful than he had ever imagined. He remembered the night he had learned of the murdered woman, wife of veteran police officer Tim Moore and loving mother of college student Mia Moore, on the news. Due to the shocking nature of the crime and the fact that it affected one of the NYPD's finest, the story went national. Although Mia never granted an interview to a reporter, the media still possessed the ability to splash her picture across multiple magazine covers.

Scott had been intrigued at first sight. He had suspected that she embraced the qualities he so admired in a woman; she had come off as intelligent, determined, and incredibly wholesome. She had her sights set on being a teacher, but changed careers in order to help solve her mother's murder. And he would have made her his if it hadn't been for Erin Whitley. Erin had been easily accessible, residing in his hometown and working alongside his father. Mia was in another state and though it irritated him to do so, he had turned his attention away from the beautiful woman in New York and focused on his Angel, now turned Whore, in Philadelphia.

But things had changed. Mia had come back to him. The problem was that Erin Whitley was still alive. And according to his number one rule, two women could not coexist. A relationship had to be resolved before another could take shape. Shaking his head, he scrubbed and rinsed his body thoroughly before exiting his immaculate glass-enclosed shower.

Scott quickly dressed for work and then concentrated on his hair. He put a few dabs of cream into his palms and ran his fingers through his thick brown locks. He knew he was a good-looking guy. Women, especially the easy, filthy ones, made it known to him that they appreciated the view. But he didn't care about those women and how he made them feel. Scott did, however, wonder how Mia's body would respond.

And he would have enjoyed completing his morning routine with the thought of Mia on her knees in front of him, but he couldn't dismiss the vision of Paul Whitley calling for her as she exited the cab. Were they dating? What were the odds that Mia and Paul Whitley just happened to find each other? He would take some time today to review the notes he had taken regarding Mia a couple years ago and find the connection.

With every hair in place, each tooth flossed and glistening, Scott grabbed his cell phone from the nightstand. He decided that his phone would remain on his person the rest of the day. He was curious to learn Montclair's ultimate destination. According to the tracker feature on his cell, Montclair's vehicle was heading south on I-95...toward the city Scott had shared with Erin Whitley.

Chapter Twenty-One

We have some time to kill before we meet up with Erin and Chase at the condo. Can I take you to a late breakfast?" Paul looked at his watch. "Or lunch?"

"Uh...yeah. Lunch sounds great," Mia said.

"What are you in the mood for?" Paul asked.

Mia knew exactly what she was in the mood for and it certainly didn't involve a sandwich. She must have zoned out for a bit, imagining exactly what she would rather be tasting, because she heard Paul ask, "Mia?"

Mia chose the first thing that came to her. "Um...Philly's known for their cheesesteaks, right?" she asked.

He smiled, as if he appreciated her simple request. "Geno's it is." Paul hung a right and drove a few city blocks before saying, "If you can handle a Monty's sandwich, you will have no problem dealing with a messy Geno's cheesesteak. Just remind me to grab some extra napkins."

Mia was thankful that Paul was acting normal. She was nervous that he would treat her differently after what she had told him about her parents. But he had just listened, asking a question from time to time, before telling her how sorry he was that she had to go through such a traumatic experience.

They pulled up to an orange-and-white building with the name of the establishment written in bold capital letters. The place was mobbed and as she looked at the orange picnic-type tables, Mia noticed that there wasn't a seat to be had. Paul must have read her mind because he said, "How about we take our food to go. We can eat in Rittenhouse Square, right across from Chase's place. Sound good?"

Mia nodded. As they stood in line, Mia read the small menu on the board behind the cashier and instantly zeroed in on the Whiz cheesesteak. Her arteries were screaming for her to rethink her decision but she held firm and when it was finally her turn, she proudly placed her order. Paul opted for the American cheesesteak, a side of fries and two bottles of water. The food came out in record time and they were back in the car within minutes. Mia held the food on her lap, which was a mouthwatering tease. Luckily the park was only five minutes away and she was able to curb the temptation to devour her entire lunch by swiping one of Paul's fries from one of the greasy white bags.

"I saw that, Mia," Paul said. Mia didn't know how he noticed, since his attention seemed to be focused on parallel parking.

"Sorry. They just smelled so good," she said, blushing.

Paul turned off the ignition. "I want to see you try to have just one. They're very addictive." He looked at her with such heat that she suddenly lost the ability to speak. She just sat there like an idiot, staring at him with a pile of food on her lap. He broke their gaze and exited the vehicle. Mia finally came to at the sound of Paul opening her car door. He took the food from her lap and then helped her out of the car. The gesture was both gentlemanly and without a doubt…sexy.

"I think I have a blanket in the trunk," he said. He pushed a button on his key ring and the trunk flew open. In an attempt to make herself useful, she walked over and withdrew a fleece blanket. Paul slammed the trunk closed and she immediately felt his hand at the small of her back. Though the sudden touch of his hand surprised her, she couldn't help but feel turned on and protected.

They crossed the street and made their way to the park. The beautiful summer weather seemed to draw even the most sedentary of individuals outdoors. Both adults and children were making good use of the grounds, whether they were playing Frisbee or just taking their dog for a walk. Mia caught sight of a wiry chocolate Lab dragging his owner down one of the many paths and instantly felt guilty for leaving Henry.

"So, who's watching that madman of yours?" Paul asked, leading her to a patch of grass beneath one of the larger maple trees. It was the release of his hand from her back that brought her back from her delirium, allowing her to answer his question. It only took her a second to realize that the madman he was referring to was her naughty toddler puppy.

"Rose finally got her wish. She graciously offered to watch him for the night. I'm sure she is spoiling him with table scraps as we speak," she said, spreading out the blanket.

"I get the sense Rose was quite the spitfire in her heyday," Paul said, taking a seat. He emptied the contents of both bags and then handed her the Whiz cheesesteak. Mia smiled when Paul placed the carton of fries in between them, signaling that he was willing to share the highly addictive guilty pleasures.

"I would have to agree with you. She seemed disappointed over my reason for needing a dog sitter," Mia said, biting into a sandwich that was nothing short of Heaven.

"Well, you must not have told her that you were spending the night with me. I suspect if you would have told her the truth, our Rose would have been very pleased," Paul said, reaching for a fry.

Mia almost choked on her cheesesteak. What was it about this man that made her body want to reject food and drink? He handed her a water bottle and she took a healthy gulp. Mia fought hard not to look at him, since she had a feeling what she would see if she did. That heated gaze would surely be there, making her burn for him. "Thank you," she said, between two smaller sips.

"Better?" he asked.

"Yes, much." Mia made the mistake of making eye contact and, as she predicted, he was watching her with those piercing blue eyes. She expected to see a smug smirk accompany his gaze, but instead she detected confidence and genuine concern…which only increased his attractiveness.

* * *

"Incoming!"

Paul reluctantly shifted his attention from Mia to the panicked voice in the direction of the field. He had less than a second to react and thanks to his quick reflexes, that was all he needed to catch the Frisbee that was just a moment away from nailing Mia in the face.

"You okay?" he asked, reaching over to touch her face. He didn't know why he felt the need to stroke her cheek and force her to focus on him.

He felt her lean into his hand for a split second before she pulled away. Her sudden withdrawal bothered him immensely, though he wouldn't dare let on, considering what she had disclosed to him earlier in the day. Between her mother's rape and murder and her father's suicide, he couldn't blame her for being guarded. It also explained why she toted a gun when walking her dog.

But what couldn't be explained away was the way she responded to him. It wasn't as if she were socially awkward or unsure of herself. She had been a competent criminal profiler for the NYPD, a position that required dedication and confidence. He had witnessed her in work mode and was impressed by how professional and insightful she was. But when they were alone and she was no longer on the clock, she came across as someone having limited exposure to the dating world.

It was out of character for him to be interested in someone who was not as worldly in the bedroom. During his college years, he had sought out women with experience, women who realized that sex didn't equal forever. In other words, he had left the sweet, and always more tempting, women alone.

"You're beautiful, Mia," he said. The words poured out of his mouth before he knew what had happened. Her face turned a fiery red, making her appear delicate and even more stunning.

"My God, I'm so sorry! Are you hurt?" The panicked Frisbee thrower drew closer, clearly concerned that he may have a lawsuit on his hands.

Paul had been so busy staring at Mia and wondering how she would respond to his honest admission, that he failed to recognize the familiar voice approaching.

Chapter Twenty-Two

Mia couldn't remember a day that she felt more frazzled and insecure. Paul had just told her that she was beautiful. And what was her response? Nothing…unless you want to hypothesize and speculate on the deer-in-headlights expression that surely had taken residence on her face.

"Paul?"

Mia broke free of Paul's gaze and looked at the man standing over them. She didn't know who this guy was, nor did she care that he had almost taken her head off with a Frisbee. Mia was just thankful for the distraction.

Paul stood and shook the man's hand.

"Of all the people I could hit in this park and I choose your girlfriend."

The man looked down at her, which made her feel even more pitiful. "I'm Josh."

Mia rose to her feet, though she nearly lost her balance as her feet tangled in the blanket, and introduced herself. "And

I'm deeply sorry for almost clocking you with my Frisbee," he continued.

Paul playfully returned the Frisbee by slapping it against his chest. "Shouldn't you be in class, as opposed to in a park, giving women the fright of their lives?" Paul asked.

"No, the semester ended a few days ago. I'm not due back for a little while. Shouldn't you be in a courtroom prosecuting or what have you?" Josh said, giving it right back to him.

"I took a few days off. Thought about catching a Phillies game and then heading to the shore for the weekend." Mia listened as the lie just rolled off Paul's tongue. She was impressed by how convincing he sounded, even for a lawyer. To solidify the charade, Paul wove his arm around Mia's waist and drew her close. Mia smiled, playing her part. The girlfriend comment had initially caught her off guard, but it was probably best they pretended to be a couple. A weekend getaway as friends was far less believable.

"So, how is Erin settling into her new place? I tried calling her but her phone number has been disconnected and my emails have all been returned to me."

Mia felt his body stiffen against her. "Yeah, her account was hacked. As a precaution, she changed her phone number, too."

God, the man could lie like no one else! He didn't need a moment to concoct a story. Deception just seemed to naturally spew forth. Mia watched Josh digest the believable explanation. So, this was the Josh in Erin's life. Mia quickly scanned her mental notes in regards to one of Erin's closest friends at Penn and compared them to the real thing. Though he'd had opportunity to commit the crime after gaining Erin's trust over several years, Mia's gut told her that Josh did not meet the profile. Meeting the aspiring doctor by day and suspected playboy by night only confirmed that belief. Erin's attacker valued purity above all else, which most likely would cause him to abstain for periods of time as he sought his next "Angel." According to Erin, Josh didn't discriminate by insisting that his women meet this particular specification. He happily opened his bedroom to a wide range of beautiful, and always willing, women.

Mia noticed that Paul didn't answer Josh's question about how Erin was settling in and suspected that the omission was most likely intentional. She wondered if Josh was going to refer back to Erin's living arrangements, but she was met with a stop-you-in-your-tracks smile from Josh instead. "Mia, it was nice meeting you, though I apologize for my rude introduction," Josh said, holding up the Frisbee.

Although Mia could appreciate a beautiful smile from a handsome man like the next girl, Josh's smile didn't spawn the feelings that Paul's evoked. Flushed against Paul's side, she felt claimed and every bit the pretend girlfriend. She didn't want the charade to end, to feel his arm retract with no desire to possess her.

"I survived. It was nice meeting you, too, Josh." Mia could have sworn she felt Paul's grip around her waist tighten as she uttered Josh's name.

"Well, I'll let you two get back to your lunch," Josh said, glancing at the food on the blanket. "You know, before I can cause further damage."

"Good idea," Paul said, shaking Josh's hand. "And I'll let my sister know that it wouldn't kill her to pick up the phone and call you once in a while."

Josh chuckled and started to walk away when Mia felt Paul turn her into him. Completely enveloped in his arms, she looked up at him. "You're a very good actor," Mia whispered.

It was meant as a compliment, but it was clear from the dark look in Paul's eyes that he didn't take it as such. And before she could retract her words or apologize for Lord knows what, he leaned in and kissed her. What started as a soft press of his lips soon turned into a kiss that demanded more. And hell if she was going to be the one to stop such a kiss, one that left her wanting in broad daylight, in the middle of a park full of people.

To her surprise and disappointment, he ended the kiss, leaving her breathless. Although he too struggled for breath, he was composed enough to ask, "Does it still feel like I'm pretending, Mia?"

Chapter Twenty-Three

Chase felt Erin grip his thigh, which was always welcome, but combined with the shocked look in her eyes, his arousal was doused by panic. He followed her gaze and was equally stunned at what he saw from the back window of his car. "Andrew, would you mind taking Erin up to the condo? I would like to meet with the concierge for a minute and unfortunately, I need to make a few calls in to work."

"Not a problem," Andrew said. He pulled over, letting Chase off at the door before driving into the parking garage beneath the impressive building.

Erin lipped the words "Thank you" through the window. Chase smiled at his love and waited until she was out of sight before retrieving his phone from his front pocket.

Instinct told Chase that it wasn't his job to put a spotlight on what he had witnessed. But he still felt the need to give Paul the heads-up that the scene in the park did not go unnoticed. Chase couldn't be certain if Andrew had seen his niece and Paul in a very heated embrace. He typed a quick text and pushed SEND: *"Sorry to interrupt, but we just arrived. Penthouse floor."*

A few moments went by before he received Paul's response: *"Did Andrew see us?"*

Chase felt like he was back in middle school passing notes, except that he was thirty and performing the task virtually: *"Hard to tell…but your sister definitely noticed."*

Chase wasn't sure if it was wise for Paul to pursue Mia, considering her involvement with Erin's case. But who the hell was he to stop them? If anyone had even suggested that he should have stayed away from Erin, he would have pummeled them. Nothing, not even Paul, would have kept him away from her. A few seconds passed before another text came in: *"Shit."*

Though Chase felt his pain, he couldn't help but smile. He texted back: *"That about sums it up. But in all seriousness, we have new info on Morris. See you in a few."*

* * *

What the hell was he thinking, kissing Mia out there in the open for anyone to see? With no thought to the consequences?

The truth was that he didn't think. He acted, not on impulse but on pure need. Paul wanted her at that moment and was determined to have her. He could still taste her on his tongue and feel her body melt into him as he deepened the kiss, which only thwarted his cock's efforts to stand down. Chase's first text prompted him to release Mia. He turned away in attempt to gain some semblance of control and responded to Chase.

Immediately after the second text, Paul gathered the remnants of their lunch and the blanket.

"That was Chase...seems like he has learned more about Scott Morris. Let's head over," Paul said, evading her gaze. He suddenly felt guilty for kissing her, though the way her fingers had thrust through his hair as his lips sealed over hers and how she'd allowed a gentle moan to escape suggested that she wasn't bothered by the kiss.

The lust in her eyes evaporated completely and it was replaced with a seriousness that he had become familiar with. And just like that, her game face was back on. Paul decided to keep Mia in the dark in regards to what her uncle may or may not have seen. No sense in causing her worry if Andrew hadn't witnessed him losing himself with his niece.

Mia took the blanket from his hands and walked next to him toward the street. She was again his competent, and very beautiful, criminal profiler.

His? Yes, that was exactly what came to mind when he thought about Mia...and it scared and excited him at the same time.

Chapter Twenty-Four

Chase's condo in the sky was built for comfort with all the amenities. Although the clean finishes reminded Erin of his penthouse in New York, there were stark differences between his two residences. The penthouse, with the exception of Chase's home office and the nursery, was a lavish dwelling with a modern flare, whereas the Philly condo had a more homey and traditional feel. She wondered if Gabrielle had some influence on the penthouse's appearance, because the Philly condo seemed much more comfortable...more like him. Erin pushed the thought from her mind, not wanting to dwell on that possibility.

Erin lounged in one of the many leather couches as she listened to Chase disclose what he had learned from Sam. The information he was relaying was unsettling, and as she looked over at Mia and Paul, who were interestingly enough sitting on opposite sides of the room, it was clear from their facial expressions that they too were bothered by the news.

According to Sam, Scott had a legitimate reason to leave Philly a year ago and set up roots in New York. No one in their right mind would pass up the career opportunity he had been presented. And as Chase explained further, the job offer was made months prior to Erin's rape, suggesting that Scott had not followed her to New York to continue from where he had left off.

That fact alone was interesting, but nowhere near as intriguing as the discovery of him having cancer. She had not heard about that before, neither from the medical community nor from her mentor, his father. But by that time, she already had completed her volunteer work two months prior to her leaving Philly. Communication with Dr. Mitchell Morris had basically ceased as a result.

Erin pulled out her cell and typed in a search for both father and son. There were hundreds of hits for Dr. Mitchell Morris, which wasn't surprising considering his noteworthy status in the field of medicine, and an impressive number of articles pertaining to Scott about his own successes. But the article that captivated her, the one she assumed Sam was referring to, was the inspiring story that discussed Scott's battle with colon cancer and the father who had helped him not only to survive, but to thrive and overcome such a devastating diagnosis. If Scott had cancer and received an aggressive treatment schedule under the direction of his father, it would explain why he had to delay his start date in New York.

Erin stared at the picture of Dr. Mitchell Morris and Scott at the top left corner of the article. She couldn't help but notice how tired her mentor looked, how that glint in his eyes was no longer present. She had noticed its absence at the benefit as well, but had chalked it up to him not feeling well. It was a very real possibility that his son's cancer had taken a toll on him, expediting the aging process due to stress and anxiety. Parents never stopped worrying about their children, no matter how old, how successful they were.

Erin's eyes gravitated over to a playful Scott Morris. He appeared relaxed in jeans, t-shirt and a Phillies cap, and was smiling at his dad. Erin assumed that he had worn the cap in an attempt to conceal his hair loss from the chemotherapy. Erin couldn't dismiss the thought that their expressions did not match. Where Scott appeared youthful and carefree, Dr. Mitchell Morris looked exhausted and defeated. That had to be one of the most challenging aspects of being a parent. The worry—the concern that the other shoe may drop, that your child's illness could return—never went away.

"Erin, when did you confirm your acceptance with NYU?" Mia asked.

"I believe it was in March." Erin watched as Mia digested that information. "Which makes it difficult to pinpoint who made the decision to move to New York first."

Mia smiled. "Maybe not. But we'll need to do some investigating to figure that out."

"I'm all ears, Mia. What do you have in mind?" Chase asked.

Mia looked over at Erin. "I don't want to exploit Dr. Mitchell Morris's death, especially knowing how much you respected him, Erin, but…the article Chase mentioned just now might be the in we need to ask a few questions without drawing attention."

Erin appreciated Mia's compassion but was also impressed by Mia's ability to remember the details. "I think we need to do any- and everything to rule out suspects, and right now the only one we have is Scott. So have at it, Mia," Erin said.

"Good. Under the guise that I'm writing my own article to memorialize Dr. Mitchell Morris, I'll have the opportunity to ask his former colleagues some questions and allow them to share some stories about their dear friend. I'll also want to talk to the staff at Scott's former place of employment. This article would be presented as a tribute to a man that was not only a diligent doctor, but a father who cared and nursed his son back to health." Mia looked down at her watch and frowned. "Well, what are your thoughts about extending our stay one more day?" she asked, looking at the group. "I wanted to spend some time at the scene, but prior to that I wanted to walk the path Erin took that night. Tomorrow, we can concentrate on our 'article.'"

Although Erin thought Mia's idea about the article was sound, she stopped comprehending what Mia was saying and a wave of nausea overtook her. Erin knew that going back to the scene of the crime was going to be difficult. How could it not be? But she was also aware that it was necessary for the investigation...and maybe for her recovery. Erin felt Chase weave his fingers through hers, as if sensing her sudden discomfort. She looked up at him and kissed him gently. Erin couldn't get over how far they had come in such a short time. This caring and accepting man was the same domineering boss she had first encountered in his office just several weeks ago. And he was all hers. She snuggled into him, savoring how protected she felt in his arms.

"I have taken off from work until further notice," Chase said.

"And I don't have a job, so no problem there," Erin said with a sheepish smile.

Erin looked over at Paul. She noticed that he had been unusually quiet during the debriefing. It was possible that he was being his typical reserved self, remaining silent while he processed some heavy information. But Erin couldn't help but think he appeared distracted.

She thought about what she had seen in the park and wondered if that was contributing to his detached demeanor. Although the visual of her brother kissing a woman with such passion was definitely awkward, she found herself hopeful that her brother was digging himself out of the hole he had been in for the past year and was allowing someone else in. On a more selfish note, she couldn't be more pleased that the woman he had been kissing was Mia. Erin had liked Mia from the moment she met her.

"I have some personal days coming to me. I'll stay as long as is needed," Paul said. Erin watched him first glance at Mia before he looked at her. She couldn't help but smirk, prompting Paul to scowl.

Paul stood and grabbed his black duffel bag. A soft chuckle escaped from Chase as she felt him release her and rise from the couch.

"I'll show you where you can crash," Chase said, smiling at Paul. "Mia, can I show you to your room?"

"That would be great. I could use a shower and a change of clothes before we head out," Mia said.

Paul didn't say anything. He didn't have to. The way his body went rigid at the sound of Mia's voice spoke volumes. Her brother, that impenetrable fortress with the flawless foundation, had begun to crack.

It was about frickin' time.

Chapter Twenty-Five

Chase had forgotten how much he liked his home in Philly. It had been two months since he had stayed in his condo and unfortunately it had been a short trip last time. The corporate office was of course in New York, but Montclair Pharmaceuticals had smaller, but very well-run, branches in multiple cities across the country. Philadelphia was home to the second-largest office, and he enjoyed his business trips to the city. In the spring and summer months, he and his father would take full advantage of their time together and frequently mix business with pleasure, sneaking a Phillies game in whenever they could. Thinking about his father saddened him. He missed him now more than ever. Chase would have loved to introduce Erin to his dad. His dad definitely would have fallen for her and her spirit, just as he had.

Chase had taken the liberty of ordering takeout for himself and his guests. They had some time to kill before the food arrived and Chase couldn't think of a better way to spend it. He entered his bedroom and found Erin out on his balcony. She didn't see him at first and he took the opportunity to just take her in and admire the woman he loved. She was sipping a glass of chilled tea while peering out over the cityscape…and looking, as always, beautiful. He had to admit that the view was fantastic. It was the main reason he had purchased the place.

"You seem relaxed here," he said, watching her lick her lips after a recent sip. He couldn't help but stare at those pouty lips and imagine what she could do with them. His cock twitched at the thought.

"This condo, this feels more like…you," she said.

They may have only been together for a month, but it was obvious that she knew him well. His penthouse did not reflect his personality as much as the condo. Gabrielle had insisted that the penthouse was in need of updating and before Chase knew it, five renovations later, the modern and streamlined penthouse no longer resembled the warm and welcoming home he had acquired as a bachelor. The only room that had remained frozen in time was his home office, his private and comfortable getaway. The nursery also reflected his tastes, as he singlehandedly prepared the comfortable space for a child that he thought was his.

"Don't get me wrong, your penthouse is gorgeous, but, well…"

Erin blushed, as if she was embarrassed for insulting his New York home. With her cheeks a pinkish hue, her blond hair flowing freely in the breeze, she looked so lovely that it was difficult to concentrate. He walked out onto the balcony. "Gorgeous, but very cold," he said, wondering if he had finished the sentence correctly.

"Um…no…ah…yes?" she asked, fumbling.

"This place is more my taste. I have neglected to make changes to my penthouse. But since I have recently learned that my girl finds the interior of our home to be, well, aversive, I think it's time for some renovations."

Her cheeks went from pink to flaming red. "Oh God, no Chase, I didn't mean that I dislike your penthouse, I just felt…" Although she looked stunning, appearing innocent and beyond mortified, he couldn't let her think that she had insulted him.

"I had plans to renovate the penthouse, Erin. I want that place to feel like home, a home that reflects us both."

"You did?" she asked, the panic receding somewhat.

"Of course. I want you to be comfortable in your home. And that goes for the penthouse as well as the other houses I own," he said. He realized what he had said could come across as arrogant, emphasizing how much money he had, but he didn't care. Chase needed her to know that what was his was now and always would be hers.

Erin sighed and looked out over the city, allowing her cheeks to return to their natural shade. "I always loved this city." She stood on her tippy-toes and squinted. "New Jersey is just a stone's throw away. See that church steeple over there, the one on the Jersey side?"

Chase followed her gaze and spotted the tip of an impressive stone structure amidst small homes. "Yes," he said.

"My parents were married in that church," she said. Her voice was filled with longing and just as he was about to console her, she continued, "And if you drive about five miles west of the church, you'll find the small town where Paul and I grew up."

Chase wanted to take her in his arms and make her forget about everything she had lost in her young life—her parents, her innocence—but he got the feeling that she wanted, or maybe she needed, to talk. He took her hand and walked her over to the set of reclining patio chairs. They each took a seat and for the next half hour, Chase listened to Erin talk about her childhood, how she lived in a modest but very happy home with a wonderful family. From her tone and how she appeared wistful when she spoke about her upbringing, it was obvious that she hoped she would be able to provide the same for her own family someday. Chase remembered what she had said the night of the benefit. Standing in front of his mother's painting, she had told him that she wanted many children.

And if he had it his way, if she would have him, he would be more than happy to give her the tree-lined street she had described, the house with the picket fence she longed for. But unlike her childhood home, the house wouldn't be modest, as it would need to be large enough to accommodate all the children that he would love to give her.

"Would you mind if...if tomorrow we could go visit my parents' church?" she asked.

Chase wasn't a psychiatrist, but he knew she was making some kind of emotional breakthrough when it came to coping with the loss of her parents. And he was happy to be at her side, helping her stand her ground while she tackled each one of her demons. "I would love to see the church. We'll grab some breakfast and head over to Jersey in the morning," he said.

Chase had already made the executive decision that Erin would not be included in Mia's investigation in regards to the "article" she was researching for. Erin had worked in Dr. Mitchell Morris's hospital and there was a great chance that people would recognize her and wonder why she was there. It was best to keep Erin far away from that. Besides, tonight was going to be very difficult for her. Although he understood why Mia wanted to go to the cemetery and see where the crime took place, what the lighting was like and so forth, it was still going to be a struggle for everyone to re-live the event.

Erin stood and walked the two steps to join him on his own lounge chair. "You were too far away," she said.

"I was thinking the same thing," he said.

Erin threw one gorgeous leg over and straddled him. Against the backdrop of the city, she looked positively radiant and, to his de-light, wanting.

"I need you, right now," she said, hovering over him. Erin tore off her t-shirt and then undid the front clasp to her lace bra. Her full breasts sprung forward and were now within inches of his mouth. His cock went from hard to complete stone at the sight of her taut, rosy nipples.

"Ah…yes," he said, taking one nipple into his mouth, while giv-ing the other the attention it deserved with his fingers. He sucked and nipped at her, enjoying her taste and the sounds she was making.

He felt her hand at his belt and was thankful that she wanted it as much as he did. With her perched on top of him and naked from the waist up, he wasn't going to last too long. To expedite the process, he lifted his ass, which allowed her to shimmy his pants and boxer briefs down low enough so he could maneuver. He needed to get inside her. He reached for the button on her thin khaki shorts when she pushed back, making him release her nipples. She slith-ered down his body and lowered her head.

"I want this," she said. She kept her eyes locked on his while she licked the underside of his cock.

"Christ!" Chase gripped the sides of the lounger. "Your mouth…Erin," he groaned.

With heavy lids and a look of satisfaction on her face, she

wrapped those full lips around his cock and took him deep. He thrust his hips, maximizing the incredible sensation within her hot mouth. Erin pried his fingers from the death grip he had on the chair and brought his hands to the back of her head. The gesture overwhelmed him, as it was her way of showing him that she trusted him with her body. He could come at any moment like this, with her head bobbing up and down on his cock at a pace that he could control. But that was not what he wanted, not this time anyway. He felt his balls tighten and knew that he had to act.

"Shorts…off…now," he said, barely able to get the words out.

Erin complied immediately and removed her shorts and panties. She resumed her original position and straddled him on the lounge chair. The lips of her sex brushed against his throbbing cock. He couldn't take it any longer. She must have known he was struggling because in one fluid movement she lifted herself onto him and let him slip all the way into her tight channel.

"Oh Chase…you feel so good," she moaned. He grabbed her hips as she bounced up and down on his cock.

He watched his girl bite down on her lower lip. She was close. Thank fucking God! "Are you going to come for me, baby?" he asked.

"Yes…yes. Please make me come," she begged.

And that was his undoing. He thrust into her with a sense of urgency and from what he heard, wonderful precision. Chase exploded into her sweet heat. With her back arched and her breasts even more pronounced, his climax seemed to go on for an eternity. He felt her cunt clench around his cock and her body quivered. Chase took her in his arms and held her quaking body against his chest.

"It will never be enough," she said, breathless.

"No baby, not with us," he said, the mixture of her perfume and sex filling his nostrils. The intoxicating scent alone had the ability to make him want to take her again. But as she nuzzled into him, he could tell his girl was spent. He swung his feet around and stood. As he carried her to their bed for a much-needed nap, he whispered, "I'll never get enough of you, Erin. Never."

Chapter Twenty-Six

Scott looked at his tracker. Erin Whitley had come home. He had wondered if she would ever return to their city, maybe take a trip down memory lane.

Scott sat back in his leather chair and processed what he had learned between patients. His internet search had been productive, giving him a better understanding of why and how Mia had become involved with the Whitleys. Scott was disappointed in himself for not having put together the connection between Erin's bodyguard and Mia until today, but he would get over it.

So, Andrew Moore's niece had joined Montclair's payroll. Was that the case? Had Mia been brought in to help build a profile? That was a more realistic explanation, and more palatable than thinking that Mia was seeing Paul Whitley. Scott would not lose his Angel again. He had waited so long for her.

It had been hours since he watched Mia leave in Paul Whitley's vehicle. Where were they headed? Had she returned home? It was possible that she had gone to Philadelphia to meet up with Montclair and Erin Whitley, but he couldn't be certain.

Scott finished with his patients and decided to head home. He picked up a salad and a green tea from his favorite organic shop on the way. He needed to refuel, but more importantly, it was essential that he prepare for what he hoped would be a memorable evening with Mia.

After dinner, Scott showered and shaved for the second time in one day. He wanted to be clean for her, his skin sensitive to her touch. He felt his adrenaline pumping, the excitement building as he thought about his Angel. He knew he was breaking his own rule by pursuing Mia while the Whore continued to desecrate herself. But he felt that the window of opportunity was closing and if he had any chance of having Mia, he would need to act now. He would take care of Montclair and his Whore upon their return.

He quickly dressed and left his apartment. He was happy to know that Mia hadn't moved from her parents' home. A top-notch medical library was conveniently located just blocks from Mia's house. Not that he thought he would need to produce one, but the library posed as a perfect alibi. He pulled up to the library, grabbed his backpack from the trunk, and exited his vehicle. The library was not slammed, probably due to the fact that the semester had concluded, but it was still busy enough for his intended purpose.

Scott made sure to greet the young librarian behind the counter. She was plain and only slightly attractive. Perfect. He smiled at her, which caused her to blush. "Is anyone using study carrel five? Need a place where I can do some research without being interrupted," he said. Scott had visited this library a handful of times for research purposes and always requested that particular carrel. It was secluded away from everyone. He could easily put his empty backpack on the desk, grab a few books off the shelf and scatter them haphazardly next to his backpack, and slip out the back door of the library.

"Um…yeah…no one has reserved it yet. It's all yours," Plain Jane said.

"Great," he said. He winked at her, in hopes that she would remember him. Her skin grew pink and blotchy. Yeah…she would remember if she was ever asked if she had seen him in the library that night.

* * *

It was about time Mia had shown some signs of life. Rose had been worried about her young neighbor. It wasn't healthy for a beautiful girl like Mia to be alone, especially after what had happened to her parents, God rest their souls. Hopefully, she was spending her evening in the company of a man, with Paul Whitley in particular, but Mia had not disclosed why she wouldn't be back the next morning as planned, but would be returning that afternoon instead. Rose told Mia that if she wanted to spend another night away, she was more than happy to watch Henry. Mia had thanked her for the gesture, but seemed confident that she would be home to retrieve Henry.

After receiving Mia's phone call saying that she wouldn't be back until later the following day, Rose decided to go next door and grab some more dog food to hold him over. Mia also told Rose that she had filled one of his hollowed-out rubber toys with peanut butter and had put it in the freezer. Mia assured her that Henry would gnaw on that frozen treat for hours if given the opportunity. Rose let herself into Mia's home with the key Mia had given her and went to the kitchen in search of the items. Instead of hauling the thirty-pound bag of food over to her house, she decided to dish out a few scoops of food into a plastic container she found in one of the kitchen cabinets. Next, she went to the freezer and found the toy gorged with peanut butter. With dog food in one hand and peanut-infused toy in the other, she made her way to Mia's porch and locked the front door.

Rose turned around and discovered that she was not alone. A very attractive man in black jeans and a white button-down shirt shared the space, and she gasped with surprise.

"Oh…I'm so sorry. I didn't mean to frighten you," he said, his brown eyes twinkling. "I was just coming to visit Mia. To see if she wanted to grab dinner."

Rose looked him over. He appeared sincere and was dressed as if he was hoping that Mia would accept a dinner invitation for a casual night out. But something about him didn't seem right.

"Well, Mr.…"

"Michael," he supplied.

"Well, Michael, Mia is out of town for the night. She should be back later tomorrow," Rose said, descending Mia's porch steps. She walked across the adjoining properties and stopped at her side gate. Henry was wagging and staring at the frozen treat in her hand. She threw it over the fence and was amazed that he caught the toy in midair, considering it was as heavy as a brick. Henry trotted off to the backyard for what she hoped would be hours of puppy bliss. "I'm dog sitting until she returns."

"No problem. I'll catch up with her at work," he said.

Something was definitely off. The man gave her the creeps,

though she had no idea why. "Oh, you two work together at Lincoln Elementary?" she asked, with her back still turned.

"Yes. As a kindergarten teacher, Mia must have the patience of a saint. That's why I opted for fourth grade. More my speed," he said.

Rose instantly felt sick. Though his answer had been quick and correct as he referenced Mia as a kindergarten teacher, she noticed one glaring problem: Mia didn't work at Lincoln. She was a teacher at Washington Elementary, and this man…whoever he was…was a liar.

Rose felt her hand begin to shake and she quickly tucked it into the pocket of her pink knit sweater. Avoiding eye contact, she turned around. "Well, it was nice to meet you, Michael. I'll be sure to tell Mia you stopped by," she said, ascending her own porch steps.

She opened her screen door and let it smack shut behind her. Her hands were shaking furiously, causing her to drop the plastic container of dog food. Henry's food pellets scattered everywhere. It was during that split second, when her attention was diverted to the mess at her feet, that she heard the familiar sound of her screen door creaking open.

"Very clever. Even I can admit that," Michael said.

This man…this "Michael" gently closed the screen door behind him. "You won't be telling Mia I stopped by…you won't be telling Mia anything ever again."

Chapter Twenty-Seven

Mia found her surroundings to be more than accommodating. Chase really knew how to make his guests feel welcome. Her room contained a king-sized bed, a walk-in closet, beautiful handcrafted matching furniture and a full bath with a garden tub and a glass-enclosed shower she had just taken advantage of. The only problem with her room was that it was directly across from Paul's.

She couldn't stop thinking about him or the way his kiss made her feel. It had been both gentle and intense, and she would be lying to herself and anyone else who may have been enjoying their show in the park if she said that she didn't want more. The man could definitely kiss. She had kissed enough guys to know. But that was the extent of her experience in that area. She didn't really have a solid reason why she had never felt the need to expand her skill set, other than she hadn't found the right guy. Mia wondered if Paul knew just how inexperienced she was and cringed. She may be a half-decent kisser, but when it came to the actual act or pleasing him orally, she didn't know where to begin. There was not a doubt in her mind that she would disappoint him in the bedroom if presented with the opportunity.

* * *

Paul needed to get Mia out of his system, which was next to impossible, especially after her casual remark about needing a shower.

The clusterfuck of emotions that he was experiencing was more than overwhelming. He would be focused one minute, giving his full attention to the morbid reason for their trip, too distracted and incapacitated due to his desire for Mia the next. Paul took her lead and decided to get a shower of his own and release his pent-up frustration.

He knew it wouldn't take long. His cock hadn't fully settled down since their kiss in the park. Paul tried to clear his mind of everything, including Mia, as he stroked his cock. He just wanted this to be quick and done with. Maybe then he would be a lot less on edge, which would enable him to think clearly when in Mia's presence. But as he felt his climax mount, all Paul could think about was bending her over on the shower bench and taking what he wanted to be his and his alone.

With his palm against the tile wall and his other hand working vigorously on his cock, he closed his eyes and visualized Mia taking it all, and filling her with his cum. Hot, demanding spurts of semen shot against the shower wall and he groaned, allowing her name to escape between breathless pants.

It took longer than usual for him to catch his breath and for his heart to return to a normal rhythm. As he finished his shower, washing off the remnants of his frustration, he realized that all he'd done was put a Band-Aid on his problem, a bandage that was already coming undone and curling at the sides. He cursed at himself, knowing that his need for her would continue to fester and increase with each passing minute.

Pissed off, he dressed in jeans and a t-shirt and decided to join the others for dinner. He opened his bedroom door and found Andrew waiting for him. Any doubt that Andrew didn't bear witness to the kiss in the park was laid to rest. Andrew's typical stone-faced expression was replaced with anger, and if Paul was being honest with himself, he couldn't blame Uncle Drew one fucking bit.

"A word, Mr. Whitley," Andrew said, walking into Paul's room.

Paul closed the door behind him and was instantly pinned against it by one powerful forearm across the back of his neck. "Mia may be a grown woman, but she is also my niece...and someone who has experienced more heartbreak than anyone I know," Andrew said, his voice so steady that it was scary.

Whatever military hold Andrew had on him was working, as it both secured him against the door and caused him just enough pain to bring him discomfort. Paul knew he deserved it. "She told me about her parents, what she went through," Paul said through gritted teeth. He may deserve to be accosted by Andrew, but he didn't have to like it.

"Was that before or after I saw you mauling my niece in the park?" Andrew asked. Andrew tightened his grip before he released him. Paul wanted to rub the arm that had been in Andrew's vice grip, but didn't.

"I'm sorry that you saw me kissing Mia. But I don't regret kissing her. I don't take advantage of women, nor do I kiss every beautiful woman I see." For a moment he thought about securing the mask he wore in court, the one that showed no emotion. But out of respect for Mia, he couldn't lie. "I have feelings for her," he said. Paul was both surprised and oddly at ease with his admission.

"You just met her," Andrew said. Andrew's anger receded somewhat, but was unfortunately replaced with disbelief.

"I'm aware...and I can't explain it. That's the truth," Paul said. The two men stared at each other. Paul knew that Andrew was analyzing him, trying to detect deceit. And it was absolutely uncomfortable.

"I brought her onto this case and I will surely take her off if I deem it necessary. She is like a daughter to me. Don't expect me to do anything less than a father would do if his child was hurt. Are we clear, Paul?"

Andrew had never called Paul by his first name. He had kept it professional, addressing him as Mr. Whitley at all times. But right now, in the middle of Paul's bedroom, he was just a man that cared for his niece, plain and simple. Paul had to give it to the man. He knew exactly how to make his point, and he didn't even need to raise his voice or throw a punch.

"We're clear," Paul said.

Andrew stared at him for a moment and then nodded.

"Mr. Montclair would like to leave in thirty minutes," Andrew said. "Ms. Whitley wanted to know if you were going to join them for dinner."

"Yes, I'll be right out," Paul said.

"Very well, *Mr. Whitley*," Andrew said before turning and leaving the room.

Although Paul was grateful that Andrew was able to shift back into his role as bodyguard, the emphasis on his name did not escape his attention.

Chapter Twenty-Eight

Some days can't make up their minds, wavering back and forth between seasons. But this evening was beautiful, warm and comfortable; the scent in the air promising that summer was here to stay. And it was an exact replica of the night Erin had been raped.

Erin felt the knots in her stomach tighten as she directed Chase toward the science building at Penn. He pulled the car into the visitor center's parking lot directly across from the building where she had spent countless hours studying, biting her nails, and even doing a little praying now and then when faced with a challenging exam. Chase raced around the car and opened her door. He took her by the hand and lifted her out of the car.

Someone had either lit a fire under Mia or she was trying to avoid Paul from duplicating the gentlemanly gesture, because she was on the sidewalk before Paul could even unbuckle his seatbelt. Erin couldn't help but smile at the possibility that Paul had finally met his match. With everything going on, including the wonderful late afternoon she'd had with Chase on his balcony, she didn't have a chance to confront her brother about the kiss she had witnessed in the park. There would be time to grill him later. For now, all she wanted to do was get through the night.

"I think we should start in the very classroom in which Erin took her last final," Mia said.

Erin nodded, keeping her eyes on the building ahead.

"You don't have to do this, Erin. I can take Mia to wherever she needs to go, including the cemetery," Paul said.

Erin reached for Chase's hand and held it with a death grip. She stopped in her tracks, only now realizing how lucky she really was. Chase, Paul, Andrew, even Mia, were here to support her and find an ending to a very gruesome story. And it wasn't without consequence. Chase and Paul were putting their own lives on the line and Mia, a woman she had recently met, had skipped work and put in some long hours to help her. "I'll never be able to thank you enough…everything you are doing for me…I…" Erin couldn't finish because Chase's arms were around her and snuffing out the sobs with his chest. He held her for a bit before she faced her support system. "I guess I just needed to get that out of my system. Now, let's do this," she said, feeling more confident as she met the loving stares of two men and a caring woman who had always shown her genuine respect.

"Lead the way, Erin," Mia said.

Erin knew that the building would be open. The accelerated summer program started about a week after graduation and, as she predicted, the campus was alive with ambitious college students who simply wanted to get ahead in their studies. Erin led her entourage down the hall to the stadium-seating classroom. A few stragglers were quickly gathering their books and Macs, probably eager to continue their night of studying at the impressive library down the street. Erin felt their pain, remembering how grueling, how intense those last remaining classes could be. After the last student had left, Erin glided down the aisle and stood where she had handed her exam in to Dr. Farrell.

"Show me where Dr. Farrell was standing," Mia instructed.

"I was standing here, with my back to the doors and..." Erin's voice trailed off. She closed her eyes and saw Dr. Farrell in her mind's eye.

Erin felt feminine fingers squeeze her hand. "It's in the details, Erin. What do you remember?"

"We...Dr. Farrell and I, were talking right here, in this spot, when I noticed him looking past me, toward the wooden doors over there," Erin said, pointing to the back of the room. "I followed his gaze, but no one was there." Erin rubbed her eyes. "I hadn't thought about that detail, until now. That maybe my attacker had been watching me, even in class."

"Erin, I know our preliminary profile suggests that we are dealing with someone who is established, older perhaps, but we can't rule out the possibility that he may have been a fellow student. Can you recall how many students were in this particular class?" Mia asked.

"Had to be around twenty-five...thirty maybe. Predominantly male of course," Erin said. "But I would only be able to name a few of them. I wasn't much of a social butterfly."

"Okay, I'll get my hands on last year's yearbook somehow and we'll put a list together."

Erin admired how Mia's mind worked. It was always churning. She wasn't afraid to explore all possible options. Although Scott Morris was a suspect, it was clear that Mia wanted to refrain from putting all her eggs in one basket. Because what if they were wrong? What if Scott wasn't the man who had attacked her? What if he was the man Sam had described? A man who had been offered a dream job at a world-renowned hospital in the same city in which she was planning to attend medical school. A man whom she had met only once while working as a volunteer and who had not contacted her again until his father had passed. A man who had suffered through cancer and lived. A man who devoted his life to helping others battle the same disease.

Chapter Twenty-Nine

A necessary evil. That was what their trip to Philadelphia was.

Paul understood why they had to retrace Erin's steps that night, starting first at the classroom and now walking the few city blocks to the cemetery, but it didn't make it any easier to stomach. He looked ahead, just in time to see Mia's arm link through Erin's. The sight was comforting and disturbing at the same time. He was happy that his sister felt at ease at the moment, but was distressed at the ominous reason why Mia had entered their lives.

Chase too looked unsettled, as he constantly scanned their surroundings. Paul had a feeling that all Chase wanted to do right now was take his sister home and barricade her in her room. Paul could definitely relate. He didn't know exactly how he would handle things if he was in Chase's shoes. It was less than a second later that he received a vision of himself throwing Mia over his shoulder and securing her in some impenetrable bubble.

Paul was so lost in his thoughts that he didn't realize that they had arrived at their destination. He almost slammed into Mia from behind, but stopped just in time. Chase started to walk toward Erin, perhaps to give her some support as she confronted her worst nightmare, but Mia gave him a look that told him to stand down. Chase stopped, and though he looked a little peeved, he obeyed and stepped back. Paul took Chase's lead and gave the girls some space. Andrew, however, did not stay with the men but dutifully carried on with his assignment and followed Erin.

Mia still held on to Erin's arm and gently swung her around until Erin's back was to the entrance of the cemetery. Standing face-to-face, Mia held both of Erin's trembling hands in hers and then asked, "Erin, I want you to look over my shoulder and tell me what you see."

The sight of his sister shaking infuriated him. Erin didn't deserve this. She had been through enough already. All he wanted to do was protect her, like he had always tried to do. But in the end he had failed her. He had let her out of his sight, just long enough for that monster to swoop down and crush her spirit.

"There's a restaurant on the corner, a used bookstore, and a deli," Erin said, surveying the establishments across the street.

"Can you recall if those stores were in business a year ago?" Mia asked.

Paul watched Erin exhale, as if she was becoming a little more relaxed. Mia's tone was soothing and patient.

"The restaurant, Celia's Soups, was definitely there, as I visited it frequently for lunch. And the bookstore, well, I worked there for a little while to earn some cash. But the deli…" Erin shook her head. "I don't remember that place at all. Must have just popped up sometime this year."

"You're doing great, Erin." Mia smiled at her. "Is the bookstore open at the moment?"

Erin shook her head. "No, it's sort of a mom-and-pop-type shop. It closes early. Seven o'clock on weekdays."

"And how about Celia's Soups?"

"It's alive and well. Actually, it looks like business has picked up since last year," Erin said, sounding surprised.

Mia squeezed her hands. "Erin, this is what I noticed. There's not a lot of foot traffic here. With the exception of the soup shop, the block is relatively quiet, especially for a summer evening."

Paul saw his sister swallow before shaking her head. "That night…it was just like this. The sounds, the smells…well, it's like I have gone back in time."

"But we're with you this time," Mia said, looking at Chase and then at Paul before putting her attention back on Erin. "Will you walk with me?" Mia asked.

Erin nodded and without explicit direction, she led Mia into the cemetery. Paul felt helpless…again. He looked over at Chase, who appeared equally miserable. Chase was pacing atop the cobblestones. Paul had seen Chase unnerved before. Finding your ex-fiancée dead in a bathtub would rattle anyone. But what had really rattled Chase, what seemed to unravel him until there was nothing left, was when he had thought Erin left him for good. And that was what he wanted for his sister: a man who would do anything for her, love her, risk everything for her. That was what she deserved.

"All I want to do is get the girls away from this place. They have five more minutes," Chase said, looking over at Mia and Erin.

Paul knew what Mia was doing. He had to admit that she chose the proper course of action by sequestering them and stealing Erin away, safely out of earshot. Chase would not have been able to handle hearing what had happened amongst the tombstones. It would have driven Chase mad. And as for himself, it was a wise decision that he wasn't invited to participate in the discussion. He had lived it and once was enough.

Chase's cell phone buzzed, sounding louder than usual in the quiet and very secluded cemetery. Paul watched as Chase withdrew his phone from his pocket and read the incoming text message. Chase's face went white at first and then changed to a fiery red within moments.

"He's here," Chase said, his voice a gravelly whisper.

Those two words had the ability to paralyze a man. But there was no time for that. All he could think about was getting the girls to somewhere safe. "Andrew, we need to get them out of here…now," Paul said.

Although he had given Erin and Mia some latitude, Andrew had remained in close proximity to them at all times. But as he heard his name pierce the silence, Andrew rushed over and calmly asked the girls to come with him.

The look of horror on their faces only fueled Paul's anger. There were already too many memories associated with this godforsaken place. The only way this nightmare was going to end, the only way he could ensure Erin's and Mia's safety, was to finish what he had started all those months ago.

Chapter Thirty

Without a signal, without an account to trace back to, it was nearly impossible for his calls to be linked to him. To increase his chances that he would remain undetected, Scott immediately powered off the burner phone and tucked it into his front pocket. He would dispose of the phone properly at another time. Right now, it was imperative that he return to study carrel five.

Scott saw two teenaged boys exiting the library from a side door. He picked up the pace, getting to the door just before it locked behind them. Scott found his study carrel and the contents he had left on the table undisturbed and sat at the desk. He had to catch his breath and give off the appearance that he was either a diligent student or a professional who took great care in fine-tuning his craft, not a man who had just murdered a woman who was too smart for her own good…

Walking along the sidewalk, Scott noticed Mia's car in the driveway. But more importantly, Whitley's vehicle was nowhere in sight. He didn't want to get his hopes up that she was home. For all he knew, she was still with Whitley, trying to connect the dots to a case that was none of her business. He quickly dismissed the thought, as he peered into the front door and detected movement within Mia's home. His Angel was waiting for him.

Scott heard the sound of whimpering to his left and found a yellow Lab wagging at him. The mutt looked as if it was going to leap over the fence he was entrapped by if he didn't get some attention soon. And although it had just been a few seconds, when his focus had been ripped away by a fucking dog, that was all it took for him to screw things up royally. The movement he had detected had not been caused by Mia, but an older woman, one who had sniffed him out in a matter of moments.

Scott opened one of the medical journals on the desk and pretended to give it his full attention. After a minute or so, he felt his body begin to relax and he actually gained interest in what he was reading. He knew that he would have to remain in the library, securing his alibi for a while longer, so he might as well pass the time engaged in a task that might increase his medical knowledge.

He was reading a case study about a thirty-six-year-old man who had the unfortunate experience of coming down with two extremely rare types of cancer when he looked up just in time to see a middle-aged man briskly walking past his carrel as he spoke into a cell phone. The side of the man's face was shielded by the phone, enabling Scott to notice other details, such as the man's build, his determined gait, the way he turned abruptly at the next aisle of books and walked in the opposite direction.

Maybe he was being paranoid. No one would blame him. He had just killed a woman. But the sight of this man unnerved him and Scott couldn't help but wonder if he had been careless. No, maybe his Angel was just that good at her job. He wouldn't fault her for it if that was the case. She was doing what she was being asked to do, submitting, complying in order to fulfil the needs of others. Ahh…Mia was perfect.

Scott couldn't be certain if he was being tailed, at least not at the moment. But it was something he could find out, quite easily actually, if he was patient. Pretending that he was something he was not would also help matters. With that thought, Scott slung the backpack over his shoulder and then gathered his books. As he walked over to the counter, he scoped out the library staff and found his Plain Jane.

He plopped the books on the counter in front of her and smiled. She stared at him, blushing like some pathetic teenager. Although she may very well be a virgin, had to be, she was not his type. She lacked the other qualities he insisted upon. But he sucked it up, forcing himself to engage in seven minutes of mind-numbing conversation with the woman. With another strained smile, he secured a date to the Starbucks down the street, thus solidifying the alibi that had already begun to take shape.

Chapter Thirty-One

Chase waited until Erin was safely tucked away in a cab with Andrew and Mia and halfway down the street when he turned to Paul. "I'll call Andrew's man in New York and ensure that Scott Morris is exactly where he was the last time we checked in... far away from here."

"And I'll check out the cemetery and the restaurant on the corner," Paul said.

No other words needed to be exchanged. Although the fucker's identity was still unknown, they both knew what to look for. But after nearly fifteen minutes of surveying the cemetery and its nearby surroundings, they begrudgingly gave up, fetched Chase's car, and headed back to the condo.

"According to Morris's tail, he's tucked away in some study carrel at a university medical library. It looks like we have the wrong guy. Obviously he can't be in two places at once." Pissed and helpless, Chase squeezed the steering wheel until his knuckles were white. "I need to get her away from here for a while, Paul. I know you may not want me to, but..."

"Leave as soon as you can," Paul interjected. Paul's eyes were constantly moving, most likely scanning the streets for something, anyone who seemed out of place. "His tone has changed. He's frustrated and more brazen."

Paul was right. Chase had never received a text from the fucker before. He had changed the rules, making the situation all the more worrisome. Chase couldn't stop thinking about the brief, but telling message: *Those memories, her virginity, will always belong to me. Your trip to Philadelphia will yield nothing.*

"We'll leave as soon as my jet is cleared for takeoff," Chase said. Anxious to get home to Erin, he weaved between traffic and then picked up speed the first chance he got.

"Where will you go?" Paul asked.

"I have a vacation home in the Caribbean. It's very secluded. It also has a security system that puts the one in my penthouse to shame," Chase said, finally turning into his parking garage.

"Keep my sister away as long as it takes. Mia and I can handle the research end of things here," Paul said.

Chase didn't like the idea of Paul and Mia being left behind to do all the dirty work. But he also knew that he didn't want Erin to spend another night in the same city as her attacker. Paul must have sensed Chase's discomfort because he said, "I need you to take care of her, Chase. Even if that means you have to fly her thousands of miles away to do so. I can't lose her."

* * *

Mia stood at Chase's breakfast bar and nervously strummed her unmanicured nails against the cool granite. She wanted to think like a profiler at the moment, using what had happened in the cemetery as a way of peering into the psychopath's mind. But she couldn't. All she was concerned with was seeing Paul and Chase walk through the door, safe and intact.

Mia heard the sound of Andrew's voice from the other room and practically sprinted to the foyer. Erin was even faster and leapt into Chase's arms. Sobbing, Erin wrapped one arm around Chase's neck while the other reached for Paul. The scene brought tears to Mia's eyes.

"We're okay, love. We're here," Chase said to Erin. Erin let go of her brother and allowed Chase to gather her in his arms. Seconds later, Chase lifted her up and carried her into their bedroom.

In an attempt to regain some composure, Mia turned around and started back toward the kitchen when she felt a familiar hand envelope hers. Paul whipped her around and looked into her eyes. Standing there, her eyes welling with tears, she'd never felt more vulnerable. And she'd never felt more thankful in her life that he had come back safe and sound.

"Are you all right?" Paul asked, his voice gentle. She started to wipe the tears with the back of her hand, when he reached up and stopped them in their place with his fingertips.

Mia swallowed. She wasn't used to fighting back this unrelenting flood of emotion. It had been so long since she had let herself feel anything. Mainly because it was just so goddamn easy to remain numb. But there she was, falling apart at the seams in front of a man who was making her feel something. "Yeah. I…I was just worried…for both of you," she said.

The tips of his fingers navigated to her chin. He stared at her for a few moments and then said, "We have some work to do. Are you up for it?" His hand fell away from her face.

Work. Yes. That was what she needed to focus on. Not the incredibly beautiful man who knew just how to touch her. "Looks like we're on our own," Mia said nodding toward the closed bedroom door.

"Chase, Erin and Andrew are leaving in a few hours for the Caribbean. We think it's best that Erin get away for a while."

Mia thought about the repercussions that Erin's leaving the country would cause. It may make her attacker even angrier, more frustrated that he couldn't obtain the closure he sought. But maybe that was just what was needed to drive the psychopath to his breaking point and lure him out of hiding.

Mia must have appeared distracted because she heard Paul say, "If this is too much, if you feel that you need to get off this case, we'll understand."

"No. We are seeing this through," Mia said. She suddenly felt new tears spring forth. "It may sound strange, especially since I just met you all...but I need this. I *need* to close this case."

Before she could embarrass herself any further, she brushed past him and walked out into the kitchen in search of a well-deserved beer.

Chapter Thirty-Two

Erin didn't argue or put up a fight. She wanted out of the city as much as Chase did. Regardless, she took a quick shower, ridding herself of the filthy memories that she'd needed to revive for the sake of the investigation. After her shower, she dressed in comfortable attire and packed her small overnight bag with the few belongings she had brought for a trip that shouldn't have spanned more than twenty-four hours.

"Don't worry, sweetheart. We can get everything we need on the island," Chase said from behind.

Erin would never get tired of his endearments, how lovingly he could speak to her. But she also loved the other side of Chase, when he took control and told her all the naughty little things he wanted to do to her. However, since he learned of the rape, he had, for the most part, censored himself and refrained from talking dirty to her. He was holding back, as if he was nervous that she was going to break. She needed to rectify the situation and soon.

Erin turned around and hugged her beautiful man. Fully dressed and ready to go, Chase dropped his own suitcase and wrapped his arms around her.

"I feel like I'm running away and dumping my problems on my brother and Mia," she said, her face pressed firmly against his muscular chest.

Chase smoothed her hair with his fingers and kissed the top of her head. "No one sees it that way. In fact, Paul has taken the varnish off my hardwood floors with his pacing. Don't take this the wrong way, but he can't wait until you and I leave, putting a thousand miles between us and Philly."

Erin appreciated his attempt to lighten the situation and smiled. "Sorry. Just having a moment, I guess. Self-pity can rear its ugly head at any time."

Erin felt one hand continue to stroke her hair, but the other found her cheek and caressed her skin. "You can have all the 'moments' you need," he said.

His voice was so loving, so gentle, that she had to fight back the urge to cry. She didn't want her brother and Mia to see tears in her eyes when she said good-bye to them. As a distraction, Erin stood on her tippy-toes and gave Chase a kiss. His lips were soft but firm and he happily returned the kiss with one that tempted her to push back their flight. But the rational side of her, the side that wasn't influenced by her arousal, decided that it was best they continue it later, possibly in Chase's private jet.

"I think we should go," she said, releasing his lower lip.

He sighed and then said, "Yeah, let's get out of here before we find it impossible to stop." Erin loved how she affected him. But she particularly enjoyed the fact that he wasn't embarrassed, nor did he try to hide just how much he wanted her. "Let's go tell Andrew we're ready to head out," he said with a sheepish grin.

With Erin trailing behind him, her hand secured in Chase's grasp, they entered the kitchen…and immediately detected that something was wrong. Paul and Mia seemed to be in deep discussion with Andrew. Before Erin could get the words out, Chase voiced his own concern.

"What's going on?" he asked.

Andrew withdrew his cell phone and showed Erin and Chase a picture of some mechanical device. Although Erin had no idea what she was looking at, it was obvious from the expression on Chase's face that it was not good. "Something felt off. And the more I thought about the text—that he had sent it to you, and not Ms. Whitley, the more suspicious I became that our guy may not have made the trek to Philadelphia," Andrew said.

Erin was frustrated with herself that she was not putting two and two together. She was also feeling pretty stupid at the moment since the rest of the group seemed to know exactly what Andrew's photograph meant. "Sorry, but what is that, Andrew?" she asked, swallowing her pride.

"It's a tracking device. I found it attached to the underside of Mr. Montclair's car," Andrew said.

Erin felt her eyes widen. "So he may not even be here…in Philly, I mean?" she asked.

"Correct. With this particular device, he can track your movements from either a few feet or hundreds of miles away."

"So, what you are saying is that we cannot rule Scott Morris out, despite the fact that his tail confirmed that he was in New York at the same time we were in that cemetery?"

"Morris fits the profile and should remain at the top of the list. But we need to be sure…which unfortunately can take some time," Mia said.

"Mr. Montclair, I left the device right where I found it. We don't want him to know that we discovered it. I would suggest you leave the vehicle in the parking garage while you are away. Maybe that will draw him out. The longer he thinks you and Ms. Whitley are in Philly, the more impatient he may become…and that is when he may make the mistake we have been waiting for," Andrew said.

"That makes sense. Did you get the chance to sweep Paul's car as well?" Chase asked.

Andrew nodded. "Yes, it's clean."

"Good. I'll drive," Paul said as he grabbed his keys off the counter.

Chase was right. Paul was chomping at the bit to have her gone. Erin didn't want a mushy good-bye, so instead, she said, "I know when I'm not wanted. Let's move, people." Mia smiled and quickly retrieved her hooded sweatshirt from the back of one of the breakfast-bar chairs.

Despite Erin's attempts at levity, the drive over to the airport was quiet, as if everyone in Paul's vehicle was lost in their own thoughts. It wasn't until they had pulled into their designated gate, when finally someone spoke. Once they exited the car, Mia pulled Erin aside as the men conversed in hushed tones. "You did great tonight, Erin. I can't imagine how difficult it was for you, and I apologize if I made you feel as if you had to come to Philly."

Mia appeared worried, as if she alone had necessitated the need for her and Chase to flee the country. "I needed to come here. It was time," Erin said. Erin hugged her and though she knew it wasn't fair, mainly because there wouldn't be time for Mia to rebuke her, Erin whispered, "Take care of him while I'm gone. He needs you, Mia."

Erin released her, but shamefully stole a quick glance to assess her reaction. Mia just stood there with her mouth open and her face flushed. Yeah, Erin was totally not playing fair. But at least she now knew that Mia was equally as affected by Paul as he was by her. Erin turned and walked toward Chase and Paul and witnessed her two men engaged in one of those handshakes-turned-half-hugs that guys often do. She cherished the scene, as the respect they had for each other was evident. Erin couldn't have hoped for anything more.

Chase must have sensed that she needed a moment alone with her brother because he excused himself and walked over to Mia and Andrew.

"Don't worry about anything. Mia and I will hold down the fort while you're away," Paul said.

Erin reached up and gave him a hug and a kiss on the cheek. "I have no doubt that you and Mia can handle things while I'm gone. Anyone can see how…compatible you two are," she said. Erin made no attempt to conceal the smirk that had formed on her face.

"You're such a smartass," he said.

"Yeah, I know." She gave him one last kiss. "And you, honey, are beyond smitten with that beautiful girl over there." Erin had enjoyed their banter, the brother–sister back-and-forth, since they were kids. But Paul, being the lawyer he had always seemed to be even in his younger years, possessed the annoying ability to exact the last word. Watching her brother's face turn a sharp shade of red and appear what she could only describe as dumbfounded, Erin couldn't help but savor the small victory.

Chapter Thirty-Three

Although he would be anxiously awaiting Chase's phone call signaling that they had arrived safely at their destination, Paul felt more relaxed than he had been in a long time. The thought that his sister was physically putting distance, over a thousand miles' worth, between her and the motherfucker eased his tension somewhat, enabling him to put his focus on the task at hand.

Mia brewed espressos while he located a canister of chocolate biscotti in the pantry. The combination of caffeine and sugar would give them the manufactured energy they needed to review Mia's notes and analyze what they had discovered over the past several hours. By two in the morning, they had formulated a well-thought-out plan for tomorrow, which included a visit to Dr. Mitchell Morris's former place of work, Scott Morris's old office and the soup shop across the street from the cemetery.

Paul watched as Mia let out one yawn followed by another. With her legs outstretched on the couch, her eyelids heavy with exhaustion, she looked like she was going to pass out at any moment. "The caffeine has clearly worn off. I think we should call it a night," he said.

Mia shook her head and said, "I'll head to bed in a bit. I just want to look over the questions I'm going to ask Dr. Mitchell Morris's staff one more time."

She was either stubborn, determined or a beautiful combination of both, because she opened her composition notebook and dove right in. Paul stood and took their miniature-sized mugs to the kitchen, where he gave them a quick wash and rinse before putting them on the drying rack.

"What time do you want to start out tomorrow?" Paul yelled from the kitchen.

No answer.

"Mia?"

Silence.

Paul rounded the corner to the living room and found Mia sleeping soundly, her composition book lying facedown on her chest. He couldn't help but stare at her, study each curve of her face. Her hair had been in a loose pony tail for the majority of the evening, but sometime over the last hour, the remaining strands of hair had finally broken free of her black hair tie and now fell naturally over her delicate shoulders. Paul was thankful that the book was covering her breasts. He might be more of a gentleman than most, but even he had his limits and would have been tempted to take a peek if they had been exposed.

Paul debated whether he should move her to her bedroom, where she might be more comfortable. But as he listened to her breathe, finding her serene and in such a deep sleep, he didn't want to risk waking her. Paul went to her room and returned with a thick down comforter. He lightly peeled her fingers from the book and placed it on the coffee table. She stirred, but only slightly, and when he rested the comforter on top of her, she nestled in, wrapping herself into a tight white cocoon.

He reached over her head and turned off the lamp. The room was bathed in darkness, which only emphasized the sweet sound of Mia's exhalations. He wanted to bend down and kiss her, feel her lips part as he slid his tongue in to mingle with hers. He had tasted her in the park that afternoon and knew the moment their lips had touched that he would never get enough of her.

"Good night, Mia," he whispered, before heading to his bed without her.

* * *

Mia's eyes flew open at the bloodcurdling scream. It took a few moments to decipher where she was, which only added to her mounting fear. She determined that they were coming from down the hall…from Paul's bedroom. Mia fumbled through the darkness and located her purse on the kitchen counter. She withdrew her pistol and then crept down the hallway. She didn't bother to knock on Paul's door, as she didn't want to give the intruder Paul was having a scuffle with forewarning.

But as she stared from the open doorway, she realized that the only thing Paul was grappling with was a nightmare, and from the looks of it, his dream was not releasing its grip anytime soon. Paul was thrashing in his bed, clutching the sheets between his fists and cursing at someone only he could see. Mia had read somewhere that it wasn't wise to wake someone while they were in that state, but she couldn't let it go on. She walked toward his bed, but the sound of her name stopped her midstride.

"Mia…Mia…Mia…No!" he screamed.

Beads of sweat pooled on his forehead. Mia didn't know for certain what was tormenting him, but in that moment it didn't matter. All she wanted to do was make it stop. Make his demons stand down…until the next time. Mia placed her pistol on the nightstand and then knelt on his bed, careful not to stir him. The anguish on his face was too much for her to bear. Against her better judgment, she reached out and touched his face, smoothing each line. His body went from rigid to relaxed at her touch and she sighed with relief. His breathing returned to a safer pace and the expletives ceased immediately.

She was just about to pull her hand away when she felt his hand grip her wrist and pull it to his chest. Panicked that she had awaken him and that he would now find her hovering over him in his bed, she looked at him for confirmation. With his eyes closed and his breathing pattern steady and deep, he was still very much asleep.

Thank God.

Mia tried to tug her wrist away but she was met with resistance and instantly stopped. What the hell was she supposed to do now? Maybe if she stayed with him, his body would relax even more and in turn, he would release her wrist. Mia gently slid next to him and lay on her side. From that angle, she had a great view of his profile. She felt like some kind of voyeur as she admired his strong jaw and full lips. His hair was mussed from all the activity his nightmare invoked, making him look young and playful. Her eyes travelled southbound and she was surprised to find that he was shirtless. She must have been completely distracted with trying to calm him. That would have been the only reason she hadn't noticed that muscular chest.

Her gaze drifted from his torso to his partially covered, ripped abs. Staring at the traitorous white sheet, which covered him from the waist down, Mia definitely felt like she was moving into pervert territory. She was tempted to pull back the sheet and see what lay beneath, but in the end refrained from making such a bold move.

With only inches between them, her hand on his chest, his wonderful scent invading her space, Mia found that she was in her own personal hell. She was so aroused and wound up that it was becoming painful to be this close to him. To alleviate the tension, she closed her eyes, snuffing out the delicious view. But within seconds, she realized what a monumental mistake that was. Her thoughts immediately took her back to the park, to that kiss, and she felt her panties become moist.

Mia had to get out of his bed. Her initial intentions for coming into his room were honorable, but now…not so much. All she wanted to do was rip that damned sheet away and feel him inside her. But if she did that, he would discover just how inexperienced she was. He would be expecting her to know certain things, like how to please him, how to position herself to maximize their pleasure. But she had no sexual repertoire to pull from…nothing.

Disheartened and feeling very pathetic, she gently pulled her hand away and was grateful that he didn't resist this time. Mia shimmied out of the bed, grabbed her pistol and walked toward the door. She looked over her shoulder, stealing one last glance. He was sleeping peacefully, the nightmare forgotten. But she would never forget how his body responded to her touch, how the sight of him made her want to give herself to him completely. Shaking her head out of frustration and angst, she shut the door behind her and went to her bedroom for what she prayed would be a dreamless sleep.

Chapter Thirty-Four

They were an hour into their flight when Chase noticed that Erin appeared distracted. She had been staring out the window, remarking from time to time how beautiful things were, how peaceful things seemed to be from thousands of feet up, when he finally got the nerve to ask her if there was something, excluding the usual, on her mind. Erin glanced over at Andrew, who was enjoying a much-needed rest, and then looked back at him.

Chase got the feeling that she needed privacy for what she was about to say. Without a word, he grabbed her hand and led her to the cavern at the back of his jet.

"Your jet has a bedroom?" she said, pleasantly surprised.

"Comes in handy on long flights," he said.

"But this isn't a long flight. We should be landing in an hour or so," she said, her eyes mischievous.

As much as he wanted to take advantage of that naughty little glint in her eye, Chase knew that something was bothering her. "I brought you back here so we could talk, not that I wouldn't enjoy using this room for other things," he said. She smiled, as if what he said set the stage for what she wanted to discuss. He walked her over to the bed and sat down next to her.

"Chase, I'm worried that you feel like…like you need to be…this is not coming out well," she said, obviously frustrated.

"Just say it, Erin. I don't want you to hold back," he said.

Her face seemed to brighten at his words. "Well, I guess that's it. I don't want *you* to hold back. I don't want you to feel like you can't be yourself around me. Before you found out about my rape, you were more…forthcoming in bed. I think you're censoring what you say, choosing your words wisely in order to avoid offending me in some way."

Chase watched his girl bare her soul and loved her even more for it. "And you miss that? The words I used to arouse us both?" he asked, aching for her. Chase felt his cock swell as he digested what she had said. She was a perfect combination of naughty and nice. And she was his.

Her face was a beautiful shade of pink when she nodded.

"After you told me what happened to you, well, I wasn't sure what to do, how far I could take things without making you feel…"

She kissed him before he could finish talking. Her leg swung over his, straddling him on the full-sized bed. "You make me feel beautiful," she said leaning over. She kissed him. "You make me feel wanted." Another kiss. "And you make me so hot for you, especially when you use those filthy little words," she whispered in his ear.

He groaned and flipped her on her back. "Hard or slow, Erin?" he asked. He had already removed his shirt and was unbuckling his pants when she answered.

"I want you to take the gloves off and give it to me hard and fast. I need it, Chase," she begged.

He practically ripped the clothes off her body and buried himself deep into her tight heat. She arched her back and screamed for him to fuck her. He lifted her legs onto his shoulders and slammed into her over and over again. Her body quaked around his pulsating cock, which only sent him down his own road to release. He didn't want the incredible feeling of her shaking beneath him from pleasure to end, but he couldn't hold back anymore, and with one forceful thrust he filled her with his seed.

"Erin...Fuck!" he yelled. His cock continued to pump inside her as she milked him of every drop.

Chapter Thirty-Five

Paul awoke at dawn and could not, despite several fruitless attempts, fall back to sleep. The nightmare he'd had still lingered and he decided it was best to put his focus on preparing breakfast. He hoped Mia was more of a salty than a sweet type of person, as he found the ingredients for a bacon-and-Swiss omelet instead of what was required to make pancakes or French toast.

He crumpled the cooked bacon into the frying pan and scattered the shredded cheese on top of the eggs. With spatula in hand, he leaned back and peered down the hallway in the direction of Mia's bedroom. He must have checked on her over a dozen times within the past hour. Each time he poked his head into her bedroom, she was sound asleep and wrapped up in her blankets. At some point during the night, she must have awakened from where he had left her on the couch and moved to her bedroom.

Paul heard the coffee machine chime, signaling that the pot of coffee he had brewed was good and ready. As if on cue, he heard the door to Mia's room open, followed by soft and careful footsteps.

Erin had similar timing. He often remarked how she could be in a sound sleep one minute and up and ready to go the next, especially if freshly brewed coffee was awaiting her.

"I hope you're hungry," Paul said, flipping the omelet over perfectly.

"Starving," she said.

Paul turned to tell her that the coffee was ready, but stopped when she came into view. It was obvious that she had just woken up. She was wearing the same clothes as last night, as was he. She had tied her hair back into a ponytail. And from the looks of it, she wasn't wearing any makeup, which he loved. She was so natural, so real, that he almost forgot what he was doing and nearly burned their breakfast. He came to just in time to remove the overly cheesy omelets form the pan, and shuffled them onto two plates.

"And you made coffee, too?" she asked, walking toward the coffee maker.

"I can't start my day without it. I'm highly addicted. I can admit it, though," Paul said, trying not to stare at her ass as she poured a cup for each of them.

Disgusted with himself, he went to the fridge and retrieved ketchup and hot sauce, as he was unsure which condiment she desired with her eggs. Mia was seated at the bar sipping her coffee when he returned. He joined her and took a gulp of his coffee. "That's perfect," he said.

"Little cream, a lot of sugar. It wasn't a lucky guess. I just overheard you ordering our drinks at Dunkin' Donuts yesterday," she said, between sips.

Paul noticed that she appeared a little tired, as if she could use a few more hours of sleep. He wondered if she'd had a restful sleep, if her dreams had been peaceful, unlike his. He couldn't get his own nightmare out of his head. It was the same recurring nightmare he had been having for over a year now, except last night it had morphed into something so horrific that even the light of day couldn't minimize its effects.

The nightmare had started off like it always did; with him walking down that cobblestone street. The scream pierced the air, prompting him to move swiftly toward whatever was making that god-awful sound. In the dream, as in what happened in real life, he found a mask-wearing man violating a young woman. He beat the shit out of him by punching and kicking him until he was barely conscious. Pleased that the bastard couldn't move, he checked on the girl, and it was then the dream had mutated. In every dream, as in reality, the trembling woman had always been his sister. But last night the frightened woman was Mia, and it occurred to him, even in his nightmare, that he had failed again. He had not kept her safe.

Paul couldn't remember anything after that. Thankfully, his nightmare had come to an abrupt end for one reason or another. Lying in his bed, trying to recall the details of that nightmare, he swore he detected Mia's unforgettable scent on the pillow next to him. It was wishful thinking of course, but it had given him the motivation to get moving and prepare for another day with Mia.

Paul smiled at her. "You passed out on me last night," he said.

Mia was in the middle of chewing her first bite of omelet when her face went fire-engine red. Paul wondered what he had said wrong to evoke such a reaction. "I just mean, one minute I was talking to you from the kitchen, and the next...out for the count on the couch."

Mia swallowed her food, though it looked like a struggle. "Do you not like eggs?" he asked. She looked like she was going to be sick.

Mia shook her head and smiled. "No, I love eggs, especially with hot sauce." She reached for the little red bottle and doused her omelet with the spicy liquid. He liked her style, as he too favored hot sauce over its safer counterpart. "Sorry for being so lame last night. I was more exhausted than I thought." Her complexion returned to normal and as much as he wanted to know what had caused Mia to blush, he knew they had more important things to discuss.

"I know I'm deviating a little from what we planned last night, but for the sake of saving time, how about we split up this morning? While you go to the soup shop and dig around to see if anyone working there recalls seeing or hearing something that night, I'll go interview Dr. Mitchell Morris's staff and Scott's," she said.

Paul didn't think and just said the first thing that came to mind. "No."

"Oh. Did you want to do the interviews and I'll go to the soup shop?" she asked, looking confused.

"I mean, no, we are not splitting up. In fact, you're not going anywhere without me," he said. Paul could only imagine what he sounded like, but he didn't care. Mia wasn't going to be traipsing around Philly unescorted. Paul wanted to blame his heightened insecurities entirely on the disturbing nightmare he'd had and the text that Chase had received, but he would be lying to himself. Even if he had dreamt of horses and rainbows last night, he would still insist that he accompany her everywhere she went.

Mia stared at him for a second with what looked like annoyance, maybe even anger. But it quickly dissipated and was replaced with concern. "I know you're worried, especially after what happened in the cemetery. So, okay, we can investigate together if you like. I was just trying to multitask, that's all," she said.

Paul felt like a total shit for being such a domineering asshole. Her initial reaction, the one where she appeared pissed off, told him that she wasn't used to, or very fond of, being told what to do. She softened, of course, when it dawned on her that he was probably behaving in such a way because of what had happened in the cemetery. Mia couldn't be more wrong. The reason why he was being a demanding prick was much more caveman-like. He already, and for no logical reason, considered her his. She belonged to him.

He reached for his coffee and took a few sips. Nodding, he said, "Good. I think we should start our day at the soup shop."

Chapter Thirty-Six

Although his patience was growing thin, Scott knew that it was in his best interest to steer clear of his Angel's house for a few days. Her neighbor's house would be swarming with police as they conducted their investigation and tried to decipher whether the clever woman's death was a homicide or just an unfortunate accident. Regardless of how the old hag died, her death would surely bring Mia home. If she was in Philadelphia working on a profile, it was just a matter of time until someone reached out to her and told her that her pet sitter was dead and that her yellow Lab was in need of his owner.

The thought of not seeing his Angel for a few days distressed him. But what sent him into a near rage, even as he sat in front of his computer at work, was the frustrating fact that Montclair and his Whore were still in Philadelphia. He had debated for less than a minute whether he should go to Philly and put an end to his misery. But he would definitely be missed and was afraid that if questions were asked, if fingers started to point in his direction, he wouldn't have a solid story to cling to.

He would await their return. And when the moment was right, when he was certain nothing could ever get back to him, he would destroy them all, starting with Montclair.

* * *

Unfortunately, the soup shop was a dead end. After a little digging around with some seemingly innocent questions for the owner, Mia and Paul discovered that the shop hadn't started serving dinner until just a few months ago. They had been a breakfast-and-lunch joint at the time of the rape and would have closed for the day by four o'clock in the afternoon. No one, at least from the establishments across the street, would have witnessed anything strange going on in the cemetery because they would have closed up for the night. The rapist had planned his attack well.

"Did you always walk Erin home from class?" Mia asked.

Paul had been quiet since they had left the place. He seemed frustrated that their trip didn't prove worthwhile. Although she didn't have her hopes up that someone in the shop would have remembered something that happened across the street over a year ago, it still was a great disappointment.

Paul pulled into the visitor' parking lot at CHOP and parked the car. But he didn't make a move to exit the vehicle, at least not immediately. "Most nights, Erin walked home with friends. But every once in a while, she would stay late to study and call me to come get her."

"What happened that night?" she asked, treading lightly.

"She stayed after class to speak with Dr. Farrell. Her friends had left, probably to celebrate the end of exams. I had been drinking with a few buddies, cheering ourselves for passing the Bar, when I received her text that she was heading home…alone. I nearly lost it. I can't explain it, but it was like I knew something bad was going to happen to her. I raced out of the pub and well…you know the rest."

Unfortunately, she did. And it was heartbreaking to know that he blamed himself for not reaching his sister in time. "It's not your fault, Paul. None of this could have been predicted."

"She's my sister. And I should have been there for her. She was raped because I chose to go out and toss a few back. She was raped because I didn't make it in time."

Mia felt like she was looking into a mirror. All she had to do was swap out the "she was raped" with "my father killed himself." What a morbid thing to have in common. Before Mia could respond, he exited his vehicle. The conversation was apparently over.

Although Paul had remained quiet as they entered the hospital, Mia noticed that he hadn't physically distanced himself from her. His hand had taken residence at the small of her back the moment she had gotten out of his car. And it remained there as they reached guest reception, during their short walk to the elevator, and while they ascended seven floors. Mia realized even in the short time that she had known him that he had a possessive personality. Paul would probably admit it freely if she voiced this observation. She imagined that it felt natural for him, comforting, to want to keep the people he was with safe. The rape only compounded his innate desire to protect.

And now that his sister was far away, safe and under Chase and Uncle Drew's protection, she could only assume that Paul had shifted his need to watch over someone onto her. She didn't want to read into the gentlemanly gesture too much. And she certainly shouldn't dwell on or allow herself to replay that kiss in her mind over and over again. Emotions were running high at the moment and for good reason. Paul and Erin hadn't returned to Philadelphia since the incident and it was expected that they would struggle with coming face-to-face with the past. Still, Mia had to admit to herself that Paul's firm but gentle hand on her back made her melt. The elevator chimed, casting Mia out of her teenaged delirium.

Mia and Paul had decided the previous night that she would do most of the talking. He would be her quiet sidekick, taking notes, even donning a camera to solidify the charade. Mia looked over at the nurse's station and was happy to see what appeared to be a veteran nurse. She seemed comfortable behind the desk as she stroked her computer keys with remarkable speed.

Mia inhaled as she approached. "Good morning. My name is Mia. I'm writing the article about Dr. Mitchell Morris," she said with confidence. The older nurse stared at her for a moment, clearly bewildered by her presence. "I called yesterday...spoke to...hmm, forgot her name, but I asked if it would be okay if I came in and asked the people that Dr. Morris was close to a few questions." Mia smiled, trying to soften the approach. "It's a tribute article, a way to memorialize a great doctor and..."

"And a great man," the nurse said, finishing Mia's thought.

That was the in Mia needed. The nurse announced to one of the assistants behind the station that she was taking her break and escorted them down the hallway. Mia thought that she was taking them to the lounge or an empty room for patients to talk, but when she unlocked the heavy oak door, Mia realized her good fortune.

"No one can bear going through his things. I suspect that his office will remain untouched for a while. Dr. Morris's passing was such a…shock…a tragedy," she said, struggling with the last word. Mia could tell that the woman was in pain and instantly felt bad for exploiting his death. But Mia pushed those pangs of guilt aside and focused on what led her here, instead: Erin.

The nurse took a seat in one of the leather chairs across from a grand desk and Mia followed her lead. Out of all the hospital staff members she could have approached, Mia had apparently picked Clara, the floor's most seasoned nurse, who had worked alongside Dr. Mitchell Morris for over twenty years. Mia learned more about Dr. Morris than she had hoped.

"And his wife, how he loved her. I've never seen someone so devoted to his family," Clara said, fighting desperately to hold back the tears.

Mia looked over at the desk and focused on an eight-by-ten-inch family photo. Dr. Mitchell Morris had his arm around his wife's waist while Scott Morris, in a graduation cap and gown, stood next to his mother, smiling.

"They must have been so proud of their son. I understand that Scott Morris has become a successful doctor in his own right," Mia said, returning her gaze on Clara.

The warmth that had been in Clara's eyes, that gentleness, left her at the mention of Dr. Morris's son. "Scott may favor his father in looks, but he's nothing like his father."

Her tone was curt, almost accusatory. Mia had hit a nerve. And it was about time. "Oh, am I mistaken? Scott Morris is not a doctor?" Mia asked, allowing her eyes to grow wide with mock innocence.

"He's a doctor, but that's where the similarity ends," Clara said. She was staring at the photo with what appeared to be utter disgust. "I never told Mitchell what I thought, not that it would have mattered, but his boy is the coldest human being I have ever met. I never understood how Mitchell and his wife could have a child like that. Scott was an unappreciative youngster that grew into an egocentric man."

Clara broke down after that last jab and Mia leaned over to hug her. The woman was clearly grief stricken over the loss of her friend, which was causing her to unload some feelings that she had been harboring for years. "I guess I'm still angry that Scott chose to have Mitchell's funeral in New York as opposed to Philadelphia, where all Mitchell's friends are. Many of us wanted to attend, but couldn't due to our work schedules and the distance. I'm beyond retirement age, so I could have easily had taken off from work. But my ninety-two-year-old mother lives with me and I couldn't leave her alone to attend the funeral in New York City." She cried into Mia's shoulder and then said, after a few sniffles, "Please don't print that part about his son. I'm just upset that my friend is gone."

"You have my word, Clara. I have no desire to paint that kind of picture. Instead, could you talk to me about how Dr. Morris helped his son during his bout of cancer?" Mia asked.

Clara wiped her eyes with a tissue she had pulled from her pocket and nodded. She told Mia and Paul that Scott had come down with cancer late last spring. Mitchell had taken four months off from work to see to his son's treatment. They had caught Scott's cancer early, resulting in a full recovery.

"Dr. Morris must have been so relieved," Mia said.

Clara stared at Mia and then said, "Even though his son had beaten the disease and was in remission, Mitchell was never the same after that."

"What do you mean he was never the same?" Mia asked, patting the woman's arm.

"Dr. Mitchell had the bedside manner of a saint, a light around him that glowed brighter with each patient he cured. But after last summer, the light dimmed more with every passing month, until it was snuffed out completely when his wife died. I imagine that the stress of it all had finally gotten to him."

Mia knew she had taken too much of this woman's time already, but thought it was necessary for the case's sake as well as Clara's to finish with a story, one that portrayed the man during happier times. "Clara, just two more questions. If you could pick his greatest professional achievement, what would it be? And on a lighter note, could you tell me a time he made you laugh?"

Clara chuckled. "Well, he made me laugh every day. And for his greatest professional achievement?" Clara smiled. "He was the heart and soul of this hospital. There is no greater achievement than that."

Chapter Thirty-Seven

As progressive as Chase was, there were some things that were nonnegotiable in regards to tradition.

He had always envisioned himself proposing marriage to the woman he loved with the ring that his father had given his mother. Chase should have known that his engagement to Gabrielle was doomed the moment she insisted that she pick out the rock of her choice. He never told her about his mother's ring. Deep down, he knew she didn't deserve it. Within hours of his proposal, Gabrielle had practically drug him to Tiffany's and picked out a diamond so obscene, so ridiculously large, that it resembled gaudy costume jewelry. God, how he hated that ring. He had every right to demand that hideous piece of jewelry back the night he found her cheating on him, but by then, he didn't care. She could keep the ring and the guy she had been riding.

Chase pushed the noxious thought out of his mind and focused on the present, which was so beautiful. The setting was so perfect, the ideal combination of romance and serenity, but he didn't have the ring in his possession. Their abrupt departure from New York prohibited him from going to his bank's safe-deposit box and reclaiming what should rightfully belong to Erin. Chase knew that men, especially in this day and age, often proposed without a ring. But no matter how petty it seemed, Chase couldn't bring himself to ask Erin to be his wife without it. That ring was a symbol of forever, a symbol that everything he had belonged to her, that his love for her would never waver but grow stronger with each passing day. He thought about having the ring flown to the island, but reconsidered. Although slight, there was a risk that the stalker would trace it somehow, leading him to their private little world. To ensure her safety, he would just have to wait until they were back in New York to propose.

Chase walked to the water's edge and wrapped his arms around Erin's waist. He had been watching her for some time from a few yards away. She seemed at peace as she gazed out at the ocean, which was a marvel considering their past month. She nestled into him and sighed.

"You look very relaxed," he said, breathing in the scent of her shampoo mixed with sea-infused air. The combination was intoxicating and he longed for a repeat of last night. Despite their explosive lovemaking on the plane, his girl had been prepared to give him more the moment they stepped foot on solid ground. Reading the lust in her eyes, he had hustled her onto his gated property. Chase still wasn't certain how he had restrained himself long enough for Andrew to secure the ten-thousand-square-foot home, but when he was given the green light to enter, Chase had rushed her to the bedroom, which was where they had remained up until an hour ago.

"You told me that you owned a vacation home, not an entire island," she said.

"Oh, I must have left that part out," he said, mischievously. Chase could feel his cock grow hard against that tight little ass of hers.

"So, how alone are we here?" she asked.

It could have been his imagination, but he swore her hips swayed into him farther, tempting him to strip her out of the thin cotton skirt and tank top she was wearing. Somehow, he managed to answer her. "This is a private island. You couldn't tell last night when we arrived because it was dark, but there are no other homes."

"Is that so?" she asked. This time it wasn't wishful thinking. She was pressing her ass against his cock with the full intention to seduce.

He was seconds away from ripping away her clothes when she broke free of his embrace. Erin walked a few steps toward the water and turned around. Her nipples were erect and piercing the white, paper-thin ribbed tank. She took another step backward, keeping her gaze fixed on his rock-solid erection. Licking her lips, she slid her skirt down and kicked it safely onto the sand. Standing there wearing only a see-through white tank with no bra to limit his view and a pink thong…well it was more than he could take. Anticipating that he was going to lunge for her, she smiled and ran into the water.

He disrobed, which allowed her to gain a bit of a lead, but he quickly caught up with her. She gasped as he took hold of her from behind. Together they fell into the water and laughed.

He turned her around so she could face him. "I will always catch you, sweetheart. You must know that by now," he whispered, before taking an earlobe between his teeth. The laugher ceased and she moaned from the sudden combination of pleasure and pain. With her firmly in his arms, he waded further out into the ocean, nibbling his way down her neck to her perfectly buoyant breasts. Usually, he would just tear the shirt from her body, but not this time. Her luscious mounds were spilling over her shirt and it was so goddamned sexy. But he also needed them in his mouth, tasting each taut nipple with his tongue.

But first that barely there layer of fabric between her legs had to go. He reached down, stripped her of the pesky thong, and wrapped her legs around his waist. Chase reached down and stroked her clit, causing her body to jolt. "Is this what you want, baby?" he asked, quickly finding the rhythm she loved.

"Um…hmm," she whimpered.

He chuckled and then turned his attention to her rounded mounds. He leaned in and caressed her nipple with his tongue, lapping gently at first. But as her body thrashed with the pleasure he was giving her between her legs, his own desire took hold and he took her breast in his mouth and sucked the rigid peak. Her whimpers turned into audible moans, telling Chase that she was close.

Chase removed his fingers from her clit and slammed into her with his cock. She locked her legs around him even tighter as he rocked into her. "I want to hear you scream, Erin," he said, forcing himself to slow down. A few more thrusts and he was going to explode inside her. He wanted to make this last, at least for another minute.

Chase glided out of her enough so only the tip of his cock remained in her tight heat. He felt her fingers grab his ass and attempt to force him back inside her. But he held firm, knowing that his girl also loved it slow and deep. "Scream for me, Erin," he said, thrusting into her with one smooth motion.

"Chase!" she yelled. She was so hot for him, stripped bare and uninhibited. His girl was beautiful.

"Tell me what I want to hear," he said, pulling out. "Now."

"I…I'm yours!" she cried. "Yours."

Her eyes were closed and her back arched. He gripped her ass and slammed into her, feeling every quake from her powerful orgasm against his shaft. "Ah…Erin…I love you!" he yelled, finding his own earth-shattering release.

Chapter Thirty-Eight

As he had done at CHOP, Paul watched Mia work the fifth floor of Pennsylvania Hospital with remarkable grace. She seemed so at ease and invested in the story she was telling Scott Morris's former staff that he almost believed she might actually write an article about Dr. Mitchell Morris at the end of all this.

It was obvious that those in the oncology department who knew Dr. Mitchell Morris respected him, noting how he had a way of inspiring new doctors and reigniting the flames of veteran physicians that might have been on their way to being snuffed out. But as polite as the nurses and doctors were to him and Mia, Paul couldn't dismiss the frigid undertones, the clipped responses they received when Mia asked questions about Scott Morris. Although not as forthcoming as Clara, each nurse and doctor had given Mia an eerily similar response. In a nutshell, Scott Morris was a good doctor who paid close attention to detail, was prompt and insanely organized. However, his bedside manner, the way he connected with patients and his colleagues, had left a lot to be desired.

Paul was in the middle of his own interview when he heard Mia's phone ring. He looked over and saw Mia glance at her phone with what appeared to be curiosity, then excuse herself from the marathon conversation she was having with a very talkative doctor. But within seconds of Mia's phone call, Paul could tell something was wrong. He quickly withdrew one of his business cards from his wallet and handed it to the young woman he was interviewing.

"Please call me if you remember anything...if there is something you would like me to know about Dr. Mitchell Morris or about his son, Scott," Paul said. He forced a smile and then went to see what was causing that horrific look on Mia's face.

"I'm coming, Ben." Mia said to the mystery caller. She ended the call and looked at him.

"What is it, Mia?" he asked.

Paul could tell she was fighting back tears because she refused to look at him. "The police just found Rose." Mia swallowed and then took a deep breath. "She's dead, Paul."

* * *

Mia had known Ian and his twin sisters, Hannah and Jillian, but they had been grown and almost out of the house by the time Mia came on the scene. Unfortunately, Rose's son and two daughters were now scattered across two countries. Ian was a naval engineer stationed in Japan. Hannah and Jillian had left New York several years ago to set up a hospital dedicated to children infected with AIDS in Numidia, Africa. It would take some time just for Rose's children to make travel arrangements and return for their mother's funeral, let alone plan the details of such a morbid event. Mia knew what it was like to lose parents. She had to do something.

Mia picked up the phone and found Ben's number in her history. He answered on the second ring. "Hi, Mia. Hitting traffic?" he asked.

Ben Rollins had been on the force at the same time she assumed her position as a profiler. The fact that he had asked her out over a dozen times suggested they could have been more than just colleagues. He was nice enough and definitely wonderful to look at, but Mia didn't want to expend the energy to start something she feared would be a dead end. There was no spark; her belly didn't do flips when they shared the same space; she didn't daydream about him or fantasize about what it would be like to touch him. Her body never ached for Ben…like it did for Paul.

"A little. We should be there in five minutes. How's Henry?" Mia asked. She had called Ben earlier, several times, in fact, to check in on her furry little man. Despite being outside for more than twelve hours from what the police estimated was the time of death, Ben assured her that Henry appeared healthy and happy.

"He's very…energetic," Ben said.

Mia chuckled. "He's not behaving, is he?"

"He definitely loves to go for walks. He and I have covered most of the east side this afternoon and he still doesn't look tired," Ben said.

"Thanks for taking care of him. He'll sleep like a champ tonight," Mia said.

"Not a problem."

Although Mia was staring out the passenger-side window, she could feel Paul's gaze weigh heavily on her. "Well, Ben, any movement on the case?" Mia asked.

"Looks like an unfortunate accident, Mia. There is absolutely no sign of forced entry. Burglary doesn't seem to be a motive, since we found a diamond ring on her finger and a jar of money on the kitchen counter in perfect view of the front door. High-ticket items such as her television, a digital camera and an iPhone were also untouched. But most importantly, there is no evidence that your neighbor was physically assaulted. It appears that she tripped and hit her head."

Mia pictured the final seconds of Rose's life and cringed. "Do you think the guys would mind if I had a look at the scene? I don't want to intrude…I know that I no longer work for…"

"I think they would welcome your expertise," he said, cutting her off.

"Thanks." Mia felt like she was overstepping her bounds, but she needed to ask for another favor. "Ben, have Rose's children been notified?"

"Yes, we called them a few hours ago. Ian and his sisters said they would be here as soon as they could. I anticipate that all three children will be delayed, however. Hannah and Jillian cannot just up and leave. They will probably have to wait until their replacements have arrived before they can fly out. Ian will also have to request leave from his superiors and that can take some time."

That was what Mia expected. "Ben, could you give me their contact information? I want to reach out to them, see if there is anything I can do."

Ben gave her the three phone numbers and she plugged them into her phone. She told Ben she would see him soon and ended the call.

"Who's Ben?" Paul asked.

Paul had been silent for most of the car ride from Philly to New York. It was like he knew she needed some quiet time to process yet another loss. So, it startled her when he questioned her about Ben.

"We worked together when I was on the force. He's watching Henry for me...or should I say, maintaining him to the best of his ability," Mia said, smiling a little as she thought about her disobedient puppy.

But Paul wasn't smiling. In fact, he looked pissed. She was just about to ask him why he looked fit to kill, when his face softened and the scowl disappeared. "I'm glad Henry's all right. You must miss the little terror," he said.

The sudden shift, the way Paul could go from brooding to compassionate, gave her reason to pause. But there was no time to analyze how or why his emotions seemed to jump around. They rounded the corner and she instantly saw two police vehicles parked in front of Rose's home. The scene was all too familiar, evoking memories that she had worked hard to suppress.

Chapter Thirty-Nine

Paul watched Henry break free of someone he assumed was Ben and come barreling toward Mia. She squatted down and clapped her hands. "Come here, buddy," she said.

Henry knocked her onto her backside and covered her with kisses. She was laughing and crying as she apologized for being away so long, for leaving him outside without food and water for hours. It wasn't her fault, none of it was, but it was obvious she was feeling very guilty.

"My dog-sitting duties have come to an end," said Ben.

With great effort, she unraveled herself from Henry and stood. Ben hugged her and she returned the gesture. The sight shouldn't have made him want to hurt something, but God did Paul want to punch that man in the face! Between his lingering hug and the way the prick blushed a feverish pink when the embrace finally came to an end, Paul determined that the man thought of her as more than just a former colleague.

"Ben, this is my friend, Paul," she said.

Never had Paul felt such disdain for a word as he did when Mia uttered the word "friend." He had no right to feel jealous, so possessive of a woman he had just met, but he didn't care. Paul shook his hand and said, "Thanks for taking care of Henry while we were away."

Paul wondered if Ben had gotten the message. Mia may not have come to the conclusion as of yet, but she was with him now. Ben was part of her past. Paul met Ben's steely glare while providing a firm handshake. Yeah, Ben had read the situation correctly. But would this ex-whatever-he-was stand down or continue to pursue Mia?

"Henry was a perfect gentleman," Ben said, retracting his hand from Paul's.

"And you're a horrible liar," Mia said, reaching for Henry's leash. She smiled at Ben. "I'm going to take Henry home and get him settled. It'll only take a minute."

"Take your time. I'll see you next door," Ben said. Her "colleague" didn't look at Paul, which only infuriated him more. Instead, Ben's eyes were fixed on Mia. Finally, Ben turned and walked away.

Once inside Mia's house, with the door secured behind them, she said, "Until we can rule out that Rose's death isn't linked to...everything else that is happening, would you mind sticking around for a bit? I know it's highly unlikely that there is a connection, but I..."

"I'm not going anywhere," Paul said.

Mia nodded. "Well, I'll just go put Henry in his room, then." Mia patted her leg and called for Henry to come. Henry actually complied and followed Mia down the hallway into what appeared to be a bedroom. Moments later, Paul heard a familiar voice come across the television. Curious, he retraced Mia and Henry's footsteps and found Henry already curled up in a ball in a plush dog bed. "He loves the Weather Channel. It's his favorite. Puts him right out," Mia said, patting her sleepy dog on the head.

"I can relate. I'll flick the Weather Channel on when I can't sleep. Has a similar effect on us humans, I guess." Mia dimmed the lights and walked out into the hallway with him. "So Henry has his own room?" he asked.

"Yeah, I consider it a big crate, really. He has his space and I still have control over my own bedroom," she said.

Paul was listening, but his attention was diverted to the few dozen photos of Mia and who he assumed were her parents and Andrew on the wall behind her. "That pier looks familiar. Ocean City Boardwalk?" he asked.

Mia turned and gazed at the grainy photo of her and whom he could only conclude was her father. Covered in sand from head to toe in a pink and green bikini with the grand wooden pier in the background, Mia couldn't have been more than six years old during that particular summer vacation. "The one and only. My parents didn't have much money, but they always seemed to squeeze a few days in at the beach every summer somehow."

"Same here. Our parents worked hard, lived paycheck to paycheck, but miraculously found a way to take Erin and me on vacation each year. The Jersey Shore was always the destination. I had spent many a night walking the boards of Ocean City, sampling the…"

"Girls?" she asked, raising a playful eyebrow.

Yeah, there had been a lot of "sampling" when he had reached his mid-teens and even more when he was in college, but Mia didn't need to know that. "I was going to say sampling the food."

"Food? Yeah, okay," she said, clearly not believing him. She looked at another photo and pointed to a Ferris wheel. "In between sampling all the 'food' that the Ocean City Boardwalk had to offer, did you take time to enjoy the rides?"

Paul loved her sass, the way she could give it right back to him. "Erin made the unfortunate mistake of devouring four slices of Mack and Manco pizza before riding that exact Ferris wheel. I told her that we should wait, let the food digest, but she insisted. Her sun-tanned face went green after the first revolution. I reached her just in time to hold back her hair. The operator of the ride was not pleased."

"Oh no," she laughed.

Paul could have spent all night asking about each photo that was hung on the wall, learning the story behind every one of Mia's smiles, but he knew that people were waiting for her next door. Ruining their lighthearted conversation, he asked, "Should we head on over?"

Her smile faded as reality crept in and took its rightful place. "Yeah, let me grab a sweatshirt." Mia moved past him and entered the room opposite of Henry's. He almost followed her, as he ached to see where she laid her head down each night and surrendered to sleep, but he refrained. Instead, he looked at the wall of photos and zeroed in on a photo of Mia, no longer six years old, no longer a child, and every bit a young woman. He couldn't decipher where the photo had been taken or what event she was attending, but regardless, Mia was stunning. Her long brown hair was pulled back, exposing her flawless neck and diamond-studded earrings. The floor-length dress hugged her ample curves as she posed for the camera with a woman whose smile mimicked her own. The mature woman at her side had to be her mother, as the resemblance was just too strong to assume otherwise.

Paul looked away at the sound of Mia's bedroom door clicking shut. "I think Henry is out for the count. Better that we leave now while he is in a Weather Channel–induced coma."

Paul nodded and with his hand firmly situated at the small of Mia's back, he led her next door.

Chapter Forty

Mia had debated with herself for all of five minutes before pushing the SEND button on her cell. Knowing her uncle like she did, he would probably blame himself somehow. Like he had planned on being away on assignment at the exact moment her neighbor was found dead. It was best he heard the news from her, rather than from some other source. No doubt he was keeping tabs on her somehow. It was just a matter of time until the news would reach him, even while taking in some rays down south.

"Mia, what's wrong?" Uncle Drew asked. He sounded nervous, a complete contrast to his typical, composed self.

"I'm fine." Mia paused. "But Rose...she's gone, Uncle Drew. Fortunately, Benny and two other guys I knew during my short time on the force received the call this morning. Ben found Henry barking incessantly in Rose's side yard, the very ruckus that prompted an annoyed neighbor to call and complain. Ben called me after he read Henry's dog tags."

"So, what are we looking at here? Have they determined cause of death?" he asked.

"I just checked out the scene for myself. The injury to her head is consistent with a slip and fall accident. I found…evidence…on the cast-iron umbrella urn just inside the front door." Mia wanted to remain in cop mode, where emotions safely took a back seat, but she found that her already-fragile walls were beginning to crack.

"I'm so sorry, Mia. I should be there with you," Uncle Drew said.

Mia shook her head. "No, you are right where you need to be. Protecting Erin." Mia sighed. "I'm all right, Uncle Drew, Paul and I…"

"Paul Whitley is with you?" he asked, cutting her off.

His clipped tone was foreign to her. She reverted back to a little girl and answered, "Yes."

"Mia, I wish to speak with him, sweetheart. Please put Whitley on the phone," he said, his voice just a touch softer, despite the term of endearment.

Mia looked over at Paul and caught him throwing dog food pellets to Henry in her kitchen. Paul had a smile on his face as he praised Henry for catching the little morsels in midair. "Good boy," Paul said, patting her dog's massive head.

"Um…Paul? My uncle would like to talk to you," Mia said, holding up her cell phone.

Paul's smile melted away. "Is my sister okay?" he asked.

Mia felt terrible. Why the hell did she not squash that fear right off the bat? "Erin is fine. Sorry to scare you."

Paul exhaled as she handed him the phone. Within seconds, Paul excused himself and walked away…out of earshot. Mia knew that Erin was physically fine, but how was she faring emotionally?

Mia heard Paul's hushed voice utter a semblance of good-bye, and he ended the call with her uncle. Paul walked toward her and handed her the phone. "What would make you more comfortable? Me sleeping on your couch? Or you and Henry sleeping in my spare bedroom?"

Paul may as well have been speaking French. What the hell was he talking about?

"Um…neither. I mean…what *did* you tell Uncle Drew?"

"Your uncle doesn't feel like you should be alone tonight. And I agreed with him," Paul said.

"My overprotective uncle, the same that jacked up one of the few high school boyfriends I had because he stared at me a little too long for his taste, asked you to partake in a sleepover with his niece?"

"In a manner of speaking," he said.

"Spill it, Whitley. You're holding out on me," she said, studying those piercing blue eyes of his.

Paul sighed, signaling that he probably had hoped she would have conceded and refrained from digging deeper into her uncle's odd request. "Mia, your uncle has informed me that he will abandon his assignment if you choose to refuse my company," he said, his tone serious. "He doesn't want you to be alone tonight."

"My uncle would never walk out…just leave Erin and Chase without protection," she said, shaking her head vigorously.

"For you, he would."

Mia was considering her uncle's terms when Paul continued, "And don't ask me to lie to Andrew. He may be over a thousand miles away, but somehow he would know if we didn't pick one of those two options."

Damn it! It was like Paul was reading her mind.

Mia was two seconds away from feigning surprise, maybe even disgust at what Paul had said, but he would see right through her. Instead, she thought about her uncle's ultimatum and tried to determine just how probable it would be for him to hop on Chase's jet and fly home to New York to be with her. It was definitely not out of the realm of possibility for her uncle to leave Erin and Chase alone on that island, considering he had secured his pilot's license years ago.

Well, shit. There was no way out of this.

"I would offer you the other bedroom, but…well, I haven't been in there, no one has, since my dad died," Mia said.

"The couch is fine, Mia."

"It's a pullout. I'll go get you some sheets." Mia walked to the hall linen closet and retrieved a queen-sized set and returned to see that he had already transformed the sofa into his sleeping quarters for the night. She had to keep reminding herself that it was just for the night. And it wasn't as if Paul really had a choice in the matter. His sister would be left without her bodyguard if he didn't comply.

Mia unfolded the fitted sheet and started to tuck the first corner in when Paul grabbed the opposite end and followed her lead. They finished the domestic task in under a minute. With the freshly made bed staring at her, beckoning to be used for more than just sleeping, Mia suddenly felt nervous and very much the inexperienced woman she was. She decided that a diversion was absolutely necessary. "I'm in the mood for some pizza and a movie in which I don't have to think too much," she said, careful not to meet his gaze. Yes, food is everybody's friend. And a good guy flick, one devoid of angst and heated stares.

The food arrived forty-five minutes later. Sitting on the couch, now pulled-out bed, Mia and Paul happily dug into their pizza. Mia didn't realize until she took her first bite that she hadn't eaten since that morning. Paul was surfing through her on-demand movies when Mia spotted the movie she always seemed to watch whenever she encountered it on regular television. "That one," she said, as Paul highlighted *Cool Hand Luke* with the remote control.

"Perfect," he said, hitting PLAY. He placed the remote on the coffee table, propped a few pillows behind him and continued with his meal. He looked so relaxed, as if he belonged there, in her home, in her bed.

Mia pushed that thought aside, knowing it couldn't lead anywhere, and focused her attention on one of her favorite movies of all time. But after several minutes, Mia realized that a sexy and very young Paul Newman was no match for the gorgeous man lying next to her. She strategically placed an invisible two-foot barrier between them, but it couldn't keep his earthy and arousing scent from invading her space.

Mia didn't want to be a lousy host, just eating and shuffling off to bed, but she couldn't endure the silent torture either. She just wanted him to reach over and tuck her beneath him. She wanted to feel his weight upon her as he kissed her with that same sense of urgency she had felt in the park. Reluctantly, Mia placed her empty plate on the table next to her and tried to spark up conversation. "Why did you become a lawyer?"

Paul had been grinning at the television when she broached the question. He looked over at her and said, "A few of us, lawyers I mean, actually are interested in the business to find the truth and act accordingly."

Mia's intention wasn't to offend him, but to distract herself from the beautiful man she wanted to touch. "Sorry, I didn't mean for it to sound like…"

"Mia, I'm playing with you." Paul smiled, which made her belly do somersaults. He folded his hands in his lap. "I knew early on that I wanted to be a civil rights attorney. But after my parents died, I shifted to personal injury."

Mia had learned from Erin that their parents had died in the horrific pier accident along the Delaware River. The news of the incident had reached all the way to New York City for a couple reasons. The fact that seventeen people in all had died that night was definitely newsworthy. But months later, when all the legal dust had settled, the restaurant, along with two construction companies, had been found negligent and ordered to pay each victim's family an undisclosed sum to compensate for the damages.

"Two of my colleagues handle medical malpractice; another focuses on product fault. I take on the personal injury cases that have resulted in serious injury or death of a family member…like what happened to my parents."

Mia cringed. A week ago, she had sat on Chase's couch and asked Paul if he was seeing a therapist. No wonder he balked at the idea of therapy. Every day, every time he went into the office and defended the rights of someone who had been wronged due to negligence, he was working through his issues in regards to his parents' passing.

But was he seeking help for what his sister's rape had invoked? Watching Paul with his sister, Mia got the impression that he could be extremely possessive and demanding. And the dream. The dream she had interrupted still lingered in her mind. He had been calling Mia's name, but in the chaos of the dream, he had probably swapped out Erin's name for hers. Made sense since they had spent the evening together planning for their case. There was so much turmoil on his face and then...rage. She couldn't be sure, but it was possible the monster that had violated his sister still haunted him, weaving his way into Paul's nightmares.

"Paul, I didn't mean to get so personal...or make you recall why you had switched your concentration from civil law to personal injury," Mia said, embarrassed that she had unintentionally pried into his business.

Paul reached out his hand and caressed the side of her cheek. Her already-flushed face must have shot to a fiery red. "I'm sure that my sister made mention that I'm not one to...share my thoughts."

"I think Erin's exact words were, 'My brother isn't very forthcoming'...and that you don't trust easily," Mia said.

His eyes focused on her mouth and she licked her lips without thinking. His eyes went dark and for a moment she thought he was going to lean in and kiss her. But, much to her disappointment, he stopped right before he met her lips with his. "Do you remember what I said to you in Chase's parking garage?"

Mia felt the words leave her. She could have that kiss again, the one that made her weak and wanting all of him at once, if she would just form a coherent thought. Sensing her sudden lack of speech, he said, "If you ever want to know how you make me feel...all you have to do is ask."

She stared at him as the pad of his thumb stroked her cheek and then her lower lip. She wanted to mold her lips and tongue around his finger, a move she had never made on a guy before. And that was the moment her cell phone decided to intervene. It also marked the end of what looked like a very promising evening.

Chapter Forty-One

Mia had been on the phone with two of Rose's children for the past thirty minutes and it didn't look like the conversation was ending anytime soon. Paul retrieved his overnight bag from the car and headed straight to the bathroom. He needed a shower...a long, cold shower.

Paul leafed through his bag and was thankful that he had packed an extra pair of boxer briefs and lounge pants for his trip to Philly. He set the items aside and entered the shower. Although the frigid water caused him to jolt, his erection stayed firm, undeterred by Paul's attempt to curb his desire. Annoyed, he adjusted the temperature and coaxed his body to relax.

But a shower wasn't going to do the trick. The only thing that would bring him satisfaction was Mia. And he had been so close. Just a second later, he would have tasted her again, felt her beautiful curves against him while he palmed her breasts. But the phone had cut him off at the knees and the harsh reality that life still pressed on cast a shadow over Mia's living room.

Paul stared down at his rock-solid cock and felt ashamed of himself for wanting her so badly. Her neighbor, a woman she had known all her life, had just died and all he could think about was touching Mia, making her body rise and fall with pleasure. He contemplated whether he should take his shaft in his hand and work it until he had nothing left, but he didn't feel right doing the deed in her bathroom, with her just outside the door. Paul quickly shampooed and was in the process of rinsing when he heard a knock at the door and then a voice. She was in the bathroom with him and he was in one of those glass-enclosed showers, the kind that offers no privacy whatsoever.

There was nowhere to hide…and he didn't want to.

"I brought you a towel and a washclo…" Mia said. Her eyes never made it to his, as she stared at his arousal. She was blushing, but Paul got the feeling that she wasn't embarrassed. She looked…turned on. "I'll just set them on the sink," she said, whipping around.

Paul didn't move. He just stood there, silently daring her to turn and look at him once more. But she didn't. Instead, she wished him good night and left the bathroom. Seconds later, he heard her bedroom door close.

* * *

Mia fell into her bed and pulled the covers up around her. She couldn't get the picture out of her mind. Unabashed, Paul stood in her shower, dripping wet, his cock standing at full attention. She had never seen a man's member up close and personal before. Movies and erotic books didn't do the male anatomy justice, especially Paul's. His body was perfection and more than a little intimidating. She couldn't believe that a woman could accommodate such…size…girth. Mia had no experience, zilch, a bit fat zero in the sex department, but even she knew that Paul was well-endowed.

In an attempt to drown out the sound of the shower, which only made her think of him standing there naked…waiting, maybe…Mia switched on her iPod. The lineup of songs proved to be cruel, as if the throaty female singers and the sexy crooners were taunting her, tempting her to throw back her covers and join Paul beneath the cascading water. Again, her fear took hold and she remained in her bed. The moment they moved beyond a kiss, he would know. There would be no way to fake it or pretend that she possessed skills in the bedroom. Mia had never resented her inexperience until now. In college, she had been focused solely on her studies and the career she had always dreamed of. She remembered thinking that sex and relationships could wait. And then her mother was murdered, and all her energy shifted to finding the man who killed her and her father's reason to live. Her parents' deaths had left her numb…until now.

The only thing that could get her mind off of Paul and what she wasn't doing with him were the phone calls she had with Rose's children. That thought grounded her. Mia suddenly grew tired and surrendered to much-needed rest. She would need a recharge, considering that she had just offered to host a houseful of Rose's friends and family that coming weekend.

Chapter Forty-Two

Mia had set the alarm clock on her phone for six o'clock in the morning. There was much to do before Ian and his sisters arrived. Their flights were due in around dinnertime, and if she worked non-stop, it might just be possible to have the house cleaned and the fridge stocked. But as chaotic as the next few days would be, she knew that opening her home to Rose's family was the least she could do. Hannah, Jillian and Ian had been oversees when both of Mia's parents had died. Upon hearing the news, each of Rose's children had hopped on a plane and come to both funerals. Mia didn't want to know how difficult it was for Ian and his sisters to just drop everything and fly home.

Mia tiptoed to the bathroom as she didn't want to wake Paul. She showered quickly and dressed in beaten-up jean shorts and a tank, appropriate attire for the kind of work she was going to take on. Although Mia knew that the clock was ticking, she needed her morning caffeine as much as her next breath. As she crept toward the kitchen, she glanced over at the pullout couch and discovered that Paul was gone…and so was her dog. She walked over to the open front door just in time to see Paul bend down and pick up a pile of poop in a plastic baggie. The scene should have grossed her out, but for some reason she found it endearing as hell. "Come on, boy," he said, gently tugging on the leash. "Let's go wake up your mom."

Mia marveled at the sight. Paul Whitley could simultaneously pull off sexy and cute like no other man. Mia opened the screen door and was almost taken out by one overly excited Lab. "Good morning, men," she said. Paul's hair may have been disheveled from sleep and he was wearing lounge parents, but he screamed sex.

Not today. Those thoughts had to be locked away until further notice.

"Morning," he said, running his fingers through his thick locks. God, he was hot!

"I'll make us some coffee," she said, escaping into the kitchen.

Mia could hear Paul transforming the bed back into a couch and wondered if she had just foolishly assumed that he was even planning to stay long enough to want to have a cup of coffee with her. And why wouldn't he want to leave? He had a job, a life she assumed he wanted to get back to as soon as possible. Saving face, she reached for the travel mug in her cupboard and filled it generously. Mia was pouring in the cream when he rounded the corner. "Kicking me out?" he asked, eyeing the travel mug with a smile that could melt any female.

"Um…no. I just thought, well, you've been away for a few days and probably need to take care of some things, do some errands, maybe even go to work?" she said. She stirred his coffee then handed him the steaming mug.

"So what's on your agenda today?" he asked, completely ignoring her question.

She poured herself a cup and was preparing it to her liking when she said, "I'm picking up Rose's kids at the airport around five thirty tonight. But before that, well, let's just say that I have a few errands and chores of my own to complete."

"Where should we begin?" he asked. He sipped his coffee and licked his lips.

Mia stared at him. We?

Coming to, she said, "As you can imagine, Hannah and Jillian are not taking their mother's passing well. Ian told me last night that Jillian seemed to be in a state of shock, as she was barely able to hold a conversation with him over the phone. He has no idea how she is going to make it through the funeral, let alone enter her childhood home again. That was right around the time I told him that they were more than welcome to stay here. I have the space, I just need to clear out a few rooms first."

"That was very kind of you to offer," he said. "How can I help?"

Mia shook her head. "You already took one for the team by babysitting me and sleeping on that lumpy pullout couch."

Again he ignored her comment. "Why don't you give me a list of what you need at the store and I'll go pick it up. That'll give you some time to work around the house." He set his empty mug on the kitchen counter and started for the living room. Mia looked around at her home and remembered how alive it once was, the warmth it generated. It no longer resembled the home where she had family dinners, where she had shared stories and discussed the day's events with her parents and Uncle Drew.

Mia wanted to tell Paul that she had it all under control, but who was she kidding? Her parents' room needed to be cleared out, Henry's room needed to be converted back into a human bedroom, bathrooms needed to be cleaned, the kitchen could use a wipe down and her fridge needed to be stocked. All before this evening. And it wasn't going to happen…unless she bit the bullet and accepted his assistance.

"You really don't have to do this…help me, I mean," she said, walking into the living room.

Paul slung his bag over his shoulder. "You have put your life on hold to help my sister and have committed yourself to helping Rose's grieving family. I can't think of anyone more selfless," he said, walking toward the bathroom. "I'll take a quick shower and then head out. Leave my list on the kitchen island." He turned and smiled before disappearing into the bathroom.

* * *

Paul loathed shopping…for clothes, for food…just about everything. But as he checked off each item on Mia's list, his disdain for standing in lines and fighting over a parking space slowly faded. He had just left Home Depot when his cell phone rang. He looked down at the name on his cell and felt his stomach twitch. Paul knew he was behaving like some lovesick teenager, but he didn't care.

Mia was rattling off a few more must-haves before he had a chance to say hello. He logged the few items in his memory and went to Kohl's for a set of bath towels, washcloths, a shower curtain and a queen-sized bed-in-a-bag, whatever the hell that was. Instead of guessing and wasting time, he went right to a saleswoman and she directed him to each item. Twenty minutes later, he was back in the car and finally on his way back home to Mia.

Mia didn't hear Paul enter, a fact that truly disturbed him. He was just about to bring to her attention that anyone could have just walked in here, but the moment he saw her face, he knew that conversation could wait. Her hair had been pulled back, but due to the unremitting scrubbing of the bathroom floor, a few stray hairs had broken free and were delicately framing her face. She tried to blow an annoying lock from her face but it just fell back into the exact same spot. Crouched on her hands and knees, Mia looked beyond sexy, but he knew that right now wasn't the time to picture her doing something else while in that position, like allowing him to take her from behind. His cock moved, straining against the coarse denim of his jeans. Luckily, the ten thousand bags in his hands covered his mounting erection.

"Hey, that was fast," she said, finally looking up at him.

"It's been three hours," he said, peering down at her. At that level, he had an unobstructed view of her breasts and the perfect valley between.

She didn't seem to notice his split-second moment of weakness, because she said, "Thanks for helping me out. I really couldn't do this without you."

He wanted to take her in his arms and tell her, show her, the power she had over him, but the clock continued to move incessantly forward. "Not a problem. I'm going to put the food away and then I'll help you in here," he said.

"Not a chance. There's no way in hell I'll allow you to clean my bathroom. I'm just finishing up, anyway."

"All right. What's next, then?" he asked.

She hesitated, signaling that she may have left the most challenging task for last. "My parents' room." The tone of her voice was solemn and full of regret. He didn't know if she wanted him there while she emptied the room her parents had shared as husband and wife, but as he turned and walked toward the kitchen, he heard her say, "I think…I think I need you to help me with that room…if you don't mind?"

He was overwhelmed that she would ask him to join her in such a difficult task. He remembered when he and Erin had tackled that same challenge. It definitely took an emotional toll on a person. But what had sent his mind reeling was her choice of words. She *needed* him with her, even if it was just to help her clean out a couple of closets.

"I'll be right in," he said, holding up the bags in his hands. She nodded and then diverted her attention to the floor for a few more swipes with the scrub brush.

Chapter Forty-Three

Mia stared at what was once her parents' room and was overcome with emotion. With the exception of her parents' wedding picture and the wooden crucifix hanging on the wall and the matching furniture, nothing from her childhood remained. Paul had remained silent as did she while they folded her parents' clothes and gently laid them in the plastic storage bins he had purchased at Home Depot. It was as if he knew that this was one of the hardest things she had ever had to do in her life. And though he didn't speak, she cherished his presence, knowing it would be impossible to store away her memories without him next to her.

With the new bedding and sweet-smelling flowers placed about, the bedroom looked fresh and alive. Mia had avoided the ungodly chore of not only cleaning out the room, but entering it, for far too long. She looked at what she would now consider her guest bedroom and reached for Paul's hand.

"I didn't think I would ever be able to do this," she said, looking at her surroundings. She felt his large hand envelop hers.

"No one should have to do this alone. Erin and I had each other when we were faced with the same daunting task."

"Does time heal all wounds, Paul? Like everyone says?"

He squeezed her hand and then brought her fingers to his lips. It wasn't sexual, but beautifully tender. "Time can dull the pain, but it never heals over completely. Family and good friends can help you with what lingers about." His words hit her like a ton of bricks. She shared his outlook, the way grief should truly be perceived.

They stared at each other until the gaze was broken by a whimper in the room next door. Paul released her hand and walked in the direction of the pathetic sound. Henry was lying on the hardwood floor where his doggy bed had once been. He was clearly out of sorts and missing the bed while it finished drying on the clothesline outside. "I've spoiled him," she said.

"Maybe just a little," Paul said. Henry wagged his tail at the sound of Paul's voice.

Suddenly, that feeling set in. The one where you know you are forgetting something, but for the life of you, that something remains a mystery, frustratingly out of reach. And then Paul asked the question that brought that "something" to the forefront.

"Does Henry get overwhelmed with a houseful of people?"

Mia had thought about that, but that was several hours ago while she was in the middle of three things at once. Would her immature, very needy and attention-craving Lab be able to behave himself this weekend while she entertained people who would clearly not be in the mood to tolerate barking or relentless licking? Not a chance.

"I meant to call the kennel, but forgot." Mia looked at her watch. "If I leave now, I might be able to make it before they close. Hopefully, they're not booked up." Mia went to retrieve her keys and purse from the kitchen counter.

Paul followed her and then reached for Henry's leash. "I wouldn't mind watching him. He can come home with me…spend some time in my man cave."

Mia had already burdened him enough. Now, she was going to strap him with her dog for the next few days? No way.

"Um…he's a bit much. You've witnessed his need for attention. He is insatiable." She smiled at him, but her lighthearted grin faded as Paul clearly looked hurt.

"The days ahead are going to be hectic enough. Please let me take Henry off your hands. He'll keep me company, while you're…here."

How could she say no to that? Why would she? And, yet another question: Could he get any cuter, any sexier than he was at that moment? Most likely, yes. And she couldn't wait to experience that.

She blushed, feeling every sixteen-year-old emotion at once. He knew exactly what to say, when to pause, when to gaze into her eyes and search her soul. Unable to answer in words, she nodded.

Chapter Forty-Four

Paul was definitely going to be in trouble with Mia. Just twenty-four hours into Paul's care, Henry had become a couch potato in between their multiple walks to the park. When bedtime arrived, he even allowed Henry to sleep at the foot of his bed.

Mia had called last night to check on Henry. At least that was what she had said was the purpose of her call, but after an hour of discussing other matters that didn't concern her pet, he had come to the hopeful conclusion that she just wanted to talk to him. Which was fine with him, since he couldn't stand being away from her. But there was little he could do. She was busy helping Rose's children settle in and plan for the funeral that was now scheduled to take place on Monday. The police had officially determined that Rose's death was accidental and as a result, the family could proceed with making the arrangements.

Paul was mixing in table scraps with Henry's kibble when Mia called. "How's my little man?" Mia asked.

Paul looked down at the big brown eyes staring up at him in anticipation. Henry's tail was wagging a mile a minute. "We're just about to have dinner and watch a ballgame," Paul said.

"Sounds like fun. I'd much rather be doing that right about now," she said.

Mia seemed exhausted and he wished he could drive over to her house, pick her up and bring her to his home for the night. Watching a game on the couch with Mia while eating a heaping bowl of chili sounded like a perfect evening. "Tired?" he asked.

"Yeah, a little. We just got back from the funeral home where we ironed out the last of the details." Mia paused. "Will you be coming to the funeral?" she asked. Her voice sounded as if she was embarrassed for even asking.

"Of course. I already called a buddy of mine to come to my place and walk Henry."

Mia sighed. "Can I put anyone else out?" she asked, sarcastically. "The list of favors continues to grow."

"Rick really doesn't mind. He's planning to take Henry to the park and use your little guy to pick up women."

"Ugh," she groaned. "Henry, the chick magnet." Mia giggled, which was music to Paul's ears. "You're spoiling him, aren't you?"

"Um...no," he lied, mixing in ground beef with the dry kibble.

"Liar. I wouldn't be the least bit surprised if I came over tonight and found him asleep in your bed."

Paul wanted to ask her to do just that, but instead held back. "We're just doing what guys do, throwing a few back, watching the Phillies and eating junk food."

"He probably doesn't even miss me," she said, playfully.

Paul placed the bowl on the floor and Henry attacked it like he hadn't eaten in a week. "He misses you." Paul hesitated, wondering if he should admit what was on his mind, and then without another thought, he heard himself say, "And so do I."

Paul either took her completely off guard or she was trying to find the words to let him down easy because a few seconds of silence passed before she finally spoke. "I wish I was there…with you." Another pause, and then, "Good night, Paul."

Chapter Forty-Five

Rose's death didn't hit Mia until she was sitting in the church pew listening to each of Rose's children speak about what a wonderful mother they had, the devoted wife she had been to their father. Mia realized right then she had been on autopilot the last few days, busy making preparations, too busy, apparently, to let the loss of her neighbor sink in until now. She finally let go and began to cry. Paul offered her a tissue and held her hand.

"Thanks," she whispered. Paul squeezed her hand in reply.

After the ceremony, Mia and Paul made their way out into the vestibule. "Are you going to the cemetery," he asked.

"No, the caterer should be arriving at my house within the next thirty minutes. Everyone is coming back to my house for a light lunch and coffee," she said. Feeling a little emotional and very selfish, she asked, "Come with me?"

"I didn't plan on leaving you, Mia." He put his arm around her and led her out of the church.

* * *

Considering the sudden nature of Rose's passing, Mia expected a more solemn atmosphere, one with uncontrollable tears and raw pain. But as the dishes from lunch were cleared away and coffee and cake were passed around, the thirty or so guests spent the afternoon sharing stories about Rose and reminiscing about happier times. Rose's children were gracious with their guests, thanking them for coming to remember and honor a wonderful woman, their mother.

Mia knew that Hannah and Jillian were barely keeping it together and she admired their strength. Ian never left his sisters' sides, which spoke volumes to how close they were, the kind of upbringing they had. Rose and her husband had instilled that sense of family in their children. Rose would have been proud to see that no matter how many miles, or continents, lay between her kids, they had remained close.

Paul was a great help, working like a machine, ensuring that every guest had what they needed. He made certain that there was a constant flow of coffee, replenished the supply of cookies and cake, and took out the trash when it filled to capacity. He had caught her looking at him a few times throughout the day and each time, he simply smiled at her. Paul had removed his suit jacket hours ago and had since rolled up his sleeves. It was while he was loading her dishwasher that she realized she was falling for him.

Chapter Forty-Six

Scott was growing impatient, which was contributing to his unpleasant mood and appearance. The prickly scruff he had neglected to shave made him feel dirty...and angry. He had stayed away from his Angel for the last several days just in case the old woman's death was not declared an accident.

But his spirits finally lifted when he learned that the police suspected no foul play surrounding one Rose Elizabeth Higgins. His courtship of Mia Ryan Moore could now resume. But this time around, he would be more controlled. He had not been thinking clearly when he went to Mia's home a few days back. And because of his stupidity, he had to kill a woman, drawing unnecessary attention and delaying the time he wanted to spend with Mia.

But there was still a loose end fit to be tied, three in fact. The Whore and her man, according to the tracker, were still in Philadelphia. He wasn't sure where Paul Whitley was at the moment, but he would make it a point today, between patients, to nail down his whereabouts. Scott had been replaying the same scene in his head for days. Each detail was important; everything had to be accounted for if he was going to pull off three deaths without anyone pointing in his direction.

Scott showered, shaved, and dressed for work. Feeling much more optimistic, he decided to deviate from his usual routine by walking to work and treating himself to his favorite black organic tea at the coffee shop down the street. But as he drew closer to his destination, Scott got the sense that he was being watched. Scott kept his focus on the pavement before him in order to not tip off the possible pursuer. With the shop to his left, he turned and slowly walked toward the glass door. His cautious movements allowed him to steal an elongated glance at the swiftly moving cars behind him in the windowpane's reflection. But one car, a black luxury sedan with tinted windows, was not keeping pace with the rest of the traffic. In fact, it appeared the owner of the vehicle enjoyed taking his time. Only when Scott entered the coffee shop did the black car speed off.

As Scott stood in line for his tea, he recalled the night in the library. He had been sitting in his study carrel when a large, dark-haired gentleman had briskly walked past him. The sight had bothered him, but not enough to put plan B into action. Had his Angel, his beautiful and obviously intelligent wholesome girl, put the pieces together? The fact that he was possibly being tailed suggested he may have made her list of suspects. Scott took out his phone and called the woman he had met in the library. For the next few days, he would have to go through the motions and pretend that their titillating night at Starbucks needed to be repeated, perhaps over dinner this time.

Spending time with the naïve twit was a necessary evil. Starting a "relationship" with Plain Jane would definitely put a wrench in Mia's profile. But what would really drive it home and take the focus off of him completely was if he found someone else to take the fall.

Chapter Forty-Seven

Thank God she had an understanding principal. Anyone else would have fired her by now. Mia had called out last week due to "illness" and had taken a bereavement day yesterday. Grateful and running scared, nonetheless Mia hunkered down and dove into her work.

Her students seemed excited to see her and she was overwhelmed with dozens of hugs and *I miss you*s. She had missed them, too. All twenty-five of them. Many of her students had made her welcome-back cards. A beautiful bouquet of flowers had even been sent to her classroom. From the wording on the card, it was clear that the principal had shared with the staff that Mia had suffered a loss. Tomorrow she would make it a priority to find out who she could thank for the thoughtful gesture, as the card simply stated in typed print: *You are in my thoughts.*

The day flew by, and she was simultaneously playing catch-up and trying to get ahead in her lesson plans when she noticed the time. "Shit!" she exclaimed to an empty room. She had told Paul she would be coming over after work to pick up Henry. Although Ian and his sisters had taken an early-morning flight out to enjoy a much-needed vacation together for a few days, Paul had graciously offered to watch Henry for an additional night.

Mia gathered her belongings, including her lesson plan book, the cards her students had made her and the card that came with her flowers and threw them into her oversized purse. She again looked at the time and cursed under her breath. Luckily, she hit little traffic and made it to Paul's apartment building in a little over twenty minutes.

Paul must have informed the doorman of her impending arrival, because he said, "Mr. Whitley is waiting for you. Please go on up."

Mia smiled at the older gentleman. "Well, thank you," she said.

Once on the elevator, she felt the butterflies in her belly spring to life. Just the thought of seeing him again made her flustered. She heard the ping of the elevator, made her exit and started down the hallway, all the while chanting silently to herself, "Get ahold of yourself." She found his apartment number and knocked on the door before she could chicken out.

Mia heard a familiar whimper and loud obnoxious sniffing from the other side of the door. The door flung open and she was almost tackled by her eighty-five pound baby. "And you questioned whether he missed you?" Paul said, grabbing her by the hand to prevent a very unladylike fall.

"Come here, Henry," he said, leading Mia into his apartment and closing the door behind them.

Mia threw her purse on the ground, allowing its contents to spill out, got down on her knees and lavished Henry with three days' worth of attention. Paul had taken good care of him, maybe too well. Henry seemed chunkier around the middle. Table scraps and watching too much television had that effect. But she didn't care; her dog appeared happy and as nutty as ever.

"Where's your bone, buddy? Go get it!" Paul exclaimed.

Henry disappeared into another room and came back with a bone larger than his head. "What is that?" Mia asked. "And what dinosaur does that belong to?"

"Henry and I went shopping today. After fifteen minutes in PetSmart, Henry made the difficult choice between what you see here and a squeaky toy. I was pushing for the bone the whole time. More manly."

Mia laughed as she envisioned Paul and Henry walking the aisles of PetSmart. Still on her knees, she started to gather together the miscellaneous items that had fallen out of her purse when Paul bent down and picked up the yellow sympathy card she had received earlier in the day.

"Where did you get this?" he asked, staring intently at the yellow piece of card stock.

Mia didn't like his tone or the dark expression on his face. "Someone sent me flowers today. Probably came from the faculty. I'll find out tomorrow so I can send out a thank-you note." Mia narrowed her eyes. "Why?"

Ignoring her, he left the room and when he returned, she was surprised to see a card identical to the one she received in his other hand. "My sister received this with a bouquet of flowers from her attacker," he said, handing it to her.

Because of her sessions with Erin, she knew about the card and its wording. She just didn't string together the possibility that the two cards could have been sent by the same person until now. "It may not be from him, Paul. He signed Erin's card. This one hasn't been signed. It could be exactly what it was meant to be. A sympathy card."

"Maybe. But I'm not taking any chances. You're staying here with me until we know for sure," he said. Paul walked over to the front door and secured the locks.

What the hell? Did he really think he could just order her to stay in his apartment, locked away from the world?

"*You are in my thoughts*," he said, staring at the card again. "If it was sent to you by a group of people, like the school faculty, it should read, "You are in *our* thoughts. Shouldn't it?"

Mia could kick herself for not catching that detail. Her first day back at work had been so crazy and with the funeral the day before, the card in that context had made sense. But it was still premature to assume that the card was sent by Erin's attacker.

"Maybe. But, that doesn't mean I should move in here," she said.

Mia stood and slung her bag over her shoulder. She was just about to call Henry so they could leave when he said, "Mia, is there a reason why Erin's attacker would send you flowers?" Paul's anger had morphed into concern and it was clear that he was uncomfortable with the question he had asked.

Mia knew what he was asking. How the hell did he connect those dots so quickly? She needed to get out of his apartment. He would learn exactly what she had in common with Erin and she wasn't ready to share that with Paul. "We have no idea who sent me those flowers. I think you're jumping the gun," she said, walking toward the door.

"Are you a virgin, Mia?" he asked.

Coming from him, the word sounded like a curse, some terminal illness that she would never be able to fight off. She was so angry that she turned and looked him straight in the eye. "Yes. As a matter of fact, I am. Happy?" she asked, her arms folded against her chest.

He didn't break their stare-down. Instead, his gaze only grew darker. "I'm happy you told me the truth. But I don't like how I'm making you feel right now."

"You have no idea how I feel," Mia said. She felt her body getting worked up. The tears would be coming any minute.

"Mia, if the card is from him, well, you know what that means. You're in danger," he said.

Mia shook her head. "You don't know that," she said. The first tear slid down her cheek…and then another.

"And we can't forget the bigger picture. I know the police ruled Rose's death an accident, but now…well, can we be certain? Your next-door neighbor died while you were out of town. This could all be a coincidence…or not. We don't know. And that's why you're staying in my guest room until further notice."

Paul was quick on his feet, piecing together things she was still muddling though. Everything he had said made sense and that realization pissed her off. Mia thought with a criminal mind. She knew that the psychopath they were dealing with was dangerous, a man with no remorse. And if it turned out that card was sent from their particular psychopath, she was definitely a target. Frustrated, she said, "I'll need clothes to sleep in…and a glass of wine if you have it."

* * *

Paul knew he had backed Mia into a corner, forcing her to admit that she was what he had suspected, a virgin. And as much as it pleased him to know that Mia had never shared such an intimate experience with a man, the graver concern was that her virginity made her a target.

He was in the process of dialing Andrew when Mia came out of the guest room dressed in one of his long t-shirts and a pair of gym shorts. Dwarfed by his attire, she looked vulnerable…and still a little pissed off. "Who are you calling?" she asked.

"I think Andrew and Chase deserve an update," Paul said.

Mia ran over and took the phone from his hand. "Not yet. Let me find out if anyone in work sent me the flowers first. No sense in worrying them."

Paul didn't like withholding information from Chase and Andrew, even if it was just speculative at this point. But she had a point and he didn't see the harm in waiting until tomorrow evening, at the latest.

"Okay. Tomorrow then," he said, turning and walking back into the kitchen. He went over to the oven and took out the bubbling lasagna.

"Thanks." She set the phone on the counter. Paul glanced over his shoulder and found her scoping out the table he had set for two. "When did you make dinner? How long was I in the shower?"

"Not long. I made the lasagna before you came over. I had hoped you would join me for dinner before taking Henry home."

"It appears you're getting your wish and a housemate," she said, sounding defeated.

Paul came over to the table carrying the casserole dish of lasagna in one hand and a tossed salad in the other. "I hope you're hungry. Living with Erin this past year, I got in the habit of making more food than was necessary. She is a leftovers junkie."

"She hides it well," Mia said, taking the salad from him and setting it on the table.

Paul dished out a healthy portion of lasagna onto each plate and then poured the wine. Despite the events of the night, they found little difficulty cleaning their plates. Mia actually went back for seconds, which pleased him greatly.

"You're a great cook," she said. "My lasagna doesn't come close to this."

"Thanks. I'm glad you like it," Paul said, watching her intently. Even in his oversized clothes, she looked amazing. The smell of her freshly washed hair was mesmerizing and he struggled to not let his own needs and desires dictate where the night should go. Mia had just told him she was a virgin and it was important that he take things slow. He didn't want to scare her in any way, even if that meant putting the brakes on. Paul kept the conversation light during and after dinner and refrained from all innocent touching, like holding her hand or brushing her cheek with his fingers.

Although Mia was grateful for dinner, mentioning several times how thoughtful it was while they cleaned up and put the kitchen back in order, she was quiet, as if lost in her thoughts. He didn't want to press her too hard about it, considering, but it bothered him nonetheless.

"It's getting late and we both have work tomorrow," he said. It was a pitiful way to end the night, but he certainly couldn't say what was really on his mind.

"Yeah, speaking of work, I can't go into class looking like this," she said, frowning at her shirtdress.

"I think you look just fine. No one will notice a thing," he said, not breaking a smile.

With her eyebrow raised, she challenged him to crack.

He couldn't resist her, especially when she threw on the sass. He smiled. "I'll drive you home in the morning and then drop you off at work. What time will you get done tomorrow?"

"Around five o'clock."

"Good, I'll pick you up then."

"And if we find out the flowers were sent by the faculty?"

Paul didn't even want to entertain the possibility that she wasn't going to stay with him tomorrow night. But he also didn't want to sound like a possessive freak, either. "Then we will adjust accordingly."

Although she nodded in agreement, he couldn't dismiss the feeling that she seemed sad, disappointed for some reason. Paul chocked up her demeanor to the fact that she just learned that she may be some sick asshole's fantasy. She needed time to digest everything that was happening and hopefully they would get some answers tomorrow. "Good night, Mia," he said. He kissed her on the forehead and retired to his bedroom.

Chapter Forty-Eight

Mia's nightmare had come true. The one where the boy meets the girl, likes the girl, is attracted to the girl, just to discover that she isn't what he had expected, or had hoped for. Paul had been respectful, showing genuine concern, but not even the stone-faced lawyer could mask his disappointment when she confirmed that she was a virgin.

But it wasn't that flicker of surprise he had allowed to escape at her admission that bothered Mia the most. What absolutely killed her was how he behaved afterward over dinner. Absent were the typical heated stares, the sexual tension and angst-filled moments. He had never tried to touch her or brush against her as they washed dishes together. Instead, Paul had been a perfect gentleman and when the clock struck ten, he had kissed her on the forehead and practically dismissed her to bed...alone.

Midnight was slowly approaching and she was no closer to sleep then when she first threw herself and her pride under the covers to hide in shame. She tossed and turned, wondering how the hell she was going to move on from this. Surely the embarrassment would fade over time, especially if he was out of her life.

Mia tore back the covers and walked herself over to the adjoining bathroom. Feeling restless, she washed her face and brushed her teeth for the second time since she had retired for the evening and returned to bed. Go to sleep, Mia. Just close your eyes and don't think about, or visualize, the man sleeping down the hall.

But as she attempted to obey her own directive, Mia heard that tortured scream flooding the apartment. She ran out into the hallway and followed the sound of his voice, his raw pain. As quickly as the yelling began, it ceased, and she wondered if she should go into his bedroom to check on him. She hesitated, turned the doorknob, stopped for a moment, turned it again, and then whispered to herself, "Screw it."

Mia entered the room to discover his bed empty and the balcony door open. White curtains whipped about, exposing only slivers of the man on the balcony. His back was to her and if she was very quiet, she could turn around and escape unnoticed. But something stopped her from making that wise decision and instead, she just stood there, as if she were glued to the wood planks beneath her bare feet. She wanted a better look, needed to see his face for just a moment, to ensure that he was okay and no longer under his nightmare's unruly grasp. Miraculously, her feet broke free of their frozen state and she took a few steps forward.

With his hands on the railing, Paul was gazing at the sky, the look in his eyes suggesting that he was a million miles away. Just a little closer, she told herself. Mia took a few more steps, close enough to feel the tip of the cotton curtains glide across her legs.

The gentle caress distracted her momentarily and when she looked up, Paul was staring at her with such intensity she felt her breath escape her.

"I'm sorry I woke you," he said. His eyes roamed to every part of her body and she suddenly felt exposed and very wanted.

"I...I wanted to make sure you were...okay," she said, stumbling for words.

"I'll be fine," he said turning around and making his way back to the railing.

No. He wasn't going to do that again. Just dismiss her...assume that she could just turn her emotions on and off like he apparently could do and do well. What did she have to lose? Nothing. Her pride had already taken a catastrophic hit and she had no secrets left to hide. "I'm asking you, now," she said.

He stopped midstride, but didn't turn around. That got his attention.

"But I don't want you to tell me how you feel." Mia felt her confidence build and she took yet another step forward and said, "I want you to show me."

Paul turned and closed the gap between them. His hands grabbed the sides of her face and he sealed his mouth over her waiting lips. He groaned as his hot, demanding tongue mingled with hers. Mia wrapped her arms around his neck and ground her body against his. His erection was easily discernable through her mesh shorts, and she moaned in anticipation.

"God, I want you," he said. Paul lifted her t-shirt, actually his t-shirt, over her head, exposing her full breasts. "You're so beautiful," he said staring at her hungrily.

"Tonight, I'm yours," she said.

He picked her up and carried her to the bed. He undressed completely and then rid her body of those very unattractive shorts. Paul tucked her beneath his rock-hard body and propped himself on his elbows. He took her face in his hands and said, "We will never be just one night, Mia."

Mia looked into his eyes and knew he wasn't kidding. The lust wasn't talking, it was him. And he wanted her tonight, maybe even every night. He kissed her slowly at first and then it grew heavy and passionate. She felt his hand slide to her breast and then to her left nipple. He flicked the tight peak between his fingers as he continued kissing her. She arched her back and felt his arousal positioned at her entrance. Mia wanted, needed, the friction against her aching clit.

"Not yet, Mia. You're not ready," he said.

Paul bowed his head and took a nipple in his mouth. He continued to knead her other nipple with his experienced fingers and she panted with desire. Paul released her breast and slipped even lower, right beneath her belly button.

Oh God, was he going to…

"Oh Paul!" she screamed at the first touch of his tongue against her slick folds. She knew she was dripping wet, her body ready and needy. He stroked her clit in a rhythm that was not meant to tease, but bring her absolute pleasure. She gripped the sheets beneath her and begged him for more. Mia felt a fingertip enter and she clenched her body.

"You're so tight, so beautiful," he said. He gently pressed the tip of his finger forward. Her climax was already mounting when she felt him add another finger. Her orgasm took hold as she thrashed beneath him and screamed his name.

"Please, I need you now," she said, as her orgasm subsided only slightly.

Groaning, he crawled toward her, positioning his cock at her entrance. He kissed her softly and then slowly she felt him enter. He was gentle, pushing in just one inch at a time. The burning sensation lasted for but a moment before transforming to a feeling of fullness.

"You feel so good, Mia," he said, his voice strained. Mia imagined that he was most likely holding back, in fear of hurting her. "Are you all right? Can you take more?"

More? How much more was there?

"Yes," she said, breathless. She wanted all of him.

He thrust deeper, and that feeling of fullness turned into indescribable pleasure. Mia spread her legs farther apart in order to accommodate him and she finally felt him exhale. Paul began to glide in and out of her in slow, deep strokes.

"My God, Mia, you were made for me," he said. The declaration made her want to weep.

Mia could tell he was still being cautious and if he was going to truly let go, she was going to have to give him an explicit signal. "I can take more...give me more."

Complying, he wrapped her left leg around his shoulder and slammed into her. The forceful thrust touched every inch of her and she whimpered at the mind-blowing sensation.

"Mia!" he screamed, plunging into her one last time. She shook as her tight channel clenched around him, making him spill every drop deep inside her. The thought of him filling her with his heat made her feel claimed...and every bit his.

She pulled him close and held him to her breasts until his heartbeat returned to normal. There was so much she wanted to say. Feelings she wanted to share, but couldn't, not yet anyway. Instead, they lay in silence, which only made their already-intimate moment intensify, suggesting that their union was much more than a physical one.

Chapter Forty-Nine

Paul eventually pulled out of her and lay at her side. She let out a small whimper, as the void his action caused left her needy and immediately craving to regain that intimacy the next chance she got.

Mia saw him glance down at himself and then look at her with such fear she believed him to be in serious pain. "How bad did I hurt you, Mia?" he asked, his voice on the verge of panic.

Mia didn't have a chance to respond because he tore back the white sheet, exposing what had invoked the troublesome expression on his face. Bright red blood marked the once-pristine sheets and she cringed at the sight. "I ruined your sheets. I'm sorry, Paul."

Paul looked like he was going to blow a gasket. "I'm not concerned about my sheets, Mia. What I care about is you and the obvious fact that I caused you pain...that I wasn't gentle enough."

He couldn't have been more wrong. Not that she had anything to compare to, but she couldn't imagine a more gentle or generous lover than Paul. "You didn't hurt me. I might be a little sore, but that's to be expected, right?" she asked, reaching for him. Although

Paul allowed her to caress his cheek, she could tell he wasn't completely satisfied with her response.

"I had every intention of taking things slow, especially after you told me you've never been with anyone before." He covered her hand with his. "But I lose myself when I'm with you, so much so that I didn't even think about using protection. I have never been with a woman without using a condom…until you."

There was no way she was going to lay blame. She hadn't cared in the moment and she didn't care now. "Paul, I trust you. I know you would never have put me at risk." Mia kissed him, hoping to smooth out a few of those worry lines that sprung up on his forehead. "I want to believe that I would have prevented us from going further than a kiss, if I knew that I wasn't on the pill. But in that moment, feeling you slide into me with nothing between us, I highly doubt I would have been able to stop."

The worry lines were less pronounced, but still evident, as if he was still uneasy. "Paul, everything is all right. I've been on the pill since I was fifteen for medical reasons," she said.

"You still have no idea what you do to me. Do you?" he asked, his voice serious and dark.

Mia didn't know what to say or what could make him look at her with such heat. Luckily, he wasn't fishing for an answer, because he continued and said, "Rational thought goes out the window when I'm with you and all I can think of is making you mine."

His admission was primal and domineering…and she loved him for it. She was just about to spill her soul, when he scooped her up and carried her to the bathroom.

"I don't like to see you uncomfortable or sore. Let me take care of you," he said. His face softened and she could tell he wanted to table the conversation. If letting him run a bath for her while he doused her back with white puffy suds made his anxiety dissipate, then she was more than willing to participate. Telling him that she was falling in love with him, that she had been *his*, at least in her mind, since the day they met, would just have to wait.

Chapter Fifty

Scott was way out of his element.

Everything his date did, the way she ate, the way she curled her mousy brown hair around her finger, the way she…existed irritated him. But no matter how much he detested her company, Scott knew Plain Jane the librarian served an important purpose.

Scott made certain to sustain visibility at all times. He had made reservations for two at La Mer, one of the best French restaurants in the city, and insisted they sit in one of the two tables by the expansive front window. Scott laughed at her absurd stories, reached for and squeezed her hand when she grew shy, and drew her chair closer to him as the night dragged on. The only highlight was the food. Presented in small, elegant portions, it was difficult to overindulge and feel like a complete glutton. A crisp white tablecloth and clean silverware also kept him satisfied.

Just a few more dates and he could put himself out of such misery. Maybe tomorrow night he would take her to a movie, where talking would be severely limited, followed by a drink at a noisy club. On the third and final date, the night he absolutely dreaded, Scott would propose to stay in, preferably at her place, and take in a movie. He would have to kiss her, maybe even snuggle a bit, to make her go to bat for him if the time came. If she was ever confronted and asked just what kind of guy Scott Morris was, she would have no choice but to paint the nauseating picture of what a respectful gentleman he was, how he had held her hand while they strolled to dinner, or enveloped her in his arms when she jumped at the horror movie they rented, how he had taken things slow, never pressuring her for more than a closed-mouth kiss.

Scott and Plain Jane finished dinner and moved on to dessert and coffee. As she savored each bite of the crème brûlée, Scott took the opportunity to glance out the window. And that was when Scott saw him and confirmed that his faculties were still firmly intact. He wasn't being paranoid. The same man who had bristled past him in the library was sitting across the street at some outdoor café sipping from a white mug.

Scott immediately put his attention back on Plain Jane and smiled. She had remnants of the sweet treat on her upper lip and he inwardly shuddered with disgust. But instead of throwing her a napkin and insisting that she clean her filthy mouth, he reached up and wiped the custard away with the pad of his thumb. Plain Jane blushed, which made her appear blotchy. Scott forced a smile, praying that the person across the street had just witnessed that stomach-churning display of affection.

Chapter Fifty-One

Paul awoke the next morning in the same position that he had fallen asleep in, with Mia tucked into his arms, the alluring scent of her hair drawing him in. She stirred slightly, which only made his hard-on ache with desire. Naked, soft curves nestled even closer and he fought the urge not to take her again right there.

But he knew that her body needed time to recuperate. He hated the fact that he had caused her pain, but it also made him feel manly in a prehistoric way, and honored that she had chosen him to be the first man she had given herself to.

Exploring her body, finding more ways to give her pleasure, would have to wait, but hopefully not for too long. Now that he had been given a taste of what each night could bring, there was no way he could be without her. Since making love was out of the question this morning, he decided to shower and then cook her a hearty breakfast before work. Carefully, he untangled their legs and shuffled out of bed. She rolled onto her back, which only made his cock throb. Her beautiful breasts lay exposed and unbound just above the white sheet. With her dark hair splayed haphazardly across the pillow, Mia looked like a very sated woman.

Thankful that he had woken up extra-early today, Paul took the time to enjoy a long, hot shower. He stood beneath the pulsating shower head and closed his eyes and thought about the woman who was sound asleep in the very next room. There had been women, many unfortunately, whom he had shared his bed with over the years. But he had never made love to a woman until last night. She was his match in every way…his love.

Thinking of Mia always caused his body to respond in ways that were completely out of his control. He ached to be with her, as his painful erection indicated. Paul heard the bathroom door open and in walked his very naked girl. She was staring at his cock with the same hunger he had detected the night she had walked in on him in her own bathroom. That night he had never felt such lust in his life, and it had taken everything he had not to swing the shower door open, drag her into the glass-enclosed space and take her against the cool tile. But now he was grateful that he had not acted on his animal instincts. She deserved to have a memorable first time, where he could take it slow, kiss every inch of her and pleasure her over and over again.

Mia smiled and joined him in the shower. She closed the glass door behind her and with her back to him, and he tucked her into his arms. She sighed as the warm droplets saturated her perfect skin. "Good morning," she purred.

"Did I wake you?" he asked.

"No, I'm just an early riser." She turned and brushed his lips with hers. Her fingertips scurried across his chest, making every drop of blood in his body rush to his twitching cock. "Do you remember when I walked in on you while you were showering at my house?" she asked, her voice throaty and sexy as hell.

Did he remember? God, if she knew just how close he had been that night to claiming her as his. "Yes, not something I'll ever forget," he said.

"There was something I wanted…to do," she said, her fingers travelling southbound.

She stood on her tippy-toes and kissed him softly at first. But as her fingers reached the space just above the head of his cock, the kiss became more demanding, and she opened her mouth to welcome his tongue. The woman knew how to kiss, nipping at his bottom lip to keep him wanting so much more. Suddenly, she broke away and stepped back. The fire in her eyes was unlike anything he had ever seen. "I wanted to taste you," she said, sinking to her knees.

"Mia, you don't have to…Ah God," he moaned as she took his cock in her hands.

She stared up at him and said, "I want you to tell me." Her soft pink tongue slipped past her teeth and stroked the underside of his cock, causing his body to quake. "And show me what you like." She lapped at the glistening head. Another jolt. "Because I've never done this before."

Was she kidding? The way she was hitting every sensitive spot, licking the pre-cum away from the head as it generously flowed forth, she could have fooled him. He loved knowing that this too was a first for her, that she wanted to give him pleasure with her wet, silky mouth.

"Just like that, Mia," he said. He reached in front of him and with one hand on the shower tile, he steadied himself before his legs could buckle.

She cupped one hand around his balls and then stroked his shaft into her hot mouth. Not wanting to choke her, he refrained from doing what his body craved—which was to slam into her mouth and come down her throat—and rocked into her slowly. But just like last night, she must have caught on that he was holding back, trying to take it easy on her, because she reached around, grabbed his ass, and took him hard and deep.

While she was staring up at him, her mouth full of his cock, he growled and with his other hand, he reached for the back of her head. She moaned while she sucked and lapped at him, bringing him into her heat. "Mia," he groaned, as he pummeled her mouth.

He spread his legs wider and took in the erotic scene with awe. She was on her knees, with her hair dripping wet, and his cock was gliding in and out of her. He felt his orgasm mount. "Christ, Mia…I'm going to come, baby," he yelled. He tried to withdraw and spill his seed somewhere other than in her mouth, in order not to overwhelm her the very first time, but it only made her hands lock onto his ass and he came so hard, with such force, that he feared she wouldn't be able to take it all.

Her eyes widened and then he saw her swallow. With every drop expelled, he stood her up and brushed her swollen lips with his thumb. "This mouth," he said. With hooded eyelids and a sheepish smile, she looked satisfied.

But not as satisfied as she could be. He reached down and gently stroked her slick folds with two fingers. "I know you're sore," he said. She moaned. "I'll take care of you. I'll always take care of you." He got down on his knees and replaced his fingers with his tongue and lapped at her clit. Careful not to pierce her tender entrance, he gave all his attention to the taut nub between her thighs.

She grabbed his head, pressed her clit against his ravenous tongue and rocked harder. "Oh, God…Paul!" she screamed.

"Let me have you," he said, spreading her folds even farther apart. He licked her vigorously and she exploded around him with his name on her sweet and most generous lips.

Chapter Fifty-Two

Lying in Chase's arms, Erin couldn't imagine her world without him in it. Which was definitely not the case a month ago. Chase Montclair had just been a name then, the invisible employer she hadn't met until the day he had summoned her to his office. And what a first meeting that was! She had experienced a thousand emotions at once during that ten-minute encounter: intrigue, frustration, anger, but mostly...intense, unrelenting attraction.

Sitting behind his desk, he had seemed regal, above her in every way. He had commanded the room, her attention, from the start, and as she looked at his firm hands now grasping her from behind in the luxurious comfort of their king-sized bed, it appeared that he hadn't lost interest in her. Erin still felt like any minute now, she was going to wake up from the beautiful dream she was having, the one where the man cherishes his woman and loves her without conditions. And God knows there were plenty of reasons to make him pause and reconsider whether she was worth the trouble. The stalker she had brought into his life would have made any sane man want to leave and cut ties completely.

Maybe it was his love for her that kept him from bolting in the opposite direction…or maybe it was because he too had a sordid past, one that still had the ability to haunt him. Until recently, Chase had believed that he had inadvertently killed his unborn child when Gabrielle chased him into a stairwell and fell down a flight of steps. But it wasn't his fault that she had been running and miscarried as a result. And it definitely wasn't his fault that he had left her so she could continue to screw another man in the bed they had shared.

And now, Gabrielle was dead. Although it was painful to think of Chase with any other woman, it didn't bring Erin any comfort or joy to know that she herself may have had a hand in Gabrielle's passing. If it wasn't for Erin, Gabrielle might still be alive, modeling expensive lingerie and enjoying the life she had rebuilt in California. Erin couldn't help but feel sorry for the people Gabrielle had left behind, the parents who would grieve for their daughter and forever question why their baby would want to kill herself. No parent should have to experience such pain.

Erin had been lost in thought when she felt Chase squeeze her tight and kiss the nape of her neck. She wanted to stay just like this, forever in his arms in this beautiful bed where they could shut out the rest of the world. But that wasn't realistic or fair to the two people back in New York who had selflessly put their lives on hold. It was time to go home and confront the problem head on.

"Coffee on the balcony?" he asked, nuzzling closer.

He was making the task of broaching the subject of leaving their island getaway and returning to a city that was home to her worst nightmare very difficult. Later. This afternoon, she would tell him that it was time to leave paradise. "I would love some," she said.

Chase gave her a quick kiss and hopped out of bed. She watched him dress in a pair of khaki shorts and a navy-blue shirt before he scooted off toward the kitchen to prepare their daily dose of caffeine. Sighing, Erin swung her legs around and stood. She suddenly felt lightheaded and reached for the nightstand to steady herself. The room was still spinning when she opened her eyes, which caused her to grow nauseous. Erin sat back down on the bed and took a few deep breaths.

After a minute or so, she rose slowly from the bed and this time the room remained intact, no longer swirling around in many different directions. She walked into the bathroom and took a long hard look at herself in the mirror…and frowned at her reflection. Although her skin had tanned beautifully and her blond locks had lightened due to many hours in the sun, her eyes, her entire body for that matter, felt tired.

Pissed that she looked worn and drained, Erin tied her hair up into a bun and washed her face, scrubbing the sleep and exhaustion away. Maybe she was coming down with something? She was generally a healthy person, though a sinus infection plagued her from time to time. Although she and sinus infections had become well acquainted over the years, she never could get a handle on them or when they were about to take hold, leaving her incapacitated for a few days with a high fever, a clogged head and feeling…lightheaded. Ugh. She'd forgotten about that last endearing symptom. That had to be it. She was getting one of her dreaded sinus infections and she was on a secluded island with no antibiotics.

Between her insatiable need to stop hiding so she could confront her own problems and a sinus infection that could land her in the hospital, as her past had proved on more than one occasion, Erin determined that it was definitely time to go home.

Chapter Fifty-Three

Scott was not a tech geek by any stretch of the imagination. But he was resourceful, and this quality, which had evolved beautifully over the years, was going to point Mia and those she was helping in an entirely different direction.

Scott wondered what Mia had thought of his flowers and the few simple words that had accompanied them. He had meant what he had said. He was thinking of her. All the time, in fact. He had to have her soon or he was going to react on impulse rather than calculated need.

Scott had never found it necessary to implement spoofing. Sending a text only to have a different phone number than the one you were texting from appear seemed like a waste of time and energy. According to the internet, most people spoofed to fuck with their friends, to catch a cheating spouse or to just be a dick to whomever they chose to victimize. But Scott wasn't intending to use it for recreational purposes. No, he was resorting to such a technique to shed himself of the tail who had been following him, giving him the freedom he needed to take care of business.

This new break in the case would surely bring Montclair and his Whore back home to New York. Any lead they had been following would be considered worthless, prompting them to regroup and re-assess. Scott predicted that they would be in a state of shock at first. Erin Whitley would perseverate on how she had missed the signs, how she had been so naïve and stupid. Mia would question her own profiling skills for a bit before conceding, and Montclair and Paul would just be angry and ready to kill. All attention would be lifted from him and onto the Whore's old friend from college, leaving the two women vulnerable and the men blinded with rage.

Chapter Fifty-Four

Mia didn't have a moment to breathe that day, let alone have a chance to track down the leader of the Sunbeam Club and thank her for the flowers that had been sent to her the day before. Between circle time, recess, and putting their alphabet skills to the test, Mia's time had been consumed by her eager-to-learn kindergarteners. And she loved it all. Mia never grew tired of watching her students' progress, how one day they might have struggled with a concept and the next day, a lightbulb switched on and they were off and running with newfound knowledge. Kindergarten set the stage for all the years to come, making her job all the more critical. She wanted her students to leave for first grade embracing school, not dreading it. To achieve that, it took solid lesson planning and a whole lot of creativity to keep her youngsters interested and engaged.

The moment the last school bus pulled away from the lot, Mia ran into the building in search of Deb Watkins. Deb was nearing retirement, which was difficult for Mia to comprehend. She still had such spunk and energy to expend on her second-grade class that it was hard to picture Deb calling it a day and retiring from the profession. Despite her impending retirement, Deb continued to follow through with her duties with vigor, which included heading up the school's Sunbeam Club. Thanks to Deb, every staff birthday, every newborn baby, every marriage announcement, every loss was recognized with flowers, fruit or candy. The club was a way to make the school function more like a family than a place of business, which was difficult to do in this day and age.

Mia found Deb in her classroom, sitting behind her computer and inputting what looked to be grades into the online grade book. Mia had concluded earlier that there was no way she was going to avoid either making herself or Deb feel embarrassed, so it was best just to get it over with. Deb was either going to confirm that the flowers had come from the Sunbeam Club, making Mia feel relieved but embarrassed for even asking, or Deb was going to deny sending the flowers, making the Sunbeam leader feel like she hadn't done her job.

Deep down, Mia knew it was going to be the latter. And as Deb apologized profusely over not knowing about Mia's loss and said that if she would have been informed, she would have made sure that the school had shared in her grief, Mia felt her stomach churn. There was only one other person in the school who knew about Rose, and that was the principal. It took almost fifteen minutes to console Deb and ensure her that she was not to blame before Mia was free to seek out her principal.

A father of four teenagers, Principal Mark Bowen was a kind and fair man who always put children first. Mia didn't know how he juggled such a rich home life and a job he clearly loved, but he did it and did it well. A parent had just left his office when Mia appeared in the doorway.

He looked up from his computer and smiled. "Hi, Mia. Come on in," he said, making time for her, as he did for all his teachers. She walked in and took a seat.

As she did with Deb, Mia just came out and asked him if he had told anyone about the funeral she had attended on Monday, because flowers were sent to the school to acknowledge her loss.

"No, Mia. If I was supposed to, then I apologize. But considering…things, how private you are about personal matters, I didn't share that information."

Mr. Bowen was the only person in the school who knew about her past. Her teaching certificate, the piece of paper that allowed her to teach in the state of New York, contained her full name. In her interview, she had decided to be honest with her prospective employer about the name discrepancy and why she'd had it legally changed to Mia Ryan.

Mia felt terrible, as if she were questioning his integrity. But she had to be certain before she made the dreaded phone call to Paul. "I'm sorry, Mr. Bowen. I just wanted to know who to thank for the flowers," Mia said, standing up. "But I appreciate your discretion."

Mr. Bowen also stood but before dismissing her, he said, "Between fighting the flu and the loss of a loved one, you definitely had a tough week. How are you holding up?"

Mia felt a twinge of guilt as he mentioned her made-up illness. She didn't like lying to him about having the flu last week, but under the circumstances, it was necessary. "It's great to be back to work. I missed my students so much," she said, meaning every word.

Mr. Bowen smiled. "That's refreshing…and not something I hear every day," he said. "Well, if you need a few days to catch up, or if you need an extension on submitting your end-of-the-marking-period grades, just let me know."

Mia was so grateful to have such an understanding boss. She thanked him and left for her classroom. Mia had passed several of her colleagues on the way, all of whom looked to be in a rush. Practically every teacher in her hallway had children of their own. They were most likely on their ways to clock out of one job, just to clock back in to their most important job: being parents.

Until recently, Mia didn't know if parenthood was in her future. She had shunned all opportunities for companionship and love for so long…until last night. Mia thought about the beautiful night she had spent with Paul and as much as she wanted to dwell on the sweet words he had whispered as he claimed her again and again, she knew that he was waiting for her phone call.

Mia walked into her classroom and shut the door behind her for privacy. She was just about to dial Paul when she received a text: *"Your beauty, your purity, shall be cherished. I am waiting for you, Mia, my Angel."*

Mia had been in denial, a foolish state to be in when lives were at stake. It was unlike her not to accept what was fact, what was staring her right in the face. She looked down at the text once more and felt the bile rise in her throat. She was now, unequivocally, a target.

Mia dialed Paul's number and waited for him to pick up. She heard a cell phone ring just outside her classroom door and turned toward the sound. Paul was just on the other side, peering through the six-inch-wide glass panel on the door. Mia rushed over, swung the door open, and flew into his arms.

He shuffled her into her classroom and kicked the door closed behind them. "What's wrong, Mia? Tell me," he urged, stroking her hair.

She didn't want to cry. She definitely didn't want to tell him she was scared. Paul was already worried about his sister. Now two women in his life were being held captive in a sense by a very sick son-of-a-bitch. But she didn't want to lie either.

With her phone still in her hand, she retrieved the text and showed it to Paul. And that was the point when he lost it for a reason she hadn't seen coming.

Chapter Fifty-Five

Although the fatigue remained, Erin didn't feel any worse than when she woke up that morning. There were still no signs of a fever or the beginnings of a clog-filled head, but sinus infections had a way of sneaking up on her when she thought she was in the clear. Erin didn't want to spoil their morning and, as it turned out, the majority of the afternoon by telling Chase that she wanted to go back to New York, but now it was time.

She peeled off her bikini, showered, and threw on a sundress for dinner. In the short time that they had been on the island, it had already become a ritual for Chase and her to take a dip in the ocean, shower together, which often turned hot and deliciously heavy, and enjoy a dinner prepared by Chase and, much to her surprise, sous chef Andrew.

But today, Erin had taken her shower alone. Chase had received a phone call just as he was about to join her and it was apparent that he had to take the call. From his serious expression at the onset of the call, Erin gathered that something had happened. He had been away from the office for over two weeks and although his company ran like a well-oiled machine and could be put on autopilot for a sufficient amount of time, it was understandable that some things still required his and only his undivided attention. Erin was overwhelmed by his sacrifice, how he had put his life, the career that meant so much to him, on the back burner for her.

Fresh from the shower and feeling more like herself, though not completely, she entered the kitchen and froze at the troubling sight. Chase was gripping the edge of the counter top as he ended the conversation with whomever was on the other line. Andrew was on his cell phone and from the looks of it, scrolling for god knows what. Both men, who were typically more reserved than most, never appearing rattled, looked shaken and besieged by fear.

"What happened?" she asked, looking from one man to the next.

Andrew didn't look up from his phone and continued with whatever he was doing. Chase on the other hand walked over to her and though she felt that he was withholding a few details, he told her enough so she could share their fury and horror.

Erin's head was spinning. Mia was in danger because of her. Erin had woken up this morning knowing that it was time to go home. Now there was no doubt, nowhere else she wanted to be than with Mia. "What time do we leave?" she asked.

"Andrew will leave as soon as my jet is cleared for takeoff," Chase said, reaching for her. "He's checking the weather conditions now."

Erin stepped back, thwarting his attempt to hold her. "No," she said, shaking her head. "We are all going home."

Chase's square jaw clenched, as if he was doing his damnedest to not get demanding or angry. "It's not safe for you, Erin. I won't risk it."

"And I refuse to let Mia go through this alone. I did this, Chase. I put Andrew's niece in jeopardy," she said, her voice escalating, gaining Andrew's attention.

Chase pulled her into his arms, which made her anxiety lessen, though only slightly. "You told me not to run, remember?" she whispered.

"That's not what I meant and you know it, Erin. I need you safe and far away from him," he said, his voice gentler and more controlled.

"You can keep me safe. Hire as many men as Andrew and you deem necessary. I won't even balk at having an entourage," she said, wiggling from his embrace. "Because we are going home...all of us."

* * *

Andrew had never been so scared. All his years of service, when his life had been constantly at risk, when at any moment he could have been gunned down while he protected another, paled in comparison to how frightened he was that his only niece had been targeted. Shortly after takeoff, Andrew received a call from Mia and though he was grateful to hear her voice, she sounded different, as if for the first time in her life, she was holding out on him.

"I've missed you, honey," he said. "Are you all right?"

"Yes, just a little pissed off is all." An attempt at levity during grim circumstances wasn't too uncommon for his niece, but even now her voice sounded strained. As if she was trying too hard to not let on that she was, as she should be, terrified of the psychopath who was planning diabolical things for her.

"Well, we should be landing in New York in about an hour or so.

We'll meet you at Chase's penthouse. We have much to discuss, with our security detail being top priority."

"We?" she asked.

"Yes, Chase and Erin are with me. Erin refused to stay, especially when she heard what happened to you." Andrew heard Mia sigh. "We need to assign more security to you and Erin. I have already put some calls in and can have men in place as quick as tonight."

"Is Erin afraid of anything?" Mia asked, her voice filled with admiration. "If the roles were reversed, I don't think I would be flying back into the lion's den."

"Yes, you would," he said, his tone serious and absolute. "Erin Whitley doesn't run from her problems…and neither do you."

Chapter Fifty-Six

Paul couldn't get Mia and Henry to Chase's penthouse fast enough. The text Mia received had changed everything. The five of them needed to process what they had learned and formulate a plan. He finally stopped for a breath as he set their bags down and engaged the highly sophisticated security system. Chase's housekeeper had been gracious enough to wait around for them to arrive and give Paul a quick tutorial and, more importantly, the code which would activate the alarm.

With a giant bag of dog food in one hand and two matching stacked bowls in the other, Paul walked Henry into the kitchen and fixed him dinner. Henry wagged his tail and looked up at him, as if needing permission to attack his bowl of kibble. "Go ahead, buddy," Paul said, patting his head. Henry was crunching away when Paul exited the kitchen to join Mia.

She was staring at her phone while her thumb scrolled away. "Did he contact you again?" he asked.

"No," she said. "I was just checking to see if we missed any calls from Erin, Chase or Uncle Drew."

"Don't worry. They should be landing soon," he said. He walked over and took her into his arms. "I missed you today."

He felt her relax a little, despite discovering less than two hours ago that her life was in grave danger. Paul wanted to kiss her, feel his tongue slide over warm, lush lips and enter her, but decided to abstain. She was most likely feeling vulnerable, or at the very least, worried that she might be the bastard's next victim.

Paul was content to just hold her in his arms and breathe in her heady scent, until she looked up at him and kissed him with so much passion that he was struggling for air. "Don't let him get to me," she said, between kisses. He felt her tears against his cheeks and though a part of him thought he should stop, the other side of him believed she needed this, to feel claimed by him. That no one else could ever touch her.

"You're mine," he said, his voice gruff and demanding. He covered her mouth with his and moaned. She fisted his hair and pulled him into her. He had to have her again, feel her come around his cock as she quaked with pleasure. He picked her up, carried her into the first spare room he could find, and kicked the door closed behind him.

Paul released her and pressed her up against the door so her back was to his chest. His hands slid to her waist and he ground his erection into her. "Yes, Paul...I'm yours," she whimpered, backing into him, making the friction unbearable.

With those words, he removed her blouse and yanked up her skirt, exposing white silk panties. "God, you're stunning," he said, taking her in. With her standing there in black strappy heels with just a thin square of fabric covering her sex, he was seconds away from losing it. "So perfect," he said.

"I need you, she said, flinging her head back and giving him her neck to taste. He trailed his lips along her skin and thrust against her. "Now," she groaned.

Paul was taken by surprise as she turned and fell into his arms. They landed on the floor and within moments her panties were gone and his pants were unzipped, his boxer briefs pulled down far enough to take her. But she had other plans. With her sexy heels still on, she mounted him and sheathed his cock with her warmth. He was prepared to see a slight wince, residual discomfort from the night before as he entered her. But all he saw in her hooded eyes was desire and intoxicating need. "Slow, baby…I'm not going to last," he said, rolling his hips to meet hers.

And just when he thought he had never experienced such beauty, she reached in front of her and unlatched the front clip of her bra. Her breasts spilled forth as she met him thrust for thrust. "Paul…I…" she moaned, riding him hard.

As much as he loved watching her bob up and down on his cock, her breasts lovely and unbound, he wanted to give her what she had asked for at the onset. Still connected, he flipped her onto her back. He entwined his fingers with hers and pressed her hands at either side of her head. "I got you, baby," he said, gliding in and out of her tight heat. Her tears had receded and she looked at him with hunger and another emotion he prayed he was detecting correctly. But he didn't want to scare her and unload feelings that she might not be prepared for or even want to hear so soon. "I'll take care of you," he said, between pants. "Always."

"Yes…take me!" she screamed. She was so snug around his cock, squeezing him relentlessly, taking everything from him…including his heart.

* * *

Mia knew that reality was going to set in very soon. But for a few more minutes, as she lay in Paul's arms on the plush carpet of one of Chase's many rooms, she could pretend that everything was as wonderful as she felt at that moment. She rested her head on his muscular chest and shamelessly took the opportunity to run her fingers delicately along his tight abs. Out of the corner of her eye, she saw his semi-erect cock twitch at her touch.

She wanted him again, to feel his hands caress her as if he worshiped her body. Although he had touched and entered her with ravenous desire, he had remained gentle and…loving. Which left her feeling both frightened and euphoric. What if he didn't feel the same? What if loving her was just…too much? A burden with years of baggage and inexperience.

Paul's cell phone broke the silence and he sighed. With one hand pressed firmly between her shoulder blades, he reached over and shook his previously discarded jeans until his cell fell from one of the pockets. "It's my sister," he said.

Mia nodded and started to pull away from him in order to give him some privacy, when he gripped her tightly and held her to his chest. "I have nothing to hide…stay," he said, kissing her just above the ear. "Besides, my sister will know we are together the moment she lays eyes on us."

Mia didn't hear too much after that because all she could think about was how her Uncle Drew was going to react. Much more than an uncle, she suspected he would be protective, wary possibly, of the fact that her and Paul's relationship could have evolved so quickly. She got a sickening feeling in the pit of her stomach. Mia thought back to her high school days, especially during her sophomore year when she had finally sprouted boobs, when her uncle had taken the liberty to threaten any boy who dared to look below her neck, and cringed. There was no way her uncle was going to be pleased or embrace their newfound romance.

"They just landed and should be here soon," Paul said, tossing the phone on his heap of clothes. He rolled her onto her back. And as much as she enjoyed being beneath him, watching the muscles in his arms flex as he dangerously hovered just above her, she knew that someone just as deadly was going to be assessing Paul's motives and what he intended for his niece.

"Erin isn't the only one with rock-solid intuition. My uncle has made a career of reading people and he will know that we...that I..." Mia wanted to believe that she couldn't find the words to finish her thought. But she would have been lying to herself. She knew exactly what she wanted to say and it scared her to realize just how deep her feelings ran.

"He'll know that you what, Mia?" he asked, linking both her hands above her head with just one of his. With a hint of a smile, he looked into her eyes, as if daring her to answer his question.

"That we...are together," she said, her voice cracking. Although it wasn't what she had intended to say, it was a believable lie and from the look on his face, he appeared satisfied with her response. "We are together...right?" she asked.

She hadn't thought about asking him that, but she had to say something. And now that she had, she regretted her assumption.

God, what the hell was she going to do if he wasn't on the same page with her or didn't feel even a tenth of how she felt about him?

"Oh, we're together, Mia. I meant what I said. You're mine, now." He lowered his head and kissed her. "Mine," he said, before peeling himself away, erection and all. Mia just stared and watched him dress. For years, Mia had considered herself an independent woman with no need to find that elusive "other half" that she had heard other women talk about in regards to their relationships with men.

Mia played the last word in her head over and over again and was amazed at how wrong she had been about herself. As Paul growled that she was his now, claiming her as his own, Mia felt her heart leap within her chest.

Chapter Fifty-Seven

Between Erin's good instincts and what he had seen in the park that day, Chase had a feeling that Mia and Paul's relationship had changed significantly while they were away. And as he exited the elevator with Erin at one side and Andrew on the other, his feeling that Paul and Mia were more than friends was confirmed. Chase saw Paul's hand leave the small of Mia's back so she could give her uncle a hug. Paul took that opportunity to embrace his sister and welcome her home. Erin squeezed him tight and said through a few tears, "I missed you." Chase couldn't help but notice that Erin was a bit more emotional than usual, which wasn't at all a surprise under the circumstances. Still, it bothered him to the core to know she was worried all the time.

The vision of Erin and her brother made him remember just how important family was, what he had been missing since his father had died. Chase couldn't imagine Erin wanting to live far away from her brother; their bond was too strong and it was obvious that frequent family gatherings were a necessity. He would take that into consideration when mapping out where they should live.

Mia released her uncle and walked over to him. She appeared nervous as she said, "I hope you don't mind dogs, Chase. I didn't want to leave Henry."

"I love dogs," Chase said, bending down and stroking the tuft of hair between Henry's ears. "He is most welcome."

Mia smiled and was then immediately accosted by Erin, who was smiling now…and looking a bit mischievous. "We need to talk," Erin said, taking her by the hand and leading her into their bedroom. Their bedroom. He loved the sound of that. Everything he had was hers. But their bedroom was about to change. While they were away, Erin had mentioned that his New York penthouse didn't feel like *him*. And she was right. Nothing in the elegant space, except for his office and the nursery, screamed his name or hers. He planned on rectifying that, especially since he now knew with absolute certainty what she wanted, where she saw herself living and raising a family. But for the time being, until their living nightmare was over, the penthouse would just have to do.

Chase was happy to see Erin looking and hopefully feeling better. Although she had been her loving and beautiful self for most of the afternoon prior to Paul's disturbing phone call, she seemed more reserved than usual, as if something, other than the obvious of course, was weighing on her. Chase was thankful that Erin and Mia had made themselves scarce to indulge in some girl talk about things that weren't as heavy.

But as he turned his attention to Paul and Andrew he noticed that maybe it was wise to give them some alone time as well. The look on Paul's face was one of stone as it had to be to defend himself against Andrew's piercing glare. "Come on, Henry," Chase said, hustling from the room and giving them the privacy they apparently needed. Although Chase knew that Andrew and Paul needed to get their feelings off their chests and identify the elephant in the room, it wouldn't be easy. Chase wouldn't be at all surprised if a punch or two were thrown. From what Erin had told him, Mia was like a daughter to Andrew. And from the looks of it, the typically reserved, even-mannered ex–secret service agent…was pissed.

* * *

Alone, but not knowing for how long, Andrew cut to the chase and asked the only question that truly mattered. "Are you in love with her?"

Paul Whitley had never been one to cower or pass the buck. Hell, it had taken some restraint to not congratulate Paul when Andrew had learned that he had severely beaten the man who violated his sister. Andrew respected how loyal Paul was to his sister, how he would put everything on the line for her and more. But all that respect could be thrown to the wayside depending on Paul's answer and his intentions in regards to Mia.

"Yes, I am," Paul said, not hesitating.

Andrew just stared at him, waiting for Paul's steely gaze to waver. But after several moments of uncomfortable silence, it was clear that the conversation wasn't going to progress unless he took the initiative. "It's been less than two weeks. I can't imagine…"

"And I can't imagine my life without her in it," Paul said, cutting him off.

Andrew's intention was to bait Paul and get him to react with raw emotion, because that was where the truth lay. With his fists clenched at his side, his tone no longer businesslike, the reserved lawyer long gone; Paul was exposed and giving Andrew exactly what he wanted.

"You know what Mia means to me, Paul."

"And you know by now that I protect those I love…no matter the cost." That was the defining moment. Andrew could have either viewed him as the man who had flown into a rage, leaving a man to bleed to death or he could see him as a man that would risk everything for someone he loved. The first option would suggest that Paul was impulsive and a danger to his niece. And the latter, well, he might as well have been talking about himself. Because if it had been him in the cemetery that night, he wouldn't have just kicked the shit out of him. He would have finished the job and would have slept soundly every night thereafter.

Andrew looked past Paul and saw Mia and Erin spilling out into the hallway giggling like two teenaged girls. The sight was refreshing, giving him a different perspective. For the first time in years, Mia looked happy, resembling the carefree girl she had been before her mother and father had died. Was it possible that Paul had helped her find her smile…the very one that could brighten a room and make everyone in it stop and stare?

But Mia's easy smile faded as she looked from him to Paul. "Everything all right?" she asked.

In one extended and very-much-needed glance, Paul and Andrew had a conversation that only they were a part of. Andrew gave Paul a nod and Paul returned the gesture. The conversation was over for now. Remarkably, there were more important things to address, such as the man who was stalking not just one but two women they cared for.

But apparently Mia wasn't finished. She looked right at him and said, "Erin, Paul, can you give us a minute?"

Paul didn't move or take that opportunity to avoid what Andrew suspected would be a very awkward conversation with his niece. Begrudgingly, he had to admit that Paul had just scored a few brownie points with him for not bailing out. The only thing that finally got Paul to leave Mia was his sister. With some gentle coaxing and shameless pleading, Erin worked her magic and forced her brother out of the room.

"So he told you that we are…together?" she asked, struggling with the last word. From her stammer, Andrew concluded that Paul had neglected for one reason or another telling her the depth of his supposed feelings for her.

"Yes," he said. Paul looked down at the woman who would always be his little girl. She may have only been his niece, for his brother had doted on her like any proud pop, but with no children of his own, Andrew's heart had been claimed by Mia from the day she was born. Andrew couldn't imagine anyone being good enough for his niece. It wasn't just a case of having impossible standards. It was the simple fact that she deserved perfection, love with no restrictions and loyalty beyond measure.

"Paul won't hurt me, Uncle Drew," she said, walking toward him. "I trust him, which, as you know, isn't easy for me." Between the deaths of her parents and her short and often-disturbing career as a profiler, she had every right to be leery of people, forever questioning their intentions and analyzing what truly made a person tick. "And as much as you may not want to admit it, you trust Paul too."

Mia reached out and touched his arm. He placed his hand over hers and said, "I trust him to keep you safe. But can I trust him with your heart?"

"I don't know where Paul and I are headed…and I like that. But if I fall, if things don't work out, then…"

"I will catch you," Andrew said, embracing his brother's child. She was so special to him, precious in every way. How the hell could he blame Paul, or any man for that matter, for appreciating her for the lovely person that she was? "And protect you."

Mia squeezed him tight and said, "I was hoping you would say that." She then stepped back and said, "I'll need all the protection you can give me…and so will Erin." Her voice went from youthful to serious in less than a second, which was where the night needed to go.

Chapter Fifty-Eight

Erin hadn't known what she had been missing all this time. Sitting on Chase's bed with Mia as they talked about the new relationship that had blossomed while she was away on the island was as natural as breathing. They were like two old friends as they giggled and swooned over their men.

Mia didn't hold back when it came to talking about the feelings she had for Paul. So, Erin was happy that Mia was having a little chat with her uncle. It was pointless to even try to hide or gloss over the attraction between Paul and Mia. The moment Erin stepped off the elevator and caught sight of Mia's pink cheeks and slightly wrinkled skirt, she knew that Mia and Paul had taken what she had witnessed in the park and had moved it to a whole other level completely.

Erin walked over and pressed her ear against the bedroom door. She felt like a child eavesdropping, but she wanted to be sure that all seemed quiet before walking out into the hallway. But the sound of claws grinding against wood forced her to open the door...only to find Mia's adorable Lab staring up at her. God, he was so cute.

She hadn't realized that she had said those words out loud until she heard Chase say, "I've been replaced."

Erin looked from Henry to her gorgeous man and said, "Henry's cute…but you're handsome…and so…"—planting a kiss on his full lips—"sexy." She whispered, trying desperately not to gross out the company, which included her brother, in the very next room.

Chase sighed. "As much as I want to lock you away with me in our bedroom for all of eternity, you know that we can't." And that was when reality really set in. Her coveted girl talk with Mia, the discovery that her brother's heart had finally thawed, seemed trivial compared to the threat against not only her but everyone under Chase's roof.

* * *

Just minutes into their conversation, Erin realized that it wasn't reality setting in; it was a nightmare spilling over into her waking hours, one she would never escape.

Erin looked at Chase and then Paul. No, there had to be a mistake. It just wasn't possible.

"I don't believe you. He couldn't have sent that text," she said, her voice escalating and filling Chase's expansive kitchen. "Josh would never hurt me. Hell, he never once made a move on me in all the years that I knew him!"

Erin shook her head as she thought about all the times Josh could have done just what her brother had accused him of and didn't. "All those late nights studying alone in his apartment, he didn't even try kissing me. Walking back from a party, when he could have easily taken advantage of my drunken state, he chose to hold back my hair while I threw up instead. Tell me, does that sound like someone who rapes women?"

Erin's hands were shaking and it was clear from the looks on Paul's and Chase's faces that she had rattled both of them with her rant. But as Mia came toward her, Erin realized that Mia did not appear flustered. Actually, she was calm and more poised than everyone else in the penthouse combined.

"No. And that is why we can't accept even the text at face value. Does it make Josh look guilty? Absolutely. Has Josh moved to the top of my short list of suspects? You're damn right he has. But always be leery of what is handed to you on a silver platter. There are only a few things in this life that come easy, like your unshakable bond with your brother, and the way my uncle continues to love me no matter how much I drive him crazy." Mia looked over at her uncle, who was giving her a knowing grin.

Mia's attempt to diffuse a tense situation that could have easily spiraled out of control was successful and truly miraculous. If there was any doubt that Mia couldn't handle the pressure, that she wasn't up for the challenge of a lifetime, it was laid to rest in that one shining moment. Erin realized that if Mia, a woman who had lived through murder and suicide, could remain optimistic as she trudged through every obstacle, then Erin could freak out less and focus more.

Erin had been standing in the middle of the kitchen when Paul had dropped the Josh bomb on her. But if she was going to share Josh's story with Chase, Erin and Mia, it was best that they all grab a bar stool and take a seat.

"So, maybe it's time you know the man behind the one I befriended within my first semester of college?"

The three of them nodded and she told Josh's painful tale, one that he hadn't shared with anyone else at Penn, but her.

* * *

Josh and Julia Graham were the children of multimillionaire Richard Graham, the CEO of White Spring. Based in New York City, White Spring was a multinational investment management corporation that was thriving, appearing in Forbes *for many years and from the looks of it, would continue to for many more to come.*

Josh and Julia had never wanted for anything, at least not when it came to material things. They were set for life. All they had to do was agree to take over their father's company when the time came. But leading a corporation that they respected but had no interest in whatsoever was never their dream, causing a permanent rift within the family.

Josh and his twin sister, Julia, made the conscious decision in their senior year to rock the boat and apply to separate colleges that would fulfill his dream of being a doctor and Julia's lifelong desire to attend Rockhill School of the Arts. Julia was an accomplished pianist with superior intellect. But to Josh, she was just his easygoing sister that enjoyed hanging out, going to a ballgame and wearing jeans, sneakers and t-shirts.

Most parents would have been proud of the careers they had chosen for themselves, but not Richard Graham and his wife, Ava. They were furious that their children had turned their backs on the family and the roles they were bred for. Considering that their upbringing was devoid of warmth, love and support from their parents, Josh and Julia were not at all surprised by their reaction. Despite their parents' threats, Josh and Julia proceeded to enroll in school the coming fall, not allowing their parents' hurtful words and pleas to tarnish their dreams.

The night after they graduated high school, Josh and Julia's parents informed them that if they weren't willing to change their minds and take their positions at White Spring, then they were no longer welcome in the home they had lived in all their lives. Josh and Julia packed their bags that night and left, never once looking back.

Their first stop was the bank, where they withdrew as much money as they could before their parents either froze or closed their accounts completely. Sadly, Josh had been preparing for this day, the day when his parents would cut them out of their lives. A few months before graduation, Josh had opened an account at a small chain bank in New Jersey. Little by little he would withdraw money, some from this account, a few thousand from another, and dump it all into this secret account in New Jersey. According to his last online bank statement, he and Julia had enough money to get them through their first few years of college. Beyond that, they would need to get jobs and work their ways through. Despite growing up with ridiculous wealth, Josh and Julia were not afraid of hard work or with what it took in this day and age to make it on their own. They would have each other to complain to when times got tough and that thought allowed them to leave everything behind, including their parents.

With money in their pockets, Josh and Julia cruised along the Garden State Parkway toward Avalon. Their maternal grandmother had been living alone in the quaint shore town ever since they could remember. Her husband's high blood pressure due to job-related stress had made her a widow, and she would forever regret not putting her foot down and forcing him to leave his high-power, high-profile job sooner. So, needless to say, it sickened her when she discovered that her only *child, her beautiful Ava, had been seduced by the lifestyle that had killed her husband.*

Julia had insisted on driving, being hopped up on adrenaline over her first taste of freedom. Tears turned to smiles, smiles turned into laughter as they realized that they had really made the leap. They were finally free of their parents, their threats and their harsh and unforgiving words of hatred. Josh called his grandmother and asked her if he and his sister could stop by for a visit. It was almost ten o'clock on a Friday night, but she was elated to hear from them and was ready to welcome them within the hour. And that was right around the time when the laughter stopped. Josh and Julia looked up just in time to see the headlights of a pickup truck directly in front of them. There was no time to swerve, curse or brace for impact.

Josh was in Bayville hospital when he came to, hooked up to a number of machines with an IV sticking out of his arm. Although his head ached from what he suspected was a concussion, he remembered the accident, how one minute they were coasting down the Parkway and the next minute, they had come face-to-face with a truck travelling into oncoming traffic. But the aches and pains he suffered paled in comparison to the loss he felt deep in his soul. Call it twin intuition, but without anyone telling him, he knew his sister was gone.

His parents had been present at Julia's funeral, but neither his mother nor father spoke to him. They were colder than usual, keeping their distance from not only him but also his grandmother, who had opened her home to him for as long as he needed. Josh prepared the eulogy, but was ready to step aside if his parents had grown a heart and wished to speak loving words about their daughter. But as he suspected, they hadn't prepared a goddamn thing and were content to be viewed as guests, rather than grieving parents. Josh stood at the podium and spoke at length about the beautiful woman who the world would never get the privilege to meet. How no one would be able to witness her fiery spirit or her unwavering persistence ever again. Although his words got jumbled from time to time due to frequent emotional breaks, his final message came across loud and clear. He had lost more than a sister that night; he had lost his twin, his best friend.

Josh was in no shape to attend college that coming fall. He continued to live with his grandmother as he took on a job at Avalon's only coffee house. His grandmother kept quiet as she watched her grandson mourn in his own way, which was working most of the day, eating dinner in silence and going to bed even before an old lady like herself. The next day, the next eleven months, were more of the same. On the one-year anniversary of Julia's death, Josh's grandmother had given him the kick in the ass he needed and told him that it was time to start living, that Julia's dream of seeing him make it and be the doctor he always wanted to be, was fading a little each day.

Josh finally understood from whom Julie acquired her fire, that feisty dose of spice that made a man reassess his life and put things into perspective. The next day, he called the college and spoke to his advisor. A week later, he went to Penn to pick up his schedule, paid for his first year of college in full, and found a one-bedroom apartment that was small but clean. His grandmother made the trip into Philly to help get him settled, which had touched him tremendously. With his sister gone, his parents unreachable in every sense of the word, his grandmother was the only family he had left.

Chapter Fifty-Nine

Mia tried desperately to distance herself from the man Erin had just described and the facts that she had in front of her, which at the moment, did not work in Josh Graham's favor. A text was sent from Josh Graham's cell phone, identifying him through the use of the word "Angel" as the rapist. Josh Graham possibly had access to mass quantities of money and resources through estranged family members. Josh Graham still had ties to New York City. Josh Graham was intelligent and, from what Erin described, persistent, patient and practical. He didn't up and leave his parents' home with just the shirt on his back. He had thought ahead and shuffled money around to sustain himself for a few years. Josh Graham could not be accounted for immediately after he and Erin finished their last final exam. Those were the facts, like 'em or not.

"Uncle Drew, have you put someone on Josh, yet?" Mia asked.

"I made a call from the plane. My guy said he would contact me when they have located him," Uncle Drew said.

"Good. Now, let's shift for a second. We have had a tail on Morris for days. Any new developments there?" Mia asked.

"Frank checks in with me hourly. Morris's routine is pretty much the same each day, but his nights differ. It appears that he has a girl-friend. He is at the movies with a Ms. Jennifer Freehold as we speak. Last night, Frank followed them to La Mer, an upscale restaurant in the city, where they dined for several hours," Uncle Drew said.

"And let me guess, Morris's phone records do not indicate any-thing of concern and he hasn't come within a mile of any of us?" Erin asked.

"Correct," Uncle Drew said.

Mia soaked in everything in order to review and dissect later. But first it was important that everyone had the same information. For the next hour or so, Mia and Paul discussed their trip to both Dr. Mitchell Morris's office and Dr. Scott Morris's former place of em-ployment. Mia relayed to the group how each Morris was perceived by those who knew the men. In a nutshell, Morris Senior was loved and respected. Morris Junior was arrogant and lacking the warmth his father so easily conveyed on a daily basis.

The conversation grew more difficult when she discussed the rea-son for their abrupt departure from Philly. Paul must have sensed her discomfort because he came over and took her hand. Mia won-dered how her uncle felt about that, but Paul didn't seem to care, so why should she?

"My neighbor's death has been ruled an accident, but I feel that we shouldn't close the book on that one. We know that Gabrielle was deemed a suicide…but she was also conspiring with someone she thought was Erin's ex-boyfriend. And let's not forget Dr. Mitchell Morris's own untimely death." Mia could tell from the looks on their faces that she hadn't said anything that they weren't already thinking.

Chase had been quiet for most of the conversation, but he suddenly sprung to life. "We'll need more men, Andrew. The girls shouldn't step foot outside this door without someone glued to their sides." Chase looked over at Erin. "In fact, I don't want you leaving the penthouse for any reason."

Erin looked annoyed at the thought of being held captive in her own home. Mia was just about to interject when Paul said, "I agree." Paul then stared at her and said, "And you shouldn't either."

This was not happening. There was no way she was going to hide away for Lord knows how long, missing work, putting a complete halt to life. "I can't do that, Paul. I won't," Mia said.

"It's the same as running," Erin said.

Mia looked over at Erin and Chase. It was obvious that Chase wanted to plead with her, make her understand that all he wanted to do was keep her safe. But in the process, while she was locked away in his penthouse, he would make her go insane. Mia looked at Paul, who also appeared to be on the verge of demanding that she and his sister remain in Chase's tower.

"You can't go home, Mia," Paul said. "It's not safe enough."

"I agree with that, Mia. There are too many points of entry to secure," Uncle Drew said. Mia knew her uncle had a point, but what was the alternative?

"You will move in with me," Paul said with absolution.

As much as Mia loved the thought of waking up with Paul every morning, she knew that wasn't a good idea. "Right now, the bastard doesn't want to kill me because he believes I'm wholesome and pure. If he discovers that you and I are cohabitating, obsession will turn to hatred and he will view me as something vile, no longer worthy of his affections or attention. Erin hasn't received a text since his perception of her changed. I don't want to cut off communication with him. The more he talks, the greater the chance he will slip."

"Let's think about this for a minute. He's not bothered that you associate with what he considers to be filth, he just doesn't want you sleeping with it. Would that be safe to assume?" Chase asked.

"It appears to be the case. Every psychopath is different, with a different set of rules. And these rules often make no sense. I once profiled a psychopath that chose his victims based on firstborn status. It took a while to discover the connection—that each of his six victims was the firstborn son, but eventually the son-of-a-bitch got sloppy and we were able to connect the dots."

"Perception is everything, then," Chase said. He looked at Mia. "What if you stayed here, a place where he couldn't know for certain if you have…for the lack of a better term…gone to the dark side? It would make him uneasy, frustratingly uncertain if you were still worthy of his affections, causing him…"

"To falter," Mia finished. She looked at her uncle for guidance, but it was clear that he was uncomfortable with the plan, as he would be with any plan that put her life in jeopardy.

So it surprised her when Uncle Drew said, "As much as I hate to admit it, that may be our best option."

"Great. Then it's settled. We have plenty of room for you and Paul," Chase said, weaving a hand around Erin's waist.

"Not so fast. I've agreed to stay, but I will go to work, I will attempt to lead a normal life and try not to get fired from a job I love," Mia said.

Mia heard Paul sigh before he said, "Okay. We will have men in place everywhere you go, which shouldn't be too difficult since you will only be going to work and then returning immediately to the penthouse."

Mia's natural instinct at such a demand was to dig her heels in and challenge the person who was trying to dictate what she could and couldn't do. But that very person was the same man she had been with just hours ago, who she had given her heart and body to for the first time in her life. And he was worth compromising for.

Chapter Sixty

If he would have left five minutes later for work, Chase would have witnessed a scene reminiscent of the morning following their first overnighter. Kneeling over the toilet, Erin expelled everything she had in her stomach from the night before. When she had nothing left, the dry heaves began and lasted for another five minutes. No fever, no stuffy nose accompanied her heaving spell. She was not fighting a sinus infection. No, what she now suspected was causing her to feel fatigue and lightheadedness, and to vomit upon waking was much more serious.

Weak and shaky, Erin washed her face and rinsed out her mouth. She needed to get to her phone. Erin walked back into the bedroom and sat on the edge of the bed. She reached for her cell on the nightstand, pulled up her calendar and scrolled back to find the date of her last injection. She had marked the date with a red dot so it would be easy to spot. But it occurred to her after a few frustrating moments that the marked date was on the phone she had discarded. Her calendar and contacts had been wiped clean.

Shit.

A quick internet search enabled her to retrieve her doctor's number and she placed the call. "Ms. Whitley, it's so good to hear from you. We've been trying to reach you for several weeks. Have you moved?" asked the medical assistant.

Erin felt irresponsible and incredibly embarrassed for not only missing her last appointment, but for appearing to have fallen off the face of the earth. "Um…yes. And I also changed my phone number," Erin said.

"And your email? Do you have a new email address as well? We sent you an appointment reminder a few weeks back, but it just got bounced back to us," the kind woman said.

"Yeah, I closed that account and haven't created another as of yet," Erin said, mortified.

"Well, no matter. I have you on the phone now and we can get your new contact info. Would you like to schedule an appointment?"

"Yes. I know this is a long shot, but do you have any openings today?" Erin asked with her eyes clenched shut and prayed that they weren't booked.

"We don't have another opening until next week. Can I put you in for Wednesday at two?"

There was no way she was going to be able to wait that long. So she decided to just tell the woman on the other line, a complete stranger whom she had never met before, why she needed to be seen immediately. "Is there any way you can fit me in tonight? I think I may be pregnant." Saying the words aloud made the possibility of her condition that much more real. What would Chase say if she was pregnant? She had told him that she was on birth control. He had every right to assume that she had lied to him or even planned for this to happen. Would he view this possible pregnancy as a way of trapping him?

"Now, that changes things, doesn't it?" the nice woman chirped. "Let's see what we can do." Erin heard the medical assistant type away on her keyboard. "Dr. Martinez cushions her schedule for situations such as these. Are you available tonight at seven o'clock?"

Erin would have kissed the woman if she had been standing in front of her.

* * *

Chase technically wasn't lying when he told Erin that he needed to go in to work today. He would eventually make it into the office, but first he had to stop off at the bank. With the small box tucked safely away in the inside pocket of his suit jacket, he couldn't wait to get the day started so he could get home to Erin.

Chase had never been away from the office for such an extended period of time. He thought that going back to work today would be stressful due to his absence as he picked up the pieces of his company. But as he walked toward his office, he didn't encounter any panic on his employees' faces. No, everyone seemed to function as if he had been there the entire time, which was wonderful to see. He knew that he had Lydia to thank for that, for putting his company on autopilot.

"Good morning, Mr. Montclair," Lydia said, looking up from her computer screen.

"Lydia, would you join me in my office? We have much to discuss."

"Of course." Lydia grabbed her iPad and followed him into his office.

He closed the door behind her and then took his place behind the desk. He couldn't believe how nervous he was, now that the little square box was burning a hole in his suit's jacket pocket. Chase needed to show someone, tell anyone who would listen that tonight he was going to ask Erin to be his wife. And what better person than Lydia? Over the years, she had proven her loyalty to both him and his father. She was devoted to the company and rarely spoke her mind or challenged him. She had never commented on his breakup with Gabrielle or probed for information about why his ex-fiancée was in his life one minute and out the next. But as tight-lipped as Lydia was, minding her own business and not falling victim to mindless workplace gossip, she was cognizant of everything that went on in his building. She was his eyes and ears and as he'd learned recently, very aware that without Erin, he was lost.

Lydia Jackson was the perfect assistant.

Chase took the box out of his pocket and opened the lid. "Do you think she'll like it, Lydia?"

Lydia leaned over and peered at the simple but flawless diamond. "That belonged to your mother, did it not?"

Chase stared at the ring and envisioned it on Erin's finger. "Yes. I can't imagine giving something so precious to anyone but Erin."

Lydia smiled and then without warning, she stood and walked over to him. "Your father would be very pleased. And he would have loved to have seen you so in love…like the way he was with your mother." She leaned over and kissed him on the cheek. The sudden display of affection was out of character for Lydia, which made it all the more special and heartfelt.

Chapter Sixty-One

Chase had called on the hour every hour to check in and ask her how her day was. As much as Erin loved hearing his voice every sixty minutes, it was becoming increasingly difficult with each passing call to pretend that everything was fine. She even found herself sighing with relief when he told her that he had to work later than anticipated, which was fortunate considering her game-changing doctor's appointment.

Erin waited until the last possible minute to tell Andrew about the appointment he was clearly going to accompany her to. She didn't want to give Andrew hours of time to inquire about the appointment and alert Chase.

"Of course I'll take you wherever you need to go. I wasn't aware that you had a doctor's appointment tonight. Does Mr. Montclair know?" Andrew asked. Erin kept her head down as she retrieved her purse from the kitchen counter. With her eyes diverted, she could feel him staring at her.

"Um…no. I don't think so. It's just an annual checkup. No big deal."

"Ms. Whitley, if the appointment isn't urgent, you should consider rescheduling it. Mr. Montclair doesn't want you leaving the penthouse right now unless it's absolutely necessary."

"No can do. I planned this appointment months ago. If I cancel, it could be weeks, most likely months, before they can see me."

Andrew pressed on, making her more flustered by the second. "I'm sure Mr. Montclair's friend, Robert, would be able to make a house call. We wouldn't need to leave the penthouse and you could still receive the medical treatment you seek."

Erin had no desire to make Andrew feel uncomfortable, but she had a feeling that if she played the woman card, he would abandon the conversation. "Robert is a great physician, but he's not a gynecologist."

Andrew actually blushed before clearing his throat. "Well, shall we go?" he asked, grabbing his car keys.

***

In just a paper gown and white socks, Erin sat back in the elevated chair and told herself to breathe. Waiting for results wasn't foreign to her; she'd voluntarily subjected herself to monthly blood tests after her rape. Actually, this month, the month that had changed everything, was the only month she had foregone testing. Her mind had been on other things, like Chase, and not her ridiculous obsession with having her blood tested.

Erin's hand rested on her belly and she wondered what she was going to say to Chase if she was indeed pregnant with his child. Several ways of unloading such news were flooding her brain when she heard a quick succession of knocks at the door. Startled and beyond nervous, she heard herself say, "Come in."

Dr. Martinez was a no-nonsense, tell-it-like-it-is physician. Which was exactly what Erin wanted and needed right now. "Okay Erin, feet in the stirrups. Let's have a look."

Erin had been hoping for an external ultrasound, but no such luck. If she was pregnant, a transvaginal ultrasound would be more effective at this early stage. Erin complied and braced herself for the discomfort from the lubricated probe.

"Try to relax, Erin," Dr. Martinez said, as she gently slid the rod into position. Erin exhaled and accepted the intrusion.

Dr. Martinez shifted the probe within her and stared at the monitor. Erin didn't know whether to look at the doctor and analyze her facial expressions as she probed away, or gaze at the monitor and attempt to decipher what looked like gray, swirling fuzz.

"Well, calculating pregnancy from conception isn't an exact science, but I would say you are right around the sixth-week mark, Erin."

Erin just stared at the monitor, trying desperately to see what the doctor was seeing. "I'm pregnant?" she asked. Suspecting pregnancy and having it confirmed were two totally different things, invoking separate fears and emotions.

It was at that moment that the door swung open and Erin met Chase's gaze. "You can't be in here, sir. This is an exam room. You must leave immediately," Dr. Martinez said, her voice firm and unwavering.

"Erin, what's wrong?" he asked, ignoring Dr. Martinez completely. He rushed over and grabbed Erin's hand.

"Erin, do you know this man?" Dr. Martinez asked. "Do you want him here?"

Erin swallowed. This was the moment of truth. Nodding, she said, "Yes, I want him here." Erin looked into Chase's eyes and saw the concern, that all-encompassing love that he never withheld from her.

"Okay, then. I want both of you to look right here," Dr. Martinez said, directing them with her finger to a slight flicker on the monitor. Chase squeezed Erin's hand with both of his and obeyed the doctor.

"The answer to your question, Erin, is yes. You're pregnant and that flicker that you two are fixed on right now is the baby's heartbeat."

"Baby?" Chase asked, staring at the flicker on the computer monitor. Erin felt him squeeze her hand even tighter. Oh God! Was he angry?

Erin wanted to look back at Chase but she was interrupted by the curious expression on Dr. Martinez's face. "What is it?" Erin asked the doctor.

"Ahh…there you are," Dr. Martinez said, her lips curling into a mischievous smile. "Twins like to hide sometimes."

"Twins?" Erin and Chase asked in unison.

"To answer your question, sir…"

"Chase," he supplied.

"It's not baby, but babies. Two healthy sprouts that are measuring equal in size." Dr. Martinez clicked a few more buttons and then provided them both with a printout of Baby A and Baby B.

"Erin, I'll be back. I think you two need a moment." Dr. Martinez withdrew the probe. "Erin, you can get dressed whenever you're ready. We're finished with the exam, but we need to discuss your prenatal care. Okay?"

Erin nodded, appreciating the doctor's discretion and sensitivity.

Once alone, Erin felt the panic set in. She closed her eyes, which didn't prevent the tears from forming, and said, "I'm so sorry."

"Look at me, Erin." It was a reasonable request. He had every right to demand her attention right now.

Staring into his deep blue eyes, she couldn't hide and that was the time the flood gates burst open. "I missed my birth control shot...not intentionally, but...Chase, I'm sorry. I wasn't trying to trick you," she said, through uncontrollable sobs.

He gathered her into his arms and said, "The only thing that could make me happier than I already am..."—Erin felt one of his arms slacken—"is if the mother of my children says 'yes.'"

Chase sat back and flipped open the top to a very small box. "Marry me, Erin," he said, extracting the ring and slipping it onto her finger. She looked at the beautiful diamond and then at the man who had captured her heart. Her typical, even-keeled, reserved businessman was overcome with emotion and she saw his eyes well.

"I love you, Chase...and our family," she said, placing her hands on her belly. His own hand covered hers as the first tear slowly ran down his cheek. "Yes, I'll marry you."

He leaned over and kissed her slowly, taking the time to show her just how much he cherished her.

Chapter Sixty-Two

Scott was tired, but not physically, as his body was in top shape—a machine fed only the finest food and drink. No, he had grown weary of going so long without obtaining closure. So much so that he taken the time to research how one can track another through the use of cell phones. As a result of his diligence and perseverance, he now knew the location of Paul Whitley, Montclair and his Whore, and, of course, his Angel.

Scott didn't know when Montclair and the Whore had returned to New York, because according to the tracker, Montclair's car was still in Philadelphia. For whatever reason, they had come back to the city by some other means. But it didn't matter now. This method was more discrete.

According to the map on his phone, his Angel and Paul Whitley were at Montclair's penthouse, which pissed him off. He knew his Angel was hard at work, trying to help people that didn't deserve her to solve a mystery that would come to an end. But it would be on his terms. Since neither his Angel nor Paul Whitley were accessible at the moment, Scott focused his attention on Montclair and his Whore. He was happy to see that the vile couple had ventured out, leaving themselves beautifully exposed and within walking distance.

"I love when you smile," Plain Jane said, sipping her coffee. Scott hadn't realized he was donning such a wide grin until she called him on it. Just a little while longer, he thought, and there would be no need to keep Plain Jane around.

"Want to take in a movie tonight and order some Chinese?" Scott asked, staring at her across the small stone-top table for two on her balcony. He had stopped over at her place after work in hopes of claiming a home base. Which seemed to be working out better than he had envisioned.

Plain Jane beamed with delight. "That sounds great. I think Lee Wu's delivers," she said.

Scott shook his head. "I have a better place in mind, but they don't deliver. I'll just run and pick it up. In the meantime..." he bent over and kissed her gently on the lips, "you order any movie you like." He could stomach watching a romantic comedy, but there was no way he was going to consume food from an establishment that didn't meet his standards.

"Swear you won't mind if my movie choice falls within the chick flick category?" she asked, her eyes wide and unsuspecting. Pitiful.

"You have my word. I'm in such a good mood, I could even stomach a Julia Roberts movie," Scott said, standing up.

"Chicken or beef?" he asked, reaching for the briefcase he now carried with him everywhere he went.

"How about a little bit of both...and dumplings?" she asked.

"A woman after my own heart." He smiled and gave her a quick kiss. "Be back soon, sweetheart."

* * *

Josh had spent months trying to forget his parents and even longer trying to forgive them for just being the cold and inhuman people they were. But his father was making it increasingly difficult for Josh to cut them out of his life. His father's phone calls had started over a year ago, the night after his father's attorney had bailed Josh out of a heap of trouble and aggravation. Still, Josh felt he owed his father nothing. Richard Graham was expecting more than a thank-you and Josh wasn't even prepared to say those two painful words. He deleted his father's voicemails without even listening to them.

The texts came next, which again he deleted, though only after reading them first. Surprisingly, his father was not waiting for his son to voice his appreciation. Rather, within each text, he had asked Josh to contact his mother because she missed him and wanted to meet for dinner in the city when he was in between semesters. Josh wanted to believe that his mother was willing to wait to see him so his studies wouldn't be interrupted, which suggested that she actually respected what he was doing with his life. Even after everything that had happened, Josh couldn't pretend any longer that her approval didn't matter or that he didn't miss being part of a family. Finally, just three weeks ago, he had picked up the phone, dialed his mother and arranged to meet her in New York at her favorite restaurant.

Driving into the city for many was a headache and a source of unhealthy stress, but for Josh, he always marveled at the city's beauty, the life it exuded, the bright lights against a darkening sky. But his appreciation dimmed significantly as he stared into a sea of taillights, which caused him to adjust his speed from seventy to a complete standstill. With some extra time to kill, Josh thought about how this night could go. It wasn't an accident that he had chosen this date, this particular night to spend time with his mother. The anniversary of Julia's death was always difficult. He had hoped that for the first time, he and his mother could grieve together and remember a woman who had left this world too soon.

Chapter Sixty-Three

Chase stared at his children in awe. They were mere specks at this stage, but they were his. They were clearly labeled, "Baby A" and "Baby B." He couldn't help but wonder if Erin was carrying boys, girls or one of each. It didn't matter; he would adore whatever combination he and Erin had created in love.

It was during their meeting with the doctor when he finally was able to introduce himself properly as the father and Erin's fiancé. The doctor didn't gloss over the importance of proper nutrition, rest, and mild exercise. Dr. Martinez must have sensed his apprehension, though he would have asked despite the embarrassment it would bring to both he and Erin, because she mentioned that sexual intercourse was still something they could partake in, but that they might want to refrain from such activity as they approached the last month of pregnancy.

He couldn't wait to get Erin home to celebrate their baby news and the fact that she was going to be his wife.

* * *

Erin, Andrew and Chase were leaving the doctor's office when Erin gasped. "I left my prenatal vitamins on the counter while we were checking out." She turned and started walking back into the building when she noticed something red splattered across her chest. Puzzled, she looked around to see Chase standing there, his back toward her, and swaying eerily. "Get back into the building, Erin, *now*!" screamed Andrew, rushing over to Chase. "And call nine-one-one."

Erin wanted to see what was causing Andrew to raise his voice in a way that sounded desperate and full of panic, but she complied and ran back into the high-rise. She withdrew her phone and made the call. It was only when Andrew reappeared with Chase's arm draped around his neck and then laid him on one of the lobby's couches that she knew what to say to the nine-one-one operator.

Erin looked down and watched Andrew apply pressure to Chase's left shoulder. There was so much blood, and it was clear that Chase was on the verge of passing out. "My boyfriend's been shot...I think. Send an ambulance to the Wallford Building on Twenty-Fourth," she said and ended the call. Erin rushed over to examine the wound. If Erin wanted to know if she had what it took to be in the field of medicine, to not crack under pressure, this was the time to find out.

Erin pushed her emotions aside and forgot for a moment that the man she hovered over to assess was the same man who had just proposed to her. "Andrew, get me some water and towels," she said, ripping Chase's bloodstained shirt open. Chase hissed from the jolting movement, which Erin considered to be a positive thing.

"Keep your eyes on me," Erin said, "Don't fade on me, now. I'll just think it's your way of getting out of marrying me, you know, to avoid me tying you down, making you off-limits to every woman in the world."

Andrew came back with a bottle of water and some hand towels. Erin splashed some water on the area in which she thought the wound was. It was difficult to tell for certain, due to the massive pool of blood, but the bullet hole finally came into view. She wanted to breathe a sigh of relief, but he still wasn't completely out of danger. Although the bullet appeared to have missed every major organ and artery, she wasn't comfortable with the amount of blood he was losing.

With Andrew's help, she pressed on the wound with the clean white towels to help ebb the flow of blood. "In my heart, we are already married," Chase said, his voice gravelly. His eyes fluttered before he passed out in her arms.

* * *

Scott was thankful that he had devoted the time to ensure that his weapon could be disassembled in ten seconds or less. He had practiced for hours in the comfort of his home, breaking down the suppressed .308 rifle and placing it back into the briefcase. In a suit and tie, coming to and from a hospital every day, the briefcase would appear to be an appropriate accessory, part of his attire.

From the dark and secluded alleyway between two impressive buildings, Scott marveled at the chaos he had created. But he knew that he couldn't linger. There was an alibi to secure and Chinese food to pick up. He grabbed his briefcase and walked in the opposite direction from the Wallford Building, where people were swarming and hunkering down in fear of more gunfire. He hailed a cab and jumped in.

As the distance grew, Scott felt more empowered, and very much at ease. But he was not completely satisfied. He had hoped to have the time to fire off a few more rounds and take out the Whore as well. But the fucking bodyguard had gotten her out of the line of fire so quickly that he would just have to settle for claiming the one life for now.

Scott directed the cabbie to pull over about a block up from the Chinese restaurant. He paid his fare in cash and walked the rest of the way. He had called on his way to the assassination and put his order in. The food should be ready by now. As he'd hoped, Scott entered the restaurant, paid the bill, and generously tipped the young waitress. If he hustled, taking a few back-alley short cuts, he could be at Plain Jane's apartment in minutes.

Just feet from her building, he hit up a flower vendor on the street and bought a huge bouquet of roses. This was going to be the only tricky part of the evening. Scott knew he couldn't just walk in through the main entrance of her apartment building. His tail needed to believe that he had been at Plain Jane's the entire evening. He had been able to leave undetected through a back entrance, but the door had locked behind him.

Earlier, when Scott had been having coffee with Plain Jane, he had taken notice of the rickety old fire escape leading from her balcony to the ground below. With the flowers secured between his teeth and the plastic bag of Chinese food in his hand, Scott climbed the death trap of steps and hopped onto her balcony. Scott peered in through the French door and noticed Plain Jane setting the kitchen table for two. He put the flowers behind his back and tapped the glass with his knuckle. Plain Jane's jaw dropped as she raced to the door and undid the latch.

"How did you get up here," she asked, clearly shocked and looking over the balcony.

"I tried out your fire escape, which by the way should be condemned, to surprise you…and to give you these," he said, unveiling the flowers.

"Oh my God! Climbing up my escape…with flowers…you're just like Richard Gere in *Pretty Woman!*"

"Let me guess, one of your chick flicks you are so fond of?" he asked, smiling.

Plain Jane gave him a kissed, which was thankfully not prolonged, and said, "A chick flick that just so happens to star Julia Roberts," she said, looking all googly-eyed and pathetic.

"Well, what are you waiting for? Press PLAY. I want to know if Richard Gere has anything on me," he said, chuckling.

Chapter Sixty-Four

Josh had been fooling himself these last few weeks into thinking that his mother wasn't the calculating, heartless woman that she was. Amidst the stop-and-go traffic, he stared at the text that she had sent him just minutes ago and cursed until he was hoarse. No, she wasn't getting off that easy.

Josh dialed his mother and waited through four rings before she picked up.

"Do you know what day it is?" he asked, barely able to contain his disdain for the woman who had given him life.

"Hello to you, too, sweetheart. Yes, I'm aware that we scheduled our date for tonight, but your father needs me to attend an impromptu business dinner with him. It's extremely important that I be there, you know, for appearance's sake. I'm sorry to tell you this on such short notice. I hope it's not a terrible inconvenience."

Josh felt ill, but he wasn't going to end the phone call without letting her have it. It was the last time he was going to speak to her, so why hold back? "You really don't know why tonight is so significant?"

Silence. It had either dawned on her that tonight was the anniversary of Julia's death or she was racking her brain for enlightenment.

"Let me help you out. I chose tonight so we could be together for Julia. You remember Julia, don't you?" he asked, no longer withholding his anger.

With a sharp tongue, one he remembered clearly from his childhood, she lashed out and said, "You have always been sentimental, never able to let go of things. It's what makes you weak."

Josh couldn't believe what he was hearing. "So remembering Julia, how wonderful she was, makes me weak in your eyes?" he asked. But he didn't really care anymore to hear her response. "Why did you ask to see me in the first place?"

His mother sighed and said, "Your father and I know that the money you stole from us, the money you were secretly transferring from one account to another, must be gone by now. We were hoping you would abandon the pipe dream and return home where you belong, at your father's side, preparing to take over the business. He wishes to retire in two years and if you would just come to your senses, like you should have years ago, his empire could be yours."

And with that, all hope for one day reuniting with his family was lost.

* * *

The police had come to the hospital and had taken their statements, which were short and devoid of anything that could suggest that Scott Morris or Josh Graham could have pulled the trigger. It killed Erin to play dumb, but she knew that Chase, Andrew and Paul had plans of their own.

Erin had told the police officer that they were leaving her ob-gyn's office, where she had discovered that she was pregnant with twins, when Chase was shot. That must have struck a chord in the man in blue, because his serious tone softened after that and he concluded the interview. Andrew's statement was brief and confirmed everything Erin had said. Chase had hung on long enough to give the police what they wanted, which was a garbled plea for them to find his fiancé's stalker, before drifting off again.

"He has lost a tremendous amount of blood, but he'll be okay. With the pain meds, Mr. Montclair should sleep peacefully for several hours," the doctor said, giving Erin a comforting smile.

"Thank you, but I would like to spend the night with him."

The doctor's face fell when he asked, "Are you family?"

Erin could have lied, but she didn't have the strength. "No, though he had proposed to me just minutes before he was shot." Erin looked at Chase, who was partaking in a chemically assisted sleep.

The doctor shifted from one foot to the other, as if he was uncomfortable to be on the receiving end of something so personal. "Well, I believe that's close enough. I'll have a nurse bring a cot in for you."

Erin smiled and thanked the doctor before he left. Once alone, Erin let the tears flow freely. They receded somewhat when Andrew took her in his arms and held her for what felt like hours. "We'll get him, Erin. I promise you," he said.

Erin stepped out of Andrew's embrace. "When, Andrew? When it's too late? How many people need to be killed or wounded because of me?" she asked. With Chase out of the woods, all that concern morphed into white-hot fury. And what she sought, what she needed, were answers…and then revenge.

"You haven't caused this, Erin," Paul said from the doorway of Chase's hospital room. Mia was standing next to him, holding his hand.

"No? Really? Look at him. He's proof that being around me is dangerous," she said, pointing at Chase. Erin suddenly felt like she was going to vomit, and pregnancy had nothing to do with it this time. It had finally hit her that if the bullet had struck just a few inches over, Chase wouldn't be lying here. He would be in a body bag in the basement of the hospital.

Erin pushed past the nausea and walked over to her purse. The days of sitting back and doing nothing were over. She took out her phone and started to dial when Paul asked, "Who are you calling?"

"I'm cutting our small suspect list down to one," she said.

"No need," Andrew said, staring at his own phone. "Just received a text from Alex, one of the men I had assigned to locate Josh Graham. Apparently, Graham showed up at your old apartment, where he is ready and waiting to be questioned."

Erin grabbed her purse and started for the door.

"You're not going there alone," Paul said, blocking Erin's path.

"I don't care who wants to join me, but I'm confronting Josh tonight," she said.

Mia, the voice of reason, spoke out. "I'll stay here with Chase while Paul goes with you. In the meantime, I'll speak with Frank to ensure that Morris's whereabouts were accounted for the entire night." Mia stood between Paul and Erin and said, "Confront him…but don't kill him, especially if you're holding him against his will." Mia kissed Paul and then gave Erin a hug. "Chase and I don't want to visit either of you in prison."

Chapter Sixty-Five

With his hands and feet tied to the chair and duct tape sealing his mouth shut, Josh looked like he was starring in some mob movie. The emotions were flying as Erin stared at her best friend and possible rapist. Erin summoned all her strength, walked over and ripped the tape away. He winced, as it couldn't have felt good to have the tiny hairs on his face peeled away from his flesh in one fell swoop.

"Jesus Christ, Erin! What the hell is going on?" he growled. Andrew and the man who had apparently apprehended him and dragged him into her old apartment stepped closer.

Erin didn't want this to take too long. She wanted to get back to Chase and take care of him. So, she decided to just put it all out on the table. "I was raped while we were in college…that last night of class, after Dr. Farrell's final exam. I never saw his face, never had an idea of who could have done such a thing."

Standing over him, she watched for a reaction, one that would go beyond the scope of normal. His eyes grew wide and she noticed that he stopped breathing for a moment.

"That's why you left like you did…I always wondered." He looked up at her. "Why didn't you tell me?" he asked.

Unable to tell if he was being sincere or if he was just the most talented actor she had ever seen, she withdrew her cell phone and showed him the text she'd had Mia forward to her own cell. "Why would you send this to my friend, Josh?" she asked.

His eyes narrowed as he read the words. "I didn't send that. Who's Mia?" he asked.

"No? You didn't send this?" Erin asked. Appearing dazed, he shook his head. "Who has Josh's phone?" Erin asked. The man to Josh's left handed over the phone.

Erin scanned his sent mail and found the text. She put his phone directly in front of his face and said, "I think you should rethink your story, Josh."

"I'm telling you I didn't send that. And I don't even know a Mia or an Angel. For Christ's sake, why don't you believe me?" he yelled.

She crossed her arms to conceal her trembling fingers. "Why are you in New York tonight?" she asked, disregarding his words completely. Her heart was racing and she felt like she was going to throw up.

"Not that I would expect you to mark your calendar for something so morbid, but tonight is Julia's anniversary. I was meeting my mother for dinner, but she cancelled at the last minute. Since I was already in the city, I thought I would come by and surprise you."

His excuse was logical and as much as she hated to admit it, very plausible. Still, that text hovered over her, demanding her attention. "You're here, tied up like this, because the evidence I have points to you."

Now it was his turn to look like he was going to be sick. The expression on his face was one of betrayal and heartbreak. "I would never hurt you, Erin. You were like a sister to me. You reminded me so much of Julia, from the way you laughed to the way you…just accepted me for who I was."

Erin felt the tears begin to form and she wanted so much to run over, cut him loose and shower him with apologies. But she could never live with even the slightest bit of doubt. It would fester and eat away at her forever.

"How can I prove it to you…that I wasn't the man who…hurt you?" he said, struggling for words.

"Where were you that night? Where did you go after you left Erin with Dr. Farrell?" Paul asked, stepping out of the shadows. He had remained quiet, giving Erin full control of the interrogation, until now.

Josh lowered his head and stared at the ground.

Before Erin realized it, Paul had Josh by the throat and was squeezing the life out of him. Josh was gasping for breath when Erin yelled for Paul to stop. Paul let go of him, but Erin could tell it was the last thing he wanted to do.

"Back off, Paul. Please," she said. It killed her to ask this of him, but she knew she had to do this her way. "Did you go to the Irish Pub…like you said?"

Josh's breathing was slowly returning to a healthy pace and the color in his face had taken on a more natural hue. Josh shook his head. "No." Josh looked her squarely in the eye. "I spent that evening in a jail cell, Erin."

Erin looked over at Andrew and saw his brow rise. "Explain, Graham," Andrew demanded.

"After class, I went to visit a woman who I had been seeing. I hadn't planned it, but she had sent me a text, and well..."

"The friend?" Erin asked. She suddenly remembered. "Right before you left me alone with Dr. Farrell, you smiled and said..."

"'She'll never hold a candle to you, sweetheart,'" Josh said, finishing her thought, a thought that was now permanently in her memory. There was so much regret in his eyes that Erin had to look away.

"I had been seeing Lindsey for a few weeks, but she had never asked me to come to her place until that night. I didn't think much of it. I didn't care enough to wonder why. She wasn't looking for a relationship, either. And she never asked for more than I could give." Josh's voice cracked, prompting Erin to look at him once more. The regret she had perceived in his eyes had been replaced with what looked like shame. Erin didn't want to think of the college boy she loved like a brother; she wanted to be strong and finish this.

"Lindsey and I were in the middle of having sex when her husband came home."

Those feelings of pity she had for Josh were in the process of fading when he continued. "I didn't know she was married. I would never have gotten involved with her if I had. She never wore a wedding band, never let on once that she belonged to someone else until her husband's fist found my jaw. I fought back, but I knew I deserved the black eye and split lip he gave me. I didn't know how much commotion we had caused until the police showed up and took me in."

Erin saw Andrew withdraw his phone from his pocket. Like always, he was one step ahead of her. "We should be able to confirm his story easily, right Andrew? Since he was arrested?"

Josh shook his head. "It's not likely you will find any record of me gracing the Ninth District Headquarters with my presence that · night. My father's attorney made sure of it."

"Ninth District?" Andrew asked.

Josh nodded.

Andrew was in the process of dialing when he walked to the other side of the room, out of earshot.

Erin didn't question Andrew and decided to focus her attention on Josh. "You told me you haven't spoken to either of your parents since…Julia. Why would your father come to your aid, Josh? And why would you accept his help?" Erin was truly perplexed. The stories Josh had shared with her, the coldness he had to endure as a child, left him completely justified to shut them out of his life for all eternity.

"I didn't have an opportunity to tell my father's attorney to get the hell out, that I would rather spend my remaining savings on hiring a lawyer to get my ass out of trouble. But everything had been taken care of before I could stop it. Why? Because my father thought that if he bailed me out, I would be grateful. And to show my appreciation, I would return to New York to run a company that has blood on its hands."

Josh's eyes grew dark and Erin could tell he was back in that place he could go to once in a great while. But as quickly as the darkness would consume him, it would leave, and the carefree and wonderful person she had grown to love would come back to her. But those shadows did not fade, not this time. He was most likely thinking of how his mother and father's greed had driven him and his sister from their childhood home and onto the Garden State Parkway, a long dark stretch of road that claimed the life of a beautiful girl. It took everything Erin had not to run over and hug her best friend and chase his demons away.

"What time did you leave the police station, Josh?" Her voice wavered, but she stood her ground.

"It was a little after midnight. By one in the morning I was lying in my bed, alone, and chasing a few Motrin with a few swigs of Jack before calling it a night."

"Paul, release him," Andrew said. He was no longer talking on the phone and was walking toward her.

Paul had been quiet, to the point Erin had forgotten that her brother was there. He had listened to her and knew that she needed to control this. And she loved him for it.

Andrew stopped and stood in front of her. He took both her hands in his and said, "I spent some time in Philly as an officer. I still have ties there, to the Ninth District in particular. I asked an officer, a friend I've known for years to dig for me, to confirm that Joshua Graham had been brought in that night. My friend, a man I trust, said Josh wasn't arrested, but there is still record of him being there and that he didn't leave until midnight. Erin, Josh's story checks out. He's not the one, honey."

Erin nodded and sobbed into her hands. Her legs grew weak. Andrew embraced her. Paul finished untying Josh and then took over for Andrew, allowing her to weep against his chest. But there was someone else in the room who deserved more attention than she did. Trembling, Erin stepped out of Paul's firm grasp and looked at her best friend. "I'm so sorry, Josh. I just…" she broke down and cried harder. Josh came over and held her, allowing her to cry a year's worth of tears.

"Shh. Don't cry," he said, stroking her hair. Erin had no idea how he couldn't be furious with her. "You could have told me what had happened to you, but I understand why you didn't," he said, squeezing her tight. "I meant what I said. You were, are, like a sister to me."

Erin didn't deserve him. What she had just put him through was unforgivable, the horrific things she had accused him of, yet there he stood, speaking words of comfort and compassion.

"God, I've missed you," she said. "More than you know."

Chapter Sixty-Six

Mia felt overwhelming relief when she received Paul's phone call. Although she knew from the start that Josh didn't meet the profile, evidence had been brought forth suggesting that he might be the man they were looking for. Paul didn't tell Mia exactly how they extracted information from Josh, satisfying Paul, Erin and Andrew that Josh was innocent, but she didn't care. Right now, the focus needed to be on their one and only suspect.

Paul and Erin were on their way back to the hospital when Frank called in, as directed. Morris's car was still parked next to Jennifer Freehold's little yellow Beetle in her apartment parking lot. Neither Jennifer nor Morris had emerged since he had arrived at her place after work.

Mia was beyond frustrated, which caused her to formulate a plan that might upset those around her, including the man she was falling madly in love with. No doubt he would try to stop her, maybe even physically if necessary. So if she was going to do this, it had to be now.

Mia walked out into the hallway and fortunately found Chase's doctor at the nurses' station. He appeared concerned that she had sought him out, so Mia quickly said, "Do you expect Mr. Montclair to wake anytime soon? I was going to run down to the cafeteria for a sandwich." She was lying through her teeth.

"Not with the level of meds we gave him. He will most likely sleep through the night, which is for the best. I think it's safe for you to go to the cafeteria, though I don't know how safe it is to eat a sandwich from there. Stick with the soup," he said, his eyes kind.

"Thanks for the warning. I'll be back," she said, turning to retrieve her bodyguard and almost slamming into a very angry-looking Paul.

He had been closer to the hospital than she thought when he had called her. "Going somewhere?" Paul asked, his eyes dark.

Yeah, he was definitely furious with her. And how in God's name did he know that she was sneaking away to pay Jennifer Freehold and her boyfriend a visit?

It didn't matter, because now she was going to have to backpedal...and fast. "I was going to grab something to eat. But now, I'd rather hear about what happened with Josh," she said, hoping he was buying even an ounce of her bullshit.

Paul took her by the hand and led her back into Chase's hospital room. Erin and Uncle Drew followed them into the room. Paul shut the door behind them and said, "Mia, tell me you weren't planning to go rogue on me. Tell me that you weren't going to take matters into your own hands and slip away, putting your life in even more danger than it already is? Because if you need a clear picture of just how serious this situation is then all you have to do is look at Chase."

"Yeah, I don't mind being the reminder you apparently need, Mia," Chase said, his voice gruff.

Erin ran over and hugged him, though she was cautious to steer clear of his left shoulder. She was kissing him and crawling into his bed when he said, "Careful, Erin."

"Oh, I'm sorry, did I hurt you?" Erin asked, her eyes worried and full of panic.

"No. I'm fine. But you need to be careful. Those little peanuts shouldn't be jostled around," Chase said, kissing her lovingly.

"Little peanuts? Erin?" Paul asked, looking from Chase to his sister.

"You didn't tell them?" Chase asked with a smile so big it took up his entire face.

Erin shook her head and then looked at her brother. "I'm pregnant."

"With twins," Chase added, as if he couldn't contain himself any longer.

Mia was on the verge of squealing with delight when Paul crushed the moment by saying, "If I would have known you were pregnant, I would never have allowed you to confront Josh tonight."

"How long have I been out of it? You went to Philly to see Josh?" Chase asked, his tone laced with anger. Gone was the love and playful giddiness.

"Josh was in New York tonight to see his mother, but had stopped by my old apartment to see me. Paul and I went with Andrew to the apartment to rule Josh out as a suspect," Erin said. Mia felt bad for Erin; dealing with one domineering man was hard enough, but two was exhausting.

"And?"

"And he's not our guy," Paul said, interjecting.

"How can you be so sure?" Chase asked, still not convinced, and still very pissed off that all this had happened while he was lying on his back in a hospital room.

"He was too busy being hauled in by the police for fighting with his then-girlfriend's husband that night. He was in jail during the time in question. Andrew called in a favor with a buddy of his at that particular precinct to confirm Josh's alibi."

Chase went silent, as he was most likely digesting what they had already had time to process. His eyes narrowed and he looked at Erin. "What do Paul and I have to do to keep you two safe? Lock you both in my penthouse and throw away the key?" Chase asked, only half kidding. Mia had the feeling that he would do just that if it came down to it.

"That's the best plan I've heard all day. Speaking of locking you in the penthouse, let's head home and leave these parents-to-be alone," Paul said, taking Mia by the hand.

"Newly *engaged* parents-to-be," Erin said, sliding off Chase's bed and holding up her left hand. The sparkling diamond was breathtaking, and this time Mia did squeal for joy.

Chapter Sixty-Seven

Alex escorted Mia and Paul to Chase's apartment, where he would remain on high alert indefinitely. Uncle Drew stayed behind with Erin and Chase, guarding that hospital room with his life. Mia got the sense when she had told her uncle good-bye for the night that he had blamed himself for what had happened to Chase. But Chase wasn't his assignment, Erin was. And she and the two babies growing inside her were safe and sound.

As much as she wanted a night alone with Paul, Mia wasn't sure where Paul's head was at the moment. Between Josh's interrogation and discovering that his sister was engaged and having twins, his mind had to be teeming with emotions. Playing it safe, she quickly showered and retired for the night while Paul discussed security with Alex in the living room.

* * *

Paul entered the bedroom with a level of hunger he had never experienced before. And what he craved was the woman who lay asleep in the plush king-sized bed. Wearing just a t-shirt, her mahogany hair draped across the satin pillow, she was breathtaking, and in every way his.

He too showered, washing away his experiences of the day, and returned to the bed. Mia hadn't moved and as he slid in next to her, she sighed and nestled closer, bringing her back firmly against his chest. Lying on her side, Paul looked down at her curvy hip and appreciated the fact that she wasn't sickly thin, that she was lush and all woman. He wove one of his legs through hers and enjoyed just how well she fit, molded around his body. His arousal was pressed against her lower back, aching to take her, and that was when he heard her whisper, "Love me tonight."

"Every night," he said, rolling her over onto her back and kissing her fiercely.

Her t-shirt and panties flew away and he was inside her in moments. He would have loved to have taken her slowly, spending hours pleasuring every inch of her body with his tongue, massaging her clit with his fingers in slow, rhythmic strokes, but he needed to be inside her now.

And the way she writhed beneath him, grasping his ass as he slammed into her, suggested that she wanted him just as much. He loved the sounds she made, that she was comfortable enough to tell him to go slow or give it to her harder. Her body was made to take what he so wanted to give her. But was her heart ready? There was only one way to find out. And as recent events proved, life was short, demanding one not to be foolish and put off what may not be there tomorrow.

Mia moaned as her tight channel clenched around his cock. Her climax, as was his, was close. "Feels so good!" she groaned, against his ear. Her hot breath against his skin almost put him over the edge. Paul pulled out of her, until just the tip remained, and then thrust into her, making her back arch. She was screaming for him to take her, to give her more. With their fingers entwined, he placed her hands firmly above her head as he continued with his deep thrusts.

"I'll love you tonight, every night if you'll have me," he said, pushing into her.

"Every night," she said, breathless, her body quivering.

He forced himself to slow down, though he remained deep inside her. She needed to know exactly what he meant, that there was no turning back. Paul kissed her and she welcomed his greedy tongue. He moaned, knowing that he wasn't going to last. She felt that good.

"You're mine, baby." He slid out and then plunged back into her, taking her by surprise and sending her into an immediate orgasm. She screamed his name as she climaxed again and again.

He watched her body shake, riding out each glorious wave. She was beautiful. "I love you, Mia," he said.

Mia wrapped her legs around him and brought him even closer. "I love you," she said, taking him deeper than he ever thought possible.

Chapter Sixty-Eight

Scott's day had started off shitty and as he listened to his voice mail, he determined that it may have gotten worse. His father's attorney, Roger Epstein, wanted to discuss his father's will as soon as possible. The tone of the message did not sit well with him. Something was wrong.

And he'd thought that learning his attempt to put Chase Montclair six feet under had failed was going to be the most frustrating part of his day. Now, he actually considered Montclair's survival to be the least of his worries. Ironically enough, his deceased father was up to something. Angry, but not wanting to neglect his health, he shut down his computer and left to have lunch at his usual Friday hot spot.

* * *

Mia had one hour to find and dine with the devil, which wouldn't be too difficult since Morris was a creature of habit. According to

Frank, he would be at the Fine Meadow, an organic beans-and-greens type of establishment, for a late lunch.

As her last student exited the back door to the playground, Mia grabbed her purse and took to the street with bodyguard in tow. She lied to Alex and told him that she was in the mood for a Carmen's sub like nobody's business. Alex looked excited and in need of a foot-long sandwich. But as she walked past the famous deli, leaving Alex confused and now two steps behind her, she hustled ahead and entered the Fine Meadow.

And just like Frank had said, Morris was there and standing in a surprisingly long line. Mia had no idea so many people loved bean sprouts. Mia turned around and told Alex, who looked understandably annoyed, to grab a table for the two of them. He was definitely smarter than he looked because within a moment of scanning the small restaurant, Alex knew what she had done. "We are leaving," he said, while staring at the back of Morris's head.

"No, we're not. He's defenseless here. Trust me," Mia said, taking her place in line before Alex could stop her. She turned to Alex and mouthed that she was sorry, but he was not in a forgiving mood. Instead, he looked downright pissed as he stood by the door. Mia also caught Frank's disapproving eye from across the restaurant and she quickly turned away.

With her gut twisted in knots and in no way able to ingest something that looked like weeds, she moved closer to Morris. There were so many things that could go wrong, but it was worth the gamble…and Paul and her uncle's wrath when they found out about what she had done. Their meager list of suspects had been cut down to one and everything, all her experience, told her that Scott Morris was the psychopath they had been hunting. Despite Frank telling her that Morris had been at Jennifer Freehold's apartment during the shooting, somehow, Morris had managed to be in two places at once.

Mia leaned in, close enough to breathe in his scent. He smelled of soap and aftershave. Clean and kept. "Would an angel recognize her demon?" she whispered.

Mia watched his back go rigid as he continued to stare ahead. When he didn't answer her, she pressed on and said, "Let me see you."

His fists clenched at his sides and then relaxed. "Please," she uttered, her voice breathy.

Finally, he turned and gave her a smile that would captivate and melt any woman in the room. But Mia was not deceived by his handsome face or his sophisticated attire. She had seen the look he was giving her more times than she cared to admit. It was the look of a killer.

"Why don't you tell me, Mia?" he said, moving so close she could smell his minty mouthwash. "Do angels sense evil?"

Mia knew this confrontation could only go one of two ways. Morris was either going to pretend he didn't know her or succumb to temptation and expose himself, all the while doing it with a smile. Mia was hoping for the latter, which would throw him off his game and make him readjust. It appeared she was getting her wish.

"Apparently, both kinds sense it, can feel it deep within," Mia said, her eyes locked on Morris's. She licked her lips and his gaze drifted to her mouth. His breathing hitched in his throat and she thought she heard a hint of a groan. Mia knew she was baiting him, pushing him to see just how far he would go, how close he was to breaking.

"Both kinds?" he asked.

"Yes. The pristine and the fallen." she said. And then she dropped the hammer. She shook her head, as if she felt sorry for him. "Are you telling me that you no longer can detect a fallen angel when you see one? Even when she is standing directly in front of you?"

His eyes grew even darker. The lust she had seen in them just moments ago had been replaced by something sinister and threatening. Despite her bodyguard only being several feet away, fear overtook her. She was looking at someone, something that murdered without rational cause and preyed on women. Scott's features morphed and she found herself staring at the man who she had let get away with murder. Scott's clean-shaven face was now marred with a scar across his right cheek, though week-old stubble concealed it a bit. His cheeks were sunken in and his hazel eyes were bloodshot. Although his brown hair flowed past his shoulders, it was scraggly and thinning on top. He smiled. Perfect teeth no longer greeted her. His remaining teeth were now stained and decaying from years of neglect and drug use.

Mia's heart pounded. She knew her mind was playing tricks on her. Scott was not the man who murdered and raped her mother. But there he stood, resembling the man Mia faced in that courtroom, the man she had made certain would never leave his prison cell. Mia's head started to spin and she stumbled backward.

Scott's smile grew and he once again was the animal who had attacked Erin and not her mother. Scott took a step toward her. He leaned in and whispered, "I can smell him on you."

Her pulse was racing. But before she could speak, he continued and said, "Where is Paul, Mia? Have you seen him lately?" His smug grin sent her into a panic.

Paul.

She hadn't spoken to him since he kissed her good-bye this morning before he dropped her off at work. Mia shook her head. No. Paul is fine. He's at work, exactly where he should be in the middle of the day. I'm the target. Not Paul. He's just fine. This is what psychopaths do best. They manipulate and play mind games.

Scott's smile was all encompassing. Despite her time on the force and all those years profiling sick, soulless killers with her dad and her uncle, dread seized her and wouldn't let go. She needed to get to Paul. Mia tore away from Scott and flew out of the restaurant. Mia was gasping for air and trying to gain her sense of balance when Alex joined her on the sidewalk.

"When's the last time you spoke to Paul!" she screamed. Mia started to rummage through her purse in search of her cell phone.

"I checked in with him at ten this morning. Why, Mia? What's happened?" Alex asked.

"That was two hours ago!" She was still wrestling with her purse when Alex retrieved his cell phone and started to dial.

Mia was hysterical. Sobbing and feeling completely helpless, she threw her purse on the ground and started to run in the direction of Paul's office building.

* * *

Paul had sprinted two city blocks before he spotted her. She turned and looked at him with both fear and relief in her eyes. The woman he was in love with was either out of her mind for confronting Morris or she had a plan that no one in their group was privy to. He thought he had made himself clear last night at the hospital, but apparently he had been mistaken.

Alex appeared frustrated and pissed, as he should for being duped by his assignment. Andrew was definitely going to hear about this.

"You're okay," she said. Mia fell into his arms and sobbed.

"I'm fine, Mia. What happened? Why the hell did you confront Morris?"

She wiggled out of his grasp and stood before him. "Paul, let me explain why I did what I did," Mia pleaded.

"You will…later," he said. Paul took her by the arm and led her in the opposite direction from the restaurant. He was so angry with her at the moment that he could barely get out the words.

"Wait, Paul, I know you're mad but if you knew why…"

Paul stopped and pulled her under the awning of the closest shop. Alex maintained his distance and gave them some privacy. "Mad? You can't begin to know just how furious I am with you, how worried I was when Alex called me and told me that you approached Morris," he whispered.

"I'm so sorry. But I had to know, we had to know for sure. I couldn't wait another day, another hour. I was afraid I would be too late…again."

Paul felt his anger recede somewhat as he looked into her haunted eyes. He didn't realize how important this case was to her, how connected she felt to it, until now. Although Mia had found her mother's killer, her dad had already given up on life, no longer wanting to live in a world without his wife. Paul could now sympathize, as he couldn't imagine spending even a day without Mia.

"Come here," he said, pulling her into his arms. He kissed her forehead and stroked her hair. "Mia, you know you have nothing to prove. You did everything you could to catch your mother's killer," he said.

"But it wasn't enough and because I couldn't put two and two together quicker, my dad had no other alternative than to join his wife."

"I have some news for you, Mia. And please don't take this the wrong way. But your dad died the day your mother did, maybe not physically, but in every other sense of the word. It probably wouldn't have mattered if you had found her killer within twelve hours of the murder or twelve months later. The end result was always going to be the same and he couldn't live with that."

Mia was crying into his chest, a sight he had rarely seen. She had always been so strong, the most put-together and level-headed member of their small group. But now, every emotion bubbled up to the surface and Paul was thankful that she had chosen him to unload upon. "How do you know that?" she asked, sniffling, her voice broken.

Paul backed away and lifted her chin with two fingers. Gazing into her eyes, he said, "If anything ever happened to you, I would be forever lost. I meant what I said last night and this morning when you awoke in my arms. I love you, Mia."

With tears streaming down her face, she threw her arms around his neck and told him she loved him and how sorry she was for taking matters into her own hands. All the anger he had felt just minutes ago dissipated and he held on to her tightly, as if his life depended on it. Paul didn't care that people may have overheard their declaration of love for each other, but it did concern him that Mia was standing on the sidewalk of a busy New York City street, exposed and vulnerable. "Let's get you home," he said, unwrapping himself from arms that he never wanted to leave.

Paul hailed a cab and was thankful to see one skid to a stop within seconds. He ushered her into the cab and Alex followed. "This will end soon," he said, pulling her so close that she was practically sitting on his lap.

Mia looked up at him. "You're right." she said. Mia leaned in and whispered, "Especially since he has made himself known."

Paul hadn't forgotten about Mia's luncheon with Morris or why she had gone there in the first place, but even that had taken a backseat to the important discussion they had had on the street. It was just further confirmation that he was in love with her, that nothing else mattered. "Mia, are you telling me that he admitted to…everything? That he's the one?"

"That's exactly what I'm saying," she said.

Paul had been dreaming of the moment when he knew with absolute certainty who had hurt his sister, the coward behind the mask. With the fucker now exposed, he and Chase, and the rest of Andrew's small army, could convene and finalize their plan to rid the world of Scott Morris.

Paul knocked on the plastic between the front and back seats. "Change of plans. Take us to Mercy General," Paul said to the driver. He withdrew his phone and within seconds, Mia could hear a man's voice on the other end. "Frank, where is Morris?" Mia couldn't make out what Frank had said, but it couldn't have been good. Paul's jaw was clenched and his fingers gripped the phone so tightly she swore he was going to crush it. "He's not in the bathroom, he's running. Find him!" he spat, through gritted teeth.

Chapter Sixty-Nine

It had been thirty-two minutes since her last mad dash to the bathroom. Her morning sickness had stretched well past the morning hours, though her bouts of vomiting were less violent now. Being a woman and an aspiring doctor, Erin knew that this particular pregnancy symptom was common. But common or not, it was still a real pain in the ass.

Erin stretched out in the hospital cot and glanced at the book her brother had left her that morning while she slept. Again, she chuckled over the book's title, *Pregnant with Twins! What the #$%! Do We Do Now?*

Erin didn't know where he found that book, but it was absolutely perfect. Finding out she was pregnant was a shock in itself. But twins? Well, that was just incredible…and so very wonderful. She looked over at the father of her children, who was sleeping peacefully in the bed beside her, and smiled. Erin couldn't believe that she'd had doubts over how he would feel about being a father, that he would think she had tricked him into all of this. It brought her such joy when she remembered just how happy he had been, how enthralled he was as he stared at the monitor and watched those two flickers of light for the first time. He had been mesmerized, as was she, by their babies' heartbeats.

Erin looked from Chase to the flawless diamond on her left hand. The platinum, diamond-encrusted band with the oval-shaped solitaire fit perfectly, and she was overwhelmed by the fact that this ring had been worn by his mother, a woman he had cherished. Erin was honored to wear his mother's ring and pleased beyond belief to learn that he hadn't given it to Gabrielle. Erin was human, after all, and though Gabrielle was dead, there were moments when she wondered why Chase not only carried on a relationship with someone like Gabrielle, but had been content to have a family with her.

Erin pushed that thought aside and refocused her attention on more pleasant things. Like the handwritten inscription on the book's jacket:

Came by this morning to give this book to you, but you were sound asleep.

You should see what I'm seeing right now. You're glowing, happy, and in love with a man that cherishes you like you deserve.

This is what I always wanted for you, what I always prayed for.

So, enjoy your rest, sweetheart, as you surely won't be getting any when my nieces or nephews come on the scene.

I love you.

—Paul

Sweet, loving, and overbearing. Erin couldn't imagine a better brother. And right on cue, Paul, Mia and Andrew appeared in the doorway of Chase's hospital room. But the smile she had been wearing as she read Paul's inscription faded when she saw her brother's and Mia's worried expressions.

"What's wrong?" Erin asked.

Paul closed the door behind them. Something had happened. The nausea she had been fighting all day raged on, and she suddenly felt cool and clammy.

"What happened?" Erin looked from Mia to Paul, pleading for one of them to answer her.

"We found him, Erin," Mia said.

Erin had waited so long to hear those words. She sat there in stunned silence, only coming to when she heard Chase rustling next to her.

Garbled but coherent, Chase asked, "What...what's going on?" With his good arm, he reached over and took Erin's hand.

"Scott Morris slipped today. He faltered, as Mia had hoped he would. There's no doubt, Erin," Paul said.

Erin shouldn't have been surprised; it wasn't like the list of suspects they had constructed was extensive. But the rapist's mask had been ripped away, which exposed him for the bastard that he was, and she became overwhelmed with emotion. Relief, fear and pain took hold of her as she replayed the scenes in which she had encountered Morris first over a year ago and then recently in New York.

She was going to be sick.

Erin stood and started for the bathroom when she felt the room begin to spin. Paul caught her right before she tasted floor. Her legs felt like Jell-O as Paul carried her limp body back to the cot.

"I'll get the doctor," Mia said, running for the door.

Chase bolted out of bed, disregarding the fact that he was hooked up to an IV and a monitor that tracked his vitals, and went to Erin. "My God, you're cold and sweaty." Erin knew that his shoulder had to hurt like hell, but he didn't show it as his focus was solely on her.

"I need a bucket...something," Erin said, putting her head between her legs.

Andrew grabbed the plastic pitcher of water from Chase's food tray, dumped it in the sink and handed her the empty container. "Thanks," she said.

Mia came back into the room just moments later with the doctor. Dr. Miller was calm as he walked over to the second patient in the room. "Let's have a look at you," he said.

"She's pregnant with twins, six weeks along," Chase said with urgency.

The doctor sat down next to Erin. "Ahh...well, let me ask you a few questions first. Have you been having morning sickness?"

"And afternoon sickness." Erin swallowed, fighting back a dry heave.

"Have you been drinking enough liquids?" the doctor asked.

Again Erin nodded, but then added, "But I haven't been able to keep anything down."

"Okay. One more question. Have you observed any bleeding?"

Erin knew what he was asking. Miscarriage was very common at this stage of pregnancy. Any bleeding was cause for concern, but luckily she hadn't noticed any blood on her many trips to the bathroom. "No, no bleeding," she said.

Erin felt Chase's tension recede, but then it mounted again as the doctor informed them both that she was in need of fluids. She was most likely dehydrated from all the vomiting and would need to be replenished through an IV. "Ms. Whitley, I'll send up the order for your IV," the doctor said. "I'm also recommending an exam and an ultrasound, just to be safe." Dr. Miller scribbled something on his clipboard and stood. "A nurse will be here soon to escort you to the fourth floor." Dr. Miller smiled and gave her arm a gentle pat. "You also need rest and some stress-free days."

Erin nodded. "Thank you," she said, embarrassed for not taking better care of herself.

The doctor shifted his attention to Chase, his actual patient, and said, "Well, Mr. Montclair, you may have earned yourself a few more hours here at luxurious Mercy General." Chase glanced at his shoulder and scowled. "Leaping out of bed like that, I'll be shocked if you didn't tear your sutures."

Chase allowed the doctor to peel away the dressing to his wound. It took less than a minute for the doctor to determine that Chase was going to be Mercy's guest for a little while longer.

"I'm sorry, Chase. I didn't mean to worry you," Erin said.

Chase's eyes did not soften as she had hoped. Instead, he looked determined, almost pissed. "The doctor wants you stress free, something that isn't going to happen if you are here with me in the hospital. After your IV, if you are discharged that is, I want you to go home and rest."

The thought of being away from Chase sent her into a tailspin. He was lying in this hospital bed because of her. There was no way she was leaving him. "No, I'm not going anywhere."

The hardened look on his face vanished and was replaced by compassion and love. "You and our babies are the most important people in my life. And you are all at risk if you stay here. Please don't fight me on this, Erin. Because I will win."

Erin loved his domineering side just as much as she adored his sweet and mushy side, though the dominance had been less frequent as of late, and understandably so. "You're so confident that I will just concede?" she asked, leaning into him.

"Yes. If you don't obey, I'll leave this hospital right now, against doctor's orders. So choose, Erin," Chase said, his lips curling into a grin.

"That's blackmail. You know I won't risk your health," Erin said, feeling defeated.

"And you won't risk yours or our babies," Chase said, pulling her into the crook of his good arm.

How could any expecting mother, a mother who was already in love with the two children growing inside her, argue with that?

Chapter Seventy

Chase waited until Erin had complied with the doctor's directive and left for the fourth floor with Alex and Mia before discussing his plan for Scott Morris. If it weren't for Erin and her near fainting, Chase would have flown out of that hospital and butchered the good doctor the moment his identity was confirmed. Now that the initial shock was over, Chase's rational side was able to intercede and help devise a plan with Andrew and Paul that would help them achieve their one and only goal: to rid their lives, the world, of Scott Morris leaving no breadcrumbs, crumbs that could lead back to them.

"Morris is on the run. After Mia outed him, he took off and successfully lost the tail we put on him," Paul said.

Chase attempted to get inside Scott Morris's head. What's he thinking right now? Where would he go? A monster that craves order and needs closure.

"No doubt he's draining his bank account as we speak," Andrew said. "He'll need all the money he can get his hands on to disappear."

"Maybe." Chase stood from his hospital bed. His shoulder hurt like a bitch but he couldn't deal with that now. "I'll ask Sam to continue to monitor Morris's bank accounts. Andrew, we need men to search his home, his office, and his girlfriend's apartment, on the off chance that he is foolish enough to think that we will not be waiting for him at these places."

"Taken care of," Andrew said. "And we were tracking his cell phone. Though, according to Frank, he's already ditched it. Frank found it in the Dumpster behind the Fine Meadow."

Something nagged at Chase. He was suddenly reminded of the night Mia had sat them down and told them what they were dealing with. "Morris will not be able to abandon his life, those that would haunt him for eternity if he up and left. We are dealing with a psychopath, where logic and reason no longer exist. What is more important to him, more fulfilling, is to remain in New York and achieve closure, even if it means he could die in the process." Chase shook his head. "Morris may go into hiding, but he's not leaving this city, not as long as we're breathing."

Andrew nodded. "The priority is the girls' safety. As soon as Ms. Whitley is discharged and cleared by her doctor, I recommend that Mia and Ms. Whitley go to the island. I'm aware that Ms. Whitley is with child...with children," Andrew corrected himself. "Mr. Montclair, would your friend Robert be willing to go along with them, just in case Ms. Whitley was in need of assistance from a doctor?"

"No question. He's practically family," Chase said.

"Good," Andrew said.

"And as for the three of us?" Paul asked, gesturing to the only three souls in the room.

Andrew withdrew two guns from his person, though Chase couldn't tell for sure where he had stashed them exactly, and distributed one revolver to each of them. Andrew patted the gun he himself was toting and said, "We stay behind…and flush the bastard out of his hole…by whatever means necessary."

Chapter Seventy-One

Scott's world was crumbling around him, forcing him to claw for solid ground. He knew what he had given up in the restaurant, but in that moment he didn't care. Just seconds before Mia had spoken, he had felt the hairs on the back of his neck stand on end, as if anticipating the jolting words she was about to utter from once-adored lips.

By her own admission, Mia had fallen, putting herself in the same category as Erin Whitley. For a brief moment, he had wondered if she was lying to him, to purposefully turn him against her, but in the end he had accepted the distasteful truth that his Angel had indeed been tainted. The discovery and acceptance that Mia would never belong to him was a blow. But it was nothing compared to the fact that he had showed his hand. As much as he hated to admit it, Mia had caught him off guard. Never in a million years did he expect Mia, a woman who had a bodyguard attached to her hip, to confront him in that manner. Fortunately, Mia had taken the bait he had dangled in front of her. Asking Mia about Paul's whereabouts, making her doubt that her man was safe, that Scott had not gotten to him, created the perfect distraction to escape the restaurant without being detected.

Despite being able to elude his tail, Scott could still admit that his life was spinning out of control. He needed to get a handle on it. And for that to happen, he needed money and lots of it. The fucker whom he had lost back at the restaurant was nowhere in sight, which allowed him to slow his pace and catch his breath. He looked up the street and saw a bank ahead. He needed to grab some cash now before his Whore went to the police and named him. Luckily the bank wasn't crowded and he was quickly able to secure enough money so he could breathe for a while. The next thing he had to do was change his appearance so he could walk around freely and not constantly look over his shoulder. It wouldn't be too difficult to morph into someone else. He had pulled it off countless times. A little makeup, a wig, and some bland clothing would make him invisible in a city with a population topping eight million.

An hour and three stores later, he was unrecognizable and feeling more centered. He took a seat at one of the many benches in Eastland Park and withdrew one of the three disposable phones he had purchased on his shopping trip.

Although Scott had planned on having this meeting face-to-face, a phone call would have to suffice. He needed to know what his father was up to. His father's attorney greeted him cordially, but from his tone, Scott knew he was not expecting this call.

"My apologies for calling, but I will not be able to come to Philadelphia and finalize things in person. My patients come first and I am needed here, I'm afraid," Scott said.

"Yes, I understand. And it's not mandatory that we conduct business in person. I just thought it would be better to meet in private since, well, since…"

Scott was in the middle of stroking his new goatee when he heard Epstein waver. "Have you met with the other beneficiaries?"

"Yes, Dr. Morris, I have already shared your father's will with them and informed them of your father's wishes and what they should expect from his estate."

Scott didn't like where this was headed and he wasn't going to wait a minute longer to learn why Rodger Epstein had wanted to meet with him privately. "Mr. Epstein, is there something wrong with my father's will?"

"Dr. Morris, there is no delicate way to say this, but your father had drafted a second will and I'm afraid to say that you are no longer a recipient of his estate."

Scott felt his blood begin to boil. This was not happening. He needed that money, now more than ever. He took a deep breath and asked, "Would you be so kind as to tell me to whom my father is leaving his fortune?"

Scott heard Epstein clear his throat. "Of course, the will is a matter of public record. A third of your father's money has been put into an endowment fund at the hospital he had worked for. Another third of the money will be distributed to the American Heart Association, in honor of your mother. But the final third of the money, the three million dollars that was originally going to you, is now slated for HOPE, one of the nation's largest anti–sexual violence organizations."

Scott fought the urge to hang up on the fucker. But before losing all control, he had a couple of questions to ask. "When did he write this? Did you know about this second will?"

"At your direction, I hired a team to clear out your father's things to prepare his town home for sale. But I personally dismantled his office and boxed away all papers or things of a delicate nature. I discovered the will, which was dated the very night he died, in the top drawer of his desk, along with two sealed letters."

"To whom are the letters addressed?" Scott asked. An unnerving feeling settled at the pit of his stomach, and he began to sweat.

"One was obviously addressed to me, the same letter that identified me as the executor. Also included in that letter, were his final wishes. One of those wishes was that I ensure the distribution of the other sealed letter to a Ms. Erin Whitley in New York City," Epstein said.

"Has Ms. Whitley received her letter?" Scott asked, his tone clipped.

"I imagine she should be receiving it either today or tomorrow." The attorney must have sensed Scott's irritation because his voice softened just a touch when he said, "You have every right to contest the validity of your father's will, but please understand that the process often takes time, as any legitimate investigation does."

Scott was in no position to partake in an investigation of any kind. His father had warned him that the world would know who and what he was, he just didn't believe a dead man was capable of such a feat. It had been a grave mistake to underestimate Dr. Mitchell Morris. Scott had never been so close to losing it. He needed to get his thoughts together. "I do not plan to contest. Thank you for your time, Mr. Epstein," Scott said and ended the call.

Scott sat back on the bench and digested what he had learned. He was left with only two options. He could easily hop on a train or plane and disappear for a long time, maybe indefinitely, if he was creative with the existing money he had in his bank account. It wasn't three million dollars, but it was a considerable amount, enough to get him by for a while. Or he could find and put an end to the one woman who had started it all.

Chapter Seventy-Two

So, you see two, right?" Erin asked, already knowing the answer. It didn't hurt to hear the doctor tell her for the fifth time in less than a minute that two heartbeats were clearly detected on the ultrasound.

"Two strong heartbeats," the doctor said, humoring her once again. "But I understand why Dr. Miller sent you to be checked out. You were definitely dehydrated and for pregnant women that can be a serious problem, especially those carrying multiples." The doctor withdrew the probe and handed her an ultrasound photo of Baby A and Baby B. "The babies look great." Erin finally allowed herself to breathe and she stared at the glossy, black and white photo. "But you do need to slow down, Erin. Drink plenty of water and eat. It would be best if you put on a few pounds. You'll need to increase your calorie intake to support those growing babies."

Picturing her belly swelling with Chase's babies made her smile. Erin felt Mia grab her hand. "If you need an eating partner, I would be happy to volunteer," Mia said, giggling.

"Sisters?" the doctor asked, looking from Erin to Mia.

"Hopefully, one day we will be," Erin said, looking at the woman who had put her life on hold, had put her life at risk, for those she cared for. Erin couldn't imagine a better sister or a better wife for her brother. Mia smiled and squeezed her hand.

"Well, let's get you two out of here, shall we? I am prescribing you both an evening in front of the television with cheesecake in hand," he said with a smile. The doctor swiftly and painlessly removed the IV from her hand. It was amazing how much better she felt from simply dumping a bag of sodium chloride into her vein.

"Erin, I think we should adhere to the doctor's orders, maybe even extend those orders into tomorrow as well," Mia said, chuckling.

Shaking his head, the doctor said, "All right, someone will be in with the discharge papers. Don't even think about running off to the nearest bakery without them."

"We promise," Erin and Mia said together.

Mia waited until the doctor was gone before taking the playful conversation to where it had to go, unfortunately. "We should get going. Paul, Chase and Uncle Drew are most likely chomping at the bit."

Feeling rejuvenated at learning that her babies were safe, Erin was able to refocus on the monster that threatened the lives of everyone she loved. But before she could allow her mind to completely perseverate on such a morbid topic, she clicked on the video app on her cell phone and pointed it at the ultrasound photo. Erin had never seen Chase as frightened as she had in his hospital room. The possibility that she and their babies were in danger had invoked a level of fear in him she never cared to experience again. Although the still shot was a bit fuzzy, Erin could still make out Baby A and Baby B perfectly. With a little commentary from her explaining that their babies were beautiful and healthy, Chase would hopefully be able to calm down and exhale.

"I'm going to hit the bathroom. By that time, your discharge papers should have been delivered and your video will be finished," Mia said, grabbing her purse.

Erin looked up and stared at the woman Paul had fallen in love with. Mia had been a godsend in so many ways. She had been a source of strength when Erin felt her own leave her. She had been the voice of reason when Erin's head was spinning out of control. And she was the woman who had the ability to heal Paul's wounded heart and soul. "Mia…thanks for staying with me…and for being what we all seem to need right now."

Mia stopped midstride. "Before you all came along, I was just going through the motions. Trust me, Erin, I need you just as much." A sheepish grin appeared on her beautiful face before she turned and disappeared into the adjoining bathroom.

Chapter Seventy-Three

Although Scott had ditched his cell, the device that allowed him to track Montclair and his Whore's whereabouts, he knew where to find them. As Plain Jane had prepped her DVD player with a chick flick and he dished out the dumplings last evening, his tracker had alerted him that Montclair had been rushed to Mercy General. Scott had been cautiously optimistic that he had silenced Montclair. But the arrogant asshole had survived the shooting and was on the road to a miserable recovery. It didn't matter, now. Without harming another hair on Montclair's head, Scott was going to destroy him. Montclair might walk out of the hospital, but his Whore would never see the light of day.

Scott climbed the hospital stairs. It didn't take long for Scott to work the woman at reception to learn Chase Montclair's hospital room. Even in his disguise, he could charm and coerce the filthiest of creatures. Scott was about to ascend the next set of stairs when he spotted the Whore's oversized bodyguard through the stairwell door's narrow pane of glass. The bloated piece of shit was camped outside a patient's room. This observation intrigued him since the fourth floor was devoted to maternity patients.

She really was a whore.

Disgusted, Scott exited the stairway and began the trek down the fourth floor hallway, looking for the magic closet. If he was on a maternity floor, then there might be a closet devoted to scrubs for fathers-to-be. And as he rounded the corner, Scott found what he was looking for. The room was not occupied at the moment, another indicator that he was going to succeed. He quickly changed out of his khakis and polo shirt and into aquamarine scrubs. He withdrew five loaded syringes from his duffle bag, secured them in the band of his pants, and made his way toward the Whore.

Scott approached the nurse's station and grabbed a random clipboard from one of the cluttered desks. There was only one nurse manning the station and she was too busy talking on the phone to notice him.

Control…Focus…Control…Act.

It was highly unlikely that Erin Whitley was in Room 404 by herself. But it didn't matter. All he had to do was get close enough to her to sink the syringe into her tainted skin and it would be over. He cared little about what happened after…if he too never saw the light of day.

Chapter Seventy-Four

Erin pressed RECORD and started to speak into her phone when she heard a knock at the door. Time to be discharged. Thank God. "Come in," she yelled as she stood from the hospital bed.

Erin couldn't tell if the man who entered was a doctor or nurse, but it didn't matter. She was getting out of there and back to Chase.

"Ms. Whitley, are you going somewhere?" the man asked rather sweetly.

Erin looked at the clipboard in the man's hands, but there wasn't anything on the clipboard resembling discharge papers. Just a notebook and pen were attached by the clip. "I'm due to be discharged," Erin said, staring at the man in scrubs. Though he wore the typical hospital attire, the man seemed out of place. Erin wanted to believe that it was the blond ponytail and goatee that threw her off, but she knew that she would be lying to herself. It was a gut feeling and the tiny hairs on the back of her neck standing on end that told her she was in danger.

"Ah, receive a clean bill of health, did you?" he asked. He

snatched the ultrasound photo from her hand and stared at her children. "You really are a whore aren't you, Erin? According to this picture, you're hovering around six weeks, which means you spread your legs for him within two weeks of knowing him." He drew closer. "Which means...you have fallen from grace, Angel."

Erin wanted to run or at the very least scream for help, but she couldn't bring herself to do either. She was in some sort of dreamlike state, where her greatest nightmare was unfolding before her eyes and she had no idea how to stop it. He peeled the goatee away from his face, then the blond ponytail, and dropped them and her photo on the bed. Although his face was caked with some sort of makeup, she would know him anywhere.

Maybe it was his choice of words that made her come to. Because when he uttered the word "grace," she instantly became aware of what she needed to do. "Just like the others?" she asked, baiting him.

The curious look on his face told Erin that he hadn't expected that particular question...which gave her hope. She needed him to talk, even if she didn't make it out alive. She needed his admission on tape. Although her hands trembled, she was still able to hold on to her phone. It was still recording, but the time allotted was limited.

"Erin, you were my favorite. Maybe it was because I had waited so long, waited for that perfect moment, to have you in that cemetery."

"To rape me?" she asked, taking a step toward the door.

"Such a vile word," he said. Morris shook his head. "Vile words are uttered by whores, by women not fit or worthy to breathe my air."

"Women like Gabrielle?" she asked, careful not to look at her phone.

Morris's lips curled to form a devious smile. He was enjoying the moment, knowing, or thinking rather, that he had nothing to lose. "Some women are born filthy, Erin. Gabrielle was repulsive, tainted, even as I held her beneath the cascading suds in her bathtub." He took a step toward her. "But she served her purpose the night of the benefit...and so did my father."

There had been speculation over Morris's involvement in regards to Gabrielle's death all along, but now that it was confirmed by the killer himself, her current situation seemed even more ominous. But she couldn't stop now, especially when he just alluded to even another murder.

"Dr. Mitchell Morris?" she asked.

Morris crossed his arms against his chest and appeared disappointed with her. "You are an intelligent young woman, Erin. I thought you would have figured that one out by now." Shaking his head, he said, "The talented and ever-respected oncologist, Dr. Mitchell Morris, had kept quiet this past year. But after seeing you the night of the benefit, I got the sense that his silence was about to be broken."

"He didn't fall?" Erin asked, taking another step, until her back pressed up against the bathroom door. And that was when she remembered...Mia.

"He fell...right after I let go of him," Morris said, his voice arrogant.

Erin silently projected the reoccurring command, Stay put, Mia. Stay where you are safe.

But Mia must not have received her subliminal message, because the doorknob rattled behind her. For a split second, she had hope that Morris hadn't heard the slight jiggle of the knob. When he closed the gap between them in two strides and grabbed her by the arm, she knew that she had been foolish to underestimate him. He ripped her away from the door and she immediately felt something prick her arm. She looked down to find the source of her discomfort and saw a loaded syringe lodged in her vein.

"Don't move, Erin. If just a few drops of what is in this syringe enter your bloodstream, you and the heathen inside of you are dead within moments." Erin wanted to warn Mia, but she also had no doubt that Scott would empty whatever poison was in that needle into her body, killing everything she loved.

* * *

The stress of the day was taking a toll on Mia. She had a pounding headache, one that wasn't going to go away without some assistance. She rummaged through her purse and found her travel pack of Advil. She popped two pills in her mouth and washed them down with water from the tap.

Mia stared at her reflection, which only made her feel worse. Although she had slept soundly, wrapped in Paul's arms last night, the stress of the day was sucking the life out of her. But who the hell was she to complain? Erin had just had the scare of a lifetime. All she had was a headache, which would subside within an hour of taking the meds. She could definitely suck it up for Erin's sake.

Mia was in the process of putting the tube of Advil back into her purse when she heard the bathroom door shake. It didn't sound like someone knocking, but more like someone brushing up or pressed up against the door. Mia almost shouted Erin's name, but her instincts told her to remain silent. A jolt of adrenaline surged through her body and she pressed her ear against the door.

She recognized the smug voice immediately, as she had come face-to-face with it and the obnoxious prick it belonged to just hours earlier. Mia was now thankful that she had such a headache, one that prompted her to bring her purse into the bathroom, a purse that contained her pistol. Mia knew what kind of monster she was dealing with. If Morris was on the other side of the door instead of having escaped when he had the chance, then he had already come to terms with the repercussions of his actions. His own death was not a deterrent. He had nothing to lose, which meant that if Mia didn't intervene, Erin was in grave danger.

Mia turned the knob and flung the door open. Although she aimed for the head, her eyes were fixed on the syringe hanging out of Erin's arm. Morris's thumb hovered over the tip of the syringe. Just a push of the thumb and that unknown fluid would flood Erin's system. Morris strategically positioned himself behind Erin making it nearly impossible for a clean shot between the eyes. Mia quickly readjusted her aim and set her sights on his brachial artery. If her shot rang true, then Morris's arm would be completely incapacitated.

"A pleasure to see you again, Mia," Morris said, his eyes sparkling.

"Release her, Morris. This will be your only warning," Mia said, zeroing in on her target.

"Aren't you afraid you will be too late…again?" Morris asked, taunting her, trying to hit her where she was the most vulnerable. "You seem to have a knack for being late to the big dance. Your father definitely fell victim as a result of your poor timing…as did your sweet next-door neighbor, Rose."

Mia had never been comfortable with the police's findings. Deep down, despite the hard evidence, Mia had known that Rose's death wasn't an accident. Mia made a promise to herself that if she made it out of that hospital room alive, Rose's children would learn the truth. They deserved it.

Mia knew that he was baiting her, attempting to rattle her enough to make her second-guess herself. But ironically, his goading only solidified Mia's unwavering determination to put an end to Morris and her own self-doubt. Paul was right. Her father didn't kill himself because she had failed to promptly produce her mother's killer. He just couldn't live without the woman he loved.

Mia knew what she had to do. There was no need to negotiate. Morris had come for one reason and one reason only. And it was clear that he was willing to die to achieve it. Mia remained calm, as calm as she could be under the circumstances, and slowly cocked her neck to the left. She didn't dare take her eyes off of Morris to see if Erin had followed her lead. Another inch would be a great help, a little more wiggle room to hit her target without taking out Erin's shoulder instead.

Out of the corner of her eye, Mia took in the ever-so-slight movement giving her the green light. "You know, I had hoped…" Mia said. She pulled the trigger, never intending to finish her thought, and found her mark. His arm went limp, leaving the syringe dangling from Erin's arm.

Mia was about to finish him off with another round when she saw Erin rip the syringe out of her own vein and slam it into Morris's neck. Erin drained the syringe and stepped away from his already-convulsing body. Morris's back arched as his limbs twitched, but he still had enough in him to speak, though it was garbled. "You had hoped?" he asked, now foaming at the mouth.

The hospital door swung open, revealing a gun-toting Alex, but Mia raised her hand to thwart his own attack on Morris. "I had hoped I would have had the pleasure to kill you." Mia looked to Erin and smiled. She then turned her attention back on the quivering mess in front of her and said, "But watching you succumb by Erin's hand…is more enjoyable."

Chapter Seventy-Five

Despite the lockdown, Chase, Paul and Andrew arrived within minutes of the gunshot. Erin didn't know exactly how the three men learned that she and Mia were linked to the hospital lockdown, but she had a feeling Alex facilitated their sudden appearance within the room. Erin was prepared for a multitude of emotions from Chase, with anger being at the top of that list. But all she felt was his love when he pulled her into his arms and kissed her until she could no longer breathe. When she finally came up for air, Erin caught a glimpse of her brother embracing Mia, with equal measures of love and worry in his eyes. The scene would have been perfect if it wasn't for the corpse at their feet.

The next hour was filled with chaos and loads of questions from both the doctors who worked on the floor and the police. Luckily it had taken a few minutes before the first of many officers arrived, giving Erin and Mia time to get their stories straight. Paul's own skills came in handy as he prepped them with what they did and didn't have to tell the police. But it all became a moot point when Erin replayed the video on her phone, first only to herself and then to Mia, Chase and Andrew. Although Morris was only visible in portions of the video, his voice was crisp and gloriously incriminating as he admitted to the murders of Gabrielle, Dr. Mitchell Morris, and Mia's neighbor. The video footage concluded after that final admission, cutting out the actual shooting and stabbing via needle. The dialogue between Morris and Mia immediately following the shooting could have caused a problem from a sympathetic juror, but somehow, by some stroke of luck, the video had stopped rolling by that point.

* * *

Regardless of the mountain of evidence pinpointing Scott Morris as the monster he was, Paul hired the best law firm in the city to defend them. Over the next several weeks, Erin, Mia, Chase and Andrew were subject to multiple interrogations. Although Erin's own testimony and Scott Morris's confession justified Mia's and Erin's actions as self-defense, it was Dr. Mitchell Morris's letter that sealed Scott Morris's guilt. The letter arrived via priority mail the morning after Erin had ended Morris's life.

Sitting on Chase's balcony, with her beautiful man at her side, Erin read the letter...

Dearest Erin,

What you are about to read is my statement, a factual account of what happened, one that can be presented to the authorities if you so choose. If you are in receipt of this letter, then it was be-

cause I didn't seize the opportunity to tell you in person what you are truly entitled to know. I apologize for what I am about to reveal, for being a coward, for being a disillusioned father. You deserve to know the truth and the role I played in the crime that must continue to haunt you. Not a day has gone by that I don't regret what I have done, all the people I have hurt.

Sworn Statement

I, Mitchell James Morris, took part in a crime. I was contacted via phone by my son, Scott James Morris. He asked me to come to Franklin Cemetery in the Old City section of Philadelphia. When I arrived, my son was lying in the shadows of the cemetery and wearing a black ski mask. He had been wounded, as he was bleeding profusely. I took my son to my satellite office and tended to him throughout the night, providing treatment to stabilize him.

That same night, I discovered dozens of pictures of my intern, Ms. Erin Whitley, on his phone, along with a detailed schedule of her daily whereabouts. When my son came to and was again coherent, he confessed to me that he had raped Erin Whitley. I did nothing with that information, keeping it secret from the world and my son's ailing mother.

The injuries he had sustained as a result of Erin Whitley trying to protect herself caused him to miss five months of work. With my help, my son concocted a story to address his absence. Scott stayed at our shore home during his recuperation, where the world thought he was taking the time off of work to battle colon cancer.

My son started his new position in New York the following winter. There has been minimal contact between me and my son *since that night, with me only reaching out to him from time to time to appease his mother. My wife ultimately succumbed to her heart condition, but not before pleading with me to reconnect with my son. Fortunately, my wife didn't know the reason for the rift, just that it existed. Adhering to her dying wishes, I agreed to attend the Maya Montclair Foundation benefit with my son. It was at this benefit that I had the pleasure and misfortune to run into Erin Whitley, where I discovered that she had given up her dream of being a doctor. It destroyed me to learn that I had helped kill that dream all those months ago.*

My son raped a beautiful young woman with everything ahead of her, and yet I did nothing. I had held on to the hope for far too long that my son was something else entirely, such as a man that respected women, a man that didn't violate and prey on others. I was selfish and in denial for so many years, too many years. I fear that there are more victims out there and more to come if my son is not stopped. So, it will be in death, when I have moved on to wherever God is gracious enough to send me, that Erin Whitley will hopefully find peace and justice.

May God have mercy on my soul,
Mitchell James Morris

* * *

Erin couldn't help but feel betrayed by her mentor. But as she reached down to caress her belly, she now understood the lengths to which parents will go for their children. Even for a child like Scott Morris. Dr. Mitchell Morris had not acted as a doctor or a concerned citizen the night he had found his son in the cemetery or during the months following. No, Dr. Mitchell Morris had just been a desperate father, trying to protect his only son. It was only when all hope was depleted, when Dr. Mitchell Morris had come to the cruel and unfair realization that nothing and nobody would change what Scott Morris had always been, that he confessed and sought forgiveness. Erin wasn't one to hold a grudge. And though Dr. Mitchell Morris's involvement would sting for a bit, she knew she would forgive him in her own time.

Epilogue

It was early September and the weather couldn't have been any more beautiful for what Chase had planned, which was much more than what Erin thought the day entailed. Yes, he would be taking her to a Phillies game, but there was one important stop along the way. Chase looked over and took in the lovely sight of his soon-to-be wife staring out the passenger window. She appeared content and youthful in her Phillies cap and Chase Utley t-shirt. At seventeen weeks pregnant, her belly was a perfect little beach ball beneath the stretched cotton. And Chase couldn't be happier.

Erin must have been in a daydream of her own, because she didn't question him when he turned in the opposite direction from the Walt Whitman Bridge, the typical route from New Jersey to Citizens Bank Park in Philly. Chase didn't know for certain how she would react, if they were on the same page with what he was about to propose, but his gut told him to go for it.

He was just about to start the conversation when Erin said

dreamily, "I have always loved this town, these tree-lined streets. I grew up a few towns over, which was wonderful, but this town, its charm…it's like something out of a postcard."

Chase took that window of opportunity and turned left at the next intersection; 428 Mulberry Lane was just ahead. "Erin, do you like living in New York?"

Erin suddenly appeared nervous, scared even, and quickly averted her eyes. Chase pulled the car over right there, which just happened to be directly in front of their destination. He lifted her chin with two fingers and forced her to look at him. "You can tell me, Erin," he said, smiling at the mother of his children.

She shook her head and said, "No, not really." Her eyes began to well with tears, a reaction he absolutely didn't want to invoke. "But your company, your home base, is New York. And I want to be wherever you are."

Her words overwhelmed him, but they were exactly what he needed to hear. "Erin, my home base is wherever I decide, wherever you want it to be. Chicago, Dallas, San Francisco…"

"Philadelphia?" she asked, cutting him off.

This was the moment of uncertainty he had been worried about. Was she ready? Was she willing to live so close to a city that she loved but one that also harbored so many horrific memories?

"Would living in a suburb like this one, just minutes away from Philadelphia, a city home to many reputable medical schools that would love to have you when you're ready, make you happy?" Chase asked.

She swallowed and then nodded. He wiped her first tear away. Chase had a feeling that there were many more to come. "Could you picture yourself and our children living in that house?" Chase let his eyes drift over her shoulder. "Watching our children take their first steps on that lawn?" he asked.

Her eyes grew wide and she followed his gaze. With her mouth agape she turned around to find him dangling a solitary key in front of her. "You can say no, Erin. If it's too much…"

She flung her arms around his neck and between sobs he heard her utter a saying that he was quite fond of. "It's always too much," she said, burrowing her face into his neck.

"I love you, Erin." He gently pulled her out of the safety of his neck. He knew she was crying and would most likely be a little embarrassed for being so emotional. But he needed to see her beautiful face. "And I love the family we made," he said, caressing her belly.

This time she didn't hide in the crook of his neck. Instead, she kissed him and then looked at him with the same passion and heat he had encountered the first time she had walked into his office. Breathless, she asked, "Is the house furnished?"

It would have been an odd question if it had come from anyone else. But he knew his girl and was well aware of what she was really asking. "The bedroom, as the rest of the house, is completely furnished," he said, unable to hold back a smile.

For her small frame, Erin was incredibly strong, and she practically dragged him out of the car and into their new home. "We have but an hour until the first pitch. Care to make good use of it, Mr. Montclair?"

He lifted her into his arms. "One hour will never be enough," he said, sealing his mouth over hers. Chase ascended the stairs and right before they entered the bedroom, he looked down at the woman he already considered his wife and said, "It'll never be enough."

* * *

The Phillies game was the perfect backdrop for the surprise engagement party Chase had planned on the sly. Erin didn't know when Chase found the time to round up the intimate group of people she loved dearly and convince them to travel to Philly and take in a ballgame, but she was thrilled beyond belief. Josh was the first to come over and hug her. He was careful not to squeeze her too hard, avoiding her ever-swelling belly at all costs. It was like nothing had ever happened in New York, that she had never accused him of such a heinous act.

Erin was grateful that Chase had convinced her just weeks after Morris's death to spend some time with Josh and mend whatever had been broken. Within minutes on that weekend trip, their relationship had been repaired and strangely enough, had grown stronger because of it. They were more than friends...they were family, and as close as any brother and sister could be.

Paul was next in line, and she embraced her brother with everything she had. Erin took a step back and stared at him. That tortured look in Paul's eyes, that somber cloud that had hovered over him for so long, had dissipated, allowing the sun to finally shine through. She hugged him again and whispered, "I'm so happy, Paul. So happy." He hugged her tight, responding without words. She knew that her own happiness meant everything to him.

As if on cue, Mia came up beside him and looked up at Paul with adoration and love. "Surprised, Erin?" she asked.

Erin looked around and took in the incredible sight. Chase, Andrew and Robert were sipping beers and laughing at something Josh had said. Ricky and Sam appeared to be sharing their own stories or maybe strategies on how to invade bank accounts without being detected. Erin couldn't believe how far they had all come. How something so horrendous could have brought them all together. "I can't believe we're here," she said, gesturing to the handful of people she could truly call her family.

"It's great to have everyone together. Erin, I hope you don't mind, but my friend Carina may be stopping by. When she called me this morning, I got the sense that she needed a friend or just a couple hours to kick back and relax."

"Are you kidding? I would love to meet one of your friends," Erin said, meaning every word.

"Thanks, Erin. So…back to the subject of surprises," Mia said, looking at Paul with a mischievous grin. "Can I tell her?" Mia asked.

Erin had no idea where Mia was going with this and looked from Mia to Paul for some sort of explanation. Before Paul could answer, Mia asked, "Did you like Chase's other surprise?"

Erin looked over at Chase and caught him midsip. She scowled at him. Did everyone know that he had given her the house of her dreams earlier that day? Chase shrugged, not letting her look of aggravation affect him. In fact, he looked downright pleased with himself.

"You both knew about the house. Didn't you?" Erin asked.

"I should hope so…neighbor," Paul said, sharing Mia's devilish grin.

Neighbor? What? Since Paul wasn't dishing, she looked to Mia to spill it. "Are you telling me that you…that you both are…"

"Moving a few streets over from your new home? That your brother landed a job here in Philly behind your back and that I was able to nail down a teaching job here as well?" Mia interrupted.

"But…what? Why? You love teaching in New York. And Paul, well, Pierce and Stone was your dream job," Erin said, clearly confused.

Mia hugged her. "I'll miss my students in New York, but I know I'll fall in love all over again with my students in New Jersey. And Paul will have no problem making his mark in Philly. And…because we want to watch your precious babies grow up and laugh as Henry chases them around the backyard. And…because we want to have family barbeques and beers on the patio."

Erin felt two hands surround her expansive belly and her body instantly responded to his touch, allowing the wonderful man behind her to claim her as his. "So, I take it you've met our annoying new neighbors," Chase said.

"This is all so…perfect," Erin said, allowing the tears to flow freely.

"Pregnancy tears?" Chase asked.

Erin turned around and shook her head. "These are happy tears," she said, going up on tiptoes and kissing him deeply.

See the next page for an excerpt from the first book in Elle Keating's Dangerous Love series.

Thrill of the Chase

Chapter One

The city was changing, the rigidity of the work day slowly unraveling and melting into night. Chase Montclair powered on the wall of screens and sat back in his leather swivel chair. He'd loosened his tie and started to roll up his sleeves when he saw her.

He reached for the intercom. "Lydia, please come here."

His secretary was at the doorway of his office within seconds. "Mr. Montclair, what do you need?" Lydia was old enough to be his mother. Her maturity and refined beauty were exactly what he wanted in a personal secretary. But her most coveted quality, the trait that Chase needed above everything else, was her loyalty. Her dedication to him was unwavering. And he couldn't... *wouldn't* have it any other way.

"Who is she?" Chase pointed to the screens on the far wall. Each monitor played the same image. Lydia stared at the large center screen. It took only moments for her to identify the mystery woman. Lydia made it a priority to know everyone on staff at Montclair Pharmaceuticals because Chase didn't have the time or desire to acquaint himself with the company's peons, though he did check on them every so often via monitor to ensure that they were doing their jobs and living up to his standards.

"She works in research and development. Her name is Erin Whitley."

He liked the sound of her name. It was both feminine and strong. Chase watched the woman tap the tip of her pen against the desk and then bring it to her lips. Her eyes remained fixed on her computer screen. There was a quiet confidence in her gaze, but there was also something lonesome about her.

"Bring her to me tomorrow…after my five o'clock," he said, rolling up his other sleeve. "And ask her to supply me with her latest report." Lydia bowed her head and left without uttering a word.

Chase had never sought out an employee to satisfy him sexually. An office relationship would be an unnecessary distraction. Instead, he chose to fulfill his needs with women he didn't need to see on a regular basis, women who didn't get attached or require him to give more than he was capable of providing. After what had happened last year, it was best he check his feelings at the door and enter each sexual relationship emotionally barren.

Chase stood up and walked over to the monitors. He watched the woman closely, his intrigue growing. Only a small strip of fabric fell below her lab coat, followed by long, athletic legs and black high heels. Her blond hair was pulled into a smart ponytail, though he could imagine what it looked like unbound, when she threw her head back at the moment of climax. The thought of her beneath him, in nothing but those high heels, aroused him. He felt his trousers grow tight around his mounting erection. And it only got worse when Erin Whitley rose from her chair and started to walk toward the other side of the lab. The swing of her hips and the sight of that tight little ass made his cock beyond stiff, and he determined that he would need to remain seated when she arrived tomorrow.

Acknowledgments

I would like to thank my husband and children for their patience and love while I pursued what I once thought was unreachable.

To my mom and dad, my very first cheerleaders, thank you for all your support and optimism during those times I allowed the doubt to creep in.

And to the wonderful team at Forever Yours, in particular my editor Dana Hamilton, thank you for giving this Jersey girl a shot at her dream.

About the Author

Elle Keating was born and raised in South Jersey, where she lives with her husband and three children. It was during her long commute to work, crossing over the Betsy Ross Bridge into Pennsylvania, that her mind drifted. Images of a world with Chase, Erin, and their friends came rapidly and set her writing to bring these intense characters to life.

When Elle is not in her favorite coffeehouse, huddled in a corner on an oversized chair and working on the next book in the series, she enjoys being a mom, taking her children from one sport to the next and challenging herself frequently to be in two places at once.

Learn more at:

Twitter: @KeatingElle